Secret of the Dragon's Claw

"If you can't take the heat, don't tickle the dragon!"

-Scott Fahlman

Secret of the Dragon's Claw

✦

Book Three

Derek Hart

iUniverse, Inc.
New York   Bloomington

Secret of the Dragon's Claw
Book Three

Copyright © 2010 Derek Hart

This is a work of fiction. All of the characters, names, incidents, organizations, and dialogue in this novel are either the products of the author's imagination or are used fictitiously.

iUniverse books may be ordered through booksellers or by contacting:

iUniverse
1663 Liberty Drive
Bloomington, IN 47403
www.iuniverse.com
1-800-Authors (1-800-288-4677)

ISBN: 978-1-4502-2423-9 (sc)
ISBN: 978-1-4502-2424-6 (ebk)

Printed in the United States of America

iUniverse rev. date: 03/29/2010

Dedication

This book is dedicated to Megan McRoberts.
She is an excellent teacher, who cares deeply about her
students, promotes the wonderful adventure of reading, and
makes learning fun!

Contents

Foreword

Secret of the Dragon's Claw continues the adventures of Gavin Kane, Emily Scott, and Bunty Digby, fourteen-year-olds who struggle with their daily lives in England during the winter of 1941 and into the spring of 1942. War has forced everyone to settle into an uncomfortable daily pattern, while England is still under siege, as U-boats relentlessly attack vital convoys. Halfway across the world, British, American, and Allied forces are now also fighting the Japanese Empire. Twice before, the teens have helped battle the forces of darkness, but once again face strange and wicked creatures sent from deep within Nazi Germany.

Secret of the Dragon's Claw further develops the friendship and alliance between this teenage trio and the eccentric Sir Thaddeus Osbert. The dragon has become accustomed to battling a myriad of dangerous foes over the ages, but protecting Gavin, Emily, and Bunty has become a full-time endeavor. Thaddeus must deal with his nagging sweet tooth, which this time gets him into several compromising situations. However, the dragon's addiction to sugar has unforeseen benefits too. The children band together with their dragon friend, of course, but they also discover magical powers are commonplace throughout the United Kingdom. Will a hasty alliance with a senile old wizard be enough to prevent something so horrible, so unimaginable, that it threatens to plunge the entire world into permanent darkness?

Preface

<u>Dragon Claws</u>

Sharp, so very sharp!
Extended to defend
Talons to protect
Dragon claws

Sharp, razor sharp!
Slice to freedom
Cut to the truth
Dragon claws

Sharp, surgically sharp!
Carve the darkness
Let in the light
Dragon claws

Sharp, witty sharp!
Open our minds
Free our souls
Dragon claws

Sharp, brilliantly sharp!
Colors of the rainbow
Protect what is right
Dragon claws

By *Ian Lenthart*
(Used with Permission)

Acknowledgements

To all the wonderful people of **Kernow, England**. More commonly known as Cornwall, many citizens of this historic region readily provided tidbits and personal anecdotes, as well as inspiration to Derek Hart. By soliciting various contacts throughout the Cornish countryside, the author was able to obtain some wonderful insights into the region during World War II, thereby balancing cultural and historical integrity with literary license.

To another **Derek Hart** (no relation, as far as we know), who resides in Chester, England and has taken the time to assist the author in conducting important research. This Derek is also a writer (it must have something to do with the name) and his skills are apparent. The American Derek enthusiastically supports the British Derek in his endeavors and hopes this acknowledgement will, in some small way, spur him to continue pursuing his passion for writing.

To **Eric Hammond**, an incredibly gifted graphic artist, who has provided moral support, artistic support, and most of all, become a trusted and valuable friend.

To **Sheila Seclearr**, who has added an entirely new dimension to the tales of Thaddeus Osbert and his teenaged friends. Her talent for visualizing their lives is profound, and soon you too will have the pleasure of experiencing the magic of her art.

Cover art by David M. Burke.

Introduction

Magic is neither good nor evil. It is the intention behind the magic, which defines it as positive or negative. Understanding the relationship between "magic" and the natural world gives power and dominance over those who do not. Magic works solely within the laws of nature. Indeed, faith is the ultimate magic. It is said that faith can move mountains and as such is truly magical.

When we believe, anything is possible.

1

The Year Ends Badly

It was late November 1941, when the German submarine *U-81* received a radio message with orders to attack a Royal Navy task force heading for Gibraltar. Kapitänleutnant "Fritz" Friederich Guggenberger plotted an intercept course and just as reported, he located the British fleet, which included two aircraft carriers and two battleships. It was night when the submarine surfaced and then closed in on the nearest target, which turned out to be one of the aircraft carriers.

Up on the U-boat's bridge, the German captain was considering the attack.

"Keep her level, Chief," Guggenberger commanded through the voice pipe.

He was surrounded with silence.

"Flood tubes one to four," the captain followed with another order.

"Flooding tubes one to four," the order was repeated.

"Watch your depth, Chief," Guggenberger harshly cautioned again.

"Bow planes up ten degrees. Stern down five degrees," the chief corrected.

"Open bow caps now."

"Caps open, sir."

"Enemy's speed is fifteen knots and steady."

"Tubes one through four are ready."

"It's an aircraft carrier. Destroyer screen is far ahead."

"Do we risk it?" Guggenberger asked aloud.

"It's worth a try, Captain," Lieutenant Konig said.

"Come left to two two five."

1

"Left five degrees rudder," the chief ordered the planesmen.

"New course is two two five."

"Steady on course two two five."

"Konig, what's your feeling?" the captain asked.

"It'll work. We've got them," the lieutenant replied.

"I'm going in," the captain decided.

"Master-sight to the bridge," the lieutenant called down.

"All ahead full. Left full rudder," the captain ordered.

"Stand by to attack!" Lieutenant Konig called down the voicepipe.

"We'll get that one over there first," Guggenberger selected. "The battleship."

"Target locked," the lieutenant said.

"Then we'll drop on the big one," the captain said next.

"Targets identified," Konig announced. "*HMS Malaya* and *HMS Ark Royal*."

"Bow caps are open?" Guggenberger needed confirmation.

"Caps are open, sir," a voice from below reconfirmed.

"Fire when matched," Konig said.

"Tube one, fire!"

Swoosh.

"Tube two, fire!"

Swoosh.

The U-boat seemed to buck a little as each torpedo launched.

"Tube three, fire!"

Swoosh.

"Tube four, fire!"

Swoosh.

"Let's get out of here," Guggenberger said, pushing his men down the ladder ahead of him.

"All torpedoes running," Konig announced.

"Alarm!" the captain shouted as he pulled the hatch down over his head.

The submarine submerged with a surge of engine thrust, as the saddle tanks quickly filled with water. The U-boat's planes angled down sharply for the emergency dive.

"How much time left?" Guggenberger asked as water dripped down onto his cap.

"Just about now," Konig replied, looking at his stopwatch.

Kaboom!

Several minutes later…

Kablam, boom, boom, boom.

"Secondary explosions," Konig commented with a smile.

U-81 had fired a four-torpedo spread at **HMS Malaya** and **HMS Ark Royal**, which were overlapping targets.

The torpedoes missed the battleship, but a single torpedo struck the aircraft carrier on the starboard side, abreast of the main island. This position was the worst possible place to be hit, being dead amidships, where the list caused would be greatest. The impact was such that four main compartments, plus most of the ship's starboard bilge, immediately began to flood.

The initial detonation punched open a huge hole, the size increasing as it took a lot of time to bring the ship to a halt, which resulted in additional hull plating peeling off. Several secondary explosions wrecked the starboard boiler room, and the adjoining oil tanks flooded, as did the main switchboard and lower steering compartment. The starboard power train was also knocked out, but the port and centerline trains kept functioning.

Deep within **HMS Ark Royal**, Sub-lieutenant John Mobley was suddenly thrown from his bunk by the torpedo's detonation. On the way down, he bumped his head against the bulkhead, but even though there was a cut over his eye, the injury wasn't serious.

Some of the blast vented up through a bomb trunk, forward of the command island. The carrier whipped violently with the explosion, which hurled many of the fully loaded torpedo-bombers on the flight deck over the side. **HMS Ark Royal** showed very little damage externally and her masts remained standing. However, the aircraft carrier quickly took on a 10-degree list to port, which increased to 18-degrees within 20 minutes.

"Get up on deck, lads, on the double," Mobley ordered his mates, Radcliff and Watkins, while wiping blood away from his forehead. "Let's see if we can get one of the Stringbags off."

Due to serious flooding, communications within *Ark Royal* were lost, which explained the delay in bringing the ship to a halt. At this point, the Captain decided to evacuate the ship as soon as possible. The order echoed throughout the ship and all maintenance and engineering personnel were withdrawn from the machinery spaces and assembled topside, in order to determine who should leave the ship and who should remain. With this further unnecessary delay, damage control measures weren't initiated until an hour after the initial impact, by which time the flooding was uncontrolled.

During this critical phase, the centerline boiler room started to flood from below. During the evacuation of the machinery spaces, several covers and armored hatches were left open, allowing the flooding to spread further than otherwise expected.

As *Ark Royal* listed even more, water came in through the uptakes of the starboard boiler room, flooding over into the centerline, and later into the port boiler rooms. This flooding further reduced the area through which funnel gasses could escape, causing severe local overheating and spot fires.

With his crewmates in tow, Sub-Lieutenant Mobley managed to reach the flight deck, which was in utter chaos. The airplanes were skidding down the slanting runway and toppling into the ocean.

"Not with my Stringbag, you don't!" Mobley exclaimed.

John sprinted along the tilting flight deck, closely followed by his crew, until they reached one of the torpedo-bombers. Mobley vaulted into the open cockpit and pumped the fuel line, while engaging the starter.

"Come on, turn over," John coaxed the engine.

The engine sputtered and coughed, then roared into life.

The Swordfish started rolling.

"Whoa," Radcliff shouted. "We're moving already?"

He was correct, but it wasn't because Mobley was ready to take off. The Swordfish was starting to roll down the deck on its own, pulled by gravity and it would eventually tumble off the edge.

"Not yet, you don't," Mobley grunted, fighting with the flaps and brakes, while revving the engine.

"Come on, John, you can do it," Radcliff coached the pilot.

Mobley continued wrenching the stick and pumping the pedals, working the Swordfish into position.

"It's now or never, sir," Watkins added, his voice shaking.

Mobley nodded his agreement and throttled back. The canvas wings flexed taut under the strain of such gravitational forces pulling in several directions. The Swordfish bumped and bounced, but kept sliding to the port side. If Mobley didn't time his take-off just right, the airplane would end up in the drink.

"Hold on!" John shouted.

Mobley didn't exactly have enough air speed, but neither did he have the luxury of waiting. Fortunately, the Swordfish was designed to lift off with minimal speed, so John had no choice but to test the airplane's true capabilities.

Flaps were at full extension.

John yanked back on the stick and prayed.

Ark Royal's captain watched in amazement as one of the Swordfish torpedo-bombers actually made it off the slanting deck. Such flying abilities were truly rare and Captain Massey recognized this fact. "Make note of that Swordfish, Lieutenant Moss. I want to speak to the pilot once we've stabilized the situation."

"Aye, aye, sir," the lieutenant complied. "He has no radio, sir, but I jotted down the tail number. The pilot will undoubtedly make for *Victorious*."

Just then, the **Ark Royal** shuddered and settled even more, dramatically increasing the already serious list to port. However, power suddenly came back on again. Captain Massey grabbed the telephone, ringing the engine room.

"Chief Digby?" the captain shouted into the mouthpiece. "I need you to take control of the damage-control parties, right now!"

"Aye, aye, sir," CPO Digby replied. "We're on it, sir."

Click.

CPO Digby was now solely responsible for damage control. Now that wasn't a pleasant thought, because if **Ark Royal** sank, it would be his fault.

"Did we get hit? Did we get hit?" one of Digby's fellow sailors kept repeating.

"Of course we got hit, you blithering fool," the chief shouted in response. "What do you think all that racket was, Piccadilly Circus?"

It was all very nerve-racking! Digby almost envied the people topside who were preparing to abandon ship, because they didn't have to put up with such bloody morons. "Move it, you lunk, we've got a ship to save."

Water came gurgling up from below. Deep inside the bowls of the carrier, there were no lights. In the complete darkness, the chief thought he was near the end of his career and his life. There was no possible way he would survive this.

As water continued surging into the **Ark Royal**, the air pressure began to rise and because of this, the hatches wouldn't close properly. This was a blessing in disguise, for as each hatch raised slightly, light filtered down from overhead. The trapped sailors saw where the hatch was and swam toward the light. CPO Digby forced the hatch open, but when the men came up, water kept bubbling up from down below. After everyone was safe, Digby's crew sat on the hatch and closed it using screws.

No matter how tightly they secured it, seawater kept swirling out from between the cracks. Digby thought the hatch was going to explode, so he braced an emergency support beam between the hatch and ceiling. Still the spray kept spewing forth.

The ship's slant from flooding was getting quite steep, so it was hard to stay standing. The torpedo had hit the port side, so **Ark Royal** was tilting to port. The chief climbed up to check things out. There had already been an announcement to go to the stern deck, but inside the ship, the PA system had failed, so none of the orders were heard.

Digby yelled, "Everyone out of here!"

At first, his men couldn't understand him, because of the racket, but he repeated the order and they understood. The sailors climbed up towards the stern and reached a small hatch. The seawater had risen so much they practically had to swim there. CPO Digby pulled them up out of the hatch, rescuing all of his damage crew.

Ninety minutes after the torpedo hit, all power within the carrier failed. Meanwhile, most of the crew was ordered to evacuate the ship. Those that departed *Ark Royal* early included the entire staff of shipwrights and key members of the electrical staff, depriving the damage control crews of much-needed expertise. There were still further delays before the repair crews returned to the machinery spaces and attempts at counter-flooding began.

Half of the available compartments on the starboard side were then flooded, which reduced the list to 14 degrees. Then a critical mistake took place, which doomed *Ark Royal*. The counter-flooding valves weren't closed, so the water in the starboard compartments began to overflow back to the port side. As more water entered the starboard side of the ship, it simply added to the ship sinking.

Flooding had already shut the ship's power plant down. Since all the generators were steam-powered, this deprived the ship of electrical power. The ship's engineers fought to get the plant back online, despite the rising floodwaters. They won that battle, when the portside boiler room was lit off.

However, by that time, the list had increased to 18 degrees and the flooding was starting to spread across the ship's boiler rooms. This was an uninterrupted compartment running across the entire width of the carrier, making the machinery spaces vulnerable. The efforts made by the engine room crews to restore power were futile. The boiler room flooded, which shut down all the boilers again.

Progressive flooding caused the list to increase rapidly, which reached a 20 degrees slant and then 27 degrees.

CPO Digby managed to find a voicepipe and shouted up to the bridge. "Chief Digby here, sir. We can't stop her listing, sir."

"Counter-flood, dammit," the Captain ordered.

"Already done that, sir," Digby regretted reporting. "She's losing bulkheads."

"It's a bloody shame," the commanding officer voiced his dissatisfaction with the entire situation. "All right, Chief, you've done everything you could. Get your people out of there, on the double."

"Aye, aye, sir," Digby replied.

"Abandon ship," the order passed down the line. "All hands, abandon ship!"

One of the deck officers had come down to see how things were progressing. He rallied the damage-control party to him. "Let's get topside, chaps."

By the time Digby and his crew reached the flight deck, the slant was so severe it was like climbing a flight of stairs, without the steps. The chief managed to scramble up on one of the railings. "Toss into the sea anything that floats."

The damage-control parties struggled up the starboard side of **Ark Royal**.

CPO Digby didn't reflect on his chances of survival. He took a deep breath and jumped. Just as he did, there was a huge explosion.

Kaboom!

Some men swimming nearby had their internal organs damaged by the reverberations of the explosion in the water. The force of the blast knocked anyone remaining off the tilting deck into the water. Most of the lucky ones had jumped off the rear of the carrier.

The entire crew had vacated the carrier by the time the list reached 45 degrees. With the force generated by boilers exploding, **HMS Ark Royal** capsized and started to go down.

The ship was still moving forward a little, very slowly, and the propeller was turning, bit by bit. Inevitably, Digby was drawn into the whirlpool created by the propeller wash. The Chief desperately pushed backwards, but no matter how hard he struggled, he was powerless. One propeller blade was 16 feet long, so with each turn it created a swirling vacuum, sucking him down.

Charles Digby was getting short of breath. He couldn't fight it and started swallowing mouthfuls of seawater. For an instant, it felt better, but there was no air coming in, so he started to get short of breath again. That happened two or three times, before Digby began to pass out. At that point, he wasn't thinking about getting rescued, but wondering how his son Bunty would manage without any parents at all.

As the chief started to lose consciousness, he saw an angel of death beckoning to him. Strange as it was, the creature looked very much like a dragon, with mighty wings and a long spiked tail. Perhaps he was going to hell. The chief stopped fighting and surrendered to death.

Thaddeus Osbert plucked CPO Digby from the whirlpool and gently breathed life into the man's lungs. Once the dragon was certain Bunty's father would live, he cast the chief adrift on a piece of broken lifeboat.

Charles Digby regained consciousness some distance away from the sinking carrier. The sun shown brightly and he looked up to see blue sky. The chief tried to clear his fuzzy mind. His mind was filled with the image of a benevolent dragon smiling down at him. Digby looked around, but couldn't see anybody else. The **Ark Royal** was now out of sight. All he could see was smoke in the far distance.

The chief was under the illusion that he was the only one who had survived. When a sudden wave raised him higher, though, he saw men floating here and there.

Digby clung to the fragment for nearly two hours. An officer in the distance called for the chief to join him on a lifeboat. Digby let go of the beam and swam to the raft. More and more people started climbing aboard the float, so the dinghy would go up and down with the smallest wave. When it got particularly bad, the whole thing would sometimes submerge. The chief petty officer was forced to turn men away.

A few of the survivors were trying to administer aid to a badly injured sailor. The boy's head was split open and blood pumped out each time he breathed.

He moaned, "Give me water."

"Don't give him anything, or he'll die," the officer warned.

Then a passing destroyer flashed a signal, which read:

***Wait a little while longer, blokes, just a little while longer.
We'll pick you up soon. The U-boat is still lurking about.***

"We might just get through this thing," Digby said for the benefit of the others.

He thought they might be rescued after all. It was two hours after ***Ark Royal*** sank when the destroyer returned and threw down ropes and rope ladders. The survivors swam to them and held on. Many of the men were black with oil from head to toe, so it was a struggle just to grasp a rescue line.

It was very difficult to climb. In the worst cases, as soon as someone held onto the ladder, they would lose consciousness at the relief of being rescued and fall right back into the ocean. When CPO Digby finally made it up, there were two officers waiting at the top.

Survivors were handed towels and quickly changed into old uniforms. Each man was issued a measure of gin and was temporarily billeted in the galley. That was more than four hours after the sinking. The people rescued after that were so stiff they couldn't speak properly. Digby's bunch were relatively energetic, so they rallied around the others, wrapped them in blankets, and rolled them back and forth like barrels, until they were able to move again.

After resting for awhile, CPO Digby started feeling neurotic, as every little noise in the ship startled him. Even the clang of a dropped wrench sounded like a torpedo exploding. He didn't sleep at all and barely ate, shaking with a nervous twitch along the entire right side of his body.

Suddenly a cat jumped up into the chief's lap. It was *Oscar*, who had survived the sinking of the ***Bismarck*** and now the ***Ark Royal*** too.

"Well, aren't you tough?" Digby said, scratching the kitty behind the ears.

The cat purred loudly and made starfish paws, extending his claws and kneading the chief's uniform pants. The obvious affection made Digby relax a little.

A call went out, "Hey, you can see Gibraltar!"

Digby figured someone was lying, but he went topside anyway. Lo and behold, he saw the British port and splendor of Gibraltar. "So, I have been saved after all."

Those who weren't injured were taken ashore immediately. At an impromptu meeting of the survivors, held on Gibraltar Dockyard, it was decided to use the balance of the ship's fund to buy a silver bell for the next ship to bear the name *Ark Royal*.

Digby and the others remained in a hotel for a week and were excused morning duties. Digby spent most of his free time staring off into space or just hanging around. The survivors arranged track-and-field competitions and talent shows, where some of the sailors put on skits or sang to entertain and help pass the time. *Oscar* the cat never left Digby's side and the pair became quite inseparable.

Chief Digby, however, would have no part of the sports or leisure activities. His brooding increased and most of his former crewmates started avoiding him. Charles seemed more interested in the cat than anything else. He did manage to write a letter to Bunty, assuring his son that his father was just fine and would be home soon. Yet most of what the chief wrote was inaccurate, as a deep depression set in. While this was common with combat survivors, the Royal Navy was very slow to recognize the symptoms, since CPO Digby was skilled at masking his negative thoughts.

It had been something of a miracle that only one crewman died during the sinking, out of a compliment of 1,600 men. Eventually the survivors of the *Ark Royal* gathered together for the trip back to England. It was dawn when the convoy departed Gibraltar for Portsmouth, where the sailors would eventually be reassigned to other ships. With CPO Charles Digby and the cat *Oscar* safely aboard, the troop ship *SS Samaria* sailed on the morning of December 7, 1941.

Later that same day, while attending a Mansion House luncheon, Winston Churchill heard a rumor that the Japanese Empire had attacked the US naval base at Pearl Harbor. The Prime Minister immediately telephoned President Franklin D. Roosevelt.

In two or three minutes, Mr. Roosevelt came through.

"Mr. President, what's this about Japan?" the Prime Minster asked.

"It's quite true, Winston," FDR replied. "They have attacked us at Pearl Harbor. We are all in the same boat now."

"No American will think it wrong of me if I proclaim the greatest joy, now that we have the United States at our side," Churchill said. "I could not foretell the course of events. I do not pretend to have measured accurately the martial might of Japan, but now at this very moment, I know the United

States is in this war, up to the neck and in it to the death. So we have won after all!"

"I will call you back later, Winston," the President said.

Click.

Churchill turned and faced his friends and advisors. "America is at war! How long the war will last or in what fashion it will end no man can tell, nor do I at this moment care. Once again, in our long Island history we shall emerge, however mauled or mutilated, safe and victorious. We shall not be wiped out. We shall not be wiped out! Our history will not come to an end. We might not even have to die as individuals. Hitler's fate is sealed. Mussolini's fate is sealed. As for the Japanese, they will be ground to powder. God bless America."

It wasn't until late evening that the terrible news reached Crackington Haven. Winifred Kane suddenly woke up Gavin and Bunty and made them come downstairs to listen to the wireless. The BBC was broadcasting a special war bulletin, which was being repeated every five minutes.

"*This is a special report and this is Alvar Lidell reading it,*" spoke the all-too-familiar voice over the radio. "*Japan has launched a surprise attack on the American naval base at Pearl Harbor in Hawaii and has declared war on Britain and the United States. The US president, Franklin D. Roosevelt, has mobilized all his forces and is poised to declare war on Japan. Details of the attack in Hawaii are scarce, but initial reports say Japanese bombers and torpedo carrying planes targeted warships, aircraft and military installations in Pearl Harbor, on Oahu, the third largest and chief island of Hawaii. News of the daring raid has shocked members of Congress at a time when Japanese officials in Washington were still negotiating with US Secretary of State Cordell Hull on lifting US sanctions imposed after continuing Japanese aggression against China.*"

Winifred sat silently, too stunned to comment, as the boys looked at each other in shocked amazement. After they had time to digest the news, Bunty and Gavin went back to bed, but not before taking a moment to comfort Mrs. Kane, who was visibly upset by this latest bit of bad news.

"How much more of this can we take?" Bunty asked as they reached the top of the stairs. "It seems like we're losing the war, even with Sir Osbert's help."

Gavin had been thinking the same thing. War was now at America's doorstep as well. He wondered if the dragon would have any insights into the matter. It was time to visit Thaddeus again, right after school.

The next morning, before Gavin and Bunty departed for another day at school, Aunt Mabel brought a letter directly from the post office. It was addressed to Bunty.

"It's from me pa," he exclaimed, ripping it open.

"What does he say?" Gavin asked excitedly, because CPO Digby's letters were very rare and Bunty truly enjoyed reading them over-and-over again. "What does he say?"

Winfred shushed her soon. "Gavin, be quiet and let Bunty read it."

"Yes, Mum, I'm sorry," the boy said.

"He's just fine, he says," Bunty summarized. "Only one man died when the **Ark Royal** was sunk. Dad will be on his way home soon, with two weeks of survivor's leave. He'll be coming to Crackington Haven for awhile."

"Oh, that's wonderful," Mrs. Kane pretended to be excited too, not allowing her true feelings to show.

Bunty smiled, but seemed uneasy with his father's impending visit.

Gavin's mother knew she should say something else, but first she gave Bunty a big hug. "We'll fix up the room over the garage, so your father can come and go as he pleases. He might get here in time for Christmas and you'll be out of school."

Her words made Bunty feel much better. "That's right."

"All right now, off to school," Winifred reminded them. "We'll make plans for your father's visit when you get home."

"Yes, Mrs. Kane," Bunty said politely. "Thank you."

She beamed. "Oh, it's my pleasure. Now shoo!"

The boys scooted out the back door and sprinted to the bus stop, just barely in time to catch the lumbering old behemoth to Launceston. There was plenty of chatter, with all the children and even the adults discussing the Japanese attack on the Americans at Pearl Harbor. The war had instantly expanded to include most of the world and Gavin suspected school would seem even less important compared to these monumental events.

After final class, as planned, the boys made a beeline to the little white cottage on the hill. Just as expected, Thaddeus was waiting for their arrival.

"I thought you might come today," the dragon said as they sat down on the earthen floor, their eyes wide.

"What do you make of the attack on the Americans, Sir Osbert?" Bunty asked.

Thaddeus shook his head sadly. "Such events trouble me greatly, son."

"Are we going to lose the war?" Gavin naturally wondered.

"Not bloody likely," the dragon roared. "Yet if this new threat isn't contained quickly, my brothers and sisters might take matters into their own claws. Such a reaction would spell doom for more than just humanity, I'm afraid."

"What will we do?" Gavin asked.

Thaddeus tried to smile reassuringly. "Whatever is necessary."

"You mustn't interfere directly, Sir Osbert," Bunty warned. "Remember your oath?"

The dragon grumbled under his breath. He knew the boy was right, but without action, things might not turn out the way he hoped. His view of the future was hazy, cast in constant motion and uncertainty.

Gavin reached up and scratched Thaddeus behind the ear again. "Be patient, you old dragon. Things have worked out in the past, sometimes without us even knowing it."

The dragon nodded and flashed his smiling teeth. "You are right, of course. We shall let things take their natural course, at least for the time being."

"That's the ticket," Bunty chirped happily. He looked at his watch, a recent present from Winifred Kane. "It's time to head home, sport."

Gavin never wanted to leave the cottage overlooking Tintagel, with its castle, Arthurian legends, and mighty dragon. He knew Thaddeus had cast a wondrous spell, which was hard to break, not that he wanted to.

"Be on your way, lad," Sir Osbert said compassionately. "We don't want to worry your mother, now do we?"

Gavin shook his head.

Out the door they ran, followed by the dragon's booming laughter.

The teenagers made their way to the coast, where the boys stopped for a few minutes on the cliffs to watch the fishing fleets returning with the day's catch. Bunty gleefully watched kittiwakes soar above the cliffs, while Gavin rambled over the crumbling ramparts of Tintagel Castle. Then they wandered past majestic waterfalls, hiking long distances past the ancient shrines of their Celtic ancestors. Wherever they went, Gavin could feel the dragon's protective eyes guarding them from unexpected dangers.

Hammered by relentless Atlantic winds, the pair traversed the rugged coastline to Boscastle, arriving just in time to see several incoming MTB's as they steered through the cliff-hung entrance to the calm safety of the harbor within. It was thrilling to feel the surge of pride well up inside them, as the Navy Ensign flapped madly in the swirling winds.

Not surprisingly, Gavin knew every nook and cranny of this landscape, and with such knowledge, there were stories to share with his pal Bunty. For years, Gavin and Emily had concocted tales of shipwrecks and smuggling adventures, which took place near Boscastle, or the enchanted medieval mysteries of Tintagel Castle. Little did Gavin realize that practically every night Emily wrote down these yarns, hoping to one day publish the entire collection.

Several times while continuing on the coast path, the teens stopped to take in the sheer scale of it all, before finally strolling down into Crackington Haven. Before them appeared the superb sandy beach, the suntrap sheltered by a dramatic cliff curtain. No matter whether they were soaking up the sun or hiking along the shore, the beauty and grandeur of the scenery always left Bunty awestruck with wonder. North Cornwall was his home now and the redheaded lad made up his mind to protect the land and her people, with his own life, if necessary.

Inside a tiny white cottage, a dragon stirred. He was perplexed. Thaddeus pondered his feelings and savored his acute senses. Lifting up his snout, Sir Osbert sniffed to catch the aromas of things yet to be. The mighty beast closed his eyes and sighed, for the message was quite clear. Shaking his head and flashing his razor-sharp teeth, the dragon reacted violently to the coming threat.

The thatched roof came apart and with a mighty roar, Thaddeus was suddenly airborne, his powerful wings spreading wide as he took flight. Immediately cloaking himself in invisibility, Sir Osbert headed north, to his birthplace and homeland. It was clear that a new threat was developing, but this time it originated in Iceland, not Germany!

2

Wizards at War

Winston Churchill dubbed the race for electronic superiority, the *Wizard War*, while secretly admitting his vaunted radar network still had serious limitations. Radar allowed the British to detect the bearing and distance of encroaching aircraft, but it could not easily determine the number of aircraft in a formation, and it also did not provide much coverage over the interior of England. Once past the electronic barrier, a network of ground spotters, known as the Royal Observer Corps, tracked enemy intruders.

From the beginning of the Chain Home effort, Air Marshall Dowding had understood that radar was useless without a command and control system to absorb and act on the information provided, and had driven the development of such a system. Although British radar was nothing special, the British had thought out the implications of the technology and made good use of it.

The RAF worked with the British Postal Service to come up with a scheme where observations from radar and from observers in the field were collected at a central command center. This information was then used to obtain a precise plot of the location of German intruders and even their numbers. The command center was known as the Filter Room, since it filtered out information from many different sources.

The RAF established their central underground Filter Room in the London suburbs, on the site of a 12th century monastery named Bently Priory. Hitler often voiced his low opinion of British radar, but his military had nothing to compete with the Filter Room system.

As the Luftwaffe pounded Britain, Bently Priory became the central operations center for air defense. Reports of German formations were tracked by radar and observer details were relayed to the Filter Room on secure military telephone lines. Officers logged the reports and assigned a battle number to each formation.

In the center of the Filter Room was a huge table, with a map of the British Isles and neighboring coastal regions of Europe. Various staffers moved markers across the map with tee sticks to track the movements of the intruders. A controller observed the movements and determined which fighter squadrons should scramble to intercept the threat. Alerts were sent to the four Fighter Command groups by telephone or teletype.

Most of the tracking staff was female, affectionately known as Wafs or Wrens, depending on which branch of the service the women had volunteered to join. After the network had been in operation for several months, the general belief arose that women were more patient and attentive than men, and were better suited to the work of tracking air battles. Most of them were just teenaged girls, but they displayed a typical British coolness under pressure.

Furthermore, Winston Churchill's chief scientific advisor Lord Cherwell, previously known as Professor Frederick Lindemann, wanted more attention spent on improving and enhancing radar capabilities. Lord Cherwell was opinionated, obstinate, contrary, in many ways like Churchill himself, but without as many redeeming features. Most people who dealt with Lord Cherwell regarded him, with some justification, as an obstructionist who tried to create problems, instead of figuring out how to overcome them. Lindemann was not always wrong by any means, but he was always annoying.

Lord Cherwell didn't want the secret of the improved magnetron-radar system to fall into German hands. Once the Germans understood it, they would not only try to duplicate it, but could quickly develop countermeasures against it. The alternative klystron radio-magnetic process wasn't as powerful as the magnetron, but it could easily be destroyed in an emergency. The magnetron's copper core could survive even large explosive charges.

To compound Lindemann's exasperation, the scientist who invented several of these alternative radar options, Dr. Lamken Rune, had mysteriously gone missing in early 1940. After an exhaustive search, which turned up nothing, authorities feared enemy agents had kidnapped the eccentric old man. However, MI-6 ascertained this theory was incorrect, because the Germans hadn't made any noticeable changes or improvements to their own radar systems. Agents for the British intelligence agencies reported it was possible Dr. Rune had met with an accidental and untimely death. Until a body was located, however, it was all just speculation.

Therefore, Lord Cherwell faced trying to expand British anti-radar capabilities without one of the foremost creative minds in all of England. This meant he must look elsewhere. To Lindemann's credit, he was able to recruit several capable scientists who had already proven adroit at testing and improving radar capabilities.

To knock out enemy radars, two basic functions were involved. The first was a search, conducted with receivers and direction finders, to determine where the enemy radar was located and as many as possible of its technical characteristics. The second was jamming, accomplished by means of aluminum-foil chaff sowed in the sky by airplanes or the transmission of signals, which interfered with the operation of the enemy equipment.

In the initial stages of the program, the two functions were separate. The search was conducted to obtain technical specifications and these specifications were sent home for use in the design of a suitable jammer. The jammer was then produced, on the fastest possible basis, and put into action.

RAVEN was the code name issued for British radio and radar countermeasures. The crewmembers operating the equipment were referred to as Raven operators and the nickname quickly caught on. Throughout all of England, the fraternity of radar wizards was thereafter simply known as Ravens. They were a secretive bunch and not at all friendly to outsiders, especially meddling government officials, who they considered bumbling bureaucrats without a clue.

Regardless of all the scientific inroads made up to this point, the war continued to go badly for the Allies, but now most of the setbacks were in the Pacific. The Japanese expanded their devastating and wide-sweeping military campaign, capturing one island after another. Only days after the attack on Pearl Harbor, Japanese airplanes sank the British battleship **HMS Prince of Wales** and battlecruiser **HMS Repulse**.

Over the Christmas holiday, Prime Minister Winston Churchill traveled to the United States, where he planned to address the US Congress, visit with influential American industrialists, and implore the President to focus his military efforts against the Germans, instead of the Japanese, who he held in contempt.

Imagine how tiresome it must have been for President Franklin D. Roosevelt to have a dinner guest of whom his wife greatly disapproved and who he had met only twice before. Then this interloper had the audacity to invite himself to stay at the White House, with every intention of being their houseguest for almost three weeks.

One morning, without asking permission, Winston Churchill summoned the President's butler, Alonzo Fields.

"Now, Fields, we had a lovely dinner last night, but I have a few orders for you," the Prime Minister began. "We want to leave here as friends, right? Therefore, I need you to listen. One, I don't like talking outside my quarters. Two, I hate whistling in the corridors, and three, I must have a tumbler of sherry in my room before breakfast, a couple of glasses of scotch and soda before lunch, and French champagne with 90-year- old brandy before I go to sleep at night."

"Yes, sir, Mr. Prime Minister, sir," the ever polite Alonzo assured the guest.

"Furthermore," Churchill then declared. "For breakfast, I require two poached eggs, bacon or ham or both, and lightly-buttered toast, with two kinds of cold meats, a generous portion of fine English mustard, not that bloody German stuff and two kinds of fruit plus a tumbler of sherry. Do you understand, Fields?"

"Oh, yes sir, I do indeed, sir," Alonzo replied, having jotted down all the particulars in his little notebook.

Is it little wonder, that two days later, Winston Churchill suffered a heart attack while straining to open a stuck window in his White House bedroom? As he was secretly whisked to a nearby hospital, President Roosevelt fretted that the Prime Minister might die on American soil. Fortunately, Churchill recovered quickly, spoke to the British people over the radio that evening, addressed both houses of the US Congress the following day, and then scampered up to Canada to address their parliament.

Due to the dire situation back in England, Richard Kane wasn't able to come home for the Christmas holidays. If that wasn't bad enough, rationing had been adjusted again, down to 3 ounces of cheese, 4 ounces of jam or preserves, 2 pints of milk, and about three eggs a month. From the beginning of December, everyone received a monthly allocation of 16 points for various goods covered by the system. One month's points could get 1 pound of luncheon meat or 1½ pounds of canned salmon.

Petrol and manpower shortages meant that shops no longer delivered goods to customers' homes, so people had to carry all their purchases. Wrapping paper was very scarce. There were no turkeys, nor gin, sherry, chocolates or fruit, while cigarettes, cigars and tobacco were also in short supply, and toys, if they could be found, were often shoddy or very expensive.

People made or renovated presents, while magazines in the lead-up to December were full of ideas for homemade gifts. One patriotic gift was a National Savings Certificate or a savings book with a few stamps attached. The typical person constructed their own decorations, or cut pieces of holly, shrub, or any available greenery and decorated them with pinecones or whitewash.

"We are pretty well on our beam ends as far as Christmas fare is concerned," Winifred complained to her sister. "There's no chance of turkey, chicken or goose, not even Bunty's least favorite, the despised rabbit. If we can get a little mutton, which is the best we can hope for, I might be able to pass it off as a roast. There are a few Christmas puddings about, but Mr. Greevy's shop in Boscastle has three puddings and eight hundred registered customers."

Still, on Christmas Eve, they managed to put things together and everyone enjoyed singing carols and playing simple games by the wireless. Gavin and Bunty helped clean the kitchen, while Mrs. Scott, Emily and Mrs. Kane brewed up a pot of real tea.

The next morning, there were only a few gifts around the tree, so each person really savored the moment when it was their turn to open. Much time was spent complimenting the creative wrapping and innovative use of colored twine or even dyed shoestrings.

The high point of the gifts was another canned ham all the way from Canada, which had become Richard's standby present to his family, creating a new tradition. Gavin's father was terribly missed and his wife shed a few tears more than once over the holidays, but her son was quick to comfort her with squeezie hugs and big kisses.

Yet it was also a time of reserved optimism, because Britain was no longer alone in the fight against Hitler. Germany had attacked Russia, diverting the Luftwaffe eastwards and away from Britain. Likewise, America had entered the war. In the public view, there was now no doubt that the Allied forces would eventually win, despite the setbacks. In fact, things looked rather bleak, for on Christmas Day, Hong Kong surrendered to the advancing Japanese, although the news was withheld from British citizens for several days.

Meanwhile in the Third Reich, over every radio station, a very nervous Joseph Goebbels, the Nazi Propaganda Minister, broadcast a Christmas message to the German people. It was no message of cheer.

After a perfunctory mention of the accomplishments of the German Army, which was actually retreating in Russia, the little Minister got down to business. What he wanted was Christmas presents for the soldiers on the Eastern Front, such as overshoes, stockings, woolen underwear, furs, blankets, gloves, earmuffs or anything, in fact, which would turn the keen winds of the Russian winter.

The German people, Goebbels admitted, had already given all they conveniently could, in consideration of the tense situation regarding textile supplies. Nevertheless, as long as a single object of winter clothing remained in the Fatherland, it must go to the front.

Although he spoke of shortages at home, Dr. Goebbels did not tell his fellow Germans the truth. He didn't share the fact that each German soldier in frozen Norway was ordered to give up one of his three blankets for use in Russia. Neither did Goebbels inform anyone of the new rubber-saving rule, which forbid workers living within two miles of their jobs to cycle to work. He didn't even explain why some German planes shot down over Britain were fitted with inefficient wooden propellers.

There were other signs that Germany's Christmas would be far from *gemütlich*, the word for warm and congenial, pleasant and friendly. French factories, even those working on German war orders, got an unwelcome holiday vacation of two weeks in the form of a shutdown to save coal. In Hungary, the food situation was so acute that hunters were permitted to use precious gasoline driving to the woods in taxis. The Reich was so short of doctors that it started advertising for more physicians in the occupied countries. The overworked doctors in Germany itself were warned not to prescribe iodine, aspirin or diets with extra food. During the previous Christmas season, Germans received extra rations of food, but in 1941, the Christmas rations were reduced to just two ounces of coffee and six ounces of lentils.

Adolf Hitler himself set the tone for the holiday when he said, "Millions of our soldiers stand after a year of the heaviest battles against an enemy who is superior in numbers and material on the front."

However, when 1942 arrived, the news was a repeat of the previous year, with even more depressing setbacks for the Allies.

First, Singapore surrendered to the Japanese in February. This failure was one of the greatest defeats in the history of the British Army.

Then the Americans felt the bitter sting of defeat, as Wake and Guam were captured, thereby isolating the Philippines from Hawaii. Their pitiful remaining forces retreated to the islands of Corregidor and Bataan, hoping to hold out until a relief force could be organized.

During these desperate times, it was very important to keep up public morale and Winston Churchill's government was well aware of their responsibility in this regard. Since women were taking up the jobs vacated by men joining the services, a great deal of effort was focused on helping the female population deal with all the difficulties created by the war.

For instance, silk stockings were in short supply. To take their place, various brands of leg make-up appeared on the market. Women resorted to drawing seams with eyebrow pencil down the back of each leg to give the appearance of wearing stockings.

Clothes rationing created a new utility fashion trend, calling for short skirts, sensible flat-heeled shoes and square-shouldered jackets, which resembled the cut of men's uniforms. Fancy clothing was out, as trousers or dungarees were worn instead of skirts and a scarf was tied around the head. The British government encouraged the slogan, *Make Do and Mend*. Older clothes were transformed into modern styles and women's magazines carried tips on how to spend clothing coupons and how to revamp old suits and dresses. Winifred even converted some of Richard's old suits to wear herself.

Heavy blankets were converted into fashionable overcoats and knitting was encouraged for all ages in school. Popular knitting patterns included slippers, socks, and jumpers. Mrs. Kane was even able to acquire a pattern for the Royal Navy, so she could knit a jumper for her husband. The sewing patterns had to conform to the same stringent guidelines as store-purchased clothes, which meant there were limits on hems, pleats and turn-ups.

Just like most British women, Winifred took great pride in her appearance and improvised with make-up and hair products. Gloves and hats were essential, but hats could be easily adapted by simply adding flowers or feathers. Unfortunately, gas masks were required, so Gavin's mother had to improvise by hiding the bulky kit in the bottom of her handbag.

It would have been understandable if the war had forced Mrs. Kane to ignore her overall appearance. However, just the opposite was true. Winifred thought it was unpatriotic not to look her best.

She summed it up best for Bunty and Gavin. "The bombs keep falling and our cities are burning, but the women of Britain are going to keep morale high by looking our very best!"

In response, the boys cheered.

Gavin hugged her and said, "You're the most beautiful woman in all of the United Kingdom, Mum."

She giggled with delight and in a flurry of kisses, smothered her son with affection. Always cognizant of Bunty's feelings, Winifred reached out and pulled the boy to her side, where he too received abundant squeezie hugs and smooching.

Off they went to play and explore, heading straight for the seashore. A few minutes later, Winifred joined them, pouring out a nice hot cup of tea. The three of them sat together, sipping and enjoying the rugged unspoiled beauty of the North Cornish landscape. Perhaps they were aware of the bond between them and the sea, to feel the energy from the pounding surf and be a part of the power the sculpted the coastline, their Cornwall. Moments like these gave Gavin pause, as he realized he wasn't afraid of the ocean, but was terrified of losing everything, including his youth, to this war.

Crackington Haven was becoming a popular place for servicemen, when so many other beaches were out of bounds, because of minefields and barbed wire. It was a wonderful place to behold, though, with a stream running down from the cliff and meandering its way in between the boulders and out into the sea at the southern end of the cove.

Yet on the west side of London, Major Traber Vickers was finally successful in arranging a meeting with a group of exiled senior Czechoslovak military officers. Their headquarters was based in Porchester Gate, where František Moravec was serving as the chief of the military intelligence service of the Czechoslovak Government in Exile.

Major Vickers was invited to step inside the old mansion, but his hosts were extremely suspicious of his motives. After all, British Prime Minister Neville Chamberlain had simply given away Czechoslovakia to Hitler to prevent war. The citizens of that nation felt betrayed by the British policy of appeasement.

"I appreciate this opportunity to meet with you and your officers, sir," Vickers said quietly, well aware of how the feelings of animosity could sabotage his plan. On top of that, he was performing this mission based entirely on the request of a dragon, no less.

"I must be bleedin' out of me mind," he mumbled to himself.

František Moravec pointed towards the dining area, which served as the chief's conference room. "We shall discuss your agenda in there."

Vickers smiled as he walked into the room. "I am honored to have a few moments to outline a top secret operation for your consideration."

"Please, Major, be seated," Moravec said, motioning towards an open chair.

Everyone in the room waited until Vickers sat down, before they also were seated. There was a moment of painful silence as the men waited for their commanding officer to open the discussion.

"There are certain legends in our country regarding three dragons that flew through the air and alighted on a great rock near Prague," Moravec finally began.

Vickers smiled uncomfortably. He hadn't expected the conversation to start with a tale about dragons.

"The story claims that one of the dragons was quite benevolent," the intelligence chief continued. "He begged audience with the king and presented the monarch with many spectacular jewels for his crown. However, there was one condition attached to these priceless gifts."

Intrigued, Vickers asked, "What condition was that?"

Moravec replied, "That whosoever placed the crown upon their head would be fair, just, and kind."

"I see," the major said. "What would happen if his warning was ignored?"

All the men around the table were obviously waiting for their commanding officer to answer. The tension in the air was thick with foreboding.

"That death would come to that wicked person within a year," Moravec answered.

"Has anyone worn the crown recently?" Vickers inquired hesitantly.

Moravec nodded. "Reinhard Heydrich."

The name left his lips as if it was snake venom.

Vickers rested his hands on the table. "Then perhaps it is destiny that has brought me here today."

Everyone waited for him to continue.

"I would like to plan for the assassination of Reinhard Heydrich," Vickers said.

Another door opened at the far end of the dining room and an older gentleman entered. He was neatly attired in an immaculately tailored suit, sporting a perfectly trimmed mustache, which might have been a failed attempt to offset his dramatically receding hairline.

Moravec quickly stood up, along with the other officers. "Major Vickers, may I introduce our President, Edvard Beneš."

The man had an unprepossessing appearance, which deprived him of physical charisma, but his voice was incredibly dynamic in tone.

"I hope to prevent my countrymen displaying hatred towards England and France, who bargained away our country, for peace in our time," Beneš stated sarcastically. "Do you think murdering Heydrich will accomplish anything positive at all?"

"Such action will revive your country's resistance movement, as well as boost the prestige of Czechoslovak principles among her allies," Vickers replied.

Vickers hoped that Beneš would feel his credibility in London and Moscow depended on such dramatic evidence of Czech defiance.

The president held up his hand. "I will *never* go on public record calling for such violence. If asked, I will deny any role in its planning or execution."

"That's fair enough, sir," Vickers said. "I will present my recommendations to the Prime Minister, without inferring your sanction."

With that, President Beneš exited the room.

"If your Prime Minister approves of such a plan and is willing to accept both the blame and responsibility for German reprisals, then we will support such an operation," Moravec stated.

Vickers said, "Then I shall proceed and report back to you."

The officers all shook hands, as if sealing a business deal.

From that moment on, the stage was set.

As Thaddeus touched down on the frozen ice wastes of central Iceland, not even he could envision what serious repercussions this operation would eventually have.

3

Ramparts of Evil

Atop a dark hillside and beneath black stormy clouds, stood Schloss Wewelsburg, fortress headquarters for Himmler's vaunted SS. High above the foreboding stone structure, cloaked in darkness and the pouring rain, perched a gigantic creature of diabolical legend and forbidden myth. As lightning flashed and thunder boomed across the valley, the black dragon changed his roost, moving towards one of the towers, where candlelight filtered through the curtained windows. He was always attracted to light, thirsting to absorb its energy.

Peering into the dimly lit room, the sinister dragon could see a man, all dressed in black, sitting at a desk. The winged beast immediately recognized his master, Heinrich Himmler. The Reichsführer was furtively writing a message destined to be read by only one man – Adolf Hitler, supreme leader of Nazi Germany.

Did the letter constitute a warning, a plea, or perhaps a dark legacy for the intended recipient? Himmler seemed nervous and on edge, glancing frequently out the window or over his shoulder. Even with his handpicked bodyguards standing nearby, the Reichsführer felt threatened.

Something was coming, something even more sinister, perhaps more evil than all of the Third Reich combined. Drawn to the Nazi dogma of cruelty and enslavement, this unearthly force thrived on suffering. In fact, at that very moment, a demonic shadow swept up the outside of the tower wall, making its way towards Himmler's room. Heinrich wrote with deliberate haste, driven to finish his scrawled letter. The man was startled, as he sensed a malignant force drawing ever closer.

The candles flickered and then abruptly went out.

The blackness deepened to an oppressive level.

Crash!

Without warning, the tower window burst open, showering the inhabitants in shards of broken glass.

A robed, shadow-like form floated into the room and flung one of Himmler's elite bodyguards out the open window. The unfortunate soldier fell screaming to his death on the spiked iron fence below.

The intruder hovered above the terrified Reichsführer, until its glowing red eyes were only inches from Himmler's face. The other guards slinked back, before one cowardly soldier managed to unbolt the door and they all fled for their lives.

The Reichsführer had been abandoned.

He was all alone.

"I have need of your services," spoke the apparition, its voice clicking like the rattling of bones.

Himmler could only manage to nod.

"Good," the shadow rasped. "Your pet dragon will soon be ready to do *my* bidding, but first, you will receive a visitor tomorrow. He too is my slave."

Again, Himmler could only nod his understanding.

As quickly as it had appeared, the spirit simply vanished.

Nothing but a cold and empty sensation remained.

Himmler could not move, shaking with fear and loathing.

The next morning, without advance notice or accompanying fanfare, Adolf Hitler arrived at Wewelsburg Castle. The man's face was ashen and he appeared gaunt, possibly ill. Himmler had never seen the Führer look so poorly.

"*Heil Hitler!*" the Reichsführer called out as Hitler walked up the steps, surrounded by members of his own personal guard.

The Führer lifted his hand in a half-hearted attempt to acknowledge the salute, but skittered past Himmler without saying a word. He acted as if he was about to faint.

Himmler followed Hitler obediently.

They met privately in the castle library.

"I am honored by your visit, *Mein Führer*," Himmler said.

Hitler couldn't stop moving, for he was highly agitated. Flitting about like a dragonfly, the man seemed less like the supreme German leader and more like a frightened child. Something serious was obviously distracting him.

"May I offer you some refreshment, *Mein Führer*?" Himmler asked.

Hitler violently shook his head, but the question did stop his frantic pacing and he spun around, abruptly asking, "What will the social order of the future be like, if we win this war?"

Himmler pondered the question.

The Führer didn't wait for an answer. "Comrade, I will tell you. There would be a class of overlords, after them the rank and file of the party members in hierarchical order, and then the great masses of anonymous followers, servants and workers in perpetuity, and beneath them all the conquered foreign races, nothing more than modern slaves. Over and above all these masses, would rule a being of exalted nobility, of whom I cannot speak. This creature is already amongst us. He is here. Isn't that enough for you? I will tell you a secret. I have seen him. He is powerful and cruel. You must know that I am afraid of him?"

Himmler knew all too well.

"We shall speak no more of this," Hitler announced. "We must deliver millions of dead to satiate his hunger, or he will consume us instead. We must prepare. We must plan for death and destruction, even of our own nation. Nothing else will appease him."

Himmler cleared his throat.

"Yes, Heinrich, what is it?" Hitler demanded.

"May I recommend Reinhard Heydrich for this monumental task," Himmler spoke up. "He is a fanatical planner, as you know. He wishes only to please you, *Mein Führer*."

"*Ja, ja*, splendid," Hitler said. "We will sit now and speak of Reinhard's part in all of this."

The rest of the day was spent discussing Hitler's grandiose plans for German expansion, once the Russians had been defeated. Maps of Europe were strewn about the floor and Himmler was enthralled with Hitler's ideas regarding a united continent, all under Nazi rule.

When they finally stopped to eat, the meal was quite simple, for Hitler preferred only soup and bread. Himmler forced himself to tolerate such pauper fare for one evening, although he grimaced after every spoonful of *Kartoffelsuppe*, or German Potato Soup. Exhausted from the day's proceedings, the Führer retired early and Himmler returned to the library to study his leader's extensive list of objectives.

Hours later, the Führer suddenly awoke in total panic over some horrific nightmare. Hitler stood in the middle of the guest bedroom, stumbling about, looking around him with a distraught and terrified expression.

He muttered, "It's him! It's him! He's here!"

Hitler's lips turned blue. He was dripping with sweat. He uttered a series of numbers, which made no sense, adding strange archaic words, and then bits of phrases in ancient languages. The man's irrational behavior only heightened his obvious fear. Hitler used terms strung together in the strangest manner, which seemed to be utter nonsense.

He became silent again, although his lips continued to move.

Then he screamed, "There! Over there! In the corner! Who is it?"

Hitler was jumping up and down, howling like a dog, when Himmler and his guards burst into the bedroom. They thought their leader was under attack, but the room was empty of any other soul.

"Go, leave us," Himmler shooed away the soldiers, many of whom had witnessed very strange events since arriving. They left without discussion.

When they were alone, the Reichsführer sat with Hitler on the edge of the bed. Neither man said anything for a moment.

Abruptly Hitler stood up, his eyes wide with demonic intensity. "I must plunge Germany into the abyss, my dear Heinrich. It is the only way we will satiate the beast. You must set forth to exterminate as many as possible, before the Allies are victorious."

"Victorious, *Mein Führer*?" Himmler asked uncomfortably. "Surely Germany will prevail."

Hitler shook his head. "No, we have already lost the war."

"Why go on?" Himmler asked quietly.

The Führer sighed and replied, "It is our destiny to change the shape of the world. Our master commands it and we shall obey."

Himmler stood up as well. "But, *Mein Führer*..."

"Leave me," Hitler commanded. "There is nothing further to discuss."

Hitler did not try to go back to sleep, but dressed and walked the halls and galleries of Wewelsburg Castle. It was mindless wandering, or the Führer might have noticed certain indications regarding Himmler's fascination with dragons. Instead, oblivious to the clues around him, Hitler was unaware that the Reichsführer had already bargained with the forces of darkness, thereby assuring the Third Reich would end in flames and death.

Skipping breakfast, Hitler hurriedly returned to Berlin.

An hour later, the Reichsführer met with his lead scientist, Dr. Schumann.

"How did your discussions with the *Führer* go?" the doctor asked.

Himmler smiled with deceit. "The *Führer* approved all of my proposals. We must continue our work with a renewed sense of urgency. Only by using our newly discovered powers, may we defeat the Allies and win eternal glory for the Third Reich!"

Dr. Schumann was very excited by the possibilities. "We shall redouble our efforts, *Herr Reichsführer*."

"That is good," Himmler replied. "We must be ever vigilant and focus our energies on new ways to assure victory, no matter what the cost."

"*Jawohl, Herr Reichsführer*," the doctor said, coming to attention. "May I offer a suggestion?"

"*Bitte, Doktor Schumann,*" Himmler replied.

"I think you should ask for volunteers from within the German scientific community," the doctor said. "The more great minds we can gather here, the more fantastic things we can create for the Third Reich. You yourself have said many times how science can be a wonderful tool to promote Germany's superiority."

Himmler was pleased. "You are brilliant, *Doktor.* I will instruct the directors of my *SS Ahnenerbe Institute* to recruit mathematicians, chemists, biologists, physicists, engineers, and visionaries to expand Germany's scientific influence upon the world."

Emboldened by this plan, the Reichsführer issued edicts to all the universities and laboratories throughout the Third Reich, extolling the virtues of working for the Fatherland. He also arranged for the German magazine *Signal,* to highlight his recruiting drive with a lead article. The cover of this special edition was adorned with a photograph of Himmler standing amongst respected scientists with bad hair and wearing wrinkled white lab coats, surrounded by liquid-filled beakers and bubbling flasks.

It was at this time that yet another player became embroiled in these strange events, one ravishingly beautiful German spy known as Vera Eriksen. She was born Vera Staritzka, but fled from Russia to Denmark with her parents following the Russian Revolution in 1917. At the age of 18, Vera married Count Sergei Ignatieff, a member of an important aristocratic Russian family that had fallen on hard times since their exile after the uprising. In 1935, she changed her legal name to Eriksen and while living in Brussels, the Germans unexpectedly approached her. Surprisingly, the Secret Police successfully recruited her to work for German intelligence.

In 1938, Vera was sent to Britain, where she easily formed casual relationships with German agents, German sympathizers, and other influential people. In early 1940, Eriksen was promoted and traveled to Norway for further training. Under orders issued directly from Reinhard Heydrich, she returned to England and managed to sneak into Scotland Yard during a bombing raid over London. Moments before the seventh floor was struck with high explosives, Vera stole a key to Wilhelm Morz's personal strongbox, which was supposedly hidden in his cottage outside Swansea, Wales.

In Iceland, Thaddeus stood before Korban Vex. The two great dragons, adversaries indeed, but also respected elders for all of Draconia, were meeting in secret. The conversation was quiet and filled with foreboding.

"I felt it," Sir Osbert repeated.

Vex nodded slowly. "Yes, they are warning us. These messages come from beyond our understanding of the known universe."

"I cannot clearly translate their meaning?" Thaddeus added with frustration.

Vex knew that the wondrous red dragon had stumbled upon one of the great secrets of the cosmos. "Perhaps you are not meant to understand, my friend."

Sir Osbert shook his head. "No, the hidden air currents carried the vision to me for a purpose. It is not only profound, but also mysterious, that such signals would only come to me. I am the last of my kind, so no other dragon would be capable of receiving the pulse of energy in the form it was delivered."

Korban Vex stirred uncomfortably. He was well aware of the significance of this event. The planet itself could sense its own destruction and was reaching out to the one species entrusted with safeguarding its survival.

The purple dragon looked Thaddeus straight in the eye, an exceedingly rare and serious action. "We have seldom agreed on anything over the years, my dear friend, but there is no dragon alive I would trust more, with my life or that of our kind. You are poised on the edge of a cataclysmic event and few will ever know the part you played. There will be a time, soon, when forces beyond our control will rise to destroy all living creatures that inhabit this sphere. It will be you, who must decide which one of us will be sacrificed to defeat this wretched enemy. I do not envy you. Yet when that moment in time is clear, I will stand at your side."

Thaddeus was stunned by this commitment. He sat back on his haunches and reached out with both forepaws, resting them on Korban's immense shoulders. "In all the years I have known you, I have never doubted where your loyalty lay, Master Vex. I swear to you, that of all the dragons of our realm, I value your support most. No matter what transpires, I know that you are good to your word."

The great dragons stood, side-by-side, and faced one wall of the secret chamber. Jutting forth their right paws, each extended a single claw, as the reflection off towering columns of ice sparkled from the deadly points.

One single plate of scale lifted away from their chests, exposing a vulnerable spot above the heart.

Slash!

With blinding speed, each dragon delivered a deep slice into the other's tender skin.

Green blood spurted to mix with blue blood.

Korban Vex growled.

Thaddeus Osbert roared.

Jets of flame blasted the opposite wound, cauterizing the damage in an instant.

The bond was everlasting.

This ritual, forbidden for eons, created a pact that no human could understand.

For if either Korban Vex or Thaddeus Osbert should die, the surviving dragon would inherit every trait of the deceased.

4

Model Makers

Even though the British military was not prepared for the demand for detailed models at the onset of war, a specialized department was formed after representatives of the Royal Navy, RAF, and the Royal Army met to discuss intelligence-gathering techniques. Commando operations relied heavily on military personnel acting with a high degree of initiative. This new notion meant officers at all levels had to know exactly what they were doing and be able to pass this information on to their men accurately. Clearly, the success of commando insertions would rely on thorough briefings with first-rate intelligence materials presented, so that all personnel would have a clear image of the target and its topographic context.

The significance of aerial photography, as a source for military intelligence, was becoming more fully appreciated. Lieutenant Commander Richard Kane's section had gathered priceless information on tides, geology, and photographs of installations and cities collected from newspapers and periodicals. Furthermore, the RAF had facilities for enlarging contour maps, aerial photographs, and mosaics to the exact size of the proposed terrain models. Aerial photography and terrain modeling were to prove an effective combination.

The idea of using relief models initially met with serious skepticism by military commanders. The problem of training military personnel to comprehend strategic and tactical briefings through reading topographic maps was both monumental and vital. The vast majority of officers had only limited experience with sand tables, which were raised rims containing a bed of coarse sand. Such primitive terrain examples had been used during military training at Sandhurst Military Academy, since the beginning of the nineteenth century. Despite the cynics, the model-making group was formed, but clearly, they required skilled model makers, with art training and experience.

Professional and commercial artists, sculptors, architects, and architectural model makers were invited to volunteer for service. After training with air photo interpretation, work began on making models of occupied airfields in Brittany near Lorient and Vannes, Brest Harbor, Cherbourg Peninsula, Guernsey, and places farther away, such as Dakar and Tobruk. Models continued to be made to support commandos for targets in Italy and Norway and, gradually, the significance of the model makers' efforts became more widely recognized.

The model shop became officially known as V-Section and was transferred to the Central Interpretation Unit at **RAF Medmenham**, Buckinghamshire. The basement of Danesfield House was set aside for model making. All personnel lived in Quonset huts within the grounds of Danesfield.

To his superiors, Lieutenant Commander Kane suggested models should be made of all significant German installations, which further proved the worth of the modelers. As with all model-making activities, they were required to create highly accurate and realistic three-dimensional models. With the enthusiastic assistance of Richard's team supplying hundreds of photographs, a close-knit bond was formed between the two sections.

"Look at these photographs until your eyes bug out and screw up into your head," Lt. Cmdr. Kane reminded the modelers one afternoon during briefing. "You must get every detail perfect in your minds, then go away and recreate them from memory, come back and check your models, correct them, then go away and make them over and over again, until they're absolutely perfect. Do you understand why I am stressing such attention to detail?"

"Aye, aye, sir," they all called out in unison.

Richard smiled. "Good. Carry on, then."

"May I have a word with you, Lieutenant Commander?" one of the young artisans requested as he stepped forward.

"Yes, of course," Richard replied. "Why don't we talk over there?"

They walked to one of the unoccupied workbenches.

"I know this is highly unusual, sir, but I needed someone of authority to talk to," the man explained himself.

"Very well," Kane said. "Let's start with introductions."

"I'm sorry, sir, my name is Rupert Thatcher," the man said.

"It's very nice to meet you, Rupert," Richard said, shaking hands. "Now, what's on your mind?"

"Well, this is going to sound daft, sir, but I keep dreaming about this ruddy big castle, which seems quite Germanic in style," Thatcher tried to explain. "I can't get it out of my head, so I was wondering if I was mentally irregular?"

Normally such a question might have put Kane in an awkward position, but there was something about the young man's description that made Richard feel decidedly uneasy. "No, I don't think that at all, Rupert. Since you're a model maker, I suggest you use some of your spare time and build the castle you see in your dreams. Once you've done that, I imagine it will stop haunting you."

Thatcher's eyes sparkled with appreciation. "Now that's a perfectly spiffing idea, sir."

"Carry on," Kane dismissed him.

Rupert went back to his assigned workstation and enthusiastically returned to whatever project he had been creating earlier. Thatcher was even whistling.

With his signature smile back in place, Kane strolled from station to station, observing the other artists at work and making suggestions whenever he could. For the most part, however, he stayed out of their way, because interruptions could prove very distracting.

Shortly after their initial deliveries, the work of the model-making section began to gain recognition with the RAF and Royal Navy. The Royal Army was not so quick to accept models, but eventually admitted that V-Section had gained a reputation for integrity and worthwhile contributions to intelligence gathering and use. Consequently, the workload for the modelers increased dramatically.

More personnel were required.

Initially the Model-Making Detachment consisted of one officer and 20 men, but that quickly increased to three officers and 85 men. Shortly afterwards a small contingent of American modelers arrived at Henley-on-Thames, where they were billeted in the once-exclusive private club called Phyllis Court. The British personnel remained at Danesfield House, but were transported to Phyllis Court by truck, or made their own way by bicycle. Phyllis Court, which was a Regency-style country house, with fine views of the River Thames through its large French windows, was a pleasant place to work. Spacious and well lit, it was quite conducive to model making.

After a short training course, the Americans joined their British counterparts to form a powerful team, which turned out remarkably fine models. Oddly, the Americans were hitherto unfamiliar with the interpretation of air photography, particularly the use of photogrammetry for intelligence gathering. Many American officers required training regarding the various uses for photographs. In Britain, by contrast, aerial photograph interpretation had become a basic source of information regarding the enemy, and the use of photographs represented a major British contribution to the Allied intelligence effort.

Modeling recruits were drawn from a variety of professions and backgrounds, including sculpture, industrial design, art, display, architecture, and model work. For the British personnel there was little formal instruction, but such was not the case with the civilian contractors, who gained considerable on-the-job training. A significant number of staff were very skilled and highly regarded craftsmen, but they often suffered from the regimen of day-to-day life dictated by the military code of behavior.

In many cases, new recruits knew at least one other person within the model-making section, which is why they joined in the first place. This fact quickly galvanized the contingent into a team, because just about everyone was aware of each other's backgrounds and skills. Richard Kane was welcomed as an integral member of the section and his advice was often acted upon quickly. In fact, Richard was successful in convincing the model-makers to assign work according to each individual's skills.

For example, junior staff were given the mechanical tasks of cutting the contours using cut-awl machines or the first stage of filling the contours with Watertex, while the more experienced senior staff carried out surface interpretation, fine detail modeling, and building construction.

To entrust such secret and serious work to artists was not an idea welcomed at first by many of those in command. In some cases, names were removed from maps and the top margins showing the latitude and longitude were sliced off. It became an unofficial war of wits. On occasion, the model making section knew the target was in Germany, but seldom where. A simple formula allowed them to determine the shadow factor on a set of photographs from the height of the plane and the focal length of the camera. With this shadow factor, the model section could measure the height of any object to a high degree of accuracy.

Given the apparent worries over maintaining secrecy, it is surprising that security at **RAF Medmenham** wasn't tighter. Personnel privy to the most sensitive secrets of the war were free to frequent the local public houses and were rarely, if ever, given a security check when leaving or arriving at the base.

Working conditions were often made worse because many of their superiors viewed them as merely having fun, which meant the model makers were ranked well below fighting men. What was worse, military administrators refused to recognize model makers as skilled craftsmen.

However, the artistic skills of the model makers, combined with their essential training in air photo interpretation, provided the hybrid skills necessary to produce reliable three-dimensional representations of the landscape. The models were created so that the viewer could learn, memorize, and recognize an object before arriving. The decision to include or exclude details was the model maker's responsibility. These professionals understood the importance of including that which governed vision and excluding whatever was a distraction.

Even though the workload varied, the pressures were immense. The workshop operated twenty-four hours a day, seven days a week, with twelve-hour shifts. Each job was top secret and quite a burden for personnel to bear. The pressure of responsibility, secrecy, and deadlines often forced members to request transfer out of the model-making section.

Keeping the model shop well supplied was also constant challenge. Richard quickly noted that the model section came last in the bitter struggle for promotions, personnel, materials, equipment, or even rations. During the early stages of model making, the modelers needed sculptor spatulas, artist brushes, and texturing materials. Yet none of these items were listed in the RAF Supply Catalog, so personnel had to scrounge materials and equipment from their own studios or buy them out of their meager wages. Initially the entire workforce was male, but as demand for models increased, recruiters began searching for women volunteers.

The relatively pleasant working environment at Danesfield House helped alleviate stress, when the modelers were actually given time off. Richard organized tea parties whenever possible and did his best to keep morale high and camaraderie tight. This attention to the team's well-being added immensely to their productivity.

The finished models were of an exceptionally high standard, because they would be used for different planning purposes and by all types of forces taking part in the combined operation. Royal Navy, Army, Commando, and RAF units requested models of beaches, gun emplacements, harbors, airfields and occupied villages.

A key reason for the timely delivery of the models to the planners was the remarkable close collaboration between Kane's Photographic Interpretation Unit and the modeling staff. Military planning was often done from models before they were completed, so that any special information required was incorporated as the work progressed, and additional sections were built when a change of plan made this necessary. A higher degree of accuracy was achieved, thanks to direct contact with those actually taking part in the operation, who asked critical and timely questions about every detail of the topography.

In London, word of these modelers reached the Prime Minister. He was intrigued and hoped to make arrangements to visit V-Section as soon as possible. While leaning over and studying an intricate model of the German harbor defenses at Calais, there was a knock on the door.

"Oh, do come in," Churchill called out between puffing his big fat cigar.

"Your appointment has arrived, Prime Minister," his aide announced.

"Very well, show him in," Churchill said.

Major Vickers stepped in and smartly came to attention.

Churchill looked up and squinted, then stood straight. "Ah, it's you, is it?"

"Yes, Mr. Prime Minister," Vickers replied. "You sent for me, sir?"

Churchill coughed and stuck his left hand into the watch-pocket of his vest. "Yes, yes, indeed I did. I have been remiss in not contacting you sooner. How is the Commando training progressing?"

"Quite well, Mr. Prime Minister," Vickers said nervously, not exactly certain what he should or shouldn't say.

"Well, it has come to my attention that graduates of your courses are doing splendidly in the field," Churchill said, suddenly surrounded by billowing clouds of white smoke. He shooed the wisps away as if they were a swarm of pesky gnats and pointed to a chair. "Sit there, if you please, Major."

Vickers hurried over and sat down, ramrod stiff. "Thank you, sir."

The Prime Minister plopped down directly across from the officer and leaned forward, as if to share a vital national secret. Churchill whispered, "Haven't seen more of that bloody dragon, have you?"

Vickers gulped. "Well, sir, I..."

He didn't get a chance to finish.

Churchill sat up straight and scowled. "I do say, this is quite unsporting, if you ask me. Everyone in this bloody country seems to bandy about with this dragon fellow, except me. What is required, a formal invitation for tea at Ten Downing Street?"

Again, Traber didn't have a clue what to say that wouldn't make matters worse.

Churchill puffed away and the mood passed. He poured them both a cup of tea and plunked several sugar cubes in each. Vickers couldn't help but think of Thaddeus Osbert just then.

The Prime Minister took a few sips and then dramatically set his cup on the saucer with a loud clank. He reached for his trusty bottle of Johnny Walker Red.

"I understand you've brought me a top-secret plan from the Czechs?" Churchill asked, while pouring a healthy measure of whiskey into his tea.

"Yes, sir, that's true," the major replied, never getting a chance to taste his tea. "The government-in-exile would like to take dramatic action against the Nazi invaders."

Churchill's eyebrows went up. "Well, it's about bloody time. What do they have in mind?"

"The assassination of Reinhard Heydrich, sir," Vickers stated very slowly.

Churchill finished off the spiked tea in one healthy gulp. The Prime Minister peered over the edge of the cup, studying the officer before him. What he was looking for wasn't obvious to anyone but Winston Churchill, but he searched for the traits just the same. Then apparently, he found what he was looking for too.

The empty cup was returned to the saucer and Churchill got to his feet. Vickers also stood up and waited.

"There will be serious reprisals," Churchill said quietly.

"Yes, they are aware of that fact," Vickers said.

"What is your opinion, Major?" the Prime Minister asked.

Vickers was surprised Churchill had asked.

"I think the Czechs need to take bold action, sir," Traber replied, well aware he was covering up for the true motivation behind his support of the proposed mission. The major had only suggested Heydrich's assassination in the first place, after meeting Thaddeus Osbert.

"There will be much resistance to such a move."

"Especially if it fails."

"Success consists of going from failure to failure without loss of enthusiasm."

Vickers grimaced a little. "What I don't lack in enthusiasm, I more than make up for by the number of enemies I've made along the way, sir."

"You have enemies?" Churchill reacted. "Good, that means you've stood up for something, sometime in your life."

Vickers smiled with renewed confidence.

"I wholeheartedly support this venture, because of the very nature of its boldness," Churchill said.

"Then I shall proceed accordingly, Mr. Prime Minister," the major said.

"Some words of advice, then, Major," Churchill added. "If you have an important point to make, don't try to be subtle or clever. Use a pile driver. Hit the point once. Then come back and hit it again. Then hit it a third time, but with a tremendous whack. That should get their attention."

"Thank you, sir, I'll try to remember that," Vickers said, coming to attention.

"That will be all, Major," the Prime Minister concluded the meeting. "Keep me abreast of progress and when this vital operation is ready to launch. Then I shall throw the entire weight of the British government behind it."

"Very well, sir," Vickers said. The major turned and departed.

Churchill picked up his private telephone receiver. "Please put through a call to Mr. Beneš, the Czechoslovak president."

"Right away, Mr. Prime Minister," Ruth, the operator, replied. "I will ring you back when I have connected."

"Thank you," Churchill said and he hung up.

Several minutes later, the telephone rang. The Prime Minister picked up the receiver and said, "Hello, Edvard, it's Winston. I've had a nice little chat with our Major Vickers and I approve of the plan without reservation. The young officer will be paying you a visit again, so don't be afraid to tell him what you need to make this a success."

Due to security precautions, the two leaders couldn't discuss anything in further detail. Churchill made a few comments regarding the weather and such, before they agreed to meet later in the month.

Click.

The Prime Minister relit his Havana and puffed away. Then he picked up the telephone again.

"Yes, Mr. Prime Minister?" Ruth inquired.

"I wish to visit **RAF Medmenham** as soon as possible," Churchill said. "I would like to tour V-Section at Danesfield House and the Photographic Interpretation Unit as well."

"I will see to it immediately, sir," Ruth said.

"Thank you," Churchill said. "Call me back as soon as you have made the necessary arrangements for today, if possible, and make certain that Lieutenant Commander Richard Kane is available."

Click.

He hung up without waiting for her reply.

At **RAF Medmenham**, Richard Kane was just returning from the modeler's briefing, when Sally Fairborne hurried to intercept him.

"I just wanted to let you know, sir, that Winston Churchill is coming for a tour this afternoon," she filled him in. "You might want to get some sleep before he arrives, because he has requested you as his personal guide."

The Lieutenant Commander looked at her with barely-repressed panic in his eyes. "Whatever would I do without you, Sally?"

"You'd manage just fine, I imagine, sir," she replied.

"I'm not so certain, Sally," Richard said candidly. "Please stay close by, in case I make a blithering fool of myself and get sacked by the PM."

Sally smiled. "I promise to protect you!"

They both laughed.

Several hours later, the Prime Minster was escorted through Danesfield House, shaking hands with the staff and asking all sorts of questions. Churchill seemed genuinely interested in each model, even making a few suggestions for improving working conditions and demanding the unit receive better supplies.

One of the lead members of the PM's entourage was Lt. Cmdr. Kane, of course. Winston Churchill had greeted Gavin's father with warm regard and their handshake expressed mutual respect. In fact, the Prime Minister insisted Richard conduct a tour of the installation from front to back.

Taking advantage of a moment when the two men where standing off to one side, the Prime Minister struck up a conversation that seemed casual on the surface.

"It's good to see you again, Lieutenant Commander," Churchill said warmly.

"Likewise, sir," Richard said.

"How is that boy of yours, Gavin is his name?" the Prime Minster inquired.

"Yes, Mr. Prime Minister, Gavin is doing just fine," Lt. Cmdr. Kane replied. "The sooner we've defeated the Germans, the sooner my son can get on with his life, without fear of war and destruction."

Churchill nodded emphatically. "Indeed, Lieutenant Commander, indeed. It is my profound dream that we will quickly be rid of this insane horror."

"With your leadership, I think that day will come sooner, rather than later," Kane said.

"Well, thank you, Lieutenant Commander," Churchill said with unusual modesty.

The group moved on a bit further, before the Prime Minister signaled his aides that he wanted to be alone with Richard Kane. The two men strolled outside to stand near one of the fountains that decorated the grounds.

"By the way," Churchill tried to sound nonchalant. "How is the boy's dragon getting on?" He added a chuckle to confirm his question was just in jest.

Or was it?

Richard detected a note of seriousness hidden within the joking inquiry. He replied, "I think the two of them are quite inseparable, if you know what I mean, sir?"

Churchill smiled. "Yes, I think I do. During my youth, I had several imaginary friends to keep me company during difficult times. Perhaps boys need such things when their fathers are away?"

Kane smiled and nodded. "It's perfectly natural, under the circumstances."

"I should like to visit Crackington Haven again soon, once this madness is over," Churchill added. "You and your lovely wife Winifred, with Gavin too, of course."

"You will always be welcome, Mr. Prime Minister," Richard said.

"Let us finish the tour, so you can get back to your vital work," the Prime Minister said, ending the friendly banter.

They went inside again, rejoining the collection of officers, officials, and accompanying bodyguards.

In London, working feverishly at Scotland Yard, Inspector Peter Grimsby was faced with the seemingly impossible task of investigating more than a dozen crimes at the same time. However, his superiors expected him to make a valiant attempt at solving them all, especially the situations that involved national security.

For instance, one of his unsolved cases concerned the unexplained disappearance of Dr. Lamken Rune, the renowned British radar scientist. The man had gone missing without a trace and while the file wasn't officially closed, no one really expected Grimsby to turn up anything concrete.

Then there was the unknown motive behind the murder of Nigel Bentley, an unassuming civil servant working at the Swansea Bay Defense Radar Station, as a radio technician. The circumstances surrounding Bentley's demise were very strange indeed, as the man had been found with incriminating evidence that he had stolen certain sensitive documents from the radar station. However, since that information was still on his body, Inspector Grimsby suspected the packet had been planted. However, no additional clues or leads had presented themselves in months.

Finally, there were the repeated reports of strange sightings in the skies over North Cornwall. Almost weekly, someone would contact Scotland Yard concerning a slow-moving aeroplane, with a tremendous wingspan, circling the Cornish Coast near Tintagel. Grimsby had contacted the RAF regarding experimental airplanes, but they denied any test flights operated anywhere near Cornwall. If time presented itself, which was highly unlikely, Peter wanted to visit the northern coast of Cornwall, just to look himself.

The next day, right after school, Bunty and Gavin made a beeline to Boscastle, intercepting Emily as she skipped off the bus. Excited to see them waiting, the girl hugged them both.

Faces red from her public display of affection, the boys were suddenly at a loss for words, which made Emily giggle with delight.

"Oh, I wish Kitto was here to see you two," their friend said.

Gavin recovered and took Emily by the hand. "We're all going to see Thaddeus. It has been ages since the three of us spent an afternoon with our splendid old friend."

"Delightful!" the girl exclaimed.

The trio scampered up the coastal road towards Tintagel, laughing and chattering every step of the way. It was a beautiful cool afternoon, with not a cloud in the sky and for a moment, the war seemed so very far away. Once they reached the little white cottage on the hill, the teens slowly climbed the path, hand-in-hand.

Bunty politely knocked on the ornately carved door and then opened it.

Stepping inside, Emily was still amazed by how tiny the hamlet really was. She smiled broadly, however, when she saw the giant stone fireplace in the corner.

Swish.

It started coming apart, as each shaped stone shifted and moved through the air. Chunks and slabs sailed around the room, almost colliding, yet mysteriously always narrowly missing each other. This magical display of invisible levitation appeared random at first, but they all knew the rocks were coming together to form an entirely new shape.

What once had looked like ordinary fireplace stones had become dragon's scales. They glistened and sparkled with the pulsating colors of native flowers, including Blackstonia yellow, Crocosmia red, Iris purple, and Muscari blue.

Thaddeus Osbert appeared before them, his teeth displayed in a radiant smile. "You are most welcome here!"

As if propelled by some unseen cannon, Gavin, Bunty, and Emily catapulted forward and threw their arms about the great beast's neck, hugging the dragon with all their might.

Sir Osbert closed his eyes and savored their greeting, his gigantic heart thumping loudly. "Ah, tis grand to be missed and appreciated."

Without being told, the two boys and girl sat before him on the earthen floor.

"What brings you here today?" the dragon asked.

"We have not been very good friends for you lately, Thaddeus," Gavin spoke up. "No matter what, we should come see you more often."

"It's true, Sir Osbert," Bunty chimed in. "You always teach us so much and we have such exciting adventures with you."

The dragon snorted. "Well, perhaps that's not such a good thing."

Emily quickly came to her feet. "No, no, dearest dragon, you are mistaken. Without you, our England would be in Nazi hands for sure."

The boys jumped up too and clambered, "It's true, Thaddeus, it's true."

The creature held up a paw to silence them all. "Very well, you have made your case. Still, I am merely your tutor. It is the three of you, who have made the difference in the end."

Perhaps they wanted to disagree with Sir Osbert's observation, but never had the chance. For suddenly out of thin air, a proper tea service appeared. It was, after all, exactly 4:00 in the afternoon and time for true English citizens to partake in teatime.

Emily stepped forward and lifted the sugar bowl. "Two lumps, Sir Osbert?"

"If you please," he replied politely.

Bunty went straight for the scones and raspberry preserves.

Gavin decided he would play mother and lifted the pot to pour.

"This is grand," Bunty managed to mumble between chewing.

Everyone agreed, in spite of the boy's bad manners.

"Thaddeus, exactly how did you become knighted?" Gavin was suddenly curious.

The dragon looked a bit sheepish.

"Oh, please tell us how you earned the title of Sir," Emily inquired sweetly.

Even Bunty smiled reassuringly, his mouth stuffed and crumbs sticking to his lips.

"Well, have you heard the tale of the Spanish Armada?" Sir Osbert began.

Three heads nodded up and down in unison, like corks bobbing in water.

"I may have had a hand in the outcome," the dragon said modestly.

Bunty harrumphed. "More than a hand I wager, you mighty big dragon."

"Behave!" Emily scolded.

The red-haired lad scrunched up his nose and waggled his head in defiance.

"Now, now, no bickering, you two," Gavin interceded, feeling like a parent.

The dragon chuckled, his laughter rumbling like an earthquake.

"Please, Sir Osbert, do continue," Emily coaxed.

"History informs us that an unusually severe September Atlantic storm had formed off the Scottish coast, and the Spanish Armada was caught in its fury," Thaddeus related his story. "Many Spanish ships beached on the Irish coast, with scores of Spanish sailors captured or melting into the Irish population. It was the storm that caused nearly all the shipwrecks and casualties associated with the destruction of the Armada."

Bunty swallowed deeply, gulped his tea, and then blurted, "You caused that bloody big storm, didn't you?"

The dragon hung his head a little and slowly nodded. "While passing over the fleet of Spanish ships, just to take a look, mind you, I sneezed, which created a terrible Atlantic gale."

"You sneezed?" Bunty reacted. "You're bloody dangerous!"

Gavin studied Sir Osbert for a moment and then said, "You got in a lot of trouble with your fellow dragons over your interference, didn't you?"

Thaddeus nodded again.

"But it was an accident," Bunty said. "How can you get in trouble for that?"

"Yes, but who knighted you?" Emily asked, still wanting an explanation.

"Queen Elizabeth, of course," the dragon replied, as if the answer was obvious.

"So you knelt before the Queen of England and she tapped you on those gigantic shoulders with the flat of a sword, while formally declaring you a knight in the eyes of God?" Emily gawked with disbelief.

"Something like that," Sir Osbert replied nonchalantly.

"The Queen knew you existed?" Bunty asked with great surprise.

"Indeed she did," Thaddeus answered. "As have most of the kings and queens of England. They just don't go around announcing the fact to all the bloody common folk."

"Who's common?" Bunty demanded.

"It's just a figure of speech," Emily said with tremendous exasperation.

"I knew that," Bunty countered.

"You did not!" Emily said, hands on her hips.

Gavin stepped in between them. "Will you two stop this constant bickering, at once!"

His voice boomed inside the little white cottage and even Thaddeus was impressed by the teen's oratory power.

"Yes, Gavin, I'm sorry," Emily whispered.

Bunty lowered his head and shuffled his feet. "Me too, chum."

"Well, all right then," Gavin said pointedly.

"What was it like, Sir Osbert, to live when Elizabeth was queen?" Emily asked, hoping to get back to the subject at hand.

"The era of Elizabeth was perhaps the most appealing period of history for England," the dragon proclaimed. "Even the mighty Queen Victoria was eclipsed by her predecessor's reign, which shaped England's emergence as a significant naval power, as well as the unprecedented growth of England's commercial, cultural, and colonial activities. Elizabeth was also the last monarch who openly welcomed the advice and assistance from dragons."

"Why did it change?" Bunty wondered.

"Oh, that's a story for a different time, my boy," Thaddeus stated firmly. "Right now it's time for the three of you to hurry home and finish your studies, help your mothers with their chores, and make England strong for the future."

The trio took turns hugging Thaddeus and Emily gave him a big kiss, even though the scales on his cheek were a bit rough. Sir Osbert was most pleased.

Bunty headed out of the hamlet first, followed by Emily, but Gavin tarried.

"Is something troubling you, Master Kane?" the dragon asked.

The boy wasn't sure what it was, but there was something in the air.

He shrugged and said, "I don't know exactly, Thaddeus, but I keep having this creepy feeling that the Nazis are going to come yet again."

The dragon studied Gavin and reflected on his own senses. Indeed, there were strange currents carrying unusual messages of dire consequences."

"Pay heed to such feelings, lad," Sir Osbert suggested.

"Yes sir, I will," Gavin agreed. He waved and skittered out the door to catch up with his friends. The trio scampered down the coast road. They agreed that every visit with Thaddeus was filled with eye-opening experiences, which also conveyed serious historical consequences. Just outside Boscastle, the friends made a pact, sworn to God, to protect Sir Osbert and all that he had shared.

Bunty summed it up for them. "We hereby do solemnly swear to protect Sir Thaddeus Osbert with our lives. We also promise to never tell a living soul what we have learned and seen, for the world is not ready for such truth."

"We swear!" they said in unison.

Inside the little white cottage, a certain dragon extended one claw and scratched an itch on his forehead. Then, before returning to the safe camouflage of the fireplace, his head cocked to one side. Just as Gavin was leaving, a long-lost memory had suddenly popped into Sir Osbert's mind. Eyebrows furled and eyes narrowed, for Thaddeus wondered why, after hundreds of years, this specific recollection had returned.

5

Revelation

It was a very special day and Tabitha Bixley didn't have much time to prepare. She wanted everything to be perfect, because her guest was exceptionally important to her. They had met under unusual circumstances, but John Mobley had been on her mind ever since. In fact, she had even gone so far as to ask her father, Dymchurch Bixley, to arrange for someone to keep an eye on John while he was in the service of Great Britain. Tabitha had no idea at the time, of course, but Mobley's guardian turned out to be none other than a dragon named Thaddeus Osbert.

Still, the young woman was also very nervous, because she had made up her mind to disclose her secret to John. As Tabitha tidied up the place, she battled mixed emotions. It was true that she had fallen in love, but such emotions were so fragile under the best of circumstances. There was a war on and young people were understandably living for the moment, because they might not live for very long. Yet this was not her motivation. Tabitha wanted to spend the rest of her life with John Mobley.

Nevertheless, there was the matter of her being a witch.

How would he react once she told him?

Would he be able to accept her heritage?

As witch-training tradition dictated, Tabitha had been required to leave home for one year to experience life in a strange place. Perhaps it had been an extreme step to volunteer for service as a Wren, but she also wanted to serve England in her hour of need. The naval base at **HMS St. Merryn** was the Tabitha's home now, probably at least for the duration of the war.

Suddenly there was a confident knock on her cottage door.

Opening it, Tabitha was thrilled to see his smiling face again.

"Hello, old girl," Lieutenant John Mobley said with a huge smile.

She found her voice. "Oh, John, hello, do come in, please."

"Are you sure?" he asked. "I don't want you accused of improprieties."

Her smile was dazzling as she reached out to take his hand. "You've been invited for a cuppa tea and there's nothing improper about that."

John interlocked his fingers with hers. "Thank you for having me."

It was then that Tabitha noticed his change in rank. "Oh John, you've been promoted! Congratulations."

"It seems someone was impressed when I managed to get one of the Stringbags off the **Ark Royal** before she went down," Mobley said. "So they made me a lieutenant and now I train other idiots how to fly obsolete torpedo bombers."

She fluffed his hair off his forehead. "Don't underestimate your contribution, John. The lessons you've learned can save lives in the future."

Mobley went inside with Tabitha and she relieved him of his great overcoat, which she carefully hung on the ornate coat-stand by the front door.

"Do come in and sit by the warm fire," she offered. "I'll put the kettle on to boil."

"Sounds marvelous, Tabitha," he said.

John sat down right before the roaring flames, which never seemed to consume any wood, but snapped, crackled, and popped, while emitting real heat. "Your fireplace is grand."

Tabitha peeked in from the kitchen. "It is nice, isn't it?"

"I'm getting lonely," he said, pouting.

She joined him, pot in hand.

"I'll play mother," he volunteered. "Two lumps?"

"Oh, yes, please," she replied, sitting right beside him.

He poured out cups of hot tea and they sipped for awhile in complete silence.

"Delicious," he commented.

"It is indeed," she agreed.

"So how is the rescuing business?" John asked. "Have you pulled any other saucy individuals from wrecked paper airplanes lately?"

Tabitha giggled. "No John, just you."

"Good," he grinned. "I wouldn't want any competition."

She looked him straight in the eye and in a serious tone said, "You have no need to worry about that, John Mobley. No man alive could come close to you."

Her candid statement gave him pause. He gazed back into her sparkling green eyes and again realized how truly beautiful she was.

Then, almost in a whisper, he said, "I've missed you terribly."

"I missed you too, John."

"We're so far apart now, with me in Scotland."

"I simply fretted during the **Bismarck** chase."

"I was in good company."

"I was so worried, when I heard the **Ark Royal** had been sunk."

"It was close, but fortune was on our side then too."

"I don't want to lose you."

"You won't. I'm too stubborn to die."

Then there was silence again.

They sipped tea and looked into each other's eyes.

Tabitha couldn't stand it any longer.

"I'm a witch," she suddenly just blurted.

"Don't say that about yourself," Mobley protested vehemently. "You are anything but that. In fact, you're the most beautiful and wonderful woman I have ever known."

She grinned and gently pet John's furled brow. "Oh, silly, I didn't mean it like that. I mean I'm a practitioner of the magical arts."

Mobley's look of confusion was obvious. "Repeat that in King's English, if you please?"

Tabitha took a deep breath and said, "I'm a practicing witch and perform spells, if necessary, but only for good causes. I am not evil in any way and I have a very devout faith, but I also believe in the spiritual and magical realm of this world."

John didn't know exactly what to say, so he held out his cup. "Could I trouble you for another cup?"

She said, "Of course."

Tabitha poured him another serving of hot tea.

Mobley tentatively sipped, not knowing what to do.

Then he set the cup down. "How does all this magic stuff really work?"

"Well, let me show you," Tabitha offered.

"All right then," John agreed enthusiastically.

"What do you miss most?" Tabitha asked.

"You," Mobley replied instantly.

She blushed. "You're so cute. No, I mean something to eat."

He pondered for only a few seconds. "Rare roast of beef!"

Poof.

There was a little puff of white smoke.

On the serving table right before John, as if delivered directly from the oven, sat a magnificent prime rib of beef. There were even all the necessary trimmings and Yorkshire pudding too.

Mobley's eyes were wide with amazement. "How did you do that?"

Tabitha held out her right hand, which gently balanced a slender ebony wand. Encased in the handle was a shimmering blue jewel and from the pointed tip protruded a golden-yellow gem that seemed to pulsate with energy.

John looked at the roast, his mouth watering, and then stared into Tabitha's huge green eyes. He was at a loss for words again.

"Are you all right?" she asked worriedly.

He nodded slowly and eyed the beef joint again. "Let's eat. I'm famished."

Tabitha threw her arms around him and hugged John with all her might. He hugged her back and then they gently kissed.

"You get the plates and I'll carve," Mobley announced after they parted.

The couple sat down and enjoyed a splendid meal.

When Mobley couldn't eat another bite, he pushed back his chair and patted his stomach. "That was the most delicious roast I have ever tasted, Senior Wren Officer Tabitha Bixley."

She was pleased. "I'm glad you liked it, John."

Suddenly a howling air-raid siren began to wail.

"Oh, bother," Tabitha said.

John stood up and took her hand. "Come on, love, let's find some shelter."

"Out back," she pointed. "I have an Anderson all equipped."

They went out the back door and down into the subterranean bomb shelter, where the couple cuddled together in one corner to wait out the raid.

The naval airbase was the target, of course.

Kaboom.

Boom…boom…boom.

Inside the Anderson Shelter, Tabitha leaned against John and closed her eyes. He held her and cooed sweet nothings in her ear. She snuggled against him and they waited for the air raid to stop.

Blam, blam, blam, echoed more distant explosions.

Then silence.

After awhile, the **All Clear** siren sounded.

As the couple emerged, they heard excited shouting from the town square and went to investigate.

The Germans had dropped a stick of incendiaries on the village as well. Several of the glowing devices had fallen near the local pub, but in response, the proprietor's wife carried out a bucket of beer-overflow from the taps, because she mistook it for water. The woman plunged in her stirrup pump and doused the sputtering bomb with suds. Her assistant, covered in beer foam, announced to the attending crowd that had gathered to watch, "Ah, what a glorious death."

Everyone laughed, perhaps Mobley the loudest.

"You like it here, don't you?" Tabitha asked, as she hooked her arm through his.

"Very much," John replied. "I could see settling down here after the war is over."

"When will that be?" she asked sadly.

He shrugged. "Soon, I hope."

"Not soon enough."

The crowd dispersed and the couple headed back to Tabitha's cottage. While walking into the sitting room, John asked, "Couldn't you use your magical powers to put an end to all this senseless killing?"

"I wish I could," she replied. "I'm afraid I'm not that powerful, as witches go."

Mobley kissed her on the cheek. "Well, in my book, you're the most powerful witch in the world."

"Why is that?" she asked.

"Because you got me to seriously consider asking you to marry me."

"Oh!" she gulped in surprise.

"Did I upset you?" Mobley asked with concern.

"No, but I didn't expect that."

"Well, what do you think?"

Tabitha leaned forward a little, looked deeply into his eyes, and whispered, "It really doesn't bother you that I'm a witch?"

"Does it bother you I'm *not* a wizard?" he asked.

"No, of course not."

"Well then, there you go."

"But I'm different than you."

"Bloody good thing too."

She giggled.

"Well?"

Tabitha took his hands in hers and said, "I'd love to be your wife, John."

Mobley did a little hop and spun around three times.

"Why did you do that?" she asked.

"It keeps away the bad spirits," he replied.

"It does?"

"That's what me mum told me and she's always right."

Tabitha giggled again.

"Are you sure you want to marry a mere mortal?"

"You are a brave and wonderful man, John."

"I love you."

"I love you too."

"I don't know when we'll get a chance to be together again."

"I know. There's a war on."

"Will you wait?"

"I promise."

"No matter how long it takes?"

"A witch is only as good as her word."

They kissed.

"I'll write every day," he said after they parted.

"Me too."

John put his arms around Tabitha's waist and said, "I rather like the thought of being with someone so talented for the rest of my life. I'm looking forward to seeing what you're capable of."

"The wielding of magic requires serious training, great restraint, deep humility, and above all, enormous compassion and love," Tabitha said seriously.

"I'm in pretty good hands, then?" John asked with a huge smile.

She nodded.

"I have to get back to Scotland," he hated saying.

Tabitha sighed. "I know."

Mobley retrieved his greatcoat and they casually strolled together to the bus stop. At first, it was very awkward saying goodbye. Tabitha just rested her head on John's chest, as he held her close.

"I'll start with a marriage license and stuff like that," Mobley said quietly.

Gently pushing away from him, so she could see his face, Tabitha said, "Please do take care of yourself. I'll make arrangements on this end, like finding a wedding dress, deciding how to bake a cake without eggs, and where to honeymoon."

John grinned. "You're a witch. You'll do just fine."

She pretended to scold him. "I must be careful when I use my skills. Otherwise everyone will figure out something is up."

"I love you," he said again.

"I know," she whispered. "It's mutual."

The bus arrived, coming to a squealing stop before them. The doors swung open and John climbed up on the first step. He turned around to face her.

She waved, tears rolling down her cheeks.

Mobley waved back, blowing her kisses.

The bus pulled away as John found an empty seat. He never took his eyes off the lovely girl jumping up and down, waving enthusiastically. As Mobley finally sat down, he sighed deeply and mumbled, "Bloody war."

He didn't realize all the other passengers had heard his comment.

"Bloody right!" they all said in unison.

John laughed.

Tabitha went into the kitchen to wash the dishes, when there was another knock on the front door. Worried that John had forgotten something, she hurried to open it, but was pleasantly surprised to discover her father standing before her.

"Oh, Daddy, you just missed John," Tabitha said, throwing her arms around Dymchurch's waist.

She gave him a big hug and a kiss on both cheeks.

He chuckled with delight.

"I saw him leaving, daughter of mine," Mr. Bixley said. "I didn't want to interrupt your time together. He is a fine looking young man."

"Come in, please," she said, stepping aside to let him pass.

"I only stopped by to deliver some things from your mother," Dymchurch said, handing over a small stringbag filled with goodies.

Tabitha took it with glee. "Oh, this is grand. Did Mum put in some of her coconut cookies?"

"Of course," her father replied. "There are a few bottles of potions at the bottom, which your mum thought might be difficult to find locally."

"I'm going on duty in just an hour, Dad," Tabitha said. "Would you stay while I change?"

"Love to, lass," he said, plopping down in the comfortable armchair.

Tabitha scurried into her bedroom and changed into her Wren uniform. When she stepped out again, Dymchurch was standing before her crystal ball. His shoulders seemed to sag under the weight of something.

His daughter came to an abrupt halt. "What's wrong, Daddy?"

Her father turned to look at her, his features grave with concern.

"What is it?" she asked.

"It seems our disgraced wizard has returned to Kernow," he replied slowly.

Tabitha turned pale.

Dymchurch stepped forward to grab her arms, afraid she might faint.

"I'm fine, Father," she whispered.

"Are you sure?"

"Yes, I'm fine."

"What do you suppose made him come back?"

She turned her back to hide her tears.

Dymchurch put his arms around her and hugged. "Hush, child. Everything will work out in the end."

"I know that," she sniffed.

"Perhaps he recovered what was taken from him," her father suggested.

Tabitha shook her head. "I don't think so, Dad. The moot would have known if that was the case."

"Yes, I guess you're right."

"He probably doesn't even remember me."

"Oh, I doubt that."

Tabitha turned to face him. "Father?"

"Yes, dearest?"

"Do you think I should seek him out?"

Dymchurch pondered her question for a few moments. Then, quite emphatically, he said, "Yes, I do. Your fallen master was once the most gifted wizard in the entire world. If there's even the inkling of hope that he can restore his former glory, then everyone would benefit from it."

"Remember, he was banished by the Council of Wizards, and Elizabeth was destroyed as punishment," she pointed out.

Dymchurch said, "Those were different times. The world is changing and our closed society must deal with such challenges or perish. Not all of us disagreed with the opinions your mentor once declared at his trial."

Tabitha had something else to tell her father. "John has asked me to marry him."

Dymchurch was understandably concerned. "Does he know who you really are?"

"Yes, I told him and showed him one of my creation spells," she replied.

"What did he choose?" her father asked.

"Rare roast beef, of course," she said with laughter.

"Ah, he's a good lad, then."

"Yes, I believe he's a very good man."

"He better be, for my daughter's sake."

They laughed together and hugged again.

"He has my full blessing, daughter."

"Thank you, Daddy."

"I must be on my way now."

"It was so nice you dropping by," Tabitha chirped. "I have missed you terribly."

"Wouldn't you like to know where he is?" her father asked as an afterthought.

"Who?"

He cocked his head and looked at his daughter with feigned dismay.

"Oh, him?"

"Yes."

"I guess so."

"According to your crystal ball, our once-famous master is drunk and staggering through the bombed-out ruins of Plymouth," Dymchurch informed her. "His future actions seem a bit cloudy at the moment, but somehow he ends up in Crackington Haven, of all places."

Tabitha sighed heavily. "I must report to the airbase now. Once I get a spot of leave, I'll head up to the north Cornish coast to see if I can locate him."

"That's my girl. Never one to back down from adversity, what."

She smiled, but it was halfhearted at best.

Dymchurch reached out and gave her elbow a gentle squeeze. "Chin up, lass. Everything will be just fine, you'll see. Come on, I'll walk you to the station gate."

Tabitha grabbed her gasmask kit and the two of them exited her cottage. With a leisurely pace, they strolled over to the base security entrance, where Miss Bixley presented her identity disc. After gaining admittance, she went to the control tower to report in.

Dymchurch, on the other hand, headed straight for the pub. Patrick Knowles, the proprietor, had been a close friend for many years and Bixley thought he would drop in for some good old-fashioned political debate and a pint of bitters.

As Dr. Bixley sat at the bar, he reflected on this turn of events. Was it possible, after hundreds of years, that the greatest wizard who had ever lived, might have regained his identity or his powers? Dymchurch sipped at his bitters and waited for the proprietor to join him.

Such a possibility was wondrous.

For if it was true, then someone had inadvertently broken a very powerful binding spell and the odds against that were monumental indeed. After all, the curse had been cast by the Grand Council of Wizards, almost 750 years ago.

Dr. Bixley grabbed hold of the handle on his pint and this time took a mighty swallow. Licking away the frothy foam, he couldn't help but smile broadly.

"Eh, what's got you in such a fine mood?" barkeep Knowles inquired.

Dymchurch leaned back on his stool and patted his stomach. "Oh, I was merely pondering on how everything is changing, Pat. There are some souls on this island that are in for a rude awakening."

"Is that good, Brother Bixley?" Knowles asked with surprise.

"Aye, indeed it is," Dymchurch replied, chuckling this time. "In fact, I hope I'm there to see their faces."

Of course, little did the bartender know that his old friend Dr. Bixley was actually talking about the world of magic, wizards and witches alike.

"Another pint, Pat, if you please. I'm feeling very chipper indeed."

6

Bombs for Breakfast

Shortly after an especially scary raid on Plymouth, the Bomb Disposal Squad alarmed Emily Scott's mother, as soldiers pounded on the front door and ordered Harriet and her daughter to evacuate the house immediately.

Evidently, a wayward bomb had made impact, but didn't explode! Mrs. Scott bundled herself and Emily off to their neighbor's house, which sat directly across from Boscastle harbor.

A single Heinkel bomber let loose a stick of six bombs aimed at several Motor Torpedo Boats docked for repairs, but the German's aim was a little off. Most of the explosives landed in the water, creating gigantic plumes of spray. One of the bombs hit a goat shed at the far end of Boscastle and the poor goat never knew what hit him! Another bomb fell into the Scott's back lawn, landing only yards away from where Emily and her mother had been hiding in their Anderson shelter in the backyard. Not only did the cylinder land very close, but it tunneled underground and beneath the house, yet never detonated.

Several hours later, the bomb disposal men arrived to dig down to where the unexploded bomb sat. Then several Royal Army engineers showed up and successfully disarmed the device, which was hauled away using chains and a lorry. After they had gone, Emily and her mother looked at the mess. Most of the people in Boscastle turned out to help them inspect the damage.

"That's a ruddy big hole, Mrs. Scott," commented one of her neighbors.

"It ruined the garden, Ma," Emily whined.

Harriet shrugged and said, "Better the vegetables than us, dearest. They'll grow back, you'll see."

"Oh bother," the girl said, mimicking Bunty.

"How 'bout a nice cuppa?" Emily's mother suggested.

"That's the ticket," one of their neighbors called out.

Emily took her mother's hand and they went inside for tea. It always seemed to make everything all right. The teenaged girl would be late for school, but that didn't seem to bother her mother. In fact, Mrs. Scott had been hinting regularly that Emily should skip her education and get a real job, to help with the serious shortage of funds.

With the German bombing raids becoming more infrequent, the Morrison Shelter in the Kane cellar wasn't used very often anymore. Gavin and Bunty had discovered the reinforced top was particularly suited for fighting battles with their toy ships and soldiers. Gavin's collection of Tillicum wooden boats was quite impressive and the boys would play for hours recreating great battles at sea.

School had become a bit tedious, because the war had interrupted all sense of serious education and learning. Good teachers were in seriously short supply, not to mention the lack of books, paper and writing utensils, especially chalk. Not only that, but both Bunty and Gavin were convinced they were learning more spending time with Thaddeus, than anything presented in the classroom.

The visits to see the dragon were almost daily again and since Sir Osbert didn't seem to mind, the boys stayed for most of the afternoon and into early evening, often arriving home to be greeted with a scolding for being late. Emily tried to join them at the little white cottage on the hill whenever possible, but because she was a teenaged girl, her mother often refused to let her go play.

"You can spend time with Gavin over the weekend, Emmy," Harriet would say. "I need your help around the house."

"Yes, Mother," the girl said, while casting a mournful look in the direction of Tintagel.

Now on this day, Bunty and Gavin wanted to talk to Thaddeus about the English Civil War, since they were certain the dragon had witnessed this monumental event in British History. As soon as they hopped off the bus from Launceston, they hurried over the hills to Tintagel Castle and then up the path to the cottage.

"We're here, Sir Osbert," Bunty announced as he opened the door.

As the boys stepped inside, they smiled.

The giant stone fireplace in the corner started coming apart, as each shaped stone shifted and moved through the air. Chunks and slabs sailed around the room, almost colliding, yet mysteriously always narrowly missing each other. This magical display of invisible levitation appeared random at first, but Gavin knew the rocks were coming together to form an entirely new shape.

What once had looked like ordinary fireplace stones, now glistened and sparkled with pulsating radiant colors, including ripe lemon yellow, ruby apple red, ancient bronze, and nighttime black.

"Greetings, lads," the dragon bellowed. "You certainly made good time today."

"We had something important to discuss with you, Sir Osbert," Bunty said.

"Well, then, have a seat and let's begin," Thaddeus beckoned.

The pair flopped down on the earthen floor, side-by-side, and waited.

"Don't keep me in suspense," the dragon said.

"We were studying the English Civil War today in school," Gavin started.

Thaddeus shook his head in dismay and mumbled, "Such a waste, such a shame, such a terrible shame."

"Tell us about it, please, sir," Bunty requested politely.

"You foolish mortals with your wars over God," the dragon began. "The English Civil War was a truly profound political event in seventeenth century Europe. During this period, the Stuart kingdoms of Scotland, England and Ireland, and the Principality of Wales were ripped apart by religious and political unrest. The conflict wasn't a purely British phenomenon, but was part of a wider struggle for supremacy between Catholics and Protestants throughout all of Europe."

"It wasn't just religious differences, though, was it?" Gavin asked.

"No, of course not," Thaddeus replied. "The war forever changed the role of the English monarchy and gave extensive powers to Parliament.

"Did you choose sides?" Bunty asked suddenly.

"Not in this case," he replied. "I refused to get involved in such utter nonsense."

"It's obvious you had strong feelings about it, though," Bunty pointed out.

Thaddeus growled, "Bloody fools, fighting over God!"

"Perhaps we should change the subject," Gavin hurriedly suggested.

"I think so too," Bunty agreed.

Thaddeus snorted, a puff of orange smoke rising from his nostrils. "Humans are too easily awed by gods. We dragons have never placed much trust in them. There is only one great power and as such, there is no need for man to define godliness. Two-legged creatures are so impressed with themselves, but they can't even conceive of how great God truly is. It's insulting to witness man's ridiculous religious wars, all fought in the name of a divine being they neither know nor understand."

"We're going to leave now," announced Bunty, frightened by the dragon's temper.

By now, however, Thaddeus was in such a terrible mood, rainbow-colored smoke wafted up from his flared nostrils. "Fine, be off with you and don't come back unless you're willing to hear a lecture or two on human idiocy!"

The boys hurried out the door.

"Well, he certainly was going spare on us, wasn't he," Bunty commented.

"I've never seen Thaddeus so shirty before," Gavin agreed. "We must have said something really irritating to get him going like that."

They both shrugged and hurried home, passing by Boscastle without stopping. Much to Gavin's disappointment, Emily had notified him of her mother's new rules, which dramatically reduced her after-school playtime. Bunty was sad too, but kept his feelings to himself, rather than add to his friend's concerns.

As the boys entered the kitchen, they were shocked to find Winifred down on her hands-and knees, scrubbing the floor. More than that, she was wearing a pair of her husband's old dungarees.

"Hello, dears," she said while flicking a wisp of hair from her face.

"You won't start wearing pants all the time, will yee?" Gavin asked.

Winifred chuckled. "Funny how my menfolk hate women in pants. I do myself, but if necessary for work, I will wear them."

Her son looked shocked. "This war is changing a lot, Mum."

Mrs. Kane nodded. "It is indeed. Women are learning to make do without our men and that's a good thing."

"We're famished," Bunty said, tiring of the present conversation. After all, he had seen his mother wearing pants many times, especially when she wore her air-raid warden uniform, before...

"I'm finished here," Gavin's mother said as she stood up. "Supper is already fixed, so we'll be sitting down to eat in just a few minutes."

"Oh, goody," Bunty replied.

True to her word, Winifred served dinner about fifteen minutes later. The boys could barely wait until the prayer was finished, before they dug in.

All anyone could hear were the satisfied sounds of three people eating.

Finally, Gavin put his fork down and wiped his mouth, before saying, "If you ever have to work for a living, Mum, you should cook for the Royal Navy."

Winifred huffed and fired right back, "What do you mean work for a living? I guess a married woman, who brings up a family alone and makes a clean home, is working jolly hard for her living and don't you ever forget it."

Gavin cowed a little. "I'm sorry, Mum, I didn't mean to suggest..."

"You two go outside and leave me to my laziness," Mrs. Kane interrupted him, for she was quite perturbed. She cleared the dishes without asking if anyone wanted seconds.

Once Bunty and Gavin were in the backyard, they looked at each other and frowned. Then they sat down and pulled weeds.

"We managed to make everybody mad at us today," Bunty commented.

"That's for sure," Gavin agreed.

"It's the war, you know," the red-haired boy offered as explanation.

"I suppose you're right," Gavin said.

Inside the kitchen, Winifred felt a little guilty for getting angry. Still, with Richard gone, she had learned to be self-sufficient. It wasn't something she was willing to apologize for and there was no doubt things would be different once the war was over. Mrs. Kane missed Mr. Kane terribly, but her loneliness had forced Winifred to accept that her traditional role was changing. When something was broken, she had to figure out how to repair it. The independence was a bit scary, but exciting too.

The days of the obedient British housewife were fading fast.

While she was aware that the future would be different, Winifred loved Richard very much and knew he was not the typical English male. His vast experience as a former international photographer and his brilliant mind always intrigued her. More importantly, her husband had always treated her as an equal, teaching her how to drive a car, when most women would never dream of getting behind the wheel.

Yet next to being a mother, Winifred loved to read most of all. There was never enough time for her to settle in Richard's big armchair and relax with a magazine or good book. So instead, she turned her attention to the boys' welfare and cooking, still able to find pleasure in making delicious meals from next to nothing in ingredients.

Gavin's mother reached over and opened the back door. "Boys, come here, please."

The pair scampered inside.

"I'm sorry I said anything to upset you, Mum," Gavin was quick to say.

"Me too," Bunty added.

"All is forgiven," she said, kissing them both.

Gavin looked his mother over once again. "In fact, Mum, you look pretty fantastic in Dad's pants."

"Do you really think so?" she giggled, turning around in a circle, as if modeling the latest Parisian fashions.

Bunty looked over at Gavin, who smiled and nodded.

"Nice bum, too!" they both shouted.

"Oh!" she exclaimed with embarrassed surprise.

The duo burst into laughter, before ducking under her grasping hands. They escaped up the stairs.

"You two ruffians take a bath," she called up after them.

Then she smiled a silly little grin. Winifred wasn't shocked by anything the boys said anymore. Perhaps she secretly blamed the lack of proper fatherly guidance or even accepted that such behavior was the end result of this terrible war. Whatever the reason, Mrs. Kane started whistling her favorite tune and sashayed back into the kitchen.

The next day, rations were cut yet again. The sugar allowance was now only eight ounces a week, and Winifred's tea was down to a paltry two ounces. The production of crockery, cutlery, and toys was severely curtailed as inessentials.

The boys were unaware of this news, until they reached the little white cottage on the hill. Much to their dismay, Thaddeus was in an even worse mood than the day before. While considering if they should leave quietly, the dragon snorted.

"What's got you so upset now, my friend?" Gavin asked quietly, scratching behind the creature's ear.

Regardless of his foul demeanor, Sir Osbert enjoyed the pleasurable sensation and growled, which was his form of purring. The noises made Bunty laugh.

The dragon ignored the red-haired boy's giggling and replied, "This sugar situation is getting completely out-of-hand. The British government has cut the ration again and I'm not going to tolerate it!"

"That's right, Thaddeus," Gavin egged him on. "I think you should go straight to London, land on top of the PM's residence at Ten Downing Street, and demand that all this sugar nonsense be stopped immediately."

Sir Osbert did not find the teen's teasing at all funny. He sarcastically said, "Oh, bravo, what a performance." Then he unenthusiastically clapped his front paws together.

Gavin looked the big beast straight in the eye. "Stop complaining, you big oaf. You're the one who must have his daily dose of sugar. Why don't you fly to Cuba and help yourself to one of their sugarcane fields?"

The dragon had already considered taking such drastic action, but having some human make this suggestion only served to irritate him again. "I'll have you know that I can do that any time I please."

"Don't get in such a dither, Thaddeus," Bunty suggested.

Gavin joined in on the laughter.

It was the wrong thing to do!

Suddenly Thaddeus roared, "If any of you so much as pass gas in my general direction and upset my delicate nasal passages, I'll burn you both to a crisp!"

The boys stopped laughing abruptly.

"Now go home and tend to your studies, this instant," the dragon added. "Shoo!"

Out the door they ran, not even bothering to shut it behind them. Before they reached the bottom of the hill, Sir Osbert had flicked it shut with his tail. Thaddeus grumbled to himself and curled up like a cat, little wisps of green smoke wafting up from his nostrils. Recent disturbing dreams and troubling memories were upsetting the dragon, who feared that something from his ancient past was about to disrupt the present.

"The last time Thaddeus was that grumpy, it wasn't just about the lack of sugar," Bunty said as the boys hurried along the coast road. "I wonder if he knows something he isn't telling us?"

Gavin hadn't thought of that possibility. "Maybe we should go back and ask him?"

The redheaded boy shook his head. "Not on your life, sport. I don't fancy getting roasted alive over whatever is bothering him. Besides, he's a bleedin' dragon. If his foul mood is caused by the lack of sugar, he can hardly blame us!"

Gavin couldn't argue with Bunty's logic, so the boys headed straight home.

Later that very night, a flying boat took off from Nazi-occupied Norway. Its mission was to drop three German agents. This operation was part of Reinhard Heydrich's plan to replace the undercover operation of Wilhelm Morz.

The Heinkel flying boat landed successfully, where three German spies, Robert Petter, Karl Drucke and Werner Walti, were placed into a dinghy. The trio rowed ashore with their luggage containing radio transmitters. They landed near Dungeness, which was all shingle, with no grass, just stones. The enemy agents were amazed that everyone lived in sheds, wooden and metal shacks, or even converted railway carriages. There were two lighthouses, surrounded by the active sea. To these foreigners, it appeared that everything was rusted or falling apart.

From there, the trio had been instructed to cycle to London, but due to the choppy seas the bicycles accompanying them had been swept overboard.

The three men decided to split up. Werner Walti, who was supposed to be a Danish exile, went off by himself. Karl Drucke, playing the part of a French refugee from Belgium, decided to accompany Robert Petter, who was pretending to be a Swiss national.

After residing in Wales for several months, Vera Eriksen had been instructed in code to meet the three spies once they reached London. She had been made leader of the operation and assumed the identity of the long-lost niece of an elderly Italian Countess living in Kensington. The Germans thought this would be excellent cover for her to meet prominent people, because the Countess had a reputation for lavish entertaining.

Drucke and Petter arrived at the railway station, intending to catch the train. The porter and the stationmaster kept a careful eye on the two strangers. Drucke asked for the name of the station, which further aroused the suspicion of the staff.

As Drucke opened his wallet, crammed full of banknotes and laid far too much money on the counter, the stationmaster noticed that the bottom of the stranger's trousers were soaking wet as were Petter's shoes. The stationmaster told the porter to keep the pair talking, while he telephoned the local constable. Within minutes, Constable Mitchell arrived. He immediately asked to see the stranger's identity cards and noticed that although both claimed to be refugees, neither pass had an immigration stamp and the style of writing on both was decidedly Continental.

These facts peaked his curiosity, so the constable requested both men accompany him to the police station. Once there, Constable Mitchell telephoned Scotland Yard and Inspector Peter Grimsby answered the call.

The prisoners were not put in the cell, because they showed no signs of attempting escape. Indeed, the constable's wife made them both a cup of tea, which they drank while waiting in the sitting room.

Several hours later, Inspector Grimsby arrived on the scene.

"Who are you?" the Scotland Yard inspector asked the men.

Petter said, "My friend cannot speak English."

Grimsby carried out a search of each man, discovering a box containing nineteen rounds of revolver ammunition. The Inspector checked their identity cards and observed that the numbers were written in the European style. Petter told the inspector he was twenty-seven years old, and a Swiss subject, adding that they had spent the night in a hotel and taken a taxi to the outskirts of town, before walking to the station. With their credibility disappearing with every utterance, they were formally arrested and charged.

Inspector Grimsby had the suspects transferred to the secure facilities at the Kent Police Station. Once behind bars, Peter Grimsby carried out a more thorough search of the luggage, where her found a Mauser pistol, wireless equipment, a list of RAF bases, batteries and a torch clearly marked Made in Bohemia. In addition, Petter's wallet contained £72 in *Bank of England* sterling notes and Drucke's wallet contained £327 in *Bank of England* sterling notes.

However, it was the discovery of a half-eaten German sausage, a delicacy unheard of in rationed wartime Britain, which sealed their fate.

The next morning, coast-watchers spotted an object floating in the sea about a quarter of a mile off Dungeness. The harbormaster rowed out and recovered a pair of bellows and, a rolled-up rubber dinghy.

The third agent, Werner Walti, had been more successful and managed to get onto the train from to Aberdeen. The Aberdeen police were alerted and they confirmed that a man matching Walti's description had boarded the train to Edinburgh Waverley. Having reached Edinburgh, Walti deposited a suitcase, containing a wireless set, in left luggage.

He was overcome by police as he went for a revolver when, returning for his case, he was confronted. The man who arrested Walti was Peter Grimsby, who had disguised himself as a railway porter.

Outside of Swansea, Wales, Vera Eriksen was not yet aware that her fellow spies had met with such misfortune. At that moment, she was heading for an abandoned cottage, which had once been rented by Wilhelm Morz. Only recently had Vera uncovered the fact that Scotland Yard had located the decomposing remains of Morz in a cave near the Cornish coast. The coroner's report listed the cause of death from multiple lacerations, perhaps as many as one hundred.

After that, the case was filed as **UNSOLVED**.

However, Vera was under very strict orders. She was to recover, at all costs, the contents of a certain strongbox. Not waiting to receive the go-ahead signal from her superiors, Eriksen set out on her journey to reach Morz's dwelling before nightfall.

The delightful bungalow stood on a hillside overlooking a spectacular panoramic sea view. Accessed by a private drive, it was the perfect place for a spy to hide away unnoticed!

Retaining much of its original quarryman's cottage charm, the hut was blessed with many quaint features, including wood burning stove in inglenook fireplace and original beams. The location provided an ideal base for all South Wales. Surrounded by huge sandy beaches, hill and coastal paths, there was easy access to the water, an ideal jumping-off point for all Wales. Due to its hillside location, the gardens were terraced and steep in places, restricting casual visitors.

At the cottage door, the woman hesitated, checking in every direction to insure no one would see her enter. Once satisfied her arrival would go unnoticed, she slipped inside.

The plain country furniture was common for the typical farm laborer. The bench placed by the fireside was an important piece, providing a draught-free sitting area. The only table was also a practical piece, being long and narrow to provide more living space and fitted with deep drawers for storage.

Steep and uneven stairs led to a tiny upper bedroom, but the German agent didn't bother to climb steps. In fact, she knew right where she was heading.

A large stone fireplace took up one entire wall of the cottage.

Slowly counting stones aloud, "Fifteen from the floor on the right, then five to the left, two up, and seven more to the left over the mantle. Her finger rested.

She pulled out the loose stone to reveal a secret hiding place. Inside the space was a strongbox, which the woman carefully slid free.

The purloined key fit perfectly.

Click.

The lid popped open.

Poor Vera Eriksen gasped.

Meanwhile, at Schloss Wewelsburg, continuous cold rain cascaded down, as if the powers of nature were attempting to wash away the evil that pervaded in that valley. SS Major Bernhard Krüger, a meticulously correct engineer, was reporting as ordered. His secret meeting with Heinrich Himmler began exactly as scheduled.

"*Heil Hitler!*" Krüger announced as he entered Himmler's private office, while raising his right hand in the traditional Nazi salute.

Himmler looked up from his desk, expressionless. As if bored, he raised his hand lazily and replied, "*Ja, ja, Heil Hitler.* Be seated, Major."

Krüger did so.

"How is your recruiting going?" Himmler inquired, peering over his spectacles.

Krüger shrugged. "I have met with some resistance."

Himmler did not like hearing such a response. Exasperated, the Reichsführer sighed. "This will not do, Major. I will not tolerate such insolence. Ever since Heydrich took over certain responsibilities, some of his cronies do not obey orders as quickly as I would like. Perhaps I should shoot a few of them?"

"If you think it would help," Kruger said quietly.

Himmler shook his head. "Probably not. Instead, I will send Muëller to accompany you to Auschwitz, where you can select your labor force. I understand you have selected Sachsenhausen concentration camp as your base of operations?"

"*Jawohl, Herr Reichsführer*," Krüger replied. "It is a small, secluded camp and offers easy access to Berlin."

Himmler nodded his understanding. "How many prisoners will you need for this operation?"

"I have calculated upwards of twenty prisoners, but they must have certain attributes, rather than specific skills," Krüger stated.

The Major wasn't just looking for specialists, but individuals of intelligence and dexterity he could train and organize for the various interlocking tasks of engraving, printing, sorting and counting that were essential to the success of his secret operation. Hairdressers, for example, wouldn't be chosen for their profession or ancestry, but for their nimble fingers.

This time Himmler managed a weak smile. "It is a bold plan, if it works."

Krüger grinned. "Oh, it will work, *Herr Reichsführer.* "It's just a matter of organizing the correct people and having access to the necessary materials."

"Which is why the SS will support your every endeavor," Himmler announced.

The major was pleased. "Then I shall renew my search with intensity, sir. I wish to get started on this project as soon as possible."

Himmler stood up.

Major Krüger did so too.

"You are dismissed, *Herr Major,*" Himmler said.

"*Heil Hitler!*" the officer said, raising his right arm in Nazi salute.

"*Heil Hitler,*" Himmler repeated. "Report back to me when you have succeeded in recruiting your people."

"*Jawohl, Herr Reichsführer,*" Krüger said. He hesitated for just a moment, clicked his boots, turned, and marched stiffly out of the room.

7

Evil's Advocate

A large ball of red light flew directly into one of the upper turret windows at Wewelsburg Castle, followed by two others, colored yellow and green. Moments later, those same three balls of light streaked out again from the castle at incredible velocity, disappearing in seconds.

These strange lights had delivered archaic and forbidden tools of darkness, to assist Heinrich Himmler accomplish his list of foul deeds. As the man's power grew, his thirst for more power increased proportionately. The Reichsführer examined the recently delivered gifts, which were artifacts from another place in time and space. Himmler cautiously picked up the first item, which was a belt constructed of a strange material.

"It will provide you with the ability to control men's minds," a deep voice spoke from the shadows.

Himmler was getting used to unexpected and uninvited visits from strange creatures in the middle of the night. He no longer felt threatened, but embraced their arrival with expectation, for with every visit came new forbidden knowledge.

"Study these scrolls," the spirit commanded, while handing over several ancient texts. "They will provide answers, as well as solutions."

"Yes, master," Himmler said.

"Next, I command you to locate a woman known as Olga Zimmer," the apparition continued his instructions. "She is currently a prisoner in one of your concentration camps, although I do not know which one specifically."

Himmler's eyebrows went up. The malignant force was not all knowing after all. This revelation came as quite a surprise.

A caustic laugh surrounded him.

"Fool!" the ghostlike creature suddenly shouted. "I have no patience for your doubts and stupid questions. The witch Olga will be released immediately or you will suffer my wrath."

"Yes, master," Himmler said, cowering. "I will issue the orders immediately."

"Good," said the spirit. "You are learning."

"What if the woman is dead?" Himmler asked.

"She is not," the shadowy voice answered.

It took several days to locate Olga Zimmer. While the Germans were highly organized and kept immaculate records regarding the unfortunate souls sent to various concentration and extermination camps throughout occupied Europe, millions of names had to be examined before the woman in question was found. As it turned out, she was located in *Ravensbrück*, a camp primarily for women.

Once Himmler was informed that Zimmer was on her way to Wewelsburg Castle, the Reichsführer arranged for a special meeting with the entire SS staff under his control. They gathered in the main conference room, curiously awaiting their commander's announcements.

"The British apparently have an advantage we were not previously aware of," Himmler opened the meeting. "We must focus our efforts bringing Britain to her knees, by the end of the year, before America's industrial might makes a difference."

"What specifically do you have in mind, *Herr Reichsführer?*" Dr. Schumann asked on everyone's behalf.

"As you suggested, *Herr Doktor*, I have been reading those old manuscripts you discovered buried under this castle," Himmler embellished his story. "They speak of a time when magic ruled the world. It is time to wield that power once again."

Everyone gathered in the great hall was surprised the Reichsführer openly admitted that such powers existed. To do so publicly was in direct violation of certain edicts mandated by Hitler and the German puppet courts. Even after they had successfully revived the orc army, many of the SS personnel were still in denial.

Himmler was well aware of this fact. "*Ja, ja*, I know what you are thinking. Yet I am only concerned with final victory. I would make a pact with Satan to win this war."

There were some people in the room that feared his words had already proven prophetic.

"I have sent a detachment of my elite guard to bring a certain woman to me from *Ravensbrück*," Himmler continued. "She was charged for practicing witchcraft and condemned to the concentration camp. I have decided to put her skills to the test, all in the name of the Third Reich, of course."

He dismissed the entourage and retired to his private study to await her arrival.

Several hours later, there was a knock on the door.

"Enter," Himmler called out.

In stepped six black-uniformed SS stormtroopers, three on each side of their prisoner. The young woman's ankles and wrists were shackled and she wore the distinctive black-and-white striped rags of a condemned person without hope.

"You may leave her with me," Himmler ordered.

"*Jawohl, Herr Reichsführer,*" one of the SS soldiers answered.

All six departed, closing the door behind them.

Himmler walked a circle around the captive, who was shaking as much from fear, as the combination of malnutrition and inhumane treatment. The Reichsführer said nothing, but continued his scrutiny.

Suddenly he stopped directly in front of her and pointed to a black triangle sewn to the front of her tattered garb.

"What is that?" Himmler asked.

"Prisoners are classified by colored patches, *Herr Reichsführer,*" she replied hoarsely. "I was grouped with the subversive enemies of the Reich."

"The official court papers list you as a gypsy," Himmler said.

"I have been labeled as such, *Herr Reichsführer,*" she said.

Himmler leaned over to his desk and retrieved a dossier, opening the flap. "What is your name?"

"In certain circles, I am known as Olga Zimmer," the woman replied. "However, I would prefer to use Agnes Olmanns, my spiritual name."

"I am pleased you agreed to meet with me, *Fraulein Olmanns,*" Himmler said.

"It isn't wise to ignore a request from the SS," she said. "Why am I here?"

"I am aware that you have been blessed with certain unusual powers."

The woman's eyes narrowed, but she said nothing.

Himmler smiled. "You are wise to admit nothing, *Fraulein.* The Third Reich does not approve of witchcraft. If guilty, the punishment is death."

The woman asked, "Does the *Reichsführer* have a different opinion?"

Himmler nodded. "I am interested in power, no matter what the source."

"Then we have something in common, *Herr Reichsführer,*" Olmanns said.

Her statement pleased Himmler immensely. "That being the case, I have a proposition to make."

"I am listening."

"In exchange for the use of your magical powers," Himmler outlined. "I will exonerate your name and return to you any property and holdings taken from you. You will be permanently freed from *Ravensbrück*."

"Bah!" the woman blurted.

Himmler was not prepared for that reaction. "Then what do you want?"

"Revenge," she replied.

The tone of her voice was cold, ugly, and hostile, which actually sent a shiver up and down Himmler's spine. He had never witnessed such loathing before.

"I cannot allow you to take action against persons of the Third Reich," he stated.

Agnes shook her head. "My hate is for the people across the Channel, *Herr Reichsführer*."

Himmler's eyes widened at his unexpected good fortune. "The English?"

She merely glared at him.

"If I agree to your terms, would you be willing to bring the British dogs to their knees before the *Führer*?" Himmler asked.

Olmanns clicked her tongue. "Perhaps, *Herr Reichsführer*, perhaps. It would depend on what forces I encounter."

"The British military is stretched very thin," Himmler replied. "Only their vaunted Royal Navy stands in our way. If we act before the Americans can send troops, England will yet fall."

Olmanns waved him off. "I do not refer to mortal forces, *Herr Reichsführer*. I was speaking of the powers of light, of white magic."

Himmler scrunched his nose and grunted.

"Do not scoff at such things," the woman corrected him with a stern voice. "Have you not already encountered unexplained setbacks? Have not your intricate plans suddenly gone awry, because the English met your invaders with unusual powers of their own?"

Himmler was amazed. "How do you know this?"

The woman smiled grimly. "I have my sources."

The Reichsführer quickly made up his mind and said, "My people will see to your needs. You shall bathe and eat a proper meal and we shall speak of this again."

Himmler clapped his hands and the door opened. In stepped a guard.

"Remove this woman's fetters, *Feldwebel*."

"*Jawohl, Herr Reichsführer*," the sergeant replied, unlocking the chains.

"Now make certain she is fed and has a proper bath," Himmler added. "Issue her with any luxury she desires and make certain the seamstress visits her promptly. When this woman returns to me, I want to be impressed!"

"*Jawohl, Herr Reichsführer*," the sergeant obeyed.

The woman followed her escort out of the room.

The door closed again and Himmler smiled with satisfaction. "*Ach so.*"

It was all he said.

Agnes Olmanns temporarily reveled in the comfort of a piping-hot bath and nibbled on a wide selection of delicious delicacies. The witch realized her good fortune would come with a price, which presently she was more than willing to pay. The Nazis were rulers of Europe at the moment, and therefore would serve her purpose.

Moreover, that of her master.

After her wonderfully relaxing bath, a dour-faced seamstress attended Agnes, lecturing Olmanns on the attributes of proper German fashions. Warning that chic, slim figures did not fit into German life, because dresses that were good-looking one season, were the same the next, and that German men didn't like to see their wives in a new dress or hat every few months.

"Women should learn to abandon a dress when it is used up and not when it becomes unfashionable," Fruma Loewe stated firmly.

Agnes didn't really have much use for clothes. The witch was far more concerned with the Tenth Fold, than earthly possessions or human trivialities.

"Other nations elect beauty queens with long legs and narrow waists, but Germany honors women with many children and therewith honors a beauty that is uninfluenced by fashion," Lowe went on.

Olmanns said nothing, obediently submitting to the degrading fitting. She then had her hair done and a manicure.

It was the afternoon of the next day when Himmler met with Agnes again.

This time she presented a completely different picture. Olmanns was wearing the traditional German dress favored by the Nazi regime, a couture dirndl.

The Reichsführer seemed amused.

Agnes was disappointed by his reaction. "You do not like my dress?"

He chuckled. "Although the Party alternately propagates the look of the fresh-faced, blond-haired Gretchen in braids, with that of the domineering Brunhilde in uniform, I prefer the more modern fashions of Paris."

"*Fruma Lowe* thinks such clothes are vulgar and immoral," Agnes said with a sly smile. "The seamstress would be very disappointed in the *Reichsführer, ja?*"

Himmler frowned. "I do not care what that ugly old hag thinks. You are an attractive woman and should look your best while in the service of the

Third Reich. I alone will decide what fashions compliment your beauty, as long as you answer to me!"

"Of course, *Herr Reichsführer*," Olmanns said quickly, surprised by his flaring temper. "I meant no disrespect."

Himmler calmed down immediately. He took her by the arm and steered Agnes to a seat at his conference table. The Reichsführer clapped his hands and was immediately attended by several waiters.

"We will dine," Himmler commanded. "Bring wine."

"*Jawohl, Herr Reichsführer*," they obeyed.

Himmler sat beside Olmanns. He unfolded a napkin in his lap and turned slightly to face her. Saying nothing, he studied the woman for several silent minutes.

Agnes squirmed under his scrutiny, for she could not ascertain what he was thinking. The little man, all dressed in black, was very astute at blocking his own thoughts.

Wine was poured, accompanied with many trays of hot and cold hors' douvres. Himmler insisted Agnes try each one, enjoying her pleased reaction. He considered himself something of a connoisseur, while many of his fellow Nazis were appalled by the Reichsführer's bourgeois behavior.

Still, Himmler feared no living man, so he continued to live the lifestyle he chose and dared anyone to do something about it. He was the sum of his appetites and doing things in excess was his way of expressing his power. The Reichsführer had also been successful in hiding his true self from Hitler, convincing the Führer that the austere picture of Himmler all dressed in black was genuine.

"When will you depart for England?" he asked after sipping the wine.

"As soon as you wish, *Herr Reichsführer*," Olmanns replied.

"Do you have a place to stay?" Himmler asked with concern.

She nodded. "Bodmin Moor is home to many of my kindred fold. I will seek sanctuary amongst the downtrodden and destitute, the condemned and reviled."

Impulsively, Himmler reached out and squeezed her hand. "You must come back to me, victorious."

Olmanns was unprepared for this show of affection and wondered if it was genuine.

The witch smiled and said, "Then I will make certain I am successful, Heinrich."

Her response pleased Himmler and he seemed to relax, while pushing back his chair. "We serve the same master, Agnes. Our destiny is intertwined. I wish to learn true power, to revel in the ability to control all the mindless slaves of the world. Will you teach me these things?"

'So, that is what he wants,' Olmanns thought to herself.

The witch stood up. "It would be a great honor, *Herr Reichsführer*. Upon my return, I will take you as my apprentice and instruct you in the ways of black magic."

Himmler was thrilled beyond description. He took the witch into his arms and hugged her, then spun away like a little child on Christmas morning. He was delighted by the implications.

Unbeknownst to the Reichsführer, Olmanns did not intend upholding her end of the bargain. She found the little man quite disgusting. He was merely a pawn in her game and not a very bright one either. The urge to tell him what she really thought was distracting, but she managed to refrain.

"I shall leave immediately," Agnes said instead.

Back in England, at **RAF Medmenham**, Lieutenant Commander Kane was just returning to duty after a few hours nap. While the long and uncertain days of impending invasion had finally passed, there was still so much to do. Richard never felt rested, but even with staffing problems and shortages with just about everything, it seemed like his team was really making a difference.

He stopped to pour himself a mug of coffee and then entered the photo-analysis room. There wasn't much activity, for it was the down time between reconnaissance flights. Sally Fairborne smiled and waved.

"Hello, sir," she greeted him. "Did you get some sleep?"

"Yes, thank you, I did," he replied.

"There's nothing on the threat-board and not any of the scheduled recon sorties have returned yet," she brought him up-to-date. "I hope you don't mind, but I gave most of the crew a few hours off."

"Not at all, Sally," he said. "I'm glad you took the initiative. Tired eyes might miss something."

Richard walked by her side, sipping at his coffee, when something grabbed his attention.

"What's this then?" Kane asked, pointing to a large, cloth-covered object sitting on one of the long photographic survey tables.

"It came over from V-Section this morning, sir," Miss Fairborne said. "Rupert Thatcher told me you might like to see what he'd built."

Kane stepped forward and flicked off the piece of muslin.

He almost stopped breathing at what he saw.

"Dear God, sir," Sally exclaimed. "It's Wewelsburg Castle!"

Lieutenant Commander Kane slowly approached the model, marveling at the detail. "I think we need to have a word with young Rupert."

In Germany, Reichsführer Heinrich Himmler decided to return to Berlin. Pressing matters required his immediate attention. Berlin's Wilhelmstrasse gloried in the name of the Kaisers of imperial Germany. The Finance Ministry stood toward its southern end. Farther down, the street was traversed by Prinz-Albrecht-Strasse, where stood the huge, L-shaped headquarters of the Gestapo. Just like the other overbearing buildings lodged behind pseudo-classical fronts, its architecture was proud and brooding. Most windows gracing this official avenue were topped by a heavy triangular tympanum. The Finance Ministry was erected in the 1870's without this classical adornment, adopting instead the Italianate style of a Medici palace.

Himmler entered Gestapo headquarters and was immediately surrounded by staff and fellow officers, who showered him with lavish praise. The Reichsführer loved the attention and basked in his glory.

While in far off Wales, Vera Eriksen managed to find a place to sit down. She stared at the contents of the strongbox for a very long time. Then, slowly, she gingerly picked up the first photograph and flipped it over.

Written in German, but not in code, where the words:

Dragon attacking German troops
Crackington Haven, North Cornwall, England

The second photograph was of three teenage children. Written on the reverse side was:

Gavin Kane
Emily Scott
Byron "Bunty" Digby

Next, there was a letter, once again written in plain text, which was highly unusual.

You have discovered and opened my strongbox. The photographs are real. I have seen the dragon with my own eyes and fear for my very life. This creature is the single greatest threat to Germany's survival.

However, do not attempt to defeat this dragon on your own. Use one of the children to bait the great creature, luring it to the Reichsführer. Himmler will know how to handle this.

W. Morz

8

Drunken Old Fool

Darkness blanketed the city, permeating along the streets and collecting in the alcoves and alleyways. An eerie silence hung heavily over the bombed-out ruins of Plymouth, the shells of buildings swathed in thick smoke-filled fog. Where the *Dingles Department Store* had once stood, there was nothing but rubble, which had been painted white to show people where to walk. Dust permeated everywhere, clouds of grit filling the air with the acrid smell of wet plaster and burnt wood. The city streets were nothing more than an urban desert, abandoned and desolate, ringed by sorrow and despair.

A drunken old man came stumbling down the street just then, avoiding the neatly stacked piles of bricks recovered from the debris and wreckage that once had been people's homes and businesses. Reaching the nearest alley, the inebriated man leaned heavily against the wall, before sliding down to plop on a pile of rubble. Reclining against the building, he violently retched all over himself. Throwing back his head, the wretched old codger began singing some unidentifiable tune and he was badly off key.

Clunk.

A piece of brick fell from a crumbling wall nearby.

"Who's there?" the drunk shouted.

A brief movement further down the narrow lane startled him even more and poised, he peered into the darkness.

"Stay away!" he slurred, trying to focus on anything in the inky blackness.

Nothing happened, however, so after a few seconds the man slumped over.

The dense smoke drifted past, swirling slightly with the faint breezes. Bunty Digby watched from his hiding place, but no other signs of life were evident on the deserted streets. Satisfied he had remained undiscovered, the red-haired boy cautiously stepped out and made his way towards the alley. The teen hugged the rough brick walls of each building and tried to stay hidden in the shadows. Bunty slipped past the wrecked and silent storefronts, carefully closing in on the snoring drunk.

The old coot was a graying gent with a scraggly beard and mustache, who wore filthy tattered clothes and stunk of ale and vomit. In fact, the smell almost made the boy turn away. Still, there was something fascinating about the bum, although Bunty was clueless as to why. A long, wooden pipe jutted carelessly from the man's coat pocket, but otherwise it appeared as if the vagabond had no other worldly possessions.

Bunty knelt down and reached for the pipe.

"Have you come to rob me?" the man suddenly asked, his eyes still closed.

Startled, Bunty jumped back and said, "No, I wouldn't think of it."

"Then why do you hover over me?"

"I saw you collapse," Bunty replied. "I came to see if you were ill."

"Bah!" the old fart grunted. "Surely you can smell?"

The boy held his nose.

"Indeed," said the man. "I thought so."

His eyes were still shut.

Bunty was amazed. "How do you do that?"

"Do what?"

"See things without opening your eyes."

Suddenly they popped open. The man's eyes were beady-black, like the eyes of a crow. They darted about, clearly focused and not bloodshot, as Bunty had imagined they would be. He certainly didn't act like the drunken old slob he appeared.

"May I be of assistance to you, sir?" Bunty asked.

"Oh, so it's *sir* now, is it?" the man grumbled. "Do I look like someone who deserves to be addressed in such a manner?"

"My father taught me to speak to anyone older than me with due respect, sir," Bunty replied defensively.

The old man started to laugh, but his sharp guffaw was interrupted by a wicked cough. After hacking and wheezing for several minutes, the man slumped back, gasping for breath.

"Perhaps you should see a doctor, sir," Bunty suggested.

"Not bloody likely."

"Well, I can't leave you here in this condition," the boy added.

"Why not?"

"Because it wouldn't be right, sir."

"Do you have a name, lad?" the man asked, his voice suddenly quite kind.

"I go by Bunty, sir, Bunty Digby."

Out stretched a hand.

"Pleased to meet you, Bunty."

The boy shook the man's hand, but immediately noticed several faded tattoos inked into the weathered skin.

"Likewise, sir," Bunty whispered.

"I'm known as Lamken Rune," the man introduced himself.

Bunty sat down on the pile of rubble and took a careful look at the fellow opposite him. Rune wore a wool overcoat several sizes too big for his frame and a rumpled floppy hat that had lost its proper shape long ago.

"Never seen the likes of me before, I venture," Lamken guessed.

Bunty shook his head.

"I could do with a drink," the man stated.

Then he belched noisily.

Bunty cringed and grasped his nose again. "What a foul stench!"

"Pardon me, lad," Rune attempted an apology.

"I don't think you need a drink, sir," Bunty said. "You need a hot bath, new clothes, and some decent food."

Rune grinned. "Sounds lovely. Do you have some place in mind?"

Bunty shrugged. "Perhaps."

Lamken grunted. "If I had my Elizabeth, I could just conjure up those things."

"Who is Elizabeth?" the boy asked.

"She was my staff," Rune replied angrily.

Bunty scooted backwards, afraid the old drunk might turn violent. The red-haired boy vaguely remembered his father sometimes getting physical after drinking too much. His poor mother had been the unfortunate one who felt the brunt, however. Thinking of his mum made Bunty sad.

"I won't hurt you," Lamken tried reassuring the boy. "I just miss my Elizabeth, that's all."

"I'm sorry she's gone, sir," Bunty said.

"Taken from me, she was," Rune said.

"That's awful. Did you report her kidnapping?"

The codger gasped with surprise, and then bellowed with laughter. "Good God, chap, who would care that some old wooden staff was kidnapped, as you said?"

Bunty was befuddled and confused. "Elizabeth isn't a living person, then?"

Rune wiped his eyes. "Alas, she didn't eat or sleep or breathe, as you would know it. Elizabeth was a wooden pole, enchanted and powerful as she was."

Bunty's eyes narrowed. "Do you take me for a fool?"

"Not at all, Bunty," Rune replied.

"Then explain yourself or I'll turn you in to the local old bill."

"Not the police," the old man pretended to protest. "In all respects, they're so immaculately turned out, so immaculately polite, so immaculately trained and so immaculately infuriating!"

"Come clean then, you smudger," Bunty demanded.

"There's nothing to explain, lad," Lamken said. "I'm a man of magic, down on his luck, who had his staff seized from him, while in the company of some questionable fellow wizards."

"You expect me to believe you're a wizard too?" Bunty scoffed.

Rune asked, "What's a wizard, besides a bloke with a big stick and tricks up his sleeve? In fact, most of my fellow sorcerers are exceedingly rude fellows, who possess little, if any, social skills whatsoever."

Bunty sighed. The addled old fool was seriously brain-damaged after years of alcohol consumption. What was he to do?

"Help me to my feet, lad," Lamken said, holding out his hand.

Bunty obliged, giving Rune a mighty tug.

The geezer brushed himself off and pointed towards the way out of town.

"As a rule, I avoid large cities," Rune said. "I was only passing through Plymouth, when my thirst overtook me. Let us depart and you can keep me company until you find a nice place to dump me."

"I would never do that, sir," Bunty said.

"We'll see," Rune grumbled.

The two of them ambled away, heading west, but avoiding the dusty rescue squads digging to get trapped people out from smoldering ruins. Soon the strange pair joined a steady parade of people shuffling along in the same direction. It was a mass exodus of the population, as they temporarily departed from the expected target area.

Some carried bundles of blankets. Some carried suitcases. Some carried nothing at all, because they traveled light and were the hardy ones. A long line of lorries waited to shuttle these refugees to the countryside. Kindly policemen had taken the law into their own hands, and urged the drivers to give these poor people a lift. They piled on, with their kiddies, their bundles, and their thermos flasks.

The children dangled their legs over the tailboard and laughed. The boys waved to the pretty girls as they passed. Neighbors crowded together with their bundles and chatted. Bunty thought it was like going to the fair. Now and then, a child stopped laughing and turned to look at her mother for reassurance.

Most of these survivors were homeless.

"Yes, I've lost my house and my furniture is gone," one old woman said to Lamken as they passed. "The only clothes I have are these I'm wearing. But I can do what no German dares do, for I can say what I think."

Many of them were women, women with children, women with bundles of goods. There were few men, and those who left the city were old. Often they had been refused shelter for the night. Yet they hadn't lost their spirit.

Each evening, before nightfall, they vacated Plymouth, without haste, without anxiety. There was no crying, no panic, no clamor, only people moving along the streets, along the highways, towards the countryside, away from the city.

Scrounging one of the last remaining gold sovereigns from his purse, Rune was able to purchase a bottle of spirits from one of the departing proprietors. Lamken had become nothing more than a beggar, living day-to-day as a destitute and inebriated old vagabond.

It was true that he was nothing more than an unemployed wizard, eccentric and easily distracted. He was a strangely erudite bumpkin, which was what he wanted everyone to think.

For in truth, Lamken guarded a dark secret, as well as a legendary past.

Yet in this modern age, wizards kept a very low profile, often journeying as country tinkers, traveling merchants, or wandering has-beens, which wasn't far from the truth in Rune's case. He spoke with a strange accent too, which brought difficulty wherever he went. To his credit, Lamken was well traveled, but he lacked certain cultural refinements. Bunty observed that the man was coarse, gruff, overly blunt and at times even quarrelsome.

Rune, for his part, often created adversity with his rude and ill-mannered ways. Recently, while wandering through Kent, he irritated the locals by expressing drunken profanities and pursuing the affections of a tavern barmaid. Later, Lamken got into a bitter argument with several RAF officers regarding the conduct of the war, when he insolently referred to them as "pitiful brutes who couldn't fly brooms."

The man often engaged in vehement debates with anyone foolish enough to participate. The topics ranged from rationing to theology, but always ended in hostile feelings and physical escorts to the road out of town.

On a more pleasant note, the wizard loved children, which was evident by how quickly he took to Bunty. Perhaps it was in desperation that the old man agreed to accompany the boy to Crackington Haven, but Lamken had seen something unusual in the lad's eyes. As strange as it seemed at the time, Rune spotted a dragon's shape reflected in Bunty's pupils. Such a vision required immediate investigation. Faintly disturbing, however, was the fact that the likeness of the dragon seemed vaguely familiar, which created all sorts of unsettling possibilities.

With Bunty's assistance, Lamken announced his intentions. "Lead on, lad. I shall journey with you to the North Cornish coast. It has been ages since I wandered the hills of Arthurian legend."

They strolled along the country lanes, stopping occasionally to steal an apple or take a short break for the old man to rest. The two of them sat on a hillside, looking up at the moon, when Lamken intently looked over at the boy.

"What?" Bunty asked, suddenly self-conscious.

"What were you doing in Plymouth alone?" Rune asked.

Bunty shrugged. "It was me home, before me mum was killed."

The wizard took pity on the boy. "I'm sorry, lad. I didn't mean to pry."

Bunty said, "I know that, sir. I lived in Plymouth for most of me life and I guess I missed the place, though there not be much left. I live in Crackington Haven now, with me best friend, Gavin Kane."

"Cornwall has a reputation for being a special place," Rune said. "The Cornish villages are different from anywhere in England, because the magic of the earth runs very close to the surface."

Bunty only nodded.

"Let's be on our way," Lamken said, standing up with a groan. "I wish to see your village, for it has been many years since I traveled these parts."

They walked in silence for a distance.

"Is something troubling you, lad?" Rune asked.

"Doesn't anyone ever suspect you're a wizard?" Bunty wondered.

"I attract few questions, due to my gentle nature and dislike of direct interference with other people's internal affairs and policies," the old man tried to explain. "However, I do feel negative human emotions, such as greed, jealousy, and the lust for power."

"How did you become a wizard?"

"Oh, it's a very long story. Let's just say I was born to it."

"I thought wizards used magic wands."

"Not me. My power resided in my enchanted staff."

"I see, I guess."

"When Elizabeth was taken, I lost my power and now I'm worthless."

"Not to me you're not," Bunty said loudly.

"Well, thank you, boy."

"Why did you name your staff Elizabeth?" Bunty started with the questions again.

"Oh, I didn't name her at all," Rune replied. "It's the name she came with. I merely inherited her from another great sage."

"I'm sorry she was taken from you, sir," Bunty said. "Elizabeth sounds wonderful."

The wizard looked at Bunty with sincere regard. He affectionately fluffed the boy's red hair and said, "Perhaps I'll find Elizabeth one day and you can meet her."

"I would like that."

"As I would enjoy having you as a student."

"Did you like being a wizard?" Bunty asked.

"It had its moments."

"If I knew magic, I would make chocolate cream pies every day and stuff myself."

Lamken laughed aloud. "I bet you would."

"I never imagined wizards still existed in this modern age."

"I'm afraid not much has changed in our world," Lamken said. "We still cling to our old and ineffective traditions. This terrible war has uncovered many of our weaknesses and as a result, even the wizard community is divided by petty rivalries and unstable alliances."

"Don't you worry the Germans might win the war?" Bunty asked.

Rune stopped walking and sighed heavily. "I can't imagine anything more terrifying, lad, to be certain. There are strange things going on in Germany, horrific things that defy description. Unearthly powers have combined to seduce the hearts and minds of weak-minded men, who now conspire to plunge this planet into permanent darkness."

Bunty had hung on every word.

The wizard mistook the boy's mesmerized expression for a look of fear.

"I'm sorry, I didn't mean to frighten you," Lamken said.

Bunty shook his head. "No, that's not it at all. I was just thinking how much you sound like someone I know."

"Oh, and who is this great orator?" Rune jokingly inquired.

"A dragon," Bunty replied matter-of-factly.

Lamken gulped, as he inadvertently swallowed his surprise. "You know a real dragon?"

"Oh, yes, indeed I do," Bunty said proudly. "Sir Thaddeus Osbert is his name."

With a jolt, Lamken Rune's face turned ashen-white, all the color leaving his features in a flash. He grabbed his heart and staggered backwards, as if he had seen a ghost. The wizard's mouth opened and out came a pitiful moan, before the man dropped to his knees, eyes shut tight and his body shaking.

Bunty had witnessed all this in a state of shock. He regained his wits and ran forward to throw his arms around the trembling old man, desperately trying to provide comfort.

"Please, sir, don't die," Bunty begged.

The wizard's lips were blue and his eyes were wide with fear.

"Thaddeus won't hurt you, sir," Bunty continued, hoping to reassure the old man. "He is a friendly and generous dragon, unless you're a German soldier, of course. The Jerries would be terrified."

It was then that the old man formed his quivering lips to speak. His words came out as nothing more than a hoarse whisper.

"Or unless your name is Lamken Rune."

9

Eccentric Guest

As Bunty and the old man strolled into Crackington Haven, morning was upon them with a brilliant sunrise. After spending the night on the train, it looked like it would be a beautiful day.

Lamken stopped in the middle of the road and patted his chest, while taking a deep breath of air. "Ah, the north coast of Cornwall. It has been so very long."

Bunty reached over and took Rune's hand. "Let's get a bite to eat, shall we?"

However, before they reached the Kane residence, Gavin emerged from the garage with his bicycle. He spotted Bunty right away and quickly came down the street, worry on his face.

"Where have you been?" Gavin demanded. "I was going out to look for you!"

"Plymouth," Bunty replied sheepishly.

"Bunty, you know my mother doesn't want you going there anymore."

"Yes, I know," his friend said. "Sometimes I miss home."

Gavin had been concerned, but now that he knew Bunty was safe, he patted his friend on the shoulder. "I understand. I won't tell Mum."

Then Gavin looked at the old geezer standing behind Bunty.

"Who's the git?" Gavin asked quietly.

"He's my friend," Bunty answered reluctantly.

"He sure looks down on his luck," Gavin observed.

"Nothing a bath and hot meal wouldn't set right," Bunty said.

"Some clean clothes wouldn't hurt either," Lamken spoke up.

Gavin looked the old codger over carefully. In the end, he liked what he saw.

Offering his hand, he said, "I'm Gavin Kane. Welcome to Crackington Haven."

Lamken smiled warmly. "Well, thank you, lad. You and Bunty have made this old gaffer feel quite welcome indeed."

"Come up to the house and let's see to your needs," Gavin offered.

"Are you sure, lad?" Rune asked. "I don't want to be an imposition and your mother might not take kindly to strangers."

Bunty and Gavin looked at each other and laughed.

"Oh, sir, you'll be part of the family before the day is done," Bunty said. "Gavin's mum is always taking in people for a spot of tea and such. She won't mind."

Lamken shrugged and followed the boys to the Kane household.

"Mum," Gavin called out as they stepped into the kitchen. "We have a guest."

Winifred hurried in from the sitting room, her knitting still in hand. She came to an abrupt halt when she spotted the sorry shape of their visitor.

"Oh," Mrs. Kane said.

"I'm sorry to make such an appearance, Mrs. Kane," Lamken spoke up quickly. "I'm afraid your son insisted."

Winifred collected herself and smiled. "Please, do come in, sir."

"Mum, Mr. Rune is Bunty's friend from Plymouth and he's had a bit of a rough time with all the bombing, as you can see," Gavin explained. "I thought we could offer him a spot of tea, a hot bath, and some of father's old clothes?"

His mother fluffed his hair and gave Gavin a kiss on the forehead. "You have a generous heart, son. Of course we can."

"Thank you, Mrs. Kane," Rune said sheepishly.

Winifred came forward and took the gentleman by his elbow. "Now don't be modest or ashamed. Let's get you into the tub, while I make some tea and we'll rummage through my husband's clothes. Then you'll have a bite to eat and everything will look much brighter."

She steered Lamken towards the stairs. "Put the pot on to boil, now be good lads."

"Yes, Mum, straight away," Gavin replied.

Bunty went for the cup and saucer, while Gavin lit the fire.

"He's a bit of a strange old fart, but really quite fascinating," Bunty said.

"Seems to be at that," Gavin agreed. "Perhaps he'll turn out to be the long lost cousin of the King of England."

They both laughed.

Mrs. Kane came back downstairs. "He's taking a nice hot bath and I want you to toss these rags in the trash."

She directed her instructions to Bunty.

"Yes, Mrs. Kane, right away," the red-haired boy obeyed.

When he was gone, Winifred looked at her son, but didn't say anything.

"He seems like a nice old man, Mum," Gavin felt like he had to explain. "I thought we could make a difference."

His mother smiled. "I'm not angry at all, son. I was just realizing how much you've grown up since your father has been away. It's a shame he's missing his little boy growing into a man."

Gavin gave his mother a big hug. "I love you."

"I love you too, Gavin," she whispered, while kissing his forehead. "You're a good boy and I'm very proud of you."

When Lamken came into the kitchen an hour later, he did indeed look completely different. Besides trimming his beard and mustache, the bath had done wonders. Add to that Richard Kane's clothes and Rune looked like a new man.

"Thank you, Mrs. Kane," the old man said. "I feel ten years younger from your generosity."

"Please call me Winifred," Gavin's mother corrected him. "You're our guest."

Bunty was staring.

Rune grinned. "Didn't realize I was so handsome, did you, son?"

Gavin and Bunty chuckled.

"Sit, sit, have some hot tea," Winifred coaxed Lamken to take a seat at the breakfast table. "There's no sugar, I'm afraid, because we can't seem to keep any for very long."

Bunty quickly glanced at Gavin, but they said nothing.

"That's quite all right," Rune said. "I'm grateful for anything."

"There's a few biscuits and jam," Gavin offered.

"Simply lovely," the old man chirped.

Lamken quickly consumed two cookies, not missing a crumb.

"Scrummy!" he announced.

Everyone laughed.

There was a knock on the back door.

"Hello," a cheerful girl's voice spoke from outside.

Emily had arrived!

"Come on in, dearest," Winifred said.

"Hello, Emmy," Bunty and Gavin greeted their friend in unison as Emily stepped inside.

Emily waved, but didn't say anything, because she was startled by the presence of a stranger in the kitchen.

"Emily Scott, this is Dr. Lamken Rune," Mrs. Kane made the introductions.

"It is a pleasure to meet you, sir," she said politely, curtsying.

The old man beamed. "Such manners. The pleasure is mine, Emily. Please, join us for a nice cup of tea."

"Oh, how lovely," Emily chirped.

"I'll leave the four of you to talk, while I finish my chores," Winifred told them. "Please stay for supper, Doctor?"

"I'd be honored, Mrs. Kane," he replied.

"Doctor?" Bunty asked incredulously as Winifred returned to the sitting room. "How did she know you are a doctor?"

"We had a nice little chat upstairs, young man," Lamken replied.

"Medical doctor?" Gavin asked.

Rune shook his head. "No, I was once a scientist, specializing in radio waves and magnetic engineering."

"Wow," Bunty oohed and ahhed.

Lamken chuckled. "Now don't get all starry-eyed over it. I merely enjoyed tinkering and fiddling with things, which usually led to some useless invention of some sort."

"Like what?" Bunty asked.

"Well, the last project I worked on was radar," Rune replied hesitantly.

"You invented radar!" Bunty exclaimed.

"No one person can be credited with inventing radar," Lamken said. "It was the result of many minds. The idea had been around for a long time, like a spotlight that could cut through fog. The problem was too advanced for years, but with British technology and a bit of magic, we Ravens put that straight."

"Ravens?" Bunty wondered.

"Our nickname," the man replied. "I think we were dubbed Ravens out of jealousy by other scientists, who likened us to scavenger birds."

"How did you get involved with these Ravens?" Gavin asked.

"Great Britain was making strides developing radar in the years leading up to this terrible war," Lamken explained. "After some fumbling about, I decided to give the lads a helping hand, because I was aware that a serious military threat was developing in Germany. With the success of several well-timed experiments, an early warning system was built around the British Isles, which used radar to warn of incoming aerial invasions. This advancement has given our RAF the edge they need to outmaneuver the German Luftwaffe."

"Bloody brilliant," Bunty said.

"I had come to have a feeling for the way the Germans did things," Rune went on to explain. "They would take simple ideas, and put them straight into practice, no matter what technical requirements were involved, because they had a far greater command of precision engineering. I wondered how the Luftwaffe was able to accurately bomb British targets, even with strict blackouts? I was pained to discover the Germans had been navigating by radio beams."

"So you helped develop a practical use for radar?" Emily surmised.

"While radar development was being pushed, because of wartime concerns, the idea of radar first came to me as a tool to help prevent seagoing collisions," Rune went on. "Ever since the *Titanic* ran into an iceberg and sank in 1912, I've been interested in ways to make such disasters avoidable."

"That's what I want to be when I grow up," Bunty announced. "A scientist!"

"Well, Britain needs good minds, Bunty," Rune said. "Otherwise the competition will run away with all our hard work."

"Why do you say that?" Emily suddenly asked.

"England has it all, including brains, ideas, and inventions," Lamken stated emphatically. "Yet we squander all the genius away. Our country's brilliance needs governmental and national protection, as well as support."

"I think Mr. Churchill is supporting the war effort any way he can," she countered. "The PM can't put his backing behind every scheme, or we wouldn't get anywhere."

"She's very bright," Bunty interjected.

"I can see that," Lamken said. "You're right, lass, of course, but we haven't even scratched the surface of what we're capable of. There are so many problems to solve, without war getting in the way. Minds should be focused on ideas that save lives, not how to kill more efficiently."

Gavin was pleased to hear the old man say that. "Please, Doctor, go on."

"I am deeply interested in the capacity and character of the human brain," the wizard tried to explain. "I'm a pacifist by nature, peace-loving, and reluctant to work on weapons of any kind, no matter how good the cause."

"Britain is fighting for her very survival," Emily stated emphatically.

"So true," the doctor agreed. "This is why I helped with radar. Ten years ago there were many learned people who scoffed at our work."

"That's ridiculous," Bunty said.

"You need to keep in mind that many ideas now accepted as commonplace, were once the ideas of uneducated eccentrics," Rune stated with a grin.

"Like you, sir?" Bunty wondered.

"Indeed, just like me," the wizard chuckled. "For instance, I'm convinced there are people in other universes trying to communicate with us."

"Wow, that's pretty neat," Gavin reacted.

Bunty and Emily both nodded in agreement.

"You don't think I'm crazy?" Rune asked with surprise.

"Remember, the three of us know a real dragon, sir," Bunty whispered quietly, so Gavin's mother wouldn't hear. "We've learned that there are lots of things in this world that are strange and unusual, but still real."

"Well, with this trio by my side, the odds are billions to four," Lamken said.

"You sound so pessimistic," Emily said sadly.

"Actually, I'm a wild-eyed optimist," Lamken said. "With such odds, we're bound to succeed."

The teens laughed.

Suddenly Bunty became quite serious, but hesitated asking his question.

The wizard could sense this. "Go ahead, Bunty, ask whatever's on your mind."

"Dr. Rune, why are you so terrified of Thaddeus Osbert?" the boy asked.

Gavin and Emily weren't aware of this fact beforehand, so with shocked expressions, they focused their undivided attention on the old man. There was no doubt they wanted to hear his answer.

Lamken took another sip of his tea. His bottom lip was quivering again. It was obvious that talking about the dragon caused a powerful emotional reaction. With incredible willpower, Dr. Rune took a deep breath and coughed to clear his throat.

"It is difficult to admit my crime, but I once betrayed that dear old dragon," Lamken said finally.

"Why would you do such a horrible thing to such a wonderful creature?" Emily demanded, before Gavin or Bunty had a chance to stop her.

The old man hung his head.

Gavin sternly wagged his finger at Emily and then said, "Please, Dr. Rune, go on. We won't judge your actions, at least not until we've heard both sides of the story."

Lamken forced a smile. "Thank you, lad. That's fair enough."

They waited.

"It's really quite simple," the wizard finally began. "I was faced with a choice and selected poorly."

"Nothing in life is simple, Dr. Rune," Gavin said, remembering a lesson from a certain dragon.

Lamken looked at Gavin with admiration and respect. "For one so young, you possess an inordinate amount of wisdom."

"He's like that," Bunty said.

"You're right, of course," Rune went on. "Life is full of choices and even when they seem simple, the outcome can be extremely complicated. I didn't listen to Sir Osbert's advice and instead followed an impulse, which in turn led to disastrous results."

He took another sip.

The three teens sitting around the table hadn't flinched a muscle. They were expectantly waiting for him to continue his story.

"Long ago I possessed many magical powers and was considered a wizard of great promise," Lamken went on. "Perhaps I was seduced by my abilities, but soon I was selected to preside over the Royal Moot of England. This body of witches and wizards advised kings and queens, assisted armies, and helped shape government policies. We have stood in the shadows for generations, offering wise council whenever approached."

Rune took another sip of tea.

"However, that power was also quite seductive and often led members of our moot to go astray," Lamken continued. "I once was imprisoned by a witch who I fancied, trapped by her beauty. It was your Thaddeus who set me free."

"I told you he was a good dragon!" Emily stated abruptly.

"Yes, you are right," Rune said. "He is a very good dragon. In fact, because of his decision to set me free from the witch's spell, Sir Osbert was condemned by his fellow dragons for meddling in human affairs."

Gavin heard this and said, "He's been known to repeat such behavior."

The wizard nodded his head. "Indeed he has. When I stopped counting, Sir Osbert had been accused of the same infraction at least one thousand seven hundred and seventy-three times throughout human history. The old boy cares about what happens to people, which is either a glorious trait or a wicked curse, depending on your point of view."

"So what was this choice you made?" Emily asked, forcing the conversation to get back on track.

Rune sighed, realizing he had to come clean. "I chose dragon over human."

"What's wrong with that?" Emily asked.

"I am a Druid, child," the wizard said. "As such, I was considered a pagan and evil. To defend dragons was an act of blasphemy and certain members of the early Christian church condemned me. In anger, I conspired with unholy forces to bring down nations. I used my magical powers to muddle men's minds, an easy thing to do. When I was summoned before the Royal Moot to answer for my crimes, however, I was a coward and blamed Thaddeus Osbert, claiming the old boy had tricked me into betraying humanity."

Then the old man buried his face in his hands.

Neither Gavin nor Emily knew what to say.

Bunty spoke up. "Have you learned any lessons from your actions, sir?"

Lamken looked up, surprise on his face. He had only expected harsh words from these teenagers, who so obviously loved Thaddeus. "Yes, Bunty, I have. That those who once betrayed dragons could easily do so again. I would rather turn my back on the entire world, than allow mankind to make war on those grand creatures. In the end, I did not protect humanity with my lies, but helped divide nations into civil war against each other, all in the name of God."

"What was Sir Osbert's reaction to all this?" Gavin asked.

"Unable to believe a wizard would betray his own kind, Thaddeus sought me out to confront me."

"What happened then?" Emily asked, scooting to the edge of her chair.

Dr. Rune quickly scanned the room and tried to listen for anything that might betray the dragon's presence, because he might be listening nearby, invisible and silent.

In actuality, Thaddeus was hundreds of miles away, in Iceland.

"Listen well, my friends and learn the truth from me," Lamken spoke softly. "For those who loved me, I loved in return, and for those who schemed to betray the dragon world, I betrayed instead. To prevent a backlash, the wizard's moot banished me forever and my magical staff was confiscated and destroyed. Even parts of my memory were erased and I have wandered the British Isles ever since. Until now, that is."

"Do you think you were treated fairly?" Bunty wondered.

"Life isn't fair, boy, and neither are the lessons," Rune replied. "I know my actions were wrong, because I betrayed an innocent creature's trust. Only a fool pursues true evil with eyes wide open, knowing full well what they are doing and choosing to betray all humanity for the sake of worldly riches. My sentence was lenient compared to the damage I caused. Yet I have learned to believe in faith and spirituality, thereby experiencing goodness and forgiveness. God created dragons, not Satan. Any fool who believes otherwise is acting as an agent of the devil."

Silent reflection followed the old man's confession. None of the teens knew what to say just then. It would take time to decide how they felt about the entire situation.

Gavin broke the silence. "Well, I think I know Thaddeus Osbert and I believe he would forgive you if you asked him to, Dr. Rune."

Lamken seemed unconvinced, but he didn't voice his doubts.

Instead, the old man said, "I'd fancy a good movie about now."

"I don't think we have enough money for all four of us," Gavin said. "Me mum works at the *Bude Cinema*, but she won't let us just sneak in."

The old man chuckled. "Oh, money's no problem with a wizard like me."

"You can make money?" Bunty asked, his eyes wide with amazed delight.

"Here, let me show you how," Lamken offered.

He took an old farthing from his pocket and with great care covered it in a piece of silver foil.

"Now just pretend it's a sixpence, throw it in the tub and make your way into the theatre, but don't tell anyone I showed you, in case you get caught."

"That's not magic!" Bunty said with great disappointment.

"Do you want to see a movie or not?" Gavin asked, jumping up from the table.

They all nodded.

"Then let's try Dr. Rune's method and see what happens."

With Mrs. Kane's permission, off to Bude they went.

No one at the movie theatre was wise to their altered-coin method. With Lamken leading the way, each of them plopped a silver-wrapped farthing into the pail and went inside. Once in their seats, they all had a good laugh.

They watched *Let's Get Tough*, starring The East Side Kids, who helped the home front in this mix of comedy, espionage, and patriotic sentiments. After being rebuffed from joining the war effort, because of their age, the Kids did some snooping and crashed an alliance between Japanese saboteurs and a German immigrant with pro-Nazi sentiments.

"That movie was funny," Bunty summed up his impressions as the screen went blank.

"I thought it was exciting too," Emily added.

Gavin wasn't sure how he felt. He had looked over at Dr. Rune several times during the film and noticed the wizard's eyes were closed. However, he was convinced the old man had been wide-awake the entire time.

Once the lights went up, Lamken stood up and said, "That was very entertaining, considering it was from the Yanks."

Everyone exited the cinema in an orderly fashion, meeting up with their guardian by the curb. Setting a leisurely pace, the group headed back to Crackington Haven. The three teens were unusually quiet again, their thoughts returning to the earlier discussion.

Suddenly Bunty came to an abrupt halt.

"What is it?" Gavin asked with concern, as everyone came to a stop.

His friend turned around and faced Dr. Rune.

"What's on your mind, lad?" the old man asked.

"I've been thinking, sir," Bunty said. "Some of the things you said earlier, just don't make sense, unless you're very old."

Lamken chuckled. "Old indeed."

"So, just how old are you?" Emily asked.

"Well, that's not the type of inquiry young people should ask," Rune replied.

"You're avoiding the question," the girl countered.

Lamken sighed. "At last count, I've seen a little over eight hundred years."

"You can't be that old!" Emily blurted.

Rune shrugged. "Give or take a few years, here and there."

The three of them just stared at him.

Emily shook her head and in quick succession said, "You're balmy, barmy, bats, batty, bonkers, buggy, cracked, crackers, daft, dotty, fruity, haywire, kooky, loco, loony and loopy!"

Gavin and Bunty stared at her with amazement, stunned that the girl could rattle off so many different words meaning just plain crazy.

Even Lamken seemed impressed. "Well done, Emmy. I think you covered all the possibilities."

Under his breath, Bunty said, "She only got as far as L. I could have thought of a lot more examples."

Gavin smiled.

"So what's the truth then?" Emily demanded.

"I have not lied to you, lass," Lamken said.

After that, everyone continued their journey in complete silence.

Supper was ready when the group reached the Kane house. Winifred was actually excited to have so many people taste her cooking. It didn't seem to matter that rationing made everything in short supply, because her guests would see what she was capable of doing.

"This meal is quite delicious, Winifred," Lamken commented after taking a few bites. "Whatever is this tasty meat?"

"Spam," Gavin blurted, crinkling his nose.

Simultaneously, Bunty and Emily laughed, for they knew only too well, what their friend thought of the processed meat.

"Well, it's scrummy, as my chum Bunty says," Rune added.

"Yes, scrummy indeed, sir," the redheaded boy chimed in.

Gavin decided it was better to stay silent and eat, because he was hungry and there wasn't any other choice. His mother leaned over and gave him a very gentle kiss on the earlobe.

"You are a sweetie," she whispered. "For being such a good sport, I have a little treat, just for you, after everyone is out of the kitchen."

That little secret spurred Gavin to finish his helping in record time.

Emily was given permission to spend the night, as long as she was up extra early in the morning to catch the bus to Truro. After her bath, the girl turned in, so she could get a good night's sleep.

After looking everywhere, Bunty finally found the old man standing outside in the garden, looking up at the sky. The teen wasn't sure he should disturb the wizard, but before he turned to go back inside, Rune spoke.

"Come here, Bunty," Lamken said. "I have something to tell you."

"Yes, sir," the boy said.

Bunty stood close to the old man, as if he it was safer being near the wizard.

"Thank you again for looking out for me, son," Rune said quietly. "I owe you a great deal."

"Not really, sir," Bunty said. "You are very interesting."

The wizard grinned. "Is that so?"

"Indeed it is. I have learned a lot from you."

"That's grand."

Lamken knelt down before the boy and said, "I must be moving on."

"You mustn't, please," Bunty pleaded.

Rune took hold of the boy's shoulders. "You are a fine lad, Bunty. I am grateful to you for setting me straight. I must go, to find my way again and perhaps begin anew the search for my Elizabeth. I will return, I promise."

Bunty pouted and scuffed his shoes against the grass. "That's what everybody says."

"My word is my bond, lad. I will pass this way again by the end of the month."

Bunty looked up. "That seems so far away."

"No, not really. The time will fly by, you'll see."

The red-haired boy held out his hand. "It has been a pleasure meeting you, sir."

They shook hands.

"For me as well," Lamken said.

The old man turned around slowly and walked away, slipping out through the back gate. Bunty ran past the garage to watch the wizard stroll up out of Crackington Haven along the coast road.

Inside the kitchen, Gavin was enjoying a piece of real chocolate. The treat his mother had given him was more than he had expected possible and the teen savored every little nibble, meant to last a long time.

Bunty came in through the back door, but didn't even notice what Gavin was eating.

"Where's Dr. Rune?" Winifred asked.

"He's moved on, Mrs. Kane," Bunty replied.

"What?" she asked with disappointed surprise.

"He told me he would come this way again by the end of the month, but I don't believe him," Bunty added.

Winifred made eye contact with her son and signaled him to leave. Gavin did so without a fuss, quickly heading up to Bunty's room, since Emily was asleep in his bed.

"Would you care for a cookie before you go to bed?" Mrs. Kane asked, once she was alone with Bunty.

"No, thank you, Mrs. Kane," the redheaded boy said dejectedly.

Winifred wiped her hands on her apron and took the boy into her arms.

Bunty leaned his head against her and sighed heavily.

"He is a wonderful gentleman," she said quietly. "You two got along famously, I think."

Bunty just nodded.

"You must have faith that he will return," she said. "Perhaps Dr. Rune is only leaving, because he knows your father is coming and doesn't want to compete for your time."

Bunty stood up straight and looked Mrs. Kane in the eye. "Do you really think so?"

She nodded and smiled. "I do indeed."

Bunty leaned in and gave her a kiss on the cheek. "Thank you, Mrs. Kane. I really don't know what I'd do without you."

That brought tears to Winifred's eyes and she gave the boy another hug. "I have been blessed by you as well, Bunty. You have no idea how terrible it was seeing you so near to death. I blamed myself for failing your mother and letting such harm come to you."

"Don't be daft, Mrs. Kane," Bunty objected. "You had nothing to do with my injury."

She shrugged. "It is a mother's responsibility to look after the children in her care. I thank God every night for sending Dr. Bixley our way."

Bunty nodded and then yawned.

"Off to bed now," Winifred said. "Tomorrow is another day."

Bunty hurried out of the kitchen, down the hallway and up the stairs. When he got to his room, Gavin was waiting.

"Here, I saved this for you," his friend whispered.

It was half a piece of chocolate.

Bunty's eyes were huge with gratitude. "Thanks, chum."

Gavin enjoyed watching Bunty eating the sweet.

They both hopped into bed under the comforter and within minutes were asleep.

As it turned out, CPO Charles Digby arrived in Crackington Haven the very next day, with a cat tucked under his arm. *Oscar* had traveled with him all the way from Gibraltar and Bunty was surprised to discover how fond of the cat his father had become.

"We rescued each other after the **Ark Royal** went down," the chief explained. "I've since learned this tabby was aboard the **Bismarck** too. He's a survivor, just like me."

Gavin's ears perked when he heard mention of the **Bismarck**. His memories of that day were still clearly etched in his mind, but learning the cat had made it through that horrible battle made the boy happy.

However, this was also the end of *Oscar's* seafaring career, because Chief Digby had arranged for the cat to be posted to the Old Sailors' Home in Belfast. There the feline could retire and live out his life in relative comfort. The CPO was sad to part ways with the tabby, but he also felt *Oscar* would have a better chance of survival away from the Royal Navy.

The boys hurried off to catch the bus to school, while Charles and Winifred sat in the kitchen enjoying hot cups of tea.

"The boy is growing like a weed," Digby said with delight. "You must be feeding him good. I hope he doesn't take more than his fair share?"

"Bunty's a very good boy, Charles," Gavin's mother said.

"I'm sure he is," Digby said.

Winifred heard something in his voice she didn't like, but it wasn't fair to jump to any conclusions. "He misses you terribly, because he'd rather be with his father."

Digby looked directly at Mrs. Kane and said, "Now, now, Winifred, don't make things up. Byron has a much better life here with you and Gavin, and you know it. I would never have wished any ill fate become his mother Marylyn, but her passing has made a world of difference for the boy. He's much better off here."

"I can never replace his mother, Charles," she protested. "No more than I can fill in for his father. My son suffers greatly not having his own father around, so think how much more difficult it is for your own son."

The chief thought about what she said, before he replied. "That may be true, Winifred, but it doesn't change the situation. I'm in the Royal Navy and gone for months at a time. I've been reassigned to another ship and who knows when I'll have leave again? There's a war on and I could get killed in action. Byron is better off with the likes of you and we both know it. I am entirely grateful for what you have done for him."

Gavin's mother appreciated the man's words, but she felt such sorrow too. Instead of belaboring the point, however, she stood up. "I must get on with my chores, Charles. Make yourself at home. Bunty will be home in a few hours."

"I think I'll take a long stroll," the chief said.

After school, instead of playing with Gavin, Bunty went straight home to spend time with his father. As the redheaded boy walked down the hill into the village, he spotted Charles emerging from the *Coombe Barton Inn*.

They waved to each other.

"Hello, Pa," Bunty greeted him enthusiastically.

"Good day to you, my boy," the chief said. "I just stopped in for a pint of bitters."

"That's all right, Pa," Bunty said.

"Let's go for a walk, son," his father said seriously. "We can have a chat, man-to-man."

"That's grand," Bunty replied, elated.

"Once my survivor's leave is over, I'll be reporting for duty on the aircraft carrier **HMS Victorious**," the chief informed his son. "Don't know much about her and she'll never replace the **Ark Royal**, but I goes where the Navy sends me."

"I'll miss you."

Charles fluffed his carrot-red hair. "Likewise, lad."

"I'm glad you spent your leave with me."

"Me too."

There was silence.

"Mrs. Kane tells me you are a very good boy and you're doing well in school."

"I guess so."

"You're becoming a man, Byron. Pretty soon you'll be telling me what to do."

They laughed.

It certainly wasn't planned, but their stroll had taken them in a circle and before long, they were standing in the Kane's backyard.

"It certainly is peaceful here on the coast," Charles said, looking out to sea.

"Do you miss the ocean, Dad?" Bunty wondered.

Unexpectedly, the chief shook his head. "Not any more."

"Was it bad?"

His father turned to face him. "Any time a ship goes down, a part of the sailor goes with it. I'm not sure I'll ever be the same."

Bunty reached over and took his father's hand.

"You probably will think your old man is losing his mind, but I keep having the strangest dreams," Chief Digby admitted in a rare moment of vulnerability.

Bunty squeezed his father's hand. "It's okay, Pa. After all you've been through, a nightmare or two seems natural to me. I have them all the time, ever since Ma…"

The boy didn't finish.

CPO Digby put his hands on his son's shoulders and looked him straight in the eye. "I miss her too, lad."

They hugged briefly.

Winifred witnessed this exchange of unexpected affection with joy in her heart. Perhaps something good would come from the war after all. The sinking of the **Ark Royal** obviously had a profound effect on Bunty's dad and it seemed for the better.

Mrs. Kane whistled a happy little tune and went into the sitting room to listen to the wireless. However, her upbeat mood didn't last very long.

Outside, Bunty stood talking to his father.

"What worries me is the nature of my dreams," Charles continued. "There's a dragon in every one."

This admission caught Bunty completely off-guard. "A what?"

"I know, it sounds daft," his father said.

"No, it's not that, Dad," his son tried to soften his earlier reaction. "I dream about dragons too."

"You do?"

Bunty smiled to himself. His statement was a bit of a tall tale, since it wasn't necessary to dream about Thaddeus. After all, that dragon was real. "Yes, Pa, I see a dragon all the time."

CPO Digby chuckled. "Well, now the both of us are crackers."

They laughed together again.

"Tell me about your dream, please?" Bunty asked nicely.

"There's not much to it, really. I'm in the water, drowning, and this big red dragon swoops down and plucks me from the sea. Then the beast sets me adrift on a piece of broken life-raft and I'm rescued."

As Bunty was listening, it struck him that it was possible his father's dream wasn't a dream at all. The redheaded boy would make a point to ask Thaddeus about it later.

"Let's go inside and see if Mrs. Kane is in the mood to whip us up a snack," Charles suggested.

"Sounds great, Pa," Bunty agreed.

They went inside, but were shocked to hear Mrs. Kane crying.

With Bunty one step behind him, Digby hurried into the sitting room.

Gavin's mother was sitting in her chair, her face in her hands, obviously quite upset.

The chief hurried to kneel before her. "Winifred, what's wrong?"

"Tobruk has fallen," she informed them. "Three years of war. Why can't we stop them? If only mothers knew their sons had died usefully, with a purpose. So many valuable lives used up, for nothing."

"Only time will tell, Winifred," CPO Digby said as he held her hands. "Perhaps their sacrifice will make a difference in the end, but only God knows that."

Mrs. Kane smiled halfheartedly. "I trust you are right, Charles. It is so good to have you amongst us again, for Bunty's sake especially."

At **RAF Medmenham**, Lieutenant Commander Kane was in his office studying a new batch of photographs taken of the German harbor defenses near Antwerp. The news of Tobruk's capture by Rommel had swept through the facility, leaving everyone a bit depressed.

There was a knock on the door.

"Enter," the officer call out.

In stepped Rupert Thatcher, the model maker who had constructed a perfect replica of Wewelsburg Castle, supposedly from his dreams alone.

Richard stood up and said, "There you are. Come on in, Rupert."

"Thank you, sir," the young man replied nervously. "You wanted to see me?"

"Relax, Rupert," Kane said in a warm friendly voice. "Have a seat."

"Thank you, sir," Thatcher said, sitting stiffly in the chair before Richard's desk.

"I just wanted to compliment you on your modeling skills, Rupert," Kane began. "The structure is magnificent. So you built it entirely from memory?"

"Yes, sir," the modeler replied.

"You've never seen that specific castle in any photograph?" Richard asked.

"Not that I know of, sir," Thatcher replied quickly, injury in his voice. "Why, is it a real place?"

Kane nodded gravely. "I'm afraid so, son. In fact, we've been keeping our eye on that castle for some time now."

Rupert looked down at his hands. "I'm sorry, sir. I did as you suggested, but the images haven't gone away. Now they're more like nightmares, with strange and horrible images."

Richard gently placed his hand on Thatcher's shoulder. "That's all right, Rupert. It's nothing to be ashamed of. I'm not sure what to make of all this, but you've got some kind of connection with that castle."

"Connection, sir?"

The officer put his hands in his pockets and slowly walked around the room. "It's difficult to explain, Rupert, but Wewelsburg Castle and Rupert Thatcher are somehow connected."

"I don't like the sound of that, sir," the young man said.

Kane smiled grimly. "I imagine you don't. However, I can't let that connection go unused or unappreciated."

"What do you have in mind, sir?"

"From now on, you're assigned to my section."

"Yes, sir."

"I want you to work on the list of projects currently requiring your skills, but once they're completed, you will work exclusively on Wewelsburg Castle."

"Yes, sir."

"I want to see if you can recall details of the interior," Richard explained.

"I'll try, sir," Thatcher replied.

"That's the spirit," Kane said with enthusiasm. "You may return to your post."

"Thank you, sir.

"Carry on."

After ten days leave, Charles Digby received orders to report immediately to Portsmouth. **HMS Victorious** would be refueling, replenishing her supplies, and taking on replacements. The chief would receive credit for his remaining survivor's leave, but this was war and the aircraft carrier's needs outweighed those of one man.

"I'm sorry 'bout this, lad," his father said to Bunty. "I'll make it up to you."

His son smiled. "It's all right, Dad. The Royal Navy needs you and that's what you do. Just write more often."

"Ah, son, you know I'm not too good with words," Digby complained.

Bunty held out his hand. "Take care, sir."

They shook hands and then hugged.

"You're becoming a man, Byron," his father said. "I'm proud of you."

"Thanks, Pa," the teen said emotionally.

Bunty helped his father pack his kitbag. As CPO Digby came down from the room over the garage, he was greeted by Mrs. Kane and Gavin.

"You are a fine woman, Winifred," the chief said, giving her hand a squeeze. "I am deeply grateful for all you've done for my Byron."

"It is the Christian thing to do, Charles," Gavin's mother said. "The next time you get leave, please know you are welcome."

Father and son shook hands again.

"I'm going to go with Pa to the bus stop," Bunty announced.

"Of course," Winifred said.

The Digby men waved as they stepped through the gate. The pair walked up the road to the bus stop.

A few minutes later, the bus from Launceston arrived. CPO Digby stepped aboard and waved through the windows, as the bus pulled away.

Bunty felt all alone again.

He sighed.

Suddenly, motion caught his eye.

Someone was strolling overland from Boscastle way, whistling an old Celtic tune that sounded strangely familiar. Bunty held up his hand to block the sun, so he could get a better look.

It was Lamken Rune!

"You've come back!" Bunty shouted.

The wizard was pleased by the boy's obvious delight. "I told you I'd come back. I think I shall stick around the northern coast for awhile, at least until I can find employment somewhere."

Bunty threw his arms around Lamken's waist and hugged.

This display of affection made the wizard uncomfortable at first, but then he patted the boy and hugged him back. "It's nice to be wanted, lad."

"I missed you, sir."

Lamken grinned. "Well, I'm here now. Let's go see Mrs. Kane and ask her if we might have a nice cuppa."

"Good idea," Bunty said.

Side-by-side, the pair walked briskly back into town and up the lane to the Kane residence.

The red-haired boy knocked vigorously on the kitchen door.

Winifred was also happy to see Rune again. She took both his hands in hers and gave them a squeeze. "It is so good to see you again, Dr. Rune."

Lamken grinned. "I took a little tour of Kernow and spent some time chatting with the little people."

"Little people?" Bunty inquired.

Rune winked. "I visited with the gnomes, fairies, elves and piskies of the land."

Winfred giggled. "Oh, you're so silly, Lamken."

Dr. Rune smiled, but Bunty suspected the old man wasn't stretching the truth. After all, wouldn't is be entirely possible that a wizard would have regular contact with other magical creatures?

10

Cursed Arrival

By now, Britain was suffering from a severe shortage of alcoholic spirits, especially bourbon and gin. Unfortunately, this was solved by the illegal production of what was commonly known as hooch. Organized gangs were busy all over the country mixing pure alcohol with juniper and almond essences. Others used potentially lethal mixtures of industrial alcohol and methylated spirits. In one incident, fourteen people died of acute alcoholic poisoning from drinking hooch at an exclusive London party. Similar cases were reported all over Britain. Many of the victims were Allied soldiers, so in an effort to protect their men from hooch, officers began issuing a free bottle of gin or whisky to each man going on leave.

At the same time, the illegal trade of goods, in violation of official regulations, became known as the Black Market. Undercover agents with the *Ministry of Food* investigated attempts by people to deal with black marketers. Parliament passed legislation, which enabled the courts to impose fines, with or without imprisonment, with damages computed at three times the total capital involved in the transaction. Inspectors made sure the statutory orders of the *Ministry of Food* were obeyed by customers, retailers, and wholesalers alike. These investigators soon discovered that unknowing farmers were often the main source of producing food for the black market, many residing in Cornwall.

Yet some people along the north Cornish coast were not so innocent.

For hundreds of years many coastal families had practiced the fine art of smuggling or shipwrecking, but were becoming proficient purveyors of black market goods. This meant the reopening of smuggler tunnels, caves, and secret warehouses throughout the British Isles. A brisk business was reborn and with it came the inherent dangers. While smuggling had provided some local people with a decent living, the black market made a new generation of criminals wealthy indeed.

Another major fraudulent scheme concerned the exploitation of children. With the outbreak of war, the British government attempted to relocate as many children from Britain's large cities as possible. For the most part, this meant the burden to take in these evacuees was placed on people living in rural areas. The billetor received monetary support from the government to help with expenses, especially food. It didn't take very long for some unscrupulous swindlers to claim these allowances, even after the children had returned home. Other crooks stole blank billeting forms and filled them in, so allowances were paid for non-existent people.

While much of the nation rallied together and put aside their social and class differences, the criminal element found entirely new avenues to pursue unlawful gains. Already strained by constant bombing and the manpower shortages war created, law enforcement officials were sorely taxed to meet the increase in criminal behavior. While Scotland Yard did its best to help out, they were busy protecting England from spies, enemy agents, and possible acts of sabotage.

It was little wonder then, that no one in Britain was prepared for the arrival of yet another threat. This woman's methods were more insidious and secretive than the German bombing raids, but they would be far more destructive if left unchecked.

Rumble…boom.

Sizzle…pop!

Crackle…snap…zing.

Out in the middle of Bodmin Moor, something strange was happening.

The winds suddenly ceased blowing and the temperature dropped almost twenty degrees. What little wildlife that was out and about, scattered in every direction.

Crash went a bolt of lightning.

Zap!

Boom, boom, boom rumbled thunder thereafter.

Agnes Olmanns suddenly appeared, standing in the bog, surrounded by swirling gray smoke and pungent odors. When the vapors cleared, she studied her surroundings for a moment, acclimating herself to the bleakness of the moor. The black witch was quite pleased, for her traveling spell had not carried her astray, but planted her feet firmly on the cursed soil of the enemy.

Olmanns made her way across dangerously marshy ground. Perpetually covered in fine, swirling mists, a nearby lake was an eerie sight. The body of water itself was approximately 200 yards long, supplied at one end by a trickling stream. Stagnant pools surrounding the lake filled the air with an unwholesome smell. Birds and animals shunned the place, and the plants were twisted and unhealthy, with shrunken trees bare and draped with slime-like moss. The place was oddly still and tainted with an atmosphere of almost tangible evil and malevolence.

The witch felt a cosmic pull from across the moor, as the wind started to pick up. The frisky breeze eddied and shifted, and abruptly grew stronger, tugging at her cloak. Waves rippled across the lake, while leaves and small sticks were thrown into the air.

Agnes wasn't afraid. To the contrary, she was delighted by her discovery.

"This place is alive with dark powers," Olmanns whispered to herself.

Kneeling down, the witch touched the earth and closed her eyes, savoring the currents that ran close to the ground. Agnes could feel the oozing energy squirming and slinking beneath the surface. The moor was alive with malignant surges.

A heavy sea fog, known locally as a *roak*, slipped across the lowlands as Agnes made her way towards Warleggan. There was someone residing in the village who could offer her sanctuary, someone who had already sided with her master.

With virtually no vegetation to stop the howling wind as it crossed the moors, the occasional tree dashed its branches together in a symphony of discordant rattling notes. The witch took shelter beside an outcrop of rocks and looked out across the heather.

Suddenly, a shadow stole slowly across the moor, but stopped directly before her.

"Why have you come now?" Agnes asked.

"To bargain for more souls," the apparition replied.

"I promised you all of Briton," she replied. "What more could you ask?"

The shadow enveloped her in an instant. Her skin crawled with its cold, clammy touch, as boney fingers clasped tightly about her throat.

"Do not question me," the spirit's voice echoed inside her head.

"Yes, master," she croaked.

The apparition released her. "Good. Do not forget your place again."

To her knees, she genuflected. "Forgive my insolence, master."

"Arise, Witch of Darkness," the ghost commanded. "Do my bidding and your master will reward you handsomely."

"I exist only to obey thee, master," Agnes said.

"I have located the portal," the ghostly shape announced. "It lies directly underneath the castle, the very place where you were burned at the stake!"

"It is as you prophesized, Master," Olmanns said.

"Yes, we are so very close to victory," the spirit stated. "Soon our slaves will have committed enough vile acts to tear asunder the rift and our allies shall be free to destroy all living things on this worthless planet."

In Crackington Haven, Gavin was holding a secret gathering of his own, with Bunty and Emily in attendance. They were discussing how to convince Lamken Rune to meet face-to-face with Sir Thaddeus Osbert.

"We can't force him to see the dragon," Bunty stated emotionally. "Besides, how do we know Thaddeus won't roast him to cinders?"

"Oh, don't be ridiculous," Emily objected. "Thaddeus isn't like that."

Bunty huffed and puffed, stumbling over himself to disagree. "Not like what? Please, you've got to be serious. You've seen him when he gets angry. Just ask those dead Germans or those barbequed orcs, what they think of Sir Osbert's temper."

"That dragon's anger is nothing compared to mine," she fired back.

During all this, Gavin just sat quietly, listening and observing, while contemplating their next course of action. It was because of his continued silence that his friends suddenly stopped their bickering and looked at him.

"Don't you have something to add?" Bunty asked.

Gavin smiled warmly. "Eventually. I just wanted you both to have your turn."

"Well, we're waiting," Emily said, while tapping her foot impatiently.

Gavin had been mulling over the situation ever since hearing Rune's side of the story. There was something about the tale that seemed overly complicated, as if the real reason for Lamken's falling out with Thaddeus had been lost over time. He doubted that the dragon would hold a grudge this long. However, the only way to find out would be to arrange a meeting between wizard and dragon.

"I think we need to bring Dr. Rune and Sir Osbert together," Gavin finally said. "I can't imagine Thaddeus will do anything rash with us there. If there's bad blood between them, it might do them some good to argue. I always feel better after I've ranted and raved for awhile, don't I, Bunty?"

The red-haired boy grinned. "I know I do!"

"I bet you do!" Emily exclaimed.

"Now don't start that again," Bunty countered.

Gavin started laughing. "You two really are something."

Bunty and Emily stopped in the midst of another flurry of insults, and then both broke into embarrassed laughter.

"That's better," Gavin said. "We're friends, remember?"

Just then, Dr. Rune came into the kitchen. "You three certainly seem to be having a good time."

Bunty took it upon himself to tell Lamken what the teens had decided. He walked straight up to the old man and said, "Gavin thinks it's bloody well time you and Thaddeus Osbert made friends again and we agree, sir."

All the color left the old man's face. This time, however, he didn't cower or retreat, but held his ground. It was obvious he was seriously considering the boy's suggestion.

Then, with a titanic display of courage, Lamken said, "I think Gavin's right too, Bunty. I must face my fears. If Sir Osbert decides to eat me, then at least his meal will have a clear conscience."

A knock on the back door interrupted their discussion.

Gavin jumped up and opened it.

There, standing all straight and proper, was a beautiful young woman dressed in an immaculate Wren uniform. She was about to say something, when Dr. Rune cut in front of Gavin, blocking her path.

Tabitha Bixley was startled, retreating a step.

The two of them just stood there, staring at each other, neither saying a word.

Watching all this unfold before them, Gavin, Bunty and Emily were quite unsettled by Lamken's rudeness, but they didn't know what to do about it either.

Just then, Gavin's mother strolled into the kitchen too. She saw everyone silently standing on the back steps, so she went to investigate. It came as quite a surprise to see a pretty, young Wren surrounded by the children and Dr. Rune.

"Why, hello, dearest," Winifred greeted the young woman hesitantly. "May we help you?" Her stomach churned a little, for she feared the Wren had come to deliver the dreaded telegram that something had happened to Richard.

Tabitha swallowed and forced a smile. "Hello. I…"

She couldn't complete her sentence, because the presence of her former teacher completed unnerved her.

Mrs. Kane observed Dr. Rune's expression and asked, "Do you and the doctor know each other?"

Tabitha regained some of her poise. "Yes, we're old friends. I wasn't certain it was him, until just now."

Lamken's head throbbed with repressed vibrant visions and myriads of impossible memories, some good and some bad. His eyes filled with tears and the old man struggled to find his voice.

"Well, now, let's not all stand out here gawking at each other," Winifred said. She reached out and took the woman's hand. "Do come in for a cuppa tea."

"Thank you," the Wren said politely. "By the way, I'm Senior Wren Officer Tabitha Bixley."

The last name caused a ripple effect among Gavin, Bunty and Emily.

"Excuse me, Miss?" Gavin asked.

"Yes, young man?" Tabitha replied sweetly.

"You wouldn't be related, by any chance, to Dr. Dymchurch Bixley?" the teenaged boy inquired.

Tabitha's face lit up with delight. "Oh, yes, he's my father."

Winifred almost fell over herself with excitement. "Oh, dear, now why didn't you say so in the first place? This red-haired boy standing beside me, Bunty is his name, owes his life to your dear father. Dymchurch is such a wonderful man! Do come inside and we'll have a nice little chat."

Tabitha felt very welcome then, but still avoided Lamken's scrutinizing glare. As she slipped by him, the old man seemed the shrink away to nothing. Once again, his past was catching up to him, in startling ways. Tabitha's arrival was no mere coincidence and this revelation made Dr. Rune consider running away in panic.

Then Bunty took Lamken's hand and said, "I'm right here, sir."

His touch settled the old man's nerves instantly. Lamken looked down at the boy and whispered, "Thank you. Stay close to me, lad."

Bunty smiled and pulled the wizard inside with him.

"Come sit here, Doctor, while I put the pot on to boil," Winifred beckoned.

Dr. Rune obeyed hesitantly, but he never took his eyes off Tabitha.

As the old man sat down, he blurted, "So, young lady, what exactly do you want?"

Gavin's mother turned around suddenly, troubled by Lamken's tone. "Dr. Rune, I'm surprised at you. Have you forgotten your manners?"

"Oh, that's all right," Tabitha spoke quickly, but it was obvious by the expression on her face, that his attitude had hurt her feelings.

Yet Mrs. Kane was no longer the timid and quiet housewife from the days before the war. She had proved herself quite capable and with this newfound confidence, no longer willing to stand aside as men made a mess of things.

"No, I will not tolerate such behavior in my house," Winifred said boldly. "Dr. Rune, you will apologize to our guest immediately, or I will have to ask you to leave."

Gavin's mouth was wide with amazement. He had never seen his mother so strong in her commitment. However, he smiled then, for he was exceedingly proud of her as well.

With such expressed conviction, Lamken was not one to argue. He stood up slowly and faced Tabitha Bixley. Clearing his throat and fully aware the three teenagers were all expectantly waiting for him to speak, he gathered courage.

"I'm afraid being alone for so many years has robbed me of the common courtesies my elders taught me, Miss Bixley," Rune said slowly. "Please forgive me for treating you in such a manner."

With tears in her eyes, Tabitha put her arms around Lamken's shoulders and gave him a very gentle kiss on both cheeks. "Oh, you are forgiven."

Winifred just beamed with satisfaction, while Gavin, Bunty and Emily sighed with relief. They expectantly awaited their tea and biscuits and when the service arrived, not a word was spoken.

"Thank you for the tea, Winifred," Tabitha said quietly.

"Oh, you are quite welcome, dearest," Gavin's mother said. "It's the least I could do, considering."

"It was yummy, indeed," Bunty chimed in and everyone chuckled.

"Now you children take Tabitha and Dr. Rune with you, while I get some work done," Mrs. Kane instructed with a huge smile. "Show them all the wonderful places you've explored."

"Yes, Mother," Gavin agreed.

"Just be back before supper," Winifred added.

Out the kitchen door they all went, Tabitha holding one on Lamken's hands, while Bunty took the other.

"Where should we go?" Emily asked when they reached the road.

"Let's go to Tintagel," Gavin suggested.

"Oh, how lovely, I haven't been there in years," Tabitha announced gleefully. "What shall we see when we get there?"

"We're going to see a dragon, actually," Bunty said, hoping to startle the young woman.

"Why, that's wonderful," Tabitha replied. "I haven't seen old Thaddeus in ages."

Her revelation was quite a surprise for everyone around the young Wren, except for Lamken Rune. With the mere suggestion of facing the mighty dragon, the wizard refused to go on.

"You must face him one day, sir," Bunty coaxed. "Might as well be today."

Tabitha was surprised and dismayed to see such fear in the old man's eyes. "Surely Sir Osbert holds no ill will towards you after so much time has passed."

Yet Rune did not move.

Gavin backtracked to stand beside Lamken. "He is a fine old dragon, sir, as you know. I will go ahead and discuss the matter with Sir Osbert, before you see him yourself. It will be just fine, you'll see."

Across the bay in Wales, Vera Eriksen was still trying to come to terms with what she had discovered. The woman had never once imagined that dragons really existed, but the photographic evidence seemed irrefutable.

Regardless of the challenges that lay ahead, Vera had to figure out a way to get the photos to her new contacts that had just arrived in England. It was vital for them to get the diplomatic pouch to Germany as quickly as possible, where Reichsführer Himmler would decide what course of action to take.

Winfred sat down in her comfortable chair and opened the most recent letter from Richard. She felt a little guilty that Gavin was unaware that his father had written, but his mother wanted some privacy with her husband's words.

Dearest Winifred:

I know it's unusual to write to just you, but being away from you for so long has left quite a void in my life. The war goes badly on so many fronts and even with the Americans, we struggle to keep ahead of the Germans.

Life here is either quite boring or quite demanding. It seems that we seldom get a break from the enemy's constant attempts to undermine our efforts. They're always up to something.

I truly miss your smile, your gentle and kind words, and your marvelous cooking. Of course, I miss you most of all and our son. He is growing up without me and I feel as if I have failed him as a father. It is why I work so hard at winning this war, so I can come home to you both. The coast is always on my mind, the smells and sounds, while I can only seem to recall vague memories.

I have requested leave, but it was denied. So, I wonder if you and Gavin might find the time to come see me? I don't know how I'll get away, but we'll manage.

I love you both very much,
Richard

11

Beast of Bodmin Moor

First farmed over 4,000 years ago by Bronze Age settlers, Bodmin Moor was one of the last great unspoiled areas in England and much of its prehistoric and medieval past remained untouched by the passing of the centuries.

The Moor was dominated by dramatic granite tors, which towered over the sweeping expanses of open land. Marshes and bogs drained into shallow valleys, rivers crossed onto softer shales and carved themselves deep river valleys, all the while providing shelter for rich, damp oak woodlands.

Historically, Bodmin Moor was a landscape which engendered fear and awe, but which also provided inspiration for writers, poets and sculptors. The moors generated folklore and legend, with fact and fiction blending into one another, as tales were passed down over the generations.

The grain of the Bodmin Moor landscape reflected the granite dominance. Standing stones, burial chambers, Cornish hedges, clapper bridges, cottages and farms, were all constructed from the boulders, which over the centuries had been cleared from the surface of the moor.

Yet Bodmin Moor was surprisingly small, extending just ten miles by ten miles. The lack of features gave the impression that the upland covered a much larger area. Equally, the wealth of archaeological remains and relatively few signs of twentieth century improvements, created the illusion of expansiveness.

Although Bodmin Moor covered a comparatively small area, the open, gently curving nature of the plateau landform, punctuated by rocky tors, created a surprising sense of scale, remoteness and even desolation. These qualities, combined with the impression of timelessness, contributed to the moor's distinctive, often depressing, character. It was a landscape where any traveler was faced with the natural environment, in its most elemental form, where the unwary could easily become lost among the bogs in swiftly descending clouds and mist.

A wild and rugged area steeped in ancient history, Bodmin Moor also had more than its fair share of myths and legends, from its strong connection with the tales of King Arthur, to mysterious sightings of eerie creatures and strange lights. Unknown to believers and skeptics alike, many of the stories originated from events perpetuated by one very persnickety dragon constantly in search of sugar.

Although small towns and villages surrounded Bodmin Moor, Agnes Olmanns was only interested in Warleggan. It was a small sparsely populated parish on the edge of the moor, dissected by heavily wooded valleys. The hamlet had the reputation of being one of the most remote areas in all of Cornwall. Mainly a cattle farming region, the town itself consisted of eleven houses, a solitary pub, with a small church and chapel.

Residing in Warleggan, the Reverend Damien Dwellan was a man, who at the very least, was considered quite eccentric. Ten years earlier, when Dwellan had first arrived, the parishioners found him strange and treated him with a great deal of mistrust. He quickly established himself as outlandish, when he painted the rectory and church in glaring obscene colors. The Bishop of Truro made the vicar remove all the paint at his own expense, which Dwellan grudgingly paid.

Fewer and fewer people turned up for Dwellan's archaic services, so to fill the empty spaces in his church, the vicar cut out cardboard figures and propped them in the pews. Then he could still preach his blasphemy to a full congregation. The Bishop of Truro was forced to order an inquiry into accusations made by the parishioners, who were getting more and more concerned at the decreasing number of people attending the church, and felt that the only way to prevent a completely empty sanctuary was to remove the vicar.

The parishioners complained bitterly that Dwellan had closed the Sunday School and had refused to hold services at reasonable and convenient times. Dwellan put up a barbed-wire fence around the rectory gardens, threatened to sell the organ, which was a memorial to those brave souls killed during the First World War, and Dwellan had even supposedly misappropriated church property for his own use. He used the gardens to grow vegetables, which he fed to a herd of pigs that wandered church grounds. The vicar was often spotted flitting about at night, gesturing at the moon in vulgar ways.

The Bishop listened to Dwellan's explanations to all these rumors and found no reason to remove the reverend from his post. With that, the entire congregation refused to enter the church ever again. This did not deter

Dwellan, who merely cut out more cardboard figures and placed them in the remaining empty pews. He became a hermit, living in seclusion and rarely venturing out.

As Agnes Olmanns entered the tiny village of Warleggan, she immediately sensed loneliness, isolation and remoteness. Its little church had an air of neglect about it, overgrown with strangling vines and dark shrubberies. It was evening as Agnes quietly flitted from shadow to shadow, cautiously closing upon the godless structure.

That night, Dwellan was sitting in his library reading several forbidden manuscripts. He was drunk, having consumed two bottles of communion wine and was wondering what to do next, when he heard someone coming up the front walk. He cowered in the chair.

Agnes knocked impatiently on the rectory door.

Several minutes later, she heard a number of locks being disengaged and the door creaked open a few inches. Olmanns could see one eye peeking out.

"What do you want?" the man on the other side demanded.

Her garments were scanty and torn, and her coal-black hair lay tangled to her shoulders. The woman's dark eyes danced with unholy delight.

"Are you Damien Dwellan?" Agnes asked.

"I am," he answered. "What business is it to you?"

"Your master sent me to seek you out," she replied.

"Why are you here?" Dwellan wondered, shivering at the suggestion that the dreaded dark apparition might be close by.

Olmanns looked at him with utter contempt. With the speed of a cobra, the witch threw open the door and stepped inside. Dwellan backed against the wall, fearful for his life.

As well he should be.

"You were told to expect me, old man," she hissed.

Dwellan didn't dare move. He said nothing.

Agnes looked into the dingy sitting room. She moved past the vicar and sat down on a dusty settee that smelled of mildew. The witch waited for him to join her.

Dwellan peeked around the corner.

"Fetch me a pot of tea, you fool," she said angrily.

He did so, scurrying off to the kitchen.

Her mouth flashed a wicked grim and cackling with laughter, Olmanns looked around the room. First, she would burn all the books, every last volume. They would make a splendid fire.

Dwellan returned with a pot of tea.

"Set it here before me," Agnes ordered.

He did so.

She poured herself a cup, but did not drink it.

"When I am finished with your jolly old England," Olmanns whispered threateningly. "The only thing remaining will be their infernal tea!"

Dwellan cringed again.

"Why were **you** chosen by my master?" Agnes asked him.

He merely shrugged.

"So, the Beast of Bodmin Moor is nothing more than a wretched and vile old man," she concluded with a sneer. "You disgust me, fool."

Dwellan said nothing, but anger seethed inside him. He fought back the urge to attack her, because he knew such a move would only end in failure and death.

"Are you prepared to do my bidding?" Agnes asked.

Dwellan reluctantly nodded.

"Good," she said. "I will use this godless church to conduct certain forbidden activities. Once completed, you shall be handsomely rewarded."

This news pleased the vicar greatly. "I live only to serve you, Mistress."

Agnes burst into ridiculing laughter. "You live to serve your own foul desires, fool. Displease me in any way and I shall slit your throat."

"Yes, Mistress."

"Have you prepared the corpus altar?" she asked.

"The dead were taken to the cemetery at night and buried without any religious ceremony," the vicar told her. "I sought only the lost, abandoned, betrayed souls without hope. They were easy to find these days."

"I shouldn't wonder."

"Do you wish to proceed?"

"I do."

"Then follow me, Mistress."

Dwellan beckoned and shuffled to a rear door, which opened on the once-beautiful gardens, which were now nothing more than infestations of weeds and decay.

Agnes reached out and snagged his elbow. "I shall go on alone."

"Yes, Mistress."

She creaked her way through the gates.

There was no light in the cemetery that night, other than moon and starlight.

With warmer weather, the winter dieback of vegetation was not as complete as in previous years. No longer cleared, weeded, and tidied, the undergrowth was thick. Many animals and birds made the cemetery their home, such as foxes, rabbits, hedgehogs, squirrels, lizards and snakes. All these brambles, prickles and thorns formed a formidable defense and deterred even the most determined vandal. Ivy and painful barbs kept the cursed cemetery's dark secrets safe, because to read the inscriptions and learn the history, a visitor would have to be very brave and risk paying the price.

The headstones differed according to denomination, region, and date of origin, but were grouped in strange archaic patterns. The carved monuments were often askew and many of the inscriptions were unreadable, worn smooth by the forces of time. Still, the church cemetery seemed perfect for the witch's needs.

Olmanns inspected an altar fashioned between two similar headstones, a plank of wood balanced on top. Unfolding a black length of cloth, Agnes began a ritualistic chant, calling forth evil powers.

Lightning flashed in the distance and thunderstorms approached from the west.

More darkness enveloped the land.

Red-robed monks floated down from the swirling clouds, armed with strong spells and the mindless will to obey the witch's commands.

"Have you brought me the essence?" Agnes inquired.

One of the newly arrived assistants nodded and handed over a small ornate cut-glass vial. The liquid inside swirled of its own accord, with red and purple fluids that never mixed.

Olmanns smiled with satisfaction. Her destiny was about to be fulfilled. Once again, she would be the most powerful sorceress in all the land, her name no longer tied to seventeenth century witch-hunts, but to times that were more legendary.

Her servants knelt before her and as one asked, "What is your will, Mistress?"

"Go forth and commit murder," she commanded. "You must slay every white witch and wizard you can find in Briton. No force of light or good must be allowed to interfere with my master's plans."

"We obey," they said as one.

Then, as quickly as they had appeared, the red-cloaked minions divided their ranks and dispersed in every direction. Their future deeds would be most foul and if successful, such criminal acts could sway the balance in favor of Agnes Olmanns.

At **RAF Medmenham**, Richard Kane was faced with the unpleasant realization that Wewelsburg Castle was far more important than anyone could imagine. However, in spite of his conclusion, how exactly was he going to convince anyone else? There must have been incredible power emanating from the castle, to cause Rupert Thatcher's dreams to be so vivid.

12

Difficult Reunion

The three teenagers gathered outside the little white cottage on the hill. They seemed uncertain what to do next and hesitant to proceed with their plan.

"I'll wait out here for the wizard," Bunty said softly.

"We'll go inside and prepare Sir Osbert," Emily tried reassuring him.

"Okay," Bunty said, wringing his hands.

Gavin pushed open the door and peered in. "Thaddeus, are you home?"

A familiar dragon's voice called out, "Yes, dear boy, do come in."

Gavin and Emily stepped inside, slowly approaching.

The enormous fireplace broke apart, each shaped stone shifting and moving through the air. Chunks and slabs sailed about the room, almost colliding, yet mysteriously always narrowly missing each other. This magical display of levitation no longer appeared random, for the teens knew the rocks always came together to form the distinctive and recognizable shape of a mighty dragon.

What had looked like ordinary fireplace stones, now glistened and sparkled with pulsating radiant colors. The scales undulated with life and vitality. In a blink, Thaddeus Osbert had reappeared, his body rippling with power and definitely not of this world.

"Good day to you all," the dragon greeted them. "Why is Bunty waiting outside?"

They had forgotten Sir Osbert's extraordinary powers.

"He's waiting for a friend, Thaddeus," Emily tried to explain.

The dragon seemed quite excited. "Oh, lovely. I do enjoy meeting your friends. You always seem to know the most fascinating people or creatures."

Gavin and Emily laughed nervously, because they didn't know how Thaddeus would react once Lamken arrived. Emily sat down on the stool, but kept looking over her shoulder.

"Is something troubling you, lass?" the dragon asked.

"What?" Emily reacted, spinning back around. "Oh, no, of course not. I was just wondering if Bunty was okay?"

"He is within the protection of this hamlet, Emmy," Thaddeus said. "Nothing can harm him as long as I am here."

"That's good," she sighed.

The dragon eyed Gavin and Emily with concern. He cocked his head and studied them for a moment. There was definitely something amiss, for he could smell their uncertainty. He was just about to investigate further, when Gavin stepped forward.

"Yes, Master Kane, what is it?" Thaddeus inquired, relieved that the boy might divulge what was on their minds without the dragon having to force a discussion.

"I have continued my studies, as you suggested," Gavin began. "I finished reading the collected works on King Arthur and also completed the *Wizard Diaries*. I was wondering if I might ask you a few questions?"

The dragon was thrilled. "Of course, lad, please do."

"What happens to wizards?" Gavin asked. "Do they die?"

"Everything dies eventually," Thaddeus replied slowly, suddenly remembering his blood pact with Korban Vex. "Yet life goes on. We shed these earthly bodies and are reborn. It is the cycle of things."

"What happens to a wizard's power?"

"In the preferred manner, the spells and knowledge are passed along, from sage to apprentice."

"What happens if that doesn't take place?"

"Then the power is lost, which is truly a shame."

"Is there nothing that can retrieve it?"

Thaddeus seemed perplexed for a moment. Then he answered, saying, "I know for a fact that at least one wizard transferred all his power and knowledge into his staff, so that it would never be lost."

Gavin was instantly aware of who the dragon was referring.

Sir Osbert frowned. "However, the staff was destroyed and the wizard was banished from his brethren, cut off from his power. To this day the poor man wanders the British Isles, in search of his soul."

"That is sad," Emily commented.

"Yes, indeed it is," the dragon agreed. "Most sad."

"Have you seen this wizard since?" Gavin tried to ask nonchalantly.

The dragon's eyes suddenly became moist. "Alas, he no longer travels where I can see him. I fear his sorrow interferes with my ability to feel his life energy."

"What happened?" Emily asked as she stood up.

"He seemed a cheerful enough fellow for awhile, always ready with a drunken smile," Thaddeus recalled. "He carried an old milk bottle filled with tea and a bottle of whisky too. Then the spark went out and a part of him died. It was tragic, really, because he needlessly blamed himself for so many of the world's ills."

Gavin looked over at Emily.

She looked back and subtly nodded.

"Thaddeus, may I be allowed to pry into your personal affairs?" Gavin asked.

The dragon's eyes grew very wide. He was quite surprised by the boy's question. Then, just a quickly, they narrowed to mere slits.

"I sense a purpose in your inquiry, lad," Thaddeus replied. "I trust you with my life, Gavin Kane, so I trust you with your questions. Please, proceed."

Gavin took a deep breath. "Were you betrayed by Lamken Rune?"

The dragon snorted, a big puff of yellow smoke belching forth from his nostrils. He wasn't angry, but had been caught off guard by the question. Lowering his gigantic head to rest just inches from Gavin and Emily, he looked deeply into their hearts and souls.

"You have recently seen this wizard?" he asked quietly.

They both nodded.

"I see."

Thaddeus closed his eyes and considered the ramifications. When he opened them again, they were bright with warmth and fond regard. Both Emily and Gavin instantly knew everything would be just fine.

Gavin jumped forward and threw his arms around the dragon's neck, squeezing hard. Emily did so too, from the other side.

Thaddeus chuckled. He craved affection and relished receiving it.

"I leap to the conclusion that Bunty is waiting for the wizard's arrival," the dragon stated finally.

"Yes, Sir Osbert," Emily answered.

"In fact, he has already arrived," a deep voice spoke from the doorway.

It was Lamken Rune.

Holding his hand tightly was Bunty Digby, his face ashen with concern.

The great dragon looked at the red-haired boy with pity. "Do not fear me, boy. Your friend is welcome in my house."

The change was instantaneous.

Bunty grinned and pulled Lamken along with him.

The wizard went to his knee before the dragon, deeply bowing his head.

"Arise, Wizard, arise," Thaddeus commanded.

"Not before I admonish all my guilt before thee," Lamken said. "I am but a fool and it has taken these many ages to learn of my failings. I beseech thee."

"I have never wished ill of you, not then and not now," the dragon said.

Lamken Rune held his reverent pose. "I am greatly moved by your compassion, Sir Osbert. Yet I have come to beg your forgiveness and I must have it."

"Then it is freely given, Wizard," the dragon said. "You are forgiven, so I would once again count you as my friend and ally."

Bunty first looked at Gavin and then Emily. They all shared smiles with immense satisfaction.

As in the olden days, Lamken Rune once again stood erect, but he felt obligated to add something more. "I must commend you on what a wonderful young man you have taken under your wing to tutor, Sir Osbert. Gavin Kane was convinced I should seek an audience with you. The boy has character and has proven his heart is driven by fairness and justice."

Thaddeus smiled proudly as he looked down upon Gavin. "Indeed those traits are reflected in his daily actions. I am grateful to you for speaking well of him, for I see great things in the boy. Vivienne herself has chosen Gavin to be Protector of the Sword and Keeper of the Lake."

From that moment on, the wizard looked upon Gavin with different eyes.

Gavin raised his hand for permission to speak.

"You are not in school, young man," Thaddeus said as he recognized the boy's right to the floor. "You must be polite when in the company of men, but in my presence, speak your mind boldly."

"As long as I don't interrupt you, isn't that correct?" Gavin pointed out.

The dragon nodded and everyone else laughed.

"Please, Gavin, do continue," Thaddeus interrupted the chuckling.

"I just wanted to make it known that Bunty deserves the lion's share of credit for bringing Lamken before you," Gavin said. "Bunty cares deeply for the wizard's well-being."

"Such actions do justice to you, Byron Digby," the dragon said. "You are proving to be indispensable to us all."

The red-haired boy blushed.

"Do not be so modest, Bunty," Thaddeus said. "You have sacrificed much to the success of our previous adventures and England owes you a debt not easily repaid."

Bunty bowed. "It is an honor to serve."

Thaddeus cocked his head again. "I also sense a very profound emotion has developed in your heart for this wizard fellow?"

Bunty looked at Rune and nodded.

The dragon cast his gaze over those in the room, to settle on the young woman standing in the doorway. His eyes locked on Tabitha and when he spoke, his words were as much for her as anyone.

"Bunty, you are a devoted soul, loyal and caring, compassionate and forgiving," the dragon proclaimed. "It is your love for this old man which will change the course of history, not the wars of man."

Indeed, Tabitha Bixley did not miss the significance. As she gasped with delight, a powerful surge of white light emanated from Bunty and traveled the distance to surround Lamken Rune. Then it was gone.

"Grrrrrr!" the dragon suddenly growled, frightening everyone there. Sir Osbert shuddered and his tail whipped about violently, as if the creature felt threatened.

"What's wrong, Thaddeus?" Gavin was alarmed.

"Someone, or something, has just arrived in England uninvited," the dragon replied. "Great evil is once more upon our dear Britannia."

"I sensed it as well, old friend," Rune agreed. "The northern moors seethe with a sordid presence I have not felt in ages."

"Your moots are in grave danger," Thaddeus announced as he closed his eyes. "I see assassins lurking in the shadows."

Rune looked over his shoulder at Tabitha. "You must raise the alarm, to warn the others."

She nodded. "I will go now."

The white witch slipped away on the wind, hoping to reach the members of her coven before disaster struck. The quickest and most efficient method relied on their intricate network of interconnecting crystal balls.

With Tabitha's departure, the little cottage became uncharacteristically quiet. Everyone was staring at the spot where she had been standing moments before.

"I hope the lass will make it in time," the wizard said.

"Why don't you do something to help her?" Emily suggested sternly.

"There's not much I can do, girl," Lamken replied. "I have no magical powers whatsoever."

"Then what good are you?" she snapped.

"Emmy!" Bunty exclaimed. "Stop being so rude."

"No, she's right," the wizard said. "I'm not going to be much help to anybody."

Before the discussion went any further, Thaddeus interrupted. "Emily Scott, may I speak to you for a moment, please?"

"Yes, Sir Osbert, of course," the girl replied sheepishly. "Excuse me, everyone."

Emily went to stand before the great dragon.

"I'm a bit surprised at your behavior, lass," Thaddeus said quietly.

"What chance have we?" she asked him, suddenly defiant again. "Gavin refuses to accept his destiny, we're allied to a wizard without any magical powers, and then there's Bunty and me, who do nothing but argue. If it wasn't for you, I don't think we'd last long."

Thaddeus smiled at Emily with pity. "Have you not paid any attention to your history lessons, my dear? England's glorious past is made up of countless situations where reluctant heroes made the difference. It was seldom about pompous monarchs and grand armies, but more often rested on the shoulders of everyday men and women. I would much rather throw my lot in with this disorganized rabble, than march with Britain's finest infantry."

Emily had listened to every word. She hung her head. "I'm sorry I doubted."

Thaddeus gently lifted her chin with just one talon. "It is your responsibility to question and doubt, Emmy. There is no harm in doing so. You only lose the battle when you give up. The three of you are a team and by sticking together, you will make a difference. Given the right opportunity, so will Lamken Rune."

"I wish Kitto was here." Emily confessed. "I miss her very much."

The dragon smiled. "Perhaps she will return when you need her most. Elves have the uncanny ability to show up at just the right time."

"Do you really think so?"

"Indeed I do."

Emily smiled broadly. "Oh, I hope so."

"Your faith will make it so, you'll see."

Arriving in St. Merryn, Tabitha Bixley cautiously and quietly entered her cottage. She looked at her watch and sighed with relief. There was plenty of time to send an alert to all the moots in England, get ready to report to the airbase, and still have time for a cup of hot tea.

Using her crystal ball, the beautiful young witch sent warning messages to all the magical creatures throughout the United Kingdom. Tabitha waited to make certain her words had been transmitted and received, before lighting the fire in the stove.

Then she went to her bedroom to freshen up. Looking in the mirror, it was difficult sometimes to balance the life of a witch with that of a Wren. In some ways, she enjoyed her duties in the Royal Navy more than casting spells. When the war was over, she would have to consider her future carefully.

The kettle whistled.

Tabitha scurried into the kitchen and poured herself a nice cup of Earl Grey tea. Sprinkling in a bit of sugar, she sat down and savored the first sip.

Closing her eyes, she whispered, "Ah, simply marvelous."

Creak.

Tabitha jumped to her feet and spun around.

There was nothing there.

"Oh, silly, behave," she scolded herself. "You're all nerves for nothing."

However, an intense shiver ran down her spine.

For something was amiss.

Reaching for her wand, Tabitha's fingers never quite made it.

A powerful force knocked her off her feet, sending the young woman slamming against the fireplace. She barely missed hitting her head on the stone mantle.

Gasping for breath, Tabitha felt long boney digits tighten around her neck, squeezing harder and harder. The white witch fought back with every ounce of strength she had, but it was no use. She was about to lose consciousness, to slip into death and beyond.

"You shall die," a raspy voice whispered in her ear.

Then, without warning, the vice-like grip came apart, releasing her!

Tabitha fell to her knees, stars dancing before her eyes.

The sounds of a struggle forced Tabitha to look over her shoulder.

Through blurry vision, she could make out a grappling pair, a dark figure in uniform struggling in the dimly lit hallway with a red-robed shape. Suddenly Tabitha realized her rescuer was John Mobley. As she regained her senses, her fiancé slipped. He barely got up from his knees, when the red-robed figure kicked him in the stomach.

"Oof," Mobley grunted.

"*Flamma dissolutus!*" Tabitha cried out, aiming her wand.

A searing blast of yellow-white light crossed the room and disintegrated the red-robed figure, leaving only smoking cloth and ashes.

Tabitha helped John to his feet. She fell into his arms with a pitiful sob.

"Everything's just fine now," he whispered, gently running his fingers through her luxurious auburn hair. "Thank you, honey. That was close."

She looked over his shoulder at the mound of smoldering clothing.

"Is he dead?" John asked, without checking himself.

"He better be," Tabitha replied, anger in her voice.

"You're pretty dangerous when you're mad," he said, smiling.

"He was about to kill you, John," she explained. "I won't let anything happen to you, do you understand?"

"Yes, honey, I do," he replied, taking time to kiss her.

She liked that and relaxed immediately.

They put their arms around each other and just stayed that way for awhile.

"I saw the look on your face when you were fighting him," Tabitha whispered.

"I figured I better take that guy out, before he cast a spell or whatever," John told her. "After all, he was in red robes, so I just assumed he was a bad wizard or something rotten like that."

Tabitha pet his grizzled cheek. "You assumed correctly."

The couple went and sat on the sofa.

"I sure could use a cuppa tea," Mobley commented.

"Coming right up," she said, swirling her wand before them.

Poof.

A pair of cups appeared, filled with steaming-hot Earl Grey tea.

John grinned and took a healthy sip. "I really could get used to your talents."

Tabitha giggled. Then she frowned, realizing that John had come all the way from Scotland. "What are you doing here, John? You aren't absent without permission, are you?"

"Not bloody likely, lass," he replied. "I came to the air station on official business, but stopped by to see if you were home. Bloody good thing I did too."

"Yes, it was a good thing."

"So, who was that guy?"

"A monk from an outlawed cult."

"Why was he after you?"

"Not just me, I'm afraid."

"Shouldn't you warn the others, whoever they are?"

"I did already, just before the monk attacked me."

"Now what?"

"I have to report for duty, John. Let's go to the base together."

Mobley hesitated.

"What's wrong?" she asked.

"The last time I was at the field, the Jerries dropped bombs," he replied. "I don't want to bring bad luck."

"Don't be silly," Tabitha pretended to scold him. "Besides, they can't hit anything anyway."

They both laughed.

Hand-in-hand, the couple walked leisurely to the airbase.

13

Secret Weapons

A long-range Spitfire, flown by the ever-reliable Wing Commander Ian Warwick, was on a routine reconnaissance mission over northern Germany. The pilot pressed the automatic camera button, as he passed over Peenemünde, on the Baltic coast, because he spotted evidence of construction activity with circular emplacements on the ground. There was no antiaircraft fire and little activity to warrant further investigation, but his previous experience convinced him the sight might be of some importance. The Spitfire continued on, heading for home.

Peenemünde was situated in a quiet, wooded region in Germany, located at the mouth of the river Peene, on the island of Usedom. Unknown to Warwick, Peenemünde was also the top-secret location of a new German scientific facility. Ian's few hasty photographs probably wouldn't reveal the scope of the massive construction project underway, involving housing for engineers and scientists, a power plant, a liquid oxygen plant, a wind-tunnel facility, barracks, two concentration camps, a rocket production facility, a development works facility, and Luftwaffe airfield. This giant installation was designed to house over 2,000 scientists and 4,000 support personnel. To the northern end of Peenemünde, between the forest and the sandy foreshore, nine test stands for test-firing rockets had also been constructed.

After Warwick's photographs were developed and delivered to Richard Kane's analysis department, the interpreters were unable to locate anything out of the ordinary from the short series of snapshots. Even to their trained eyes, the construction appeared to be a logging operation and paper mill, nothing more.

However, Peenemünde was soon to become the most important installation in all of Germany. A number of seemingly fantastic projects were simultaneously under production, well funded and supported by Nazi fanaticism. Hundreds of gifted and innovative scientists were pursuing development of jet and rocket engines, as well as futuristic aircraft designs.

One of those men was Dr. Rudolph Schriever, along with his loyal engineer Otto Habermohl. They were dedicated to a vision and determined to design a flying saucer. Their initial blueprints were met with skepticism from their fellow scientists, but undeterred, the duo proceeded collecting the necessary materials to construct a prototype. Mauthausen concentration camp supplied technically oriented prisoners for the project, while one prototype was successfully constructed and the initial flight-test scheduled.

The craft had retractable undercarriage legs padded with inflatable rubber cushions. It was structured to carry a crew of three. Habermohl and Schriever chose a flat hoop, which spun around a fixed pilot's cabin in the shape of a dome. It consisted of steerable disc wings, which enabled, according to the direction of their placement, in horizontal takeoff or flight. Their first model attained a height of 12,400 meters in three minutes and a horizontal flight speed of 1000 miles per hour.

The vanes were held together by a band at the outer edge of the wheel-like device. The pitch of the vanes could be adjusted so that during take off more lift was generated by increasing their angle from a more horizontal setting. In level flight, the angle would be adjusted to a smaller angle.

The wing-vanes were set in rotation by small rockets placed around the rim like a pinwheel. Once rotational speed was sufficient, liftoff was achieved. After the craft had risen to some height, horizontal jets were ignited and the smaller rockets shut off. After this, the wing-blades would be allowed to rotate freely as the saucer moved forward. At the discretion of the pilot, the lift-power could be increased by directing the adjustable horizontal jets slightly upwards to engage the blades, thus spinning them faster.

Massive stress tests and research work were involved prior to undertaking the manufacture of a real working prototype. Due to the high rate of speed and the extraordinary heat demands, it was necessary to find particular materials in order to resist the effects of the high temperatures.

If water or air is rotated into a twisting form of oscillation known as colloidal, a build up of energy results, with immense power, which created levitation. On their first experiment of this theory, the test apparatus rose upwards, trailing a blue-green, and then a silver-colored glow. The motion, in turn, created an atomic low-pressure zone, which developed when the surrounding air was rotated at high speeds, wither radially and axially.

The day arrived and the weather was perfect for flying.

However, the pilot soon reported having difficulty controlling the craft. It appeared that the rotation process was malfunctioning and he was losing power.

Kaboom!

Seconds later the disc exploded.

The wreckage came hurtling to earth, pieces of the flying saucer scattered in every direction. By the time the test team made it to the crash site, there was little remaining. Between some wires and a tangle of supporting struts in the middle, the remains of the partially destroyed cockpit protruded. The pilot and copilot had been burned beyond recognition.

The test had ended in complete disaster.

Otto Habermohl and Rudolph Schriever were suddenly the laughing stock of the military scientific community. Rejected and shunned by their peers, the two engineers considered committing suicide. While sitting side-by-side, pistols in hand, Dr. Schriever looked down at a copy of *Signal*, the German propaganda magazine. The folio-sized publication had been created in an effort to rally other European nations to the Nazi cause.

The cover immediately caught Schriever's attention. There was a photograph of Heinrich Himmler, all dressed in black, surrounded by men in wrinkled white lab coats.

The headline read:

Reichsführer Supports Scientific Community

Schriever set down his pistol and picked up the magazine. Quickly flipping to the lead story, Rudolph read every world with fascination. Himmler insisted that science, like everything else, was meant to serve the Nazi party. When the Reichsführer discovered the cause of death of most SS soldiers on the Eastern Front was from the elements, he ordered his scientists to discover a way to protect his men from the weather. He was calling together all the scientific minds throughout the Third Reich, imploring them to use their minds to discover great solutions that would lead to victory.

In fact, Himmler was quoted as saying, "*No idea, no matter how outlandish, will be ignored. The Third Reich seeks innovation.*"

Dr. Schriever gently lifted the gun away from his colleague's hand. "Do not be too hasty, *Herr Habermohl.*"

Otto wasn't really in the mood to end his life anyway. "*Jawohl, Herr Doktor.*"

"We must seek an audience with the *Reichsführer*," Dr. Schriever said. "Perhaps he will support our theories."

"And if he does not?" Habermohl asked.

"Then we will shoot ourselves, but not before!" the doctor replied. "Let us make arrangements to travel to Berlin on the very next train."

Several days later, British intelligence became aware that the Germans had developed a new weapon, when a Danish naval officer discovered an early test version had crash-landed on a small island between Germany and Sweden. The officer sent a photograph and a detailed sketch of the "bomb" to Britain, where quiet preparations began to deal with the new threat, which some experts warned had the potential to win the war for Germany.

In far away Iceland, the members of the Grand Dragon Council were holding an emergency meeting. Hundreds of dragons, from all over the world attended, but noticeably missing was Sir Osbert.

"The Chronicler will read aloud Section Ten of the official Draconian history," commanded Drasius Flylander, the council leader.

Twizzler Binoculus, a small bespectacled blue dragon, stepped up before the gathering of dragons and cleared his throat. Then, quite carefully, the creature opened a magnificent gilded book and began to read aloud.

"Centuries ago, human armies ventured across Europe to wage war against those who followed a different religious faith," the chronicler read. "During the horrific battles before the holy city of Jerusalem, the fabric of reality was torn asunder, allowing a devastating influx of dark magic through the rift, which allowed demons to wander the planet unopposed.

"As the space continuum of this planet was ripped apart, a dark plague swept aside goodness and light. Hordes of demons and strange creatures sprung up throughout the land, which led the human era known as the Dark Ages.

"After heavy losses, a small band of heroic knights managed to battle their way through the forces of darkness. With incredible valor, these men defeated a black wizard, known to be a mage of considerable power. The enemy fled, along with a host of evil creatures, allowing the knights to seal the breach.

"Realizing that the discovery of certain powerful relics had caused the forces of evil to take such desperate action, the knights agreed to forever protect the religious artifacts, while seeking out the enemy and driving them back to where they had come.

Fortunately, these hordes of magical creatures returned to the other side. The most powerful of these dreaded creatures were Void Dragons, immense reptilian beasts capable of unleashing terrible destruction with their claws, breath weapons, and magic spells, which could control the weather and summon natural disasters.

"Near the end of the human twelfth century, certain gifted humans discovered physical and scientific truths unknown to the commoner. These special ones would become the first human wizards, people who could shape a new form of energy channeled through their spirits. These magical people would prove to be dangerous to Draconian society, as their defensive magic could protect troops against our scorching dragon-fire and their offensive spells could pierce our tough scales.

"As the years went by, the last of our brethren gathered within our impregnable glacial fortress. The final battle between dragons and mankind took place at *Húnaflói*. Just when it appeared as if annihilation was the only outcome possible, the greatest wizard of all time arrived at the scene. His birth name was Myrddin, but was more commonly referred to as Merlin the Magician.

"This wizard put a stop to the war and negotiated the first treaty between man and dragon. While all dragons are sworn to avoid the affairs of mankind, our species will never forget the sacrifice and loyalty that Myrddin showed the Dragon community.

"So states the official doctrine."

Twizzler stepped back, removed his spectacles, and blended into the gathered masses of his fellow dragons.

"Why was it necessary to bore us with a story we have all heard since childhood?" demanded Wasabi Watanabe, elected ambassador from the Eastern Clan of dragons.

"It is necessary, because Myrddin has returned!" Chief Council Drasius Flylander announced. His yellow scales vibrated as if on fire.

Without exception, every dragon in attendance was instantly amazed to silence.

"It isn't possible," Watanabe spoke finally. "The wizards placed a powerful curse within the mage's soul and destroyed his enchanted staff."

"Or so we were informed," Korban Vex said from within the ranks. "Humans are very capable of distorting the truth, even within the magical community. I would hazard to guess that someone told a lie."

Many dragons laughed, but not because the statement was humorous.

"Then what shall we do?" Brianna, the sky blue ice-dragon demanded.

"We should do nothing, but only observe how this unfolds," Baron Goch, the former council leader, suggested strongly. "To do otherwise would violate our code."

"We could always ask Thaddeus Osbert what he knows," Watanabe blurted.

The reaction from his fellow dragons was less than enthusiastic.

Chief Council Drasius Flylander scowled. "I do not think your suggestion was made in jest and neither do I think it is honorable for you to cast dispersions on a fellow elder."

Watanabe was not apologetic. "Based on previous history, my observation is not without merit, no matter how bluntly stated."

Flylander dismissed any further discussion. "These proceedings are hereby adjourned. The Council will meet again within the moon's cycle, but only if necessary."

The gigantic yellow dragon did not wait for objections or motions, but merely lumbered away. The other council members followed his lead and disbanded, leaving Wasabi Watanabe and Korban Vex. Neither creature spoke to the other, but it was painfully obvious that the two influential elders were destined to meet again soon.

14

A Wizard's Failings

Inside the little white cottage on the hill, Bunty, Gavin and Emily, joined Lamken Rune and Tabitha Bixley, all guests of Sir Thaddeus Osbert. Everyone enjoyed several cups of hot tea, with plenty of sugar, by the way. It was 4:00 in the afternoon, the accepted time for high tea and with biscuits, it was a perfect little gathering.

"The terms wizard and witch are used in magical society in more or less the same context," Tabitha explained.

The teenagers had been quizzing Lamken and Tabitha on what it was like to be a member of the community magicians. The dragon especially watched Gavin absorb all the information and noted how often the young man's questions centered on Arthurian legends.

"I have read that wizards created dragons," Gavin said. "Have you ever done so?"

For only a fleeting instant, the old man looked directly at Thaddeus, and then focused on the ceiling, as if searching for the right answer. Gavin didn't miss a thing, but decided his observation could wait for a later time.

"No, Gavin, I have not dabbled in such magic," Rune finally replied. "Such power takes days and days of meditation and spells. I have learned to leave such conjuration work to God."

"Tabitha has such a beautiful wand," Emily observed and everyone focused on the white witch, who blushed a little.

"A wand serves as a focusing tool that enhances a wizard's capabilities to perform magic," Lamken Rune explained to his rapt audience. "While performing magic without wands is possible, a point of origin is required for most spells. Wands come in many colors and varieties, and are made of different woods, such as holly, vine, and oak. They also contain magical cores, which defines their character, power, and relationship with the wielder."

"Have you ever used a wand?" Bunty wondered.

"Never carried one, lad," the wizard replied. "All my magical powers were encased in my staff Elizabeth. Since she was taken from me, I am powerless."

"Isn't there something we can do to find your Elizabeth?" Emily wondered.

Lamken shook his head. "No, lass, I'm afraid there is nothing we can do. I have spent decades looking for her, but I think she was either burned or broken in two, thereby snuffing out her spark of life."

"You should make a new staff," Bunty suggested. "We'll go out and find a perfect length of wood. You could conjure up the necessary spells and presto!"

The old wizard chuckled good-naturedly. "Oh, if only it were that simple. Elizabeth was carefully selected for her unique character and charm. Since red cedar was naturally resistant to moisture and decay, the receding bark revealed signs of other life in an intricate display amidst the grain. Once I had cleaned the wood, I spent months studying Elizabeth, to determine the best way to match her unique personality to mine. I added crystals and precious gems, wrapped her in gold and silver wire, before bonding us forever with drops of my blood. I cannot make such a pact again in this lifetime or the implications would be disastrous."

"I see," Bunty said, without understanding at all.

Lamken could see the boy wasn't satisfied with the old man's answer.

"A wizard's staff is a specially created device, made for a specific wizard," Rune went on. "Only the wizard for whom the staff is made may use that staff. A wizard's staff is bonded by a secret creation spell. This spell requires the sacrifice of the true nature and soul of the wizard for whom the staff was made. I am forever linked with Elizabeth and even though she may have been destroyed, I cannot create another."

Bunty nodded his acceptance of the wizard's thorough explanation. "I'm sorry I was so insistent, sir. It just seems such a shame that you have to exist without your magic."

Rune fluffed Bunty's carrot-red hair again. "Indeed, it is a shame. The handiest attribute of my staff was Elizabeth's ability to store all my spells. She was so attune to me that she could foresee the spells I would need and cast them, even before I thought of them. It was a friendship and partnership like no other."

"Elizabeth sounds wonderful," Emily said wistfully.

Tabitha Bixley changed the subject. "What should we do about the rip in the continuum, Master?"

"Repair it, of course," Rune replied. "Failing that, we must prevent anything from escaping."

"What exactly is wrong with this continuum thingamajig?" Bunty wondered.

"An effect in which a temporal anomaly causes distortions in the local space-time continuum, which caused time to slow to a gradual halt, allowing the forces of darkness to enter our realm," the wizard answered.

Bunty sighed. "Could you tell us that again in King's English, please?"

Tabitha laughed. "Yes, Master, help us uneducated servants understand what you are talking about!"

"Space and time travel along a path that is curved," Lamken tried to explain, using his hands to accentuate his words. "The curvature occurs as a result of the influences of mass against movement in time. As three-dimensional beings, we perceive time only because of our memory. We remember what was, as a variable interval from what is now. If we had zero memory, we could not detect time, because we would exist only for the moment. The result of this is our perception that time progresses in a straight line, always going forward. This is similar to primitive peoples perceiving the Earth as flat. It could be infinite, because the horizon always kept bringing something new, no matter how far we've traveled. Or, it could be finite, in which case there was the risk of falling off the edge."

Open-mouthed, everyone in the room just stared at the wizard.

"In its simplest form, a curve, extended infinitely, becomes a circle," Rune decided to continue, hoping he would get somewhere eventually. "This sphere, when looked at microscopically, without precision, would appear as a flat surface, just like primitive people perceived the Earth. Only when enough of the Earth was explored and technology was developed adequately, could the true form of Earth be correctly determined. The same holds true for three-dimensional beings trying to grasp the dimension of time. It travels in a gigantic circle."

"What happens if something interrupts time?" Gavin asked.

The wizard smiled grimly. "Anything powerful enough to disturb time would cause it to separate, or come apart, allowing the different elements of time and space to intermingle."

"Which isn't good?" Bunty guessed.

"That's right, son," Lamken said.

"Then what?" Emily asked.

"Horrible creatures, not meant for this place or time, might cross into our realm," the wizard answered.

"Such as?" Bunty wondered.

"Rift dragons, or worse," Tabitha interjected.

The teens simultaneously shrugged, communicating their lack of knowledge regarding these threats.

Thaddeus took up the conversation. "Rift dragons are entirely evil creatures that enter other worlds through holes in the space-time continuum. From a rift dragon's head, to the very tip of its tail, the creature is solid black, but even more than that, the beast absorbs all light that hits it. This is how the dragon feeds, by actually swallowing the light it comes in contact with."

"That's pretty serious," Emily said.

"Indeed it is," Rune said.

"Rift dragons are cruel and merciless," Thaddeus went on. "They are worse than the Nazis, who are the enemy of all that is good, because Void Dragons are the enemy of all that is living. A rift dragon will eventually attack any living creature, regardless of alignment. I believe the Germans have unwittingly freed a Void Dragon from its lair in another dimension."

"If what you say is true, then how can we defeat it?" Gavin asked.

"That's a very good question, my boy," the wizard said. "As far as I'm aware, only one human has ever defeated a rift dragon before, and that was a long time ago."

"Who was that?" Bunty innocently asked.

Lamken looked at Thaddeus, who looked at Tabitha. Then the three of them looked at one specific teenaged boy.

"King Arthur," the dragon replied.

On either side of Gavin, Bunty and Emily also turned to face him.

The young man just sighed and shook his head. "Not this again."

Without waiting for further discussion, Gavin stood up and marched out the front door. He was in no mood for kings and queens, bold tales of brave knights, or magical adventures to save and protect the bloody British Empire!

Emily excused herself and quietly followed him outside.

Tabitha spoke to Rune, "I must report for duty within the hour, so I'm on my way. Blessings be to you all."

Poof.

In a cloud of purple smoke, the white witch disappeared.

Bunty stepped up to Thaddeus, "Pardon me, Sir Osbert?"

"Yes, young man, what's on your mind?" the dragon replied, only mildly perturbed that the red-haired boy had prevented him from making sure Gavin didn't need a good lecture.

"I've been meaning to ask this for some time, but did you rescue my pa after the *Ark Royal* sank?"

"Well, I wouldn't exactly call it a rescue," the dragon replied modestly. "I merely plucked him from harm's way and set him on a piece of flotsam to be rescued by his own kind."

Nevertheless, Bunty threw his arms around the creature's neck, hugging Sir Osbert with all his might. "Thank you, Thaddeus. I just knew it was you!"

The dragon frowned and quickly said, "Let's keep this secret between you and me, if you don't mind? I don't want my fellow dragons to find another reason to complain about my constant interference."

"Mums the word, Sir Osbert," Bunty promised, pretending to zip shut his lips.

His innocent mimed action made the dragon chuckle. "There's a good lad, Byron. Go now and join your friends."

Emily found Gavin near Tintagel Castle, where he stood on the cliffs overlooking the sea. She didn't say a word, but just slipped her fingers in between his. There they stood, side-by-side, silently sharing thoughts and emotions, without uttering a word.

She felt his doubts, his loneliness without his father, the pain of growing into a young man, all his emotions suddenly very real and poignant. Closing her eyes, Emily couldn't help but remember all the wonderful memories of their youth.

Inside her cottage in St. Merryn, Tabitha smiled to herself, for she could sense the power of young Emily's compassion, born from a heart of kindness. There was something else about the girl that intrigued the white witch even more. It seemed that Emily possessed certain gifts usually associated with those who practiced the art of magic.

Bam, bam, bam.

Suddenly there was rude knocking on the front door.

Tabitha scurried excitedly to open it, hoping it would be her fiancé John.

To her utter amazement, she almost ran smack into the scaly left leg of a dragon.

Looking up, she saw Thaddeus looking down. "Oh, Sir Osbert, to what do I owe the occasion?"

He grinned. "May I come in?"

"Of course," she replied.

Vooooooooooooooooooooom.

Shrinking down, down, down, the dragon was eventually no bigger than the typical domesticated housecat. Thaddeus stretched and then strolled into the house, making straight for the fireplace, where he curled up near the heat.

Tabitha giggled and joined him, sitting down on the floor nearby and staring into the roaring flames. There was a moment of uncomfortable silence.

The miniature Thaddeus spoke up, saying, "You got away before I had an opportunity to tell you how wonderful it is to see you again, lass. I have missed your laugh all these years."

She hung her head. "I'm sorry, Sir Osbert. I'm afraid I haven't been a very good friend since…"

"It was so marvelous when your father agreed to help save Bunty's life," the dragon interrupted her train of thought. "The red-haired lad's destiny is tied to a great many things."

Tabitha nodded. "Yes, your companions have incredible significance, much of which was foretold. It is not by chance that you are guardian over all three, rather than just Master Kane?"

The dragon grinned. "Still as sharp and observant as ever, eh lass?"

That statement made her smile.

"England no longer stands alone fighting this war, but her position is still quite perilous," Sir Osbert went on. "I have been watching over this country and her people, for century after century, well aware that the empire would one day fade from importance. That time is almost upon us."

Tabitha was noticeably sad, yet she still reached out and scratched Thaddeus under the chin.

The dragon growled, but this time it really did sound like purring.

"What will come of us?" Tabitha asked.

"Do not trouble yourself with former glories," Sir Osbert replied. "There are battles yet to fight and trouble brews in cauldrons black as night."

Tabitha detected something profound in the way the dragon was speaking. "What exactly are you not telling me, Sir Osbert?"

Thaddeus grew a little, now the size of a dog. "There are forces at work behind the scenes, as we all know. This time, however, my fellow dragons are choosing sides and taking action, contrary to our laws. I am no longer alone in disobeying my elders."

Tabitha was deeply concerned and surprised.

"We are headed for the defining moment in our long mutual history, lass," the dragon continued. "My vision of the future is cloudy at best, as if the universe does not wish me to see a clear path. Therefore, I must act on my instincts."

Tabitha shook her head. "There is another way, Sir Osbert."

Thaddeus was quite intrigued. "Tell me, please."

"Trust in Gavin," the white witch said quietly. "In him you will find the answer you seek. The boy has been chosen to wield the blade, a sword your father watched forged in the volcanic fires and then presented to Arthur. In his youth, Gavin does not yet understand the power that lies within his reach. With your guidance, he will discover the role he plays. Until then, you must be patient and wait."

The dragon nodded and said, "I have missed your wise council, Vivienne. The boy does not know your true identity yet."

"Mayhap he shall never know, Sir Osbert," Tabitha said quietly. "Only time will tell."

15

Plans of Retaliation

Without any indication as to the reason, Heinrich Himmler was suddenly summoned to Berlin. The Reichsführer departed Wewelsburg Castle in all haste, certain that Hitler had discovered what he had been doing. To his relief, upon arriving at the German Chancellery, Himmler was greeted with unusual fanfare and celebration.

After all, it was April and the Führer's birthday was fast approaching.

The city, however, was showing the effects of British night bombing, as buildings here and there were nothing more than ruins. A pall of smoke drifted over the rooftops and antiaircraft batteries were emplaced on practically every street corner. The capital was under siege and this fact struck Himmler hard.

The Reichsführer and Reinhard Heydrich met privately with Adolf Hitler, before the scheduled cabinet meeting. In the course of their discussions, Hitler reminded his closest aides of his requirements in conducting the extermination of millions of innocent people. The Jews were his primary target, but he included a long list of intended victims, based solely on his edict that they were somehow inferior to pure Germans.

The full cabinet meeting followed, which was secret, of course.

In one of Hitler's rare moments of complete objectivity, the supreme leader confided with all in attendance. "We are doomed, of course. There will be no victory, only misery and death for my beloved Germany."

Himmler urged Hitler to seek a diplomatic solution.

The Führer rejected the suggestion out of hand. "It is too late for that! Do you think that drunken bulldog would allow Germany to keep her honor? Never! I will never sue for peace, even if we all go down in flames."

Then Hitler flew into an insane tirade, screaming vile curses, while ranting and raving about being betrayed. He completely lost his temper and spewed insult after insult, stomping his feet and pounding the table.

No one dared say a thing.

Eventually exhausted by his tantrum, Hitler marched out of the conference room, exiting through a door in the rear. His cabinet members were dumbfounded by this behavior, but quietly dispersed.

Himmler slipped away from Heydrich and went into his private office on the second floor. Once at his seldom-used desk, the Reichsführer picked up the telephone and rang for Heinrich Muëller.

"I wish to speak to you now, alone," Himmler said, before hanging up.

Moments later, Heydrich's aide was standing nervously before the Reichsführer. "You wished to see me, sir?"

"What have you learned in my absence?" Himmler asked.

"The mission to seize the magical sword went awry on the beach near Crackington Haven, North Cornwall, *Herr Reichsführer*," Muëller replied.

"Crackington Haven is of no military importance whatsoever," Himmler said after looking at the map of England.

"Not in the normal sense of the word, *Herr Reichsführer*," Muëller said.

Himmler drummed his fingers on the desktop and asked, "What are you suggesting?"

"I believe the men you sent to snatch the fabled sword met with disaster, because our forces were ambushed by something other than traditional British stiff, upper lip tenacity," Muëller explained.

The Reichsführer quietly said, "Go on."

"Accurate intelligence gathering in England is still handicapped by various unexplained factors, but I've been able to piece together some startling coincidences," Muëller said.

"I don't believe in coincidences," Himmler stated angrily.

"Neither do I, *Herr Reichsführer*," Muëller said in his defense. "That is why these factors stand out. Certain events can't be explained away by mere chance."

"Continue," the Reichsführer said impatiently.

"There are forces in the universe that we don't fully understand," Muëller nervously went on. "I believe the British have harnessed some of those unusual powers, which is why your brilliant plans keep failing."

Himmler was listening. Agnes Olmanns had come to the same conclusions. Perhaps there was truth in what the witch had said after all. "How do we combat such forces?"

Muëller wasn't comfortable with his answer, but neither did he shy away from expressing his conclusions. Both Heydrich and Himmler had taught him to speak his mind, no matter how unpopular that opinion might be.

"Your subsequent operations were on the right track, *Herr Reichsführer*," Muëller replied. "What was lacking were effective counter-measures to offset the British ability to respond to such attacks."

"How would we gather such counter-measures?" Himmler asked.

"I could create a list of people who possess certain unexplainable powers, *Herr Reichsführer*," Muëller replied hesitantly. "It would require sifting through the human garbage incarcerated in concentration camps, prisons, and mental institutions, for these facilities are where we send such enemies of the State."

"Can you gather such a unit of subversives for me?" Himmler inquired. "I wish to possess such an inventory."

"*Jawohl*, it can be done, *Herr Reichsführer*," Muëller replied.

"Then do so immediately," Himmler ordered. "Once you have located these unusual gifted people, have them immediately transferred to a holding camp, so that they are not executed by accident."

Heydrich's aide knew better than to argue with the Reichsführer. He would make the task his first priority, as long as no one else was the wiser. Muëller was also concerned with watching his back.

Himmler wrapped up his business and planned to leave Berlin as soon as possible, when his telephone rang. The call was from the Reichstag receptionist. "Yes, what is it?" the Reichsführer asked.

"There is a Dr. Schriever here to see you, *Herr Reichsführer*," the woman said.

"What is his business?" Himmler demanded.

"He is responding to the scientific recruiting you are undertaking," she replied.

Himmler looked at his watch and impatiently said, "If the man is qualified, then I will arrange an interview. Take his card and assure Dr. Schriever that he will be contacted as soon as possible."

"*Jawohl, Herr Reichsführer*," the receptionist replied.

Click.

Himmler was impatient to return to Schloss Wewelsburg. Before he left, however, Muëller caught up with him at the train station.

"Here are the partial results of my preliminary research, *Herr Reichsführer*," the aide said, handing over a fat accordion file. "I made copies of dossiers of any of the names of subversives known to practice magic or accused persons listed as conducting unusual religious ceremonies or being involved with the occult."

Himmler was impressed. "Well done, *Herr Muëller*. I am very pleased."

The balding Prussian smiled. "Thank you, *Herr Reichsführer*."

"Order the immediate transfer of every individual in this file to my new camp outside of Wewelsburg," Himmler commanded. "Make certain that no one is overlooked, unless they have already been exterminated, of course."

Muëller clicked the heels of his boots together. *"Jawohl, Herr Reichsführer."*

Then the obedient aide went off to make sure Himmler's instructions were followed to the letter.

16

Conspiracy in the Far East

Wasabi Watanabe was a brilliantly hued Eastern dragon, the majority of his scales colored orange and red, but shimmering with golden luster. Wasabi was similar in appearance to a gigantic lizard, with short legs, long neck and tail, and a very long body, which had all the suppleness of a serpent. His feet were shaped like those of a reptile, with three long digits on each foot. He also had an opposable toe on the forefoot, used to grasp prey with hooked claw.

Ambassador Watanabe reluctantly welcomed Korban Vex to his volcanic lair in northern Japan. The caves steamed with poisonous gases, while flowing lava passed within feet of the dragons, but they were quite comfortable, impervious to such dangers.

"As I attempted to point out to the Grand Council, humans cannot be trusted," the ambassador growled emotionally. "Even the superior peoples of Asia are killing each other in droves."

Vex knew the exotic dragon was correct in his summation, but he was also aware that the majority of dragons felt strongly they should stay out of human affairs. Korban decided not to voice his opinion, at least not right away.

"I invited you here to witness firsthand the war being waged in the Pacific," Watanabe continued. "Perhaps once you've seen these barbarous acts, you will advise the Council to take action, before it's too late."

"I doubt anything I see will change their minds, Ambassador," Vex reacted. "We have watched men butcher each other for ages."

"It must be stopped!"

"How, by exterminating all humans?"

"If necessary, yes."

"So we stop the mindless killing by indiscriminate killing?"

"If our single act of evil prevents a greater evil consuming us all, then so be it."

"Your logic is askew, my friend."

Watanabe sighed and stomped his many feet in frustration. "You're infuriating with your damn logic."

Vex couldn't help but smile, as he thought of Thaddeus Osbert. "So I've been told before."

"The humans are tampering with the power of the universe," Wasabi growled.

Vex was painfully aware that both the Allies and Germans were racing to invent atomic weapons capable of massive destructive power.

"This fact is known to me," Korban said. "As long as the Germans do not succeed in developing this energy first, then we must let things flow as they will."

"No human should be allowed to split the atom!" the Eastern dragon roared. "Do they think themselves gods?"

Korban shrugged. "Perhaps."

"Unchecked, mankind will destroy this planet," Watanabe protested.

"If that is their destiny, then so be it," Vex stated the official Council's position.

"Then what of us?" Wasabi demanded. "What will become of us?"

"We shall survive, as we have always survived," Vex replied with a sigh. "Have we not vacated other planets throughout the eons?"

"I'm tired of moving on," the Eastern dragon said candidly.

Vex understood. "As am I."

There was a long moment of silence, as the two great dragons contemplated distant memories and future possibilities.

"Perhaps we should take an active role in shaping the things to come?" Wasabi suggested.

Korban looked at Watanabe from the corner of his eye. "We cannot do such a thing without the Council's approval."

Wasabi nodded. "Perhaps we can steer the Council in the right direction. I have many close friends who agree with my views, but bide their time for the right moment."

"What exactly are you suggesting?" Vex asked.

"An incident," Watanabe replied. "There must be a catalyst to create the fervor we need. The elite members of the council must be made to feel threatened by the humans."

"What kind of *incident* did you have in mind?" Korban probed.

The ambassador hesitated answering right away. He wasn't absolutely certain where Korban's loyalties lay. In the end, however, he decided it was worth the risk. "I know you made arrangements for the assassination of the German known as Reinhard Heydrich. I also know you conspired with Sir Thaddeus Osbert to complete this necessary act. If such information were openly known to the council, it could prove embarrassing."

Vex's eyes narrowed to mere slits. "Blackmail, is it?"

Watanabe shook his great head. "No, not at all. I merely wish to create an outcry on Sir Osbert's behalf. Because of your foresight, Thaddeus will make certain a terrible threat is removed. Such action should be decorated and applauded."

"It is more likely that Sir Osbert would be condemned for his actions," Korban countered. "He is acting in good faith, because I asked him to. Only a few of the Council elite sanctioned this drastic step. To disclose this might bring down the current administration."

The ambassador smiled gravely. "Yes, that is one outcome."

"So that is your plan, to change the leadership?"

Watanabe nodded slowly.

Vex pondered this revelation. He was a law-abiding dragon. He had never sided with revolutionaries, nor tolerated the many civil wars that had divided Draconian society over the millennia. He believed in justice and freedom, even though he disagreed with Sir Osbert's opinion regarding the basic goodness of humanity.

Very slowly, Korban also began to nod. "I fear you are right, Ambassador. Reluctantly I will support your movement to oust the present council leaders."

Watanabe was surprised, but elated. "This is excellent. I will make certain the news of Sir Osbert's part in the assassination is leaked to the general population."

"We have just conspired to implicate an innocent dragon," Vex stated.

"I would hardly describe Thaddeus Osbert as innocent," Watanabe objected. "He has been found guilty of such interference many times before."

"He never once denied his participation in those situations," Korban pointed out. "This time, however, we would be committing the crime and someone else will take the blame. Such actions do not sit well with me."

"It is sometimes necessary to do distasteful things to assure the betterment of our species, Korban Vex," Wasabi said.

"Perhaps, but it still leaves a bad taste in my mouth."

"It shall pass," Watanabe assured him. "No harm will come to Thaddeus, for you and I will see to that. You have my word."

The covert meeting ended abruptly, as Vex returned to his chambers in Iceland.

Watanabe was painfully aware that the Japanese Empire was now in sole possession of the whole of Southeast Asia and the majority of the western Pacific. Only Australia stood in her way. Japan needed to act quickly and decisively, before America could rebuild her fleets and counterattack.

The Imperial Japanese Navy had operational responsibility for the Pacific Ocean, including Australia and its island territories. To counter the perceived threat from Australia as an American ally, the admirals of Japan's Navy General Staff and Navy Ministry wanted to invade key areas of the northern Australian mainland. However, to invade Australia, the Japanese Navy would require troops from the Japanese Army.

Once completely isolated from the United States, the Japanese military leaders believed that Australia could be forced to surrender to Japan, using blockade and intense psychological pressures, including an intensified military onslaught against cities on the Australian mainland.

Japanese Admiral Yamamoto, who had planned the successful attack on Pearl Harbor, proposed an immediate invasion of Australia. He began with bombing raids on Darwin in the Northern Territory. He proposed landing two Japanese Army Divisions on the northern coastline of Australia, which was supposedly poorly defended. They would follow the north-south railway line to Adelaide, thus dividing Australia into two fronts. Once Adelaide had been taken, a second force would land on the south east coast of Australia and drive northwards to Sydney and southwards to Melbourne.

To see if such an operation was even feasible, a special Japanese reconnaissance team departed from Koepang, Timor aboard a 25-ton fishing vessel named *Hiyoshi Maru*. The party included Lieutenant Susuhiko Mizuno, Sergeant Kendo Morita, Sergeant Tashi Furuhashi, and Lance Corporal Kazuo Ito, along with 6 Japanese Marines and 15 Timorese, who were used as decoys.

Their orders were to land on the northwest shores of Western Australia to gauge if the Australians had any defensive forces in place. Lieutenant Mizuno's role was to look at the possibility of landing in Australia, while investigating the location for a landing place and searching for the existence of any military establishments.

The *Hiyoshi Maru* was given air cover for part of the voyage by a single Type 99 light bomber. The aircraft was heading directly for Cartier Islet, when it spotted an American submarine heading in the direction of the *Hiyoshi Maru*. The submarine also saw the Japanese aircraft approaching and immediately began to dive. The Japanese aircraft only managed to fire two bursts of machinegun fire, before it submerged. The Japanese then dropped six bombs on the submarine. They circled around the area three or four times to determine if they had hit it with one of their bombs, but could only surmise that the submarine might have sustained some damage.

The aircraft continued south flying low to avoid Australian radar situated along the remote coastline. They sighted the ***Hiyoshi Maru*** and continued south, eventually locating Cartier Islet.

Hiyoshi Maru dropped anchor near a coral reef only visible at low tide. The landing party went ashore on Browse Island, where they discovered an abandoned watchtower.

The Japanese remained on Browse Island for only three hours. This was to synchronize their arrival on the nearby Australian mainland. The recon team left the island the next morning, using fog to camouflage their entrance into an inlet on the West Australian coast. They spotted white smoke rising from a mountain on the mainland east of their location. They dropped anchor again and went ashore. The barren landscape in the area consisted shrubs and red-colored rocks. The Japanese camouflaged their boat with tree branches and ate dried biscuits.

Landing parties were led by Sergeant Morita and Sergeant Furuhashi, who went ashore and explored different areas of the Australian coast.

Wasabi Watanabe was waiting for them. He hoped the sight of a dragon would scare them off, for otherwise they would discover how vulnerable Australia really was. If accurate reconnaissance reached the Imperial forces, the invasion might be approved, which would negatively alter the course of the war.

To the Japanese landing party, the dragon looked something like a crocodile and was not less than eighteen feet in length. The most striking aspect of the monster were its multiple legs, six on each side, and its invulnerability to bullets, which merely caused it to utter a cry similar to that of a calf and bear combined. The bullets, when hitting the dragon, merely made a sound as if they were striking against a thin piece of sheet metal. What kind of animal was this, whose image bore an uncanny resemblance to the classic Eastern depiction of a dragon, but which couldn't be harmed by bullets?

The Japanese sailors took some handheld movie-camera footage of what they saw. They returned to the ship and reported to Lieutenant Mizuno on what they had seen. Besides the frightening beast, all they spotted were some old campfires, many red rocks and small trees. They slept on the ship that night and the next morning set sail for home, convinced Australia was inhabited by dragons. Of course, no one in the Imperial Navy would believe them, so the special Japanese reconnaissance team agreed to misreport their findings, hoping to convince their superiors that the Australians had constructed vast beach defenses.

17

Operation Anthropoid

The covert operation had been approved at the highest level, with Winston Churchill's personal blessing. Seven Czechoslovak agents gathered at Cholmondeley Castle in Malpas, Cheshire, England. Their British counterparts had arranged this final briefing, before the team would be parachuted behind enemy lines.

As Adolf Hitler's handpicked successor, Reinhard Heydrich was one of the most dangerous men in all of Nazi Germany. His death would be a huge loss to the Third Reich and a profound psychological victory for the Allies. With Major Vickers promoting the operation from its very conception, the proposed assassination might lead to reprisals on a massive scale. It had been decided, by the Czechoslovakian government in exile, that Heydrich's death was worth the monumental risks.

Standing before Traber were two of the Czech operatives who had graduated from his commando school. There was no doubt they were dedicated to their cause.

"Good luck, gentlemen," Vickers said, shaking their hands.

"We have not forgotten what you taught us, Major," Gabcik said in a thick accent.

"I have been instructed to give you something extra to make certain your endeavors are successful," Vickers told them.

"What would that be?" Jan Kubis asked.

Without saying another word, Vickers handed Gabcik a strangely customized Gammon grenade, tightly wrapped with adhesive tape and covered with an aluminum water canteen.

"What is that?" Kubis asked.

"An added precaution," Vickers replied. "Use this and the target will die, even if he's only wounded."

Neither Czech agent questioned the information, or the deadly gift.

A few moments before take-off, the operatives hurried out to the aircraft. There followed a few terse greetings between the Czechs and the aircrew. Hours, many hundreds of miles, and perhaps a word or two later, the commando team would parachute into the night as silently and as mysteriously as they had originally appeared.

The engines rumbled, as the aircraft flew over occupied territory. There was hardly any moonlight and the stars were shielded by intermittent clouds.

Eventually they neared the landing zone. The pilot had flown to a distinctive landmark and from there was initiating a timed run to the drop spot, designated only by latitude and longitude, where a Czech reception party was waiting.

The passengers sat perched, awaiting the signal that would send them shooting into space, into the night, to an uncertain landing below. According to the navigator's calculations, they were directly over the designated drop zone. There was nothing but pitch black darkness.

Gabcik sat with his legs over the edge, holding on with one hand.

The red warning light flashed on. This was the alert.

It would only be a matter of moments now and everyone had to be ready and quick. The Hudson was flying very low, traveling very fast, and with only a tiny space into which to drop the Czech agents, so even a fraction of a second could spell success or failure.

Suddenly they were there.

The green light flashed and Gabcik felt a slap on his back.

Out they went.

For just a brief moment, the crew could see the parachutes deploy. The Hudson gained altitude and turned for home. Down below, their former passengers were being greeted by the men with whom they would share the dangerous job ahead.

A week passed and Reinhard Heydrich continued to drive around in an open car through the streets of Prague, without military escort or armed guards. When his SS peers advised that such actions were extremely unwise, Heydrich told them the Czechs wouldn't dare harm him, because of the reprisals. For the most part, his observation was accurate, but he hadn't taken into account the British influence on Czech resistance.

On top of that, it was highly unlikely that Heydrich would have had an inkling of his standing amongst the dragons of the world. Perhaps if he had been aware that his death had been solicited by certain magical and mystical forces, he would have taken more precautions.

Then again, perhaps not.

In fact, Heydrich ignored a directive from Berlin ordering his limousine be outfitted with armor plating to the bodywork and seats. Reinhard believed the Czechs had abandoned their futile attempts at resistance and he would soon be recalled and assigned other duties. With his tyrannical success well publicized, he dreamed of assuming control of all military forces in occupied France.

Several days earlier, the British-trained covert teams had been dropped into Czechoslovakia, to orchestrate the assassination of SS-Obergruppenführer Reinhard Heydrich, who was the highest-ranking Nazi in command of the region. Heydrich's savagery and ruthlessness in suppressing the population, had earned him the nickname - Butcher of Prague.

Jan Kubis was Czech, while the other agent, Sergeant Josef Gabcik, was from Slovakia, which wasn't accidental, because the choice of one man from each country was intended to show national unity against the Nazis.

Heydrich proceeded on his daily commute from his home in Panenské Břežany. In a hurry, he didn't wait for the customary police escort. Heydrich's black Mercedes Benz convertible was on the way to Prague's Hradcany Castle for a staff meeting.

Valchik and Opalka were keeping lookout. Heydrich was unusually late, but an hour after the expected time, Valchik and Opalka gave the signal that the German staff car was approaching. The ambush spot had been carefully chosen, at a point where the vehicle had to slow down to negotiate a very steep turn in the road. Gabcik and Kubis waited at the bus stop at the curve.

As the open-topped car approached along a quiet street in the Prague suburb of Kobylisy, Josef Gabcik snatched aside his overcoat, lifted his concealed Sten submachine gun and clicked the trigger.

At that crucial moment, it jammed and failed to fire. The surprised Germans, believing Gabcik was a lone assassin, reacted quickly, braking to a stop and reaching for their weapons. Jan Kubis, realizing that Josef's gun had misfired, hurled the special grenade Major Vickers had given him, which exploded against the right rear wing of the Mercedes, puncturing the tire and blowing a huge hole in the body.

The ensuing blast and shrapnel severely wounded Reinhard Heydrich. Both Germans returned fire with their pistols, but the Czechs fled. Kubis was injured in the head and face by splinters from the exploding grenade. He forced his way past a crowd of witnesses, some of whom, uncertain of what was happening, tried to hinder his escape. As Jan stumbled along, the wounded man waved his pistol, shooting into the air, while trying to hide his face.

Opalka and Valchik escaped unnoticed, as Kubis fled in the opposite direction on his bicycle. He later abandoned it outside a shoe shop and was able to find sanctuary in the home of the Novak family. Heydrich, who had pinned Gabcik down with pistol fire, slumped against the bonnet of the car, too wounded to continue the fight.

"Get them!" Reinhard ordered.

Oberscharführer Klein took off to pursue Gabcik. The uninjured chauffeur was a formidable man and soon a running gun battle ensued, during which Klein's automatic also jammed. Fighting at close quarters, hand-to-hand in the doorway of a nearby butcher's shop, Gabcik wounded the SS sergeant in the thigh and ankle, and was able to make good his escape.

Mrs. Novak sent her young daughter to collect the bloodstained bicycle, but she was spotted and identified by the Gestapo. Gabcik made his way to another safe house. Slowly the Czech Resistance pieced together the apparent chaos and managed to assemble the assassins to aid their escape.

A terrible series of reprisals followed the attack on Heydrich. The Gestapo offered 10 million gold crowns for information leading to the arrest of the assassins. Eventually, two of their own men, Karel Curda and Vilem Gerik, betrayed Gabcik and Kubis. The Germans recovered enough evidence at the scene of the attack to allow them to identify key members of the Resistance, who were tortured, interrogated and executed.

The surviving Czech agents took refuge at the *Church of St. Cyril and Methodius*, but the information wrung out of the Gestapo's victims gave away their hiding place. The Germans quickly surrounded the church. Soldiers attacked, but the seven parachutists held them off for fourteen hours.

The trapped Czechs fought bravely. Opalka was killed in the fierce firefight, which occurred in the church. Jan Kubis and Svarc were fatally wounded and removed to hospital by the Germans, but they both died without regaining consciousness. The Germans then discovered that the other four men, Valchik, Gabcik, Bublik and Hruby, were hiding in the subterranean crypt. Many soldiers were killed in attempts to storm the crypt via the entrance hatch. Eventually the stone stairway entrance was discovered and the Germans blew it open, sending in more soldiers, but these too were easily picked off by the defenders.

Having decided the crypt was virtually impregnable, the Germans noticed it was served by an external ventilation slot. The Nazis tried to fill it with smoke, and then water. Finally, their ammunition exhausted and unable to tunnel their way to safety, the four Czech agents committed suicide, rather than be taken prisoner. Fourteen German soldiers had been killed and many more wounded in the series of attacks. If the crypt defenders had started tunneling earlier, they would have escaped via the sewers.

In Iceland, news of the assassination attempt quickly spread through the dragon community. At first, the announcement was greeted with elation, but as rumors spread of direct dragon involvement, the possibility created an outcry of concern. It quickly became apparent that, once again, most of draconic society was seriously divided over the issue of intervention.

On the other hand, in far off Asia, Wasabi Watanabe was pleased the necessary "incident" had gone off without delay. He quickly traveled through the subterranean tunnels leading to Iceland, in hopes he would reach there in time to speak with the Grand Council and perhaps lead to their overthrow.

18

School Pranks

Meanwhile, Gavin and Bunty were continuously bored at school, so they started playing harmless pranks on their unsuspecting classmates. They weren't really trying to be malicious, but focused these tricks on students who seemed deserving.

Such was the case with Reginald Sands, the obnoxious upper-crust lad who had relocated from London, but seldom forgot to remind everyone of his class superiority. Bunty was tired of Reginald's constant blabbering about royalty and privilege. To get even, the boys planned a series of tricks designed to embarrass Sands as much as possible.

"He deserves a good debagging today, "Gavin suggested one morning.

Bunty was delighted. "Oh, yes, this will be grand. Bet he wears pink bloomers."

Debagging was done by males to other males, but was even more humiliating when done in front of girls. The practice could be quite humiliating, especially since many boys didn't always wear underpants due to rationing and short supply.

At the designated location in front of school, at the predetermined time, Reginald Sands waited in front for his personal driver. He was surrounded by his entourage of lackeys and admirers.

Gavin and Bunty were hiding behind a bush, waiting for just the right moment.

"One should always be aware of one's surroundings," Reginald was heard to say. "My father, a brilliant man, always knows what is going on, as one should."

"Now!" Gavin whispered loudly, spurring his friend to action.

Bunty ran up behind Sands, waited for all his fellow classmates to take notice, and then reached out to grab Reginald's waist.

Whoosh!

Down went the boy's pants to his ankles.

This was followed by a noisy crescendo of laughter.

Poor Reginald turned several shades of red, before he regained control of his pants and tugged them back up into place, cinching the belt tightly. The private car arrived moments later and Sands scrambled into the backseat, laughter still echoing in his ears.

"Bravo!" Gavin congratulated Bunty.

The perpetrators were surrounded by thunderous applause.

Of course, it was just a matter of time before these pranks started escalating into school-wide events. The boys didn't find much satisfaction in picking on their peers, so they aimed their sights higher.

The next day, Bunty scraped out a tiny hole into the front end of his language teacher's precious piece of chalk. Then he placed a match-head inside and covered the top with chalk dust. Mrs. Drew began to write with the chalk and there was just enough friction to spark the match. Smoke came billowing out from the chalk.

The teacher screamed and dropped her piece of chalk, which shattered into a million little fragments.

The students burst into laughter.

Next, Gavin snuck the headmaster's milk cow into his office and left her there overnight. When Mr. Coopersmith opened up the school the next morning, his office desk was covered in fresh cow dung.

With each prank and the accolades that followed, the boys were challenged to think up even more spectacular stunts. It wasn't common knowledge who was actually instigating these events, but the children were definitely entertained.

For their next display of rebellion, Gavin and Bunty took an old buggy apart and lifted it, piece by piece, up to the roof of the school building, where it was re-assembled and left for everyone to see.

The student body was impressed.

The boys looked at each other and smiled with wicked pride.

Two days later, Bunty purchased three chickens from a local farm and labeled them 1, 2, and 4. Then he released them in the school hallway. All three chickens were quickly captured, of course, but the teachers went to great lengths looking for #3, which didn't really exist.

To top that, Gavin carefully hand-printed official-looking signs that read, **Please Use Other Door**. During literature class, he politely requested permission to be excused to use the restroom. Gavin hurried from here-to-there, placing the signs on all the doors in the building that led outside. When school was dismissed later that afternoon, students and teachers alike were befuddled, scrambling around looking for an exit that didn't have a sign on it.

All of this was strictly frowned upon, held stiff penalties if they were ever caught, but boys will be boys, and neither this nor any of the inherent dangers seemed to deter them. After a continuous week of these tricks, Bunty and Gavin decided to go bragging to a certain dragon, who lived in the little white cottage on the hill. They were still laughing about their escapades while entering Sir Osbert's domain.

The enormous dragon was indeed waiting for their arrival.

However, it didn't take a fool to see that Thaddeus was displeased.

"What did we do this time?" Bunty wondered.

The mighty beast extended one claw and pointed to a spot before him. "Sit!"

The boys obeyed immediately, running to the site and sitting on the hardened dirt floor, with legs crisscrossed and hands in their laps, looking up expectantly.

Bunty swallowed.

"I never expected either of you to be so cruel," Thaddeus stated coldly.

"What did we do?" Bunty asked again.

"You debagged that young man."

"Oh, that," Bunty laughed.

"Grrrr," the dragon roared.

They covered their ears and hung their heads.

"Do you think your behavior warrants praise?" Thaddeus asked.

Both boys shook their heads.

"I am especially disappointed in you, Gavin," the dragon said harshly. "Do you think it is a sign of leadership to embarrass and humiliate a fellow human being?"

Gavin cowered under the tongue-lashing. "No, Sir Osbert."

"Reginald Sands is not entirely without redeeming qualities," the dragon continued. "Put yourself in his shoes for awhile. The boy has not seen his parents in many months, while his older brother languishes in a German POW camp."

"We didn't know that," Bunty tried to argue on their behalf.

"That's no excuse."

"But…"

Thaddeus cut him short with another stern look.

"You didn't know, because you didn't bother to ask," Sir Osbert said. "There's no doubt the lad is a pompous bore, but perhaps he has reason to be. You might try to offer your hand in friendship and see what happens."

"Yes, Sir Osbert," Gavin said. "I'm sorry I've disappointed you."

The mighty dragon regained a sympathetic smile. "Do not take this lecture too hard, Gavin. You are young and impetuous at times, like your father before you. If anything good does come of this war, it will see the end to this ridiculous class system you bloody Brits are so fond of. England is a great country, because of her differences. The Empire will fade, but Britain is evermore. Always exercise fairness and compassion, for then you will have earned the right to wield that bloody great knife."

The next day at school, Bunty and Gavin took the time to seek out Reginald Sands during the daily air-raid drill. Huddled in one corner of the bomb shelter, they struck up a whispered conversation.

"Look here, Reggie," Gavin began, using his adversary's preferred nickname. "We've been very unsporting lately and it's just not right. We need to be in this together."

The Sands boy seemed totally taken aback.

Bunty quickly took up the cause. "That's right, chum. We've had our differences, it's true, but what we did the other day was bloody unsporting."

Reginald was suspicious, doubting their sincerity. "What gives, chaps?"

Gavin was afraid this might happen. He sighed and tried again. "Listen, Reggie, we're trying to apologize for being such louts. This war is no excuse for treating you badly. It's just not right to pick on you. After all, you haven't seen your parents in ages and your brother William is in a German prisoner of war camp."

Sands was shocked. "How do you know that?"

"It's not important," Bunty said. "What is important is that we stick with each other. The Jerries will win for sure, if we fight with each other."

Considering what had been said, Reginald first looked at Bunty, and then Gavin. He studied their eyes, looking for some hint of treachery.

Gavin added one more thing. "We're not just apologizing and that will be that. We want you to join us on our adventures too."

It was a good thing Sands didn't see Bunty's shocked reaction. Instead, he beamed with delight. "Well, I must say, that puts this in an entirely different light."

Out jutted Reggie's hand. "Jolly good show, what."

Gavin shook hands first, followed hesitantly by Bunty.

The ***All Clear*** siren wailed and all the students got into line to exit the shelter. Several of the teachers noticed immediately that Reginald Sands was having a friendly conversation with Gavin Kane and Byron Digby.

"Will wonders never cease," Mrs. Drew commented.

"Indeed," Mrs. Peabody said. "They're growing up fast."

After school was dismissed, Bunty and Gavin waited at the bus stop for the trip home. When nobody was near, the red-haired teen viciously poked his friend in the upper arm.

"Ouch!" Gavin exclaimed. "What was that for?"

"You blithering idiot," Bunty said as loudly as he dared. "What do you mean by inviting Sands to join us?"

Gavin smiled with pity. "Oh, now, don't be so upset, sport. Reggie will never take us up on the offer. It was just the right thing to say to convince the old boy that we really were apologizing."

"Don't be too sure," Bunty said. "Sands has an irritating habit of doing just the opposite of what we expect."

Gavin started to respond, but the bus pulled up and everyone started queuing up to board. The more he thought about it, the more convinced Gavin was that he done the right thing. Who was to say whether Reginald Sands might turn out to be a very good chum after all?

Who was to say?

Inside the little white cottage on the hill overlooking the ruins of Tintagel Castle, Thaddeus Osbert smiled with pride and satisfaction. Gavin Kane's thoughts were known to the dragon and he was immensely pleased.

"Now you've grown into a man," Sir Osbert said to himself. "You will need both courage and wisdom for the trials that still face you. Yet I would say you're off to a smashing good start."

Yet in another place, far away, there was only darkness.

Consuming everything, this pitiless spirit spread like a wave.

The land was blanketed in darkness, not from the night, but from evil pervading. Everywhere the blackness crawled across Europe, absorbing the light and stealing humanity's soul.

"*Aufstehen!*"

In the hour before dawn, the daily wake-up call ended the restless sleep of every prisoner in each freezing, lice-infested hut within every Nazi concentration camp throughout Hitler's Third Reich. Whether weary, ill, or actually dying, each miserable inmate had to tumble instantly from a wooden bunk and run, not walk, to the camp's central square, there to stand silent, motionless and utterly vulnerable for the ceremony of roll call.

The humiliating ritual was designed to demonstrate the absolute power of the SS guards over the very existence of everyone present. Some prisoners keeled over and literally breathed their last, robbing the SS of their prey as they paced wordlessly up, down, and across the mute rows.

Sometimes the guards doubled back to review those who thought they had been passed over this time, weeding away the weakest with a death sentence in a nod, the flick of a finger, or one horrifying word, "*Raus!* Out!"

There was much dust on the road, and the grass was dull, a sickening-grey color. The camp was separated from the road by several rows of barbed-wire fences, but these fences didn't look particularly sinister. However, the facility was enormous, as if an entire town of barracks had been painted a pleasant soft green.

Sachsenhausen was originally a punishment camp for Russian prisoners of war, who built it with their own hands on the train line north of Berlin. It quickly developed into a slave labor camp, where prisoners were worked to death, although thousands died from the harsh discipline and mass executions. Captives were assigned to such exacting tasks as repairing shoes and watches, and recycling captured equipment into raw materials.

The camp was laid out in a semicircular grid of 56 barracks inside a triangle enclosing 18 acres. This triangle was delineated by a wall rising almost nine feet and studded by nine watch towers armed with machine guns. With slightly peaked roofs, these blocks hugged the ground, but were separated by wide spaces to enhance visibility from the principal control tower.

The barred windows of Block No. 19 were painted over, and the building itself, the last one in the first row closest to the SS officer's quarters, was enmeshed in a barbed-wire netting to await its troop of specialists and their machines.

The tension and fear were evident in the men's faces as Major Krüger began his inspection of the prisoners. He slowly examined each man, looking for things unknown and unimagined.

Kruger halted abruptly and pointed at one.

"How old are you?"

"Sixty years."

"What was your profession?"

"Paper expert."

"Where do you come from?"

"Eichenberg in Bohemia."

"Why are you here?"

"I am a Jew."

"Step forward."

Krüger had begun the methodical work of selecting the men on whom the future of his secret operation depended. They had no idea for what they were being selected at this decisive roll call, but they immediately noticed something different, because the German officer addressed them by the formal and polite German *Sie*, instead of the familiar and demeaning *du* reserved for children, servants, and Jews under the Nazis.

Down the line he walked, selecting a professional engraver in precious metals, a banker, a paper salesman, even a Polish doctor to help preserve his work force. Contrary to his expectations, he found four men from the building trades, including two carpenters, an electrician, and a mason, but also discovered several specialists in the graphic arts, and four printers.

"Where did you work before?" Krüger asked another wretched being.

"At several printers," the prisoner replied.

"Do you want to join the others?"

"*Jawohl, Herr Major.*"

"Then join the others!"

In the end, Krüger finally picked 29 inmates instead of his planned 30, mainly middle-aged men, of whom about half were from various graphic trades, including a well-known fashion photographer.

Just as he was leaving, Krüger stopped suddenly and pointed to another man.

"You, over there, come here. I'd like to talk to you."

Norman Jablonski ran over to stand before the German.

"How old are you?"

"I'm twenty-five, sir."

"What kind of work did you do?"

"I was an accountant."

"Let me see your hands."

Although roughened by forced labor, they remained soft enough to convince Krüger the man was telling the truth.

"Take down his number, too."

Jablonski became the thirtieth and final selection.

Of those thirty men, nineteen of them had been chosen earlier that morning for the gas chambers.

Not until they reached *Sachsenhausen* did any of the prisoners know why they were there. Jablonski, quick and wily, needed little time to discover the purpose of the secret print shop.

A boastful SS sergeant picked up a counterfeit British five-pound note and said, "We have beaten England in the military field. Now, with these notes, we shall also ruin their economy. They have dropped counterfeit bread-ration coupons over Germany from the air. We shall reply with these notes, until inflation is over them like a storm."

Kruger's complicated plan was to create exact copies of existing British banknotes, including signatures, issues dates and serial numbers. The work of engraving the complex printing plates, developing the appropriate rag-based paper with the correct watermarks, and breaking the code to generate valid serial numbers was extremely difficult. Particularly hard to recreate was the paper used for printing the banknotes. The mixture had to be right to pass a common test for validity.

In England, currency in the denomination of £5, £10, £20, £50, £100, £500 and £1,000 was in general circulation. The team of forgers would only work on values up to £50. The notes were aged to give them a used touch and some were sent to neutral countries, with a request to have them checked. Only when the answer came back that the notes were regarded as real, did the Germans start to circulate them.

Although the initial plan was to destabilize the British economy by dropping the notes from aircraft, on the assumption that while some honest people would hand them in, most people would keep the notes, this plan was never put into effect. Instead, notes were transferred to a former hotel near Merano in northern Italy, from where it was laundered and used to pay for strategic imports and German spies.

In North Cornwall, however, everyone was oblivious to what was happening in *Sachsenhausen* Concentration Camp, just as they knew nothing of the millions of people being exterminated throughout Nazi Germany and the occupied countries. However, this wasn't true of a certain dragon. Thaddeus could foresee the suffering of countless innocent people, but was prevented from taking direct action, both by the law of his species and by the sheer vastness of the situation.

However, the dragon had already decided there was one exception to this rule. For reasons known only to Thaddeus, he was determined to rescue Rachel Heller, a teenaged Jewish girl languishing in *Ravensbrück* Concentration Camp. It was just a question of when.

What lay in the balance was the very nature and definition of humanity and Thaddeus never doubted that he must take direct action in this case. So many times through the course of human events, Sir Osbert could not remain idle. In truth, perhaps he was indeed meddling, by altering the destiny of a species bent on their own destruction.

In the end, it didn't matter. Sir Thaddeus Osbert had made up his mind, centuries before, that the stakes were too high not to intercede.

19

Shift in Power

In Prague, it was quickly discovered that Reinhard Heydrich's spleen had been seriously damaged and shrapnel from the grenade explosion critically wounded him. Bleeding profusely, he was immediately whisked away to Bulovka Hospital.

Heinrich Himmler, Heydrich's direct superior, took it upon himself to see to the welfare of his brilliant, yet difficult subordinate. No Czech or German Army doctors were allowed to operate on Heydrich, because Himmler sent his personal physicians to conduct the surgery themselves. Himmler's specialists declined to remove Heydrich's injured spleen right away, preferring to administer experimental drugs instead.

Heydrich died later that same afternoon.

Himmler's physicians claimed it was from blood poisoning. They insisted that some of the horsehair, which lined Heydrich's car, was forced by the blast of the grenade into his body, causing a systemic infection, which their medicine could not fight. In light of the rumors that Heydrich was the one man, of whom Himmler was both jealous and truly afraid, the validity of this diagnosis, and the intentions of Himmler's doctors was immediately suspect. Himmler's detractors, however, were wise enough to keep their suspicions to themselves.

In truth, Vicker's Gammon grenade, which killed Heydrich, contained deadly botulinum toxin. Purification and concentration of the deadly culture was added by British military scientists at Porton Down. The symptoms that Heydrich suffered before his eventual death mystified the doctors treating him and were the prolonged results of botulinum poisoning. The neurotoxin was so powerful that even the most minor flesh wound would have been sufficient to kill Heydrich.

Reinhard Heydrich's body was laid in state on the forecourt of Hradcany Castle, before removal to Germany. The Nazis put on an extravagant state funeral, consisting of a military procession using a gun carriage and the obligatory SS honor guard all dressed in black.

Yet one glaring fact remained. Heydrich's assassination took place exactly one year, to the day, from when the Nazi officer had entered the Treasure Chamber of Prague Castle, took the crown out of the display case, and placed it on his own head.

Was Heydrich cursed as soon as he placed the crown upon his brow?

Korban Vex still remembered his gift of the sparkling jewels that adorned that crown. He also felt a certain sense of vindication regarding the outcome.

When Reichsführer Himmler returned to Wewelsburg Castle, he immediately arranged for a secret memorial service to honor his fallen ally. It was all an act, of course, for with Heydrich removed, the path for more power was open for Himmler. With great pomp and circumstance, the SS put on quite a ceremony to impress their fellow comrades. Immediately following Reinhard Heydrich's entombment, the Reichsführer gathered his personal aides to him.

"The Allies have struck at the heart of Nazi Germany," Himmler stated for the record. "We must retaliate in kind!"

The SS officers all agreed, of course. What else would they dare do?

Subsequent orders for severe and brutal retaliation were approved by Adolf Hitler.

The assassination of Heydrich had not been without controversy. The plan was rumored to have originated with the exiled president of Czechoslovakia, but other sources were quick to point out how the British were deeply involved as well. The plot went ahead despite the fears of some, who predicted bloody reprisals from the Germans.

Those fears were well founded.

The Nazis reacted to the killing of Heydrich with extreme brutality. Reprisals took place immediately, with thousands of innocent Czech citizens murdered outright. The ramifications were very serious, as the news quickly reached the dragon society.

In Iceland, a great purple dragon lumbered slowly along the labyrinth of tunnels that led to the chambers of the Draconian Grand Council. Korban Vex had just returned from his meetings with Wasabi Watanabe and was just now on his way to discuss certain disturbing developments, when he was summoned to appear before a secret emergency meeting.

It had come to the council's attention that Sir Thaddeus Osbert had taken direct action to influence the actions of men, by openly approaching Major

Traber Vickers to arrange the assassination of Reinhard Heydrich. While it was true that justice had been served and a monumental threat had been removed, it was a violation of dragon law to intercede in human affairs.

For the benefit of the dragon community, many members of the Council had voiced public apprehension regarding Sir Osbert's apparently flagrant disregard for these rules. After all, he had recently been pardoned of identical crimes in the past and they just naturally thought Thaddeus had learned his lesson. This latest infraction led many to question Sir Osbert's true motivations.

While others, were convinced that such impudence must be severely punished.

In private, however, members of the elite Security Directive were greatly relieved that Heydrich was dead. The Grand Council still demanded a public hearing, to discuss alternatives and options, even if that meant covering up the truth. It was because of these issues that the influential purple dragon had been summoned.

"Korban Vex has arrived, Grand Councilor," one of the dragon guards announced.

"Approach, if you please, Korban Vex," beckoned Drasius Flylander.

The Dragon Court was primarily concerned with secretly promoting the proper use of magic, while covertly punishing vampirism, whenever the forbidden practice raised its ugly head. However, on rare occasions, the court members would hear critical arguments concerning dragon law, especially when accusations of human interaction arose.

The purple dragon drew nearer to the gathered council. "I am your humble servant, sir."

Wasabi Watanabe was standing to one side, watching, waiting and hoping for something dramatic. Then it would be his turn to strike fear in the hearts of the timid and useless elders.

"Is it true that Thaddeus Osbert conspired with humans to arrange the assassination of the German officer known as Reinhard Heydrich?" Flylander asked.

Korban Vex nodded and replied, "It is true, sire."

A tremendous murmur swept through the throng of dragons gathered there.

The Grand Councilor closed his eyes and sighed.

Vex looked over at Watanabe and immediately noticed the orange dragon seemed quite pleased. At that same moment, the purple dragon suddenly felt very guilty. After all, he had specifically asked Thaddeus to take such action, thereby saving the planet from total darkness.

"May I have permission to speak to the Council members in private?" Vex suddenly asked.

From the corner of his eye, Korban could clearly see Watanabe's worried reaction, but he no longer cared. This was a matter of honor and friendship, regardless of how many centuries Osbert and Vex had been competitors. They seldom agreed on any issue, but they shared considerable respect for each other and a blood bond recently formed.

The council members hurriedly discussed Vex's unusual request.

"We grant you this opportunity, Korban Vex," Flylander announced after his fellow members agreed to the terms of the meeting.

The mighty dragons, ten in all, retired to the private council meeting caves.

When all were settled, Vex once again approached them. "It is important that all of you are made aware of the extenuating circumstances surrounding Thaddeus Osbert's actions."

"No information you might offer can excuse Sir Osbert's blatant disregard for our laws, Korban," Agnostic Reptilian growled. She was more snakelike than most dragons, but carried with her tremendous authority on the council. Agnostic despised humans with a passion, and even though outnumbered in her convictions, held to them religiously.

Her statement incited the council members into a bitter argument.

Korban waited for a few minutes, before growling, "Enough!"

Well now, that shut them up.

"Agnostic, since you believe nothing which cannot be demonstrated by the senses," Vex lashed back. "Then perhaps you'll be willing to accept that I was the one who asked Thaddeus Osbert to kill Reinhard Heydrich."

"Why would you do such a thing, pray tell?" demanded Drasius Flylander.

"For it was I that presented those jewels so many eons ago," Korban reminded them all. "That putrid abomination placed the crown upon his sordid head and cursed an entire nation to death and misery. I, for one, could no longer watch as these wretched men lay waste to the land they were given mastery over. If you dare condemn Thaddeus for his actions, then you shall also condemn me!"

Within his towering office at Wewelsburg Castle, Heinrich Himmler watched the arrival of several trucks to *Niederhagen*, his privately constructed and maintained concentration camp. This was to be first of many deliveries of the "special" laborers targeted on Heinrich Muëller's unique list. The vast majority of accused prisoners were gypsies, condemned by Nazi courts as subversives and sub-human. However, since the Reichsführer was in charge of the disposition of all prisoners held by the Third Reich, it was up to him to decide their ultimate fate. Until Himmler had a chance to study the skills and habits of these unusual people, they would serve their sentence under his personal scrutiny.

To this end, Himmler was hoping to find a few magically gifted specimens who would agree to collaborate with the Nazis in exchange for their lives. The Reichsführer was convinced his winning methods of persuasion would win them over.

20

Dangerous Implications

"There are more than just your customary bad guys at work here," Lamken concluded. "The rift in the time-space continuum seems to keep widening."

"The careless meddling of the Third Reich made this possible, Master Rune," Tabitha Bixley said. "The portal sits underneath Wewelsburg Castle, in the Alma Valley. The dreaded SS have made the castle their headquarters."

The wizard grunted his disgust. "Bloody fools! Don't they realize what they've done?"

"There is something else you should be aware of," she hesitated mentioning.

"Yes?"

"Reichsführer Heinrich Himmler has made contact with a German witch who claims to be the reincarnation of Agnes Olmanns."

Lamken's bushy eyebrows went up at steep angles. "Is that so?"

"Is it even possible?" Tabitha asked.

"Anything is possible," Rune replied.

"Who is this Agnes woman, sir?" Bunty asked politely.

"With little concern, respect, or compassion for human life, Agnes Olmanns was the most dangerous of the former German *Witches of Darkness*," stated Lamken. "If she has joined ranks with the Nazis, it's because they've obviously promised her some of her former glory."

"Why would this woman want to help the Nazis?" Bunty asked.

"Agnes Olmanns was the last woman to be executed as a witch in 1738," Rune answered. "Her motivation might simply be revenge."

"That was more than two hundred years ago, so there's no one alive that had anything to do with her trial or conviction," Emily was quick to point out. "Surely this woman can't be serious?"

"I'm sure she's quite serious and if Agnes has assumed this woman's body, then she still blames the community of magic for not coming to her aid," Tabitha tried to explain. "She was burned at the stake."

"How horrible!" Emily blurted.

"Yes, it was," Rune said quietly, having actually witnessed those horrible times. "Thousands of innocent women were killed all over Europe, because of overzealous religious fanatics. However, in the case of Agnes, she *was* guilty of practicing the black arts."

"Does she have enough power to make a difference in this war?" Gavin asked.

"The outcome is still in doubt," Tabitha replied. "The forces of darkness are very strong, but thus far, not strong enough. The forces of light have proved better prepared to bounce back from adversity. However, Agnes could change that balance."

"Then she must be stopped at all costs," Gavin said emotionally.

The conviction in his voice caught everyone's attention.

Including Thaddeus Osbert. "Master Kane, why do you feel so strongly about this black witch? I detect a revelation you're not sharing."

Gavin didn't understand his intuition, but the correlation was impossible to deny. He faced the dragon and said, "Agnes isn't simply an evil witch from Germany's past. She is much more than that. The conflict she wages has gone on through the ages. In fact, this woman once battled Merlin, while her illicit son Mordred tried to usurp the throne from Arthur."

The silence that followed had the same impact as a thunderclap. No one dared to say a thing. Everyone stared at Gavin, shocked by the very nature of his conclusions.

It was the dragon, of course, who pursued the subject further.

"Are you suggesting that Agnes Olmanns was once Morgause?" Thaddeus asked.

Gavin nodded emphatically.

Lamken Rune came to his feet and stared into the blackened fireplace. His face was etched with worry as he pondered the possibilities.

When the wizard spoke, everyone listened. "The boy should know of what he speaks. Arthur's enchanted sword gives Gavin certain powers that only the blade can bestow upon him. Perhaps Vivienne returned *Caladfwlch* to him, because she suspected Morgause would return one day."

"More bad witches in Cornwall?" Bunty wondered.

"There have been several famous witches living in Cornwall, probably the best known being Madgy Figgy," Lamken replied. "Yet none of them compare to Morgause."

"What made her so terrible?" Bunty asked.

"Morgause was a constant thorn in King Arthur's side, casting black spells and making mischief," Lamken told them. "It could be argued that Morgause was indeed the cause of all Arthur's troubles, not Morgan le Fey, who usually gets the blame. Morgause herself tried to undo all that Arthur had accomplished."

"Whatever happened to her?" Emily wondered.

"Legends claim she was murdered by her son Mordred, but that is highly unlikely," Tabitha answered. "Within the community of magic, we assumed Morgause passed her knowledge from one apprentice witch to another, down through the ages. There is some evidence to suggest that Agnes Olmanns was the recipient."

"It is this connection to King Arthur that young Gavin has felt," Rune suggested.

Bunty was not as familiar with the Arthurian legends, but Emily was well versed in the tales and quickly went to Gavin's side. "I told you that you were destined to wield the blade of King Arthur."

Gavin was very uncomfortable with the possibility that what Emily was saying was in fact true. He shook his head.

"Why must you be so difficult, Gavin Kane?" Emily wondered. "Why won't you accept your destiny?"

He looked into her eyes.

"I am no knight in shining armor, Emmy," he whispered. "I am only Gavin Kane, from Crackington Haven, nothing more."

"Only if you believe that to be true," she countered.

"What would you have me be?"

Emily took his hand. "What you've always been."

"Which is?"

"My knight in shining armor," the girl said.

Gavin quickly averted his eyes and blushed.

"It is nothing for you to be ashamed of, Gavin," Emily said. "You are my dearest friend, who has been there for me whenever I needed you. You are fair and just, kind and friendly, giving and loyal. What better traits are there for a knight?"

"Well said," Lamken chimed in. "Gavin Kane is as much a man of honor today, as those brave souls once seated around the Round Table."

Gavin looked up at Thaddeus.

The dragon nodded. "It's true, young man. While no history books shall ever be written about what transpires here, the actions you take will have cosmic implications. By noble birth, you are from the House of Kane, Protector of the Blade and Guardian of the Lake. It is your destiny that you must fulfill."

Gavin then looked at Bunty and Emily. "I can't do it alone. Will you stand by me?"

"Of course we will, chum," Bunty said enthusiastically. "Haven't we already proven our friendship?"

Gavin said, "Yes, of course you have."

The three teens stood together, hands clasped in unity.

"Well, now that everything is settled, let's eat!" Thaddeus announced.

Everyone laughed.

"You silly old dragon," Emily said, while scratching the big beast under the chin.

"Rrrrrrrr," Thaddeus purred, stretching like a cat.

Tabitha twirled her wand and in an instant, a scrumptious meal appeared before them. Gavin, Emily, and Bunty stood with wide eyes, amazed at all the wonderful treats they hadn't seen in ages, due to strict rationing.

Everyone sat down on the earthen floor and soon there was only the sound of hungry people enjoying their meal. There was plenty to go around and even Thaddeus seemed satisfied by his portions, including several pounds of pure granulated sugar for his dessert.

After the meal, Rune headed for the door.

"Where are you going, sir?" Bunty wondered.

"Tabitha and I must scour the countryside," Lamken replied. We must find a suitable place where we can evaluate the magical options available to fight the coming scourge."

"There's an old abandoned cottage near Boscastle, Dr. Rune, if that might meet your needs," Emily offered. "I can show you."

"Well, that's simply marvelous," the old wizard chuckled. "Come along then, sweet child, and show us this humble abode."

Emily jumped up and with Bunty in hand, the teens escorted Tabitha and Lamken along the coast road to Boscastle. It was a beautiful evening, the sky filled with stars.

Their sudden exit left Gavin alone with Thaddeus. The young man sat quietly studying the dragon's immense paws. The more he examined them, the more unusual they appeared.

"Is there something different about you, I mean from other dragons, Sir Osbert?" Gavin suddenly asked.

"I'm not sure what you mean, son," Thaddeus replied. "I am a dragon in every regard."

"Well, I've never looked so closely before, but your claws look like they're made from metal," Gavin stated. "They glisten with blue-steel intensity, just like Arthur's sword."

The dragon held up one paw and extended each claw, one at a time. "As the talons grow, I file them on a daily basis, maintaining razor-sharp points."

"They still look different," Gavin said again, after touching one.

"You are very astute, lad," the dragon said with a huge smile.

"Are you avoiding answering me?" the teen asked with his own knowing smile.

"My claws are made of keratin," Thaddeus sighed in surrender. "It's the same protein that forms human hair and fingernails, but combined with a mineral secretion that is unique to my species. However, I also produce a special enzyme as part of my body's normal digestion process, and metal alloys are absorbed directly into the bloodstream. This natural formula produces talons that are more resilient and tougher than my fellow dragons, with unusual magical powers as well."

"You are so amazing, Sir Osbert," Gavin commented, eyes wide with wonder.

In Boscastle, Emily pushed open the old door to a crumbling and dilapidated hut.

Lamken peered inside and said, "Well, it's a bit dusty and damp, but it'll do."

Tabitha crinkled her nose and extended her wand over the old wizard's shoulder. "*Purgo!*" she commanded.

A brilliant flash of white light filled the room and suddenly the cottage was like new, spotless and neat, clean and tidy. Even the roof had been magical repaired.

"Wow," Bunty reacted. "Me Mum sure would have liked that!"

The four of them stepped inside.

Tabitha followed with another spell, "*Inflammo!*"

Instantly a warm, crackling fire ignited in the fireplace and they all gathered round the flames, warming their outstretched hands.

"Let's go back and get Gavin," Emily said.

"Oh, must we?" Bunty complained.

"Yes, we must," the girl replied sternly. "I don't want him to get in trouble with his mum and neither do you. Now let's leave Dr. Rune have some peace."

The two teens waved and scampered back up the road towards Tintagel to collect their friend. It was a good thing too, because Winifred Kane was quite upset at their late arrival for supper. However, with some well-timed puppy-dog looks from the trio, all was forgiven.

21

Future, Past, and Present

It was the next evening, now that Lamken Rune was all settled within the purloined abandoned hut near Boscastle. Tabitha looked into the fire and watched the dancing flames create all sorts of disturbing images. She was well aware that magical powers were unleashed every minute around the world, for enchanters seldom slept. However, the dark arts were flourishing from deep within conquered Europe and the implications were foreboding indeed.

"What you say is true," she whispered. "The rip in the vortex is large enough to allow passage for many creatures, perhaps even rift dragons."

Lamken was horrified. "Please, say it isn't so."

Tabitha frowned, but said, "I'm afraid it is. All that stands between eternal darkness and the morning sunrise is the size of the hole. It is too small yet for anything of great power to pass, but it won't be long before the passage widens."

Rune announced, "We must band together to fight this curse."

Tabitha averted her eyes and sighed with pity.

"What is it, child?" the wizard asked.

"Oh, Master Rune, don't you understand?" she replied. "None will follow you, not without your staff to prove who you really are."

Lamken sat back in dejected silence. Based on the look upon his face, it never occurred to him that his status amongst his fellow wizards might be less than satisfactory.

"When they took your staff, they took everything," Tabitha added.

Lamken looked at her with curiosity. "Then why do you still follow me?"

She averted her eyes again, but said, "Because I still regard you as the greatest wizard who has ever lived. Your wisdom and kind heart assured your use of magic was always for the good of mankind. I don't think you will ever find your Elizabeth. I'm convinced there was a conspiracy to steal her away from you, thereby subtracting your lightside power from the rest of the world."

Rune leaned forward, intrigued. "If what you say is true, how do these conspirators keep Elizabeth from contacting me? Even if they managed to destroy her, which is highly unlikely, the essence of her personality would eventually reach me."

"I don't know," she said. "I have spent hours studying this matter, but haven't been able to find an answer. The only possibility is that Elizabeth is bound by a spell that prevents her from calling out to you. Black magic, for certain, and a spell unknown to us."

Lamken rested his chin in his upturned hands. "Thank you, lass, for your loyalty. Your mother's integrity flows within your veins."

His words made the young woman smile. "She still speaks of you with love and devotion."

"A grand witch indeed," he said wistfully. "Your father is a most fortunate man!"

"They fell in love," Tabitha said. "It is so romantic."

The wizard's eyes widened then. "I also detect an unusual and profoundly spirited beating of your heart as well. In fact, I would hazard to say you've fallen in love!"

Tabitha blushed.

"Who is this most fortunate lad?" Rune asked.

"Sub-lieutenant John Mobley," she answered. "He's with the Royal Navy."

"No, you don't say?" Rune teased her.

"It's true, I do love him," she said.

"Does he know you are a witch?"

Tabitha nodded.

"Then he is a rare human indeed," Rune decided. "Do not let him get away!"

"I have no intention of losing him, believe me."

"Splendid."

"We're getting married soon."

"Delightful."

"Will you come to the wedding?"

"Wouldn't miss it for all the tea in China, lass."

"When this is over, you must go see my father. He never lost faith in you."

Rap, rap, rap.

There was a knock on the door.

"Oh, who is that?" Rune asked with exasperation.

Tabitha smiled. "Three young people, I believe. Your students have returned."

"What do you suppose they want at this hour?" the wizard wondered.

Bunty's voice came through the door. "Please let us in, sir. We have some important questions to ask you."

Tabitha opened the door and stood aside. "Enter, my youthful allies. We were just about to have some tea."

"Bloody marvelous," Bunty blurted.

Emily punched him in the arm.

"Ouch!" Bunty exclaimed.

"Stop talking like a sailor," she suggested.

"What's on your mind, Bunty," Rune asked as the teenage trio gathered by the crackling fire.

"We want to know why the wizards and witches in England aren't using their magical powers to make a difference in this war?" Emily asked.

"The human war doesn't matter to them," Lamken answered bluntly.

"It sounds like the Germans are getting help," Bunty suggested.

"German wizards, on the whole, could care less about Adolf Hitler and his fellow criminals, just like most British wizards ignore the actions of Winston Churchill," Rune said with irritation in his voice. "Unless human ambitions are a direct threat to members of the magical realm, they will stay out of it."

"Sounds just like the dragon world," Gavin said.

"So true, young man," Lamken said. "Ninety percent of the blessed ones would just as soon you humans eradicated yourselves and be done with it!"

"If the Nazis win, that might just happen," Bunty was quick to point out.

"Yes, it might," the wizard agreed.

Emily spoke next. "Don't wizards ever fight?"

Lamken laughed, but it was not because he found the question funny. "There has been a never-ending magician gang-war in the wizard world for centuries. In fact, my fellow spell-casters are fighting at the same time their human compatriots are engaged in this terrible world war."

Tabitha spoke next. "It has all the makings for a crackerjack conspiracy theory, with opposing magical forces operating under the cover of this human war."

"Exactly," Rune said. "There are forces working vigorously to thwart whatever good we have accomplished. They lust after power in the world of visible, material beings. Their goal is the total domination of the planet, not just us wizards!"

"Who, or what, are these forces?" Emily wondered.

"It's not easy to explain to anyone who isn't part of the world of magic, but I'll try," Tabitha answered after Lamken signaled that she should do so.

The teens all sat in a semicircle on the floor, balancing cups of hot tea on their laps, while wizard and witch stood before them. Emily squirmed impatiently.

Tabitha continued, saying, "The wizard war, which Master Rune speaks of, has been going on for centuries. As in all great contests, both sides seek power over the other, but in this case through magical means."

"How are we supposed to know the difference?" Bunty wondered.

This time Lamken answered the question. "*Accendo* magic is the power of adding to something that is already there, multiplying it or turning it into something new. When wizards alter a person or weapon, they use *Accendo* to add to or change the traits that were required.

"*Accendo* magic is associated with light and goodness, as the magic of life.

"*Despero* magic is the power to take away something that is there, dividing it or turning it into something useless. When wizards destroy a person or weapon, they use *Despero* to subtract or diminish the traits that were required.

"*Despero* magic is associated with darkness and evil, as the magic of death.

"Where *Accendo* magic is the creation of things, or the positive, *Despero* magic is the destruction of things, or the negative. Judge not the magic itself, but the outcome!"

"Any wizard born with the gifts of both *Accendo* magic and *Despero* magic is very rare indeed and usually such a mage will assume a position of great power and influence," Tabitha explained. "Many years before the age of printed books, the vast majority of wizards were born with both *Accendo* and *Despero* powers, but were only proficient in one or the other. It was a natural way of keeping such power in balance."

"Is *Despero* like black magic?" Bunty asked.

"Black magic is invoked to kill, injure, or cause destruction, or for personal gain without regard to harmful consequences to others," Rune stated. "Its roots are not of this world, but come from another place, a dark and evil place beyond your comprehension."

"Are the Nazis using black magic?" Emily was almost afraid to ask.

"Yes, I'm afraid they are," Lamken replied.

"Then the forces of evil will win?" Bunty asked with shock.

"Black magic only wins in appearance," Tabitha explained. "You will see it dominate the established institutions, glorified by formal rites and astonishing shows. Yet it is white magic that actually makes the world go round, even if it requires discernment to see that. It is white magic that continuously adapts to the world, from which stems all creation, which serves as the basis for civilization itself. In the end, goodness and light always are victorious."

"I'm frightened by these wars, both human and wizard," Emily said.

"As well you should be, lass," Rune said quietly. "The forces of evil never seem to run out of ways to meddle and interfere. In fact, my senses tell me that Sir Osbert was quite accurate in his pronouncement that a new dark force has arrived upon our shores."

"Not again," Bunty sighed.

Gavin stood a little straighter when he countered with, "Oh, we'll be ready. With Thaddeus on our side, those Nazis haven't got a chance."

Lamken ran his fingers through his graying hair. "Who said anything about the Germans?"

22

Purest Evil

Agnes Olmanns was convinced that Heinrich Himmler was a man of severely limited intelligence, who had no notion of the intricacies of true magic. She was painfully aware that the Reichsführer was convinced the sole task of science was to gather proof of revealed political propositions, rather than fact. Eventually Agnes would be considered a threat and done away with. For her, the Nazi regime was merely a tool and as such, was expendable when the time was right.

Therefore, the evil witch immediately set about to change her appearance.

Consulting her spells and incantations, she prepared the stages of transformation with care. Olmanns sipped her concoction slowly, savoring the wicked flavors of deceit, avarice, lust, greed, and betrayal. This was the wine of discontent and disharmony, its taste bitter and foul. Yet she drank it all, enjoying it to the very last drop.

Agnes was never some old hag, being ugly, bald, uncouth, or loathsome to behold. She had once been the victim of a previous changing, but never sought deliverance from her spells gone awry. The woman accepted her fate, but now the time had come to reverse the path taken so long ago to hide her mystic identity.

"The time is upon me," the witch said, waiting for the potion to take effect. "For I have returned from beyond the ages!"

A burst of flames signaled the beginning of a dramatic alteration.

The witch passed into another form, where she assumed the physical attributes of wondrous beauty. Gazing into the mirror, she was quite pleased with the result.

"Now let my gift of spells and potions yet govern the outcome," Olmanns proclaimed. "My tormentors shall suffer the same fate they once refused to spare me."

She emerged from the library and Dwellan immediately noticed the change. To his knees he went, bowing before her.

"Rise, slave, rise," she commanded.

The tainted vicar did so.

"The time has come to make amends for all the past injustices," Olmanns told him. "I will go forth and sweep this land of the old ineffective ways. I will bring a new order, where the dark arts shall rule once again and mere mortals shall be our slaves."

"What about me, Mistress?" Dwellan asked.

"By embracing the forces of evil, you can gain power beyond your wildest dreams," she explained to the fallen vicar.

"What must I do?" he asked. "Is there some ritual?"

Her ridiculing laugh made him cringe.

"Fool. You have already sold your soul. You are a slave, nothing more. If you wish to live and reap the benefits of servitude, then obey me without question."

"Yes, Mistress."

She smiled, although it was without warmth or compassion. "So, you are capable of wisdom after all?"

"I only wish to serve thee," Dwellan said.

"We shall see," the witch said.

"I swear allegiance only to you, Mistress."

Olmanns lifted the vicar's chin with a long, wicked fingernail. "Be forewarned, little man. If I fail, my master will seek revenge and he will consume your wretched and pitiful soul first."

"Then I shall see that you don't fail," Dwellan said.

The witch spun away from him, laughing hysterically.

Elsewhere in Cornwall, Lamken Rune had taken up temporary residence in an abandoned farmhouse outside of Boscastle. While trying to be useful, he was forced to rely entirely on Tabitha to accomplish his list of tasks.

To his delight, however, Bunty was a daily visitor, full of curiosity and wonder.

The wizard enjoyed teaching the redheaded boy an alternative history of England.

"Did ye know that our brave Prime Minister, Winston Churchill, hosted the Ancient Order of Druids at Blenheim Palace?" Rune inquired.

"No, sir, I did not," Bunty answered with surprise.

"Some claim England's PM is a wizard," Rune added.

"Well, is he?"

Lamken grinned. "It does seem that our beloved leader is blessed with many magical skills, not the least of which is his oratory talents."

"That's not magic!" Bunty protested.

"To motivate an entire nation to hold out against the horrible onslaught raining down on them is nothing short of magical, my boy," Lamken pointed out. "It isn't all about waving a wand and chanting spells."

"I never thought of magic that way before," Emily spoke up. "It seems to me that there are many wonderful things happening every day, which could be described as magical."

Tabitha placed a gentle hand on the teenaged girl's shoulder. "That is a very enlightened way to look at the world, Emily. You see things in a different light than most. Good for you!"

"I just want to escape from dull school routines and boring chores," Emily said. "I love to shut the door to my room and write stories of adventure and romance. Writing is my escape. However, I know that before I can truly be a good writer, I must venture out into the world and experience what life is all about. I must feel true emotions, be they happy or sad, before I can bring them to the written page."

"Life as a teenaged girl is tough enough," Tabitha agreed. "For a young witch like me, training is not just a matter of learning about the rules for magic, but it was also a time to develop creative abilities."

"How did you become a witch?" Emily asked.

"Generally, a girl gets picked as a successor by a senior witch or wizard, receives training from that person, and then inherits the cottage and duties of the village assigned," Tabitha explained. "It's a practice handed down over the centuries. I answered the call, but my country also needed me, so a Wren I became."

There was something in Emily's expression that Tabitha recognized. "If magic intrigues you, then we shall speak of it again."

Emily nodded. "Oh, yes, I should like that very much."

Suddenly, something began to hum and a soft glow shown from Bunty's pants.

Lamken pointed at the teen's back pocket. "What have you got there?"

The boy looked down and jumped with surprise. He gingerly slipped his fingers inside the pocket and slowly withdrew an oddly shaped piece of quartz. It was the old rock he had found in a seaside cave months ago, but left it in Gavin's room in his treasure box. Bunty wasn't sure why he had brought it with him this time? Now the gemstone pulsated with a dazzling rainbow-spectrum of lights, beating with a slowly measured rhythm, as if in perfect sync with an unknown piece of music.

Ever since finding the rock in the cavern's tide pools, the red-haired boy had secreted his lucky stone in his secret stash. That morning, Bunty had felt an unspoken urge to bring the prize with him. However, instead of a dull chip of quartz, it glowed with beautiful prisms of light.

"Why is it doing this, sir?" Bunty asked, holding it up.

"Where did you find that?" Lamken asked with barely controlled excitement.

"It was in a cave near the ruins of Tintagel Castle, sir," the boy replied.

His words galvanized the old man. "What did you say?"

Bunty was frightened by Rune's reaction. "I'm sorry, sir. I found it lying in seawater inside an old cave, nestled amongst the stones."

Lamken tried to control his emotions. "I'm not angry with you, lad. I just need to know exactly where you found that crystal."

Bunty closed his eyes and let the memories flow over him. "I was with Gavin and Emily. We were exploring several seaside caves and I spotted a reflection of something pretty under the water. I picked it up, but it was just this piece of quartz. It didn't start glowing like this until just now."

Tabitha looked at Lamken and slowly smiled. "Do you think it's possible?"

Rune was afraid to venture a guess. He took a tentative step closer to the teen and the stone throbbed even more, growing brighter still.

"What's this then?" Bunty wondered. "It seems to respond to you, sir."

"May I see your gem, please?" Rune asked politely, his hands shaking.

"Of course, sir," Bunty replied, gingerly handing over the crystal.

As soon as the stone touched the wizard's palm, it blazed with brightness, filling the room with sparkling fingers of stunning lights. In fact, everyone had to shield their eyes from the dazzling aura.

Everyone except Lamken Rune.

His eyes were filled with tears.

"Oh," the wizard sobbed. "Oh, my Elizabeth. You live!"

Tabitha reached out to steady the old man. "There, there, Master Rune, take it easy. You can't be certain it is her."

He struggled to sit down. "Oh, it's her, alright. I would know her essence anywhere."

Bunty looked very concerned.

Lamken saw the boy's expression and smiled. "Thank you, Bunty, from the bottom of my heart. You have given me hope, when I had none."

Then the carrot-topped teenager smiled.

"Do you think you will be able to locate your staff with just that?" Tabitha asked.

Rune nodded emphatically. "Somehow Elizabeth made certain one of her crystals would end up in the caves of legend. I will start my search from there."

"It might take years, sir," Bunty said.

"Do not fret, lad," Rune said. "Elizabeth will make herself known to me. It's just a matter of knowing where to look."

"I will go with you," Tabitha said.

"Me too," Bunty chimed in.

Lamken shook his head. "No, my lad, you must stay here with Emily, where it's safe. I have no magic to protect you."

Bunty understood, but he was disappointed just the same.

"We will start in the cave where Bunty found this crystal and work our way along the coast," Rune suggested. "The crystal should give us some guidance."

"Under Castle Tintagel was where we began our adventures that day, sir," Bunty informed the old man. "Yet this crystal was inside one of the many caves we explored after that, I think. I wish I could remember exactly which one."

The wizard shook his head. "Never mind, my boy. This is a journey I must make on my own. The vital clue has been provided, but it is up to me to solve the puzzle. Only then can I truly be at peace with my dear Elizabeth."

"We must be on our way, sir," Tabitha suggested. "The sooner you are reunited with Elizabeth, the sooner you can use your awesome powers to make a difference."

"Indeed, lass, you are correct," Rune agreed with a heartfelt chuckle of delight. "Let us be on our way."

Bunty followed them to the door.

The old wizard turned around and offered the boy his hand. They shook hands with mutual respect and admiration.

"Thank you again, Bunty," Lamken said. "I owe you so much."

"I would do anything for you, sir," Bunty said.

"While we're gone, please go tell Thaddeus what has transpired," the wizard requested. "The old boy might be able to buy us some time."

"Yes sir, I will."

As Tabitha and Lamken walked briskly towards the shore, Bunty waved. When they were out of sight, the red-haired teen took Emily's hand and they scampered down the coast road towards the little white cottage on the hill.

When they reached the ornate door, Bunty hesitated knocking.

"You may enter, son," spoke a familiar voice.

Bunty and Emily ran to the great dragon.

"You bring me exciting news?" Sir Osbert inquired.

"Months ago Bunty found an old crystal in a cave," Emily was first to speak. "Dr. Rune thinks it might have come from his enchanted staff."

Bunty didn't seem to mind that Emily has stolen all his thunder. "It glowed brightly when Lamken took it, as if sending a message."

Thaddeus smiled warily as he pondered the possibilities. "This seems a most fortuitous discovery. Wondrous indeed, as if we are being guided along a path not of our choosing."

His words troubled Bunty. "Do you suspect a trap?"

The dragon nodded slowly.

"Then we must go warn Lamken and Tabitha!" Emily exclaimed.

Sir Osbert shook his mighty head. "While they may experience an adventure or two, the trap I speak of is for Gavin."

Bunty and Emily were shocked to silence.

"Speaking of whom, where is the lad?" Thaddeus asked.

His guests merely shrugged.

One eyebrow went up and the mighty beast frowned, before closing his eyes to search his projected senses. In a matter of seconds, he located his young charge.

Emily and Bunty sighed with relief, for they too could suddenly visualize what the dragon wanted them to see. Gavin was sitting comfortably in the kitchen at home, enjoying biscuits and jam.

"Why aren't you playing with Bunty and Emily, dearest?" his mother asked.

He shrugged.

Winifred immediately sensed something was troubling her son. She sat beside him and fluffed his hair, before giving him a big hug and kiss. "What's got you in such a sour pickle?"

Gavin shrugged again, but said nothing.

His mother was quite perceptive and after silently reflecting for a moment, she said, "I miss your father too. He hasn't had a spot of leave for ages."

Gavin smiled and nodded.

Winifred grinned. She had identified the problem, right on the head. Unfortunately, she didn't have any ideas of what to do about it. Instead, she stalled for a little time and inspiration.

"I'll brew us up a nice hot cuppa tea and we'll noodle on this," his mother announced, springing into action.

Gavin loved his mother very much, but with all this constant banter about King Arthur, he really wanted to talk with his father. It just wasn't fair that he had to face these challenges without his dad, the one person whose council was most important.

As Winifred rejoined him with steaming hot cups of Earl Grey, she had thought of a grand solution, though quite daring and impossible. Gavin could see the sparkling light in her eyes.

"What?" he asked.

"Just as soon as we can arrange it, we're going to take the train to **RAF Medmenham**, in Buckinghamshire," his mother said, in no uncertain terms. "We will camp outside the gate until your father comes and spends a few hours alone with you."

"You too, Mum," Gavin was quick to say.

She smiled, but tears formed in her eyes, as emotion welled up inside.

Gavin reached out and took her hand in his. "It's a perfectly spiffing plan, Mum."

"We'll see to Bunty staying with Emily for a few days and purchase tickets in advance," Winifred said, regaining her composure. "Let's go to Launceston straight away, before we have second thoughts."

They jumped up and scurried off to the bus stop. The journey seemed very short, for a change, and after buying train tickets, mother and son wandered along the shops in Launceston for a few hours, before returning to Crackington Haven. It was a splendid time, filling Gavin with renewed hope that everything would turn out just fine.

23

Broom Closet

The shoreline on the north coast of Cornwall was historically less favorable for smugglers, because there were fewer gently sloping sandy beaches, and many of the suitable coves were too exposed to the wind, making approach more hazardous. The heavy surf, for which the area was infamous, was another problem. Still, the promise of easy money during these times of stringent rationing, made black market goods quite appealing.

Lamken and Tabitha scoured through one cave after another, but found nothing. Undaunted, they continued their search. After a light supper, the pair made their way towards Newquay, planning to spend the night there. They lost track of time, so fully involved in the challenge. Finally, taking a break, Lamken and Tabitha were sitting by the seashore by Crantock Bay, only a few miles from their final destination of the day. It was midnight, as they gazed out to sea. There was an unidentified craft offshore, which suddenly began signaling with lights, which snapped on and off in Morse code.

Tabitha looked across to the Newquay side of the bay and one of the big hotels had lights on in the windows, which flashed on and off as well, spelling the word **YES**.

The pair watched in amazement and watched this take place, back and forth, where lights continued flashing from the boat!

"A German U-boat?" Tabitha whispered.

"Perhaps," Lamken replied, but he didn't sound convinced.

They decided to spend the night right where they were. The wizard built a small fire and they huddled together, gazing at the hypnotic dancing flames.

"I am so pleased you finally returned, Master Rune," Tabitha whispered.

"If not for a red-haired boy with the heart of an angel, I would still be wandering the Isles," Lamken replied. "I hope my redemption lies ahead."

"Sir Osbert has forgiven you," the woman pointed out. "Now the crystal holds promise of Elizabeth. I think the signs are fairly obvious. Soon you shall be free of the curse."

"All in good time, lass," he said after yawning. "All in good time."

They drifted off to sleep.

The next morning, by rowing-boat ferry, the pair crossed the river that separated Crantock from Newquay, and strolled up to the hotel to see if they could figure out where the lights came from. It didn't seem possible that all the guests in the bedrooms could have taken part in a plot to make the signals, so Lamken looked for lights on the outer hotel brick walls. There were a few hidden among the ivy leaves, but he wasn't sure they might have spelled out the dotted letters. One of the hotel gardeners spotted them snooping about and asked them to leave at once.

"I think it was black market smugglers," Rune decided. "They were arranging for their contraband to be delivered at a certain time."

Tabitha listened, but didn't comment.

On the way back, Lamken stopped to talk to the old ferryman. Rune related what they had seen the night before, but the aged geezer was very taken aback and refused to discuss it further.

In a broad Cornish accent the boatman warned, "Listen to me, you'd best not go poking your nose into other people's business or you might get hurt."

Lamken said, "No bother. We know when to look the other way." He smiled and waved, taking Tabitha's hand.

When they were out of earshot of anyone, Rune whispered, "That hotel is nothing more than a front for smugglers, or worse. I plan to visit their cellar tonight!"

Tabitha wanted to object, but never got the chance.

Lamken opened his hand and Bunty's crystal was throbbing with green light.

It was obvious to them both that Elizabeth was nearby.

That evening, right after a quick supper at a nearby pub, Lamken and Tabitha made their way back along the road to Newquay. The town was situated in an area of natural beauty, with scores of nearby smuggler caves and soft, golden sands stretching for several miles in either direction.

Once inside the hotel, Tabitha went to inquire about a room, while Lamken searched for the correct doorway leading down to the cellar. He found it quickly and was successful in picking open the lock. Then the wizard joined his assistant in the lobby.

"We have a room on the second floor, Father," Tabitha announced for the proprietor's behalf.

"Well done, daughter," Lamken said in character. "Let us retire."

They headed for the stairs, but once out of sight of the front desk, Rune reached out, grabbed Tabitha by the elbow, and steered her towards a door at the end of the hallway. They both slipped through, the door closing quietly behind them.

Phssst.

Lamken lit a match.

Carefully they proceeded down the rickety staircase.

There were low ceilings, wobbly walls, and creaking steps.

In fact, Lamken turned to look at Tabitha and grinned.

"Seems like there should be witches and wizards gathering here, with all this atmosphere," he whispered.

She nodded nervously.

They reached the cold stone floor and discovered a candle.

"How convenient," Tabitha said.

"We're looking for a smuggler's tunnel, secret passageway, or hidden room," Lamken restated for their mutual benefit. "Do you see anything out of the ordinary?"

The girl ran her delicate fingertips over the surface of the stone wall, while closing her eyes to concentrate with her acute sense of touch.

Secret passages usually were protected by hidden doors, which were camouflaged so they appeared to be part of the wall, or as an architectural feature, such as a fireplace or built-in bookcase. Some entrances were more elaborately concealed, and could only be opened by engaging a hidden mechanism or locking device. Other hidden doors were much simpler, such as a trapdoor hidden under a rug, which could easily conceal a secret passage.

Tabitha stopped suddenly.

"Did you find something?" the wizard asked.

She flicked her fingernail along the leading edge of one brick, which looked exceedingly smooth on three sides.

Click.

The distinctive sound of a mechanism engaging made Rune grin with delight.

"You are indeed most gifted, lass," he said.

The stone wall swung open, revealing a dark passage beyond.

Tabitha swirled her wand counterclockwise, casting a spell. "*Illuminare!*"

An orb of energy burst from the tip and traveled along the narrow hallway, effectively lighting their way. There didn't seem to be any monsters or hideous villains waiting for them.

"Ladies first," Lamken offered.

"Not on your life," she replied. "I'm not that brave."

He chuckled and stepped inside, following the floating beacon before him.

After about thirty feet, the subterranean passageway opened into a large vault-like room, which was lined with planked shelving. It was immediately obvious this storage area hadn't been used or visited in decades. The smell of rotting wood was powerful and inches of dust encrusted everything. There were ancient kegs and crates stacked in several corners and all sorts of contraband were stacked on each level of shelving.

"It's only an old smuggler's den," Lamken decided disappointedly.

Unable to contain her curiosity, Tabitha went to look at some of the bottles.

The wizard was dejected and started to leave.

"Wait a minute, Master Rune," she said.

"What is it?" he asked.

"This bottle is labeled," she replied.

"So?"

"In Latin, sir. The contents are black lichen."

Rune spun back around. "You're not serious?"

Tabitha nodded.

As a reflex, Lamken pulled the gem from his pocket. In a searing flash of blue light, the crystal levitated up from his open palm and floated towards a dark corner. It hovered before a narrow broom closet, vibrating with barely-contained power.

The wizard stopped breathing.

"Go on, Master Rune," his able assistant coaxed.

Very slowly, the wizard approached the rickety door. The handle was rusted and worn. Carefully, Lamken pressed his thumb down against the trigger and pulled.

It was locked.

"Bloody hell!" he exclaimed.

Tabitha gently pushed him aside and cast another spell. "*Clavis Locus!*"
Click.

"There. I think it will open for you now."

The wizard sighed. "There is nothing more useless than a wizard without his spells or magic."

She gave him a gentle kiss on the cheek. "That's not true. Now let's cut out all the suspense and take a look inside."

So Rune took a deep breath again and yanked it open.

It was full of...brooms.

"Well, that's just bloody marvelous," he complained.

"I don't know," Tabitha wondered. "Witches often disguise their wands as broomsticks to avoid suspicion. It was also a tradition that brooms were used by some as receptacles to temporarily harbor a particular spirit."

Tabitha reached in and pulled out a broom.

Rune was instantly intrigued. "Let me see that, please?"

She handed it over to him.

Zap!

A bolt of lightning created a thick cloud of blue-black smoke, which surrounded them for a moment.

Then it cleared.

In his hands was no longer a broomstick, but a long slender wooden pole. It was ornately carved with runes and symbols, ending in a hooked end, which encased several large green and purple gems.

The wizard grasped the staff with both hands, wiping away inches of dust and cobwebs that covered its once-polished surface.

Tears rolled unimpeded down his cheeks.

"Oh, dear Elizabeth, forgive me for taking so long," he sobbed.

"Master Rune, we must flee this place," Tabitha spurred him to depart. "They will surely discover we went down into the cellar. I fear this place may be protected with unfriendly spirits or hexes."

"What makes you say that?" he asked.

Tabitha sighed and said, "Because the three chaps standing behind you look exceedingly unfriendly."

Rune spun around to discover that indeed there were three burly men in the doorway. They were armed with guns, which were all pointed at Tabitha.

"Make any sudden move old man and the pretty girl dies," one of them said in a gruff voice. Then he held out his hand. "We'll take that, if you please."

"Not bloody likely," Rune said.

"Then we'll kill both of you and take it anyway," another man said.

"There's no need for violence," Lamken said as he stepped closer, holding the staff out before him. "I just thought we could settle on a price. You know, a little lolly for our time? After all, this staff has magical powers, but only I know its secrets."

All three men hesitated.

"What did you have in mind, old man?" the apparent leader asked.

"Two hundred quid and not a farthing less," the wizard said confidently, pushing Tabitha to stand behind him.

"Coo, are ya daft?" one thug reacted.

"Look at the fine workmanship," Rune said, getting even closer.

Three heads leaned in to take a better look.

Swish.

The wizard deftly twirled the staff around.

Whack!

Wham!

Thunk!

Lamken hit each of them over the head with Elizabeth, knocking them out cold. Three unconscious forms hit the floor.

"Oh, Master, you are truly amazing," Tabitha cheered.

Rune puffed up a little and beamed. "I am rather."

She grabbed his arm. "Now it's time to leave."

"Yes, yes, of course."

The pair hurried down the dark passageway, up the stairs, and out the front door, ignoring the impassioned cries to stop from the proprietor. They scampered to the ferry landing and once on the other side of the bay, the pair celebrated with hugs.

"This is a monumental day," Lamken proclaimed. "I shall take Bunty as my apprentice to honor his service to me."

Tabitha suddenly looked dejected.

Lamken reached out and took her left hand. "There is no need for sadness, Tabitha Bixley. You have long since passed the status of apprentice. You are a fine witch in your own right. As soon as I am able, I promise to elevate your standing to sorceress."

Tabitha's eyes were wide.

"Come now, let's be off to Tintagel," Rune declared.

Thunder rumbled in the distance.

The sky grew darker by the second, as unholy storm clouds swirled overhead, and green lightning stabbed earthward. The wizard and white witch looked skyward, watching the heavens discolored by the advent of evil.

"So cometh the queen of air and darkness," Tabitha said quietly.

"She is nothing more than a villainous, seductive, megalomaniacal sorceress, who wishes to enslave our beloved home," Lamken said.

"That's not the only reason she's returned, Master Rune," Tabitha added. "The black witch is convinced you betrayed her, so many ages ago."

"Of that I am well aware," the old wizard said.

"Young Gavin has proven to be very wise indeed," Tabitha said, remembering the teen's prophecy.

"He is part of our heritage," the wizard said. "The hag must kill the boy to sever the link to Sir Gawain, her own son."

"Does she know that?"

Rune shrugged, but said, "I doubt it. She isn't the sharpest pencil in the box."

"What will you do?" the white witch asked.

"I will protect Gavin, of course."

"How?"

"I must face her."

"You cannot," Tabitha pleaded. "You don't even know if Elizabeth is still empowered."

Lamken turned to face his beautiful young ally. "You are right, lass, I don't know if Elizabeth's voice will sing again. However, until I find out, I'll have to rely on three mortal teenagers and a sugar-fixated dragon."

Tabitha giggled. "Such strange alliances speak well of you, sir."

The wizard couldn't help but grin as well. "I don't need an army, just the stout hearts of boys and girls who believe in compassion, love and magic."

"Does that include me?" Tabitha asked.

"Of course it does," Lamken laughed. "You are a maiden fair, in the service of her country, and deeply in love."

Across from Tintagel Castle, inside the little white cottage on the hill, Gavin and Thaddeus were spending time together, although their conversation seemed uncharacteristically strained. The boy was distracted by his troubled thoughts.

"Is everything all right?" the dragon inquired after awhile.

"Sometimes I think I would be better off not knowing you," Gavin said quietly.

Sir Osbert didn't take it personally, but understood the boy's reservations.

"It's not you, Thaddeus, believe me," Gavin was quick to add. "I love you dearly. It's just that damned sword and all this King Arthur stuff. I don't like the way this has turned out, especially with this war."

"The lessons are difficult for a reason, lad," Thaddeus said. "You were chosen because of your good nature, stout heart, and strength of purpose."

"Where does my destiny lie?"

"It is not for me to say. In time, you will discover your true calling. Until then, the fate of England lies in your hands. Accept this truth and you will sleep better."

Gavin shook his head. "But why me?"

Way off in the distance, as if by design, a solitary church bell tolled. However, as Gavin counted the echoes, the tone struck fourteen times.

"That's odd," the teen commented.

Thaddeus, however, easily deciphered the code. The elves had sent the predetermined signal for a reason.

The dragon gently picked the teen up and placed him on his shoulder. Gavin hugged him with all his might and rested his head on Sir Osbert's neck.

The roof of the hamlet parted and Thaddeus was suddenly airborne.

"I think an afternoon flight over the countryside will do us both good," the dragon roared. "Sit back and we'll have a nice little trip."

With protective scales elevated and Gavin all settled in, the boy looked down with unbridled delight. He loved flying with Thaddeus, seeing the world from so high above. With such perspective, things seemed to make more sense for awhile.

With tucked wings and tail angled upwards to gain maximum lift, the dragon soared with the wind. The air flowed past his scales, whistling and moaning as if alive. Thaddeus snapped out his mighty wings and the muscles flexed with massive power as the currents tugged and filled the membranes.

Back on earth, when Bunty reached the little white cottage, he was surprised to find it empty. The boy sat on the stool to await the dragon's return. Little did he know that Thaddeus Osbert already had a very specific destination on target.

"Bunty, my lad, there you are," called out Lamken Rune. He was accompanied by Tabitha and Emily too. "Come here, my boy, for we have many miles yet to travel."

"Thaddeus isn't at home, sir," the redhead apologized.

"No bother," Rune chuckled. "The wise old dragon has gone before us, for our friends the elves sent a warning message to Thaddeus for us."

Bunty looked at Emily. "Where's Gavin?"

"With Sir Osbert," she replied.

Bunty sighed.

The wizard put his arm about the boy's shoulder and said, "What's bothering you, Byron?"

Bunty shrugged. "I feel cold, as if I will never be warm again."

Tabitha looked over at Rune.

The old man knelt before Bunty. "There is an evil spirit on the move and you feel her malignant power. That is why Gavin and Thaddeus are together, to confront the harbinger of wickedness. We must join them."

Tabitha held out her hands, closed her eyes and slowly chanted, "*Viator Bodmin Velox!*"

For just a blinding instant, they were surrounded with an intense white light.

Overhead, a gigantic winged creature circled lower and lower.

"It is time, Gavin," Thaddeus announced as he prepared to land, losing elevation quickly. The mighty dragon set down on the far western edge of a desolate and wild place, the winds howling all around them.

"What is this place?" Gavin asked as he dismounted.

"Bodmin Moor," the dragon answered.

The boy shivered. "Why here?"

"Another piece of your destiny will fall into place on this very spot of ground," Thaddeus informed him. "I have foreseen it."

Gavin stepped down from the dragon's shoulders and surveyed the surrounding area. The landscape engendered fear and awe, but also strangely inspired him. Bodmin Moor was dominated by dramatic granite tors, which towered over the sweeping expanses of open bog.

The teen turned to look at Thaddeus. "You have been here before, in your past. I can feel the history of this place."

"In the war between good and evil, I must always choose sides," the dragon replied. "I could not pass by, when an innocent life was in need of help."

"What happened?" Gavin asked.

"Two great armies faced each other here," Sir Osbert explained. "The Romans entered the battle from your right and the blue-painted Picts stood to your left. The barbarians had massed their forces and taken up position at the top of that rise, leaving the Romans an uphill fight on a slope that gave the Picts a tactical advantage. The plan was to conceal the larger part of the Pictish army in the adjacent forest and to lure the Romans onto the moor. The boggy land would look firm enough to the Romans, right up to the point where it would be too late for them to get out. The remainder of the Picts engaged the enemy in battle, gradually allowing their force to be pushed back, before they broke rank and pretended to flee down the slopping ground of the battlefield. As they ran, they drew the chasing Romans into the mire, where the Picts sprang their ambush."

"A brilliant plan," Gavin decided.

The dragon nodded.

"I assume you sided with the Picts," the teen added.

The dragon nodded again.

"Who won?"

"The Romans."

His answer came as quite a surprise. "What, even with you involved?"

Thaddeus frowned. "I did not participate in the battle, Gavin."

"Why not?"

"I was forbidden to participate by the Druid magician who accompanied the Picts," the dragon answered.

"Why would this magician prevent you from helping?" Gavin countered.

"On that day, a Roman centurion would fulfill his destiny instead, young Gavin," the dragon replied. "For Arthur was victorious and changed the course of history."

"Is that why we are here, in this place?"

Thaddeus nodded.

The dragon crouched down, crossed his paws and waited. Gavin leaned against him, taking shelter behind one of Sir Osbert's ears. It was obvious to the boy that they were waiting for something.

Or someone.

As Agnes Olmanns crossed the moor in silence, she pondered the millions of British citizens she was prepared to exterminate. It was all a question of where and when.

Suddenly she halted.

The witch hadn't expected to encounter a dragon, least of all Sir Thaddeus Osbert.

Gavin was startled by her arrival as well.

"Well now, isn't this just lovely?" the woman said warily.

The dragon did not reply.

The sorceress looked at the boy and noticed there was a sword sheathed across his back. Still, she did not recognize the blade's jewel-encrusted hilt.

"Why are you here?" Agnes demanded.

Thaddeus yawned and then said, "To seek a peaceful resolution."

"Bah!" the witch grunted. "I seek revenge, nothing more."

"Yet you make war against the innocents?"

"Innocents? There are no innocents here."

"Even for such a powerful witch, hate has made you blind," the dragon roared, flashing his teeth.

Such a display of anger startled Gavin, but it seemed to have no effect on the mysterious woman standing before them.

Agnes stood her ground and said, "Before this day is done, history will forever be changed."

"Oh, there's no doubt of that," Thaddeus replied confidently.

Several miles away, Lamken Rune, Tabitha Bixley, Emily Scott and Bunty Digby suddenly appeared on the low hills overlooking Bodmin Moor. The air was heavy with the stench of rotting things and despair. The howling wind didn't stay very long, but moved on, as if to escape this wretched spot.

"Why must we come to such a sorrowful place?" Emily asked quietly.

"It is here that the past and present and future must meet," Lamken announced. "Bodmin Moor holds the key to ages unimagined. We are just in time."

"In time for what, sir?" Bunty asked.

"In time to prevent evil from grasping more than just a foothold on our dear English soil, my lad," the wizard answered. "Here is where the forces of light will battle the forces of darkness, as has happened so many times before."

24

Secret of the Dragon's Claw

Cornwall was a land of granite, tin and historic legends. The flag of Cornwall, with a white cross on a black background, represented the tin embedded in the rock, and was known as St. Piran's Cross, after the patron saint of Cornwall. Never fully colonized by the Romans, much of Cornwall was still wild moorland, unsuitable for cultivation.

On this wild plain of Bodmin Moor was found a most unusual site, punctuated by three stone circles close together. They lay on a north to south line, but were not the same size. Nine, seventeen, and sixteen stones respectively, they were carefully erected so that they all appeared the same height.

Uncommonly, the stones of the central circle were smoothed by hammering, the crystals from the breakages being spread over the interior of the central circle. The tallest stones were at the south in the two northernmost circles.

The wind rushed by, whistling and howling, as if demons were trapped within the currents of air. Bodmin Moor was stirring with activity, though none of it was tangible. In the midst of the swirling mists and eerie bogs, Thaddeus Osbert and Gavin Kane stood facing an unwelcome visitor, the blackest witch.

"Your spells have great power," the dragon said. "Why not use them for the benefit of mankind?"

The evil woman sneered and said, "You can't be serious?"

"Evil will only beget more evil," the dragon said. "Surely you know that by now."

"Why should I care?" she screamed. "They burned me at the stake!"

Sir Osbert was well aware of her personal tragedy. Such cruelty was committed in the name of justice and righteousness. There was no denying that humans were capable of great wrongs.

"You cannot condemn all of humanity for those vile senseless acts," Thaddeus said. "Besides, you did more than just dabble in the black arts. Even the Grand Wizard's Council found you guilty of practicing forbidden spells."

Agnes spat. "Death be upon them all!"

The dragon shook his head. "Don't you get tired of uttering the same old ridiculous lines? You should try to think of a new delivery."

Gavin couldn't help his laughter.

"The boy dares mock me?" Agnes exclaimed, stepping forward threateningly.

"As he should, you old hag," Thaddeus growled as he stood ready to defend the boy against any attack.

The black witch screamed out her cursed rage. She lifted her arms high over her head and beckoned for the forces of darkness to come forth. The witch walked along in the dark gleefully throwing teeth over her shoulder, while an army of skeletons spring up from the ground behind her.

"Now you will face the minions of the dark ages before me," Agnes proclaimed. "Arise, my brethren, arise."

The moor shuddered, as if disturbed by an earthquake. The bog erupted and spewed forth great globs of mud and slime. As the sun suddenly turned blood red, an army of foul creatures rose up from the ground.

"Behold, you witless dragon, my army of the unliving and undead," the witch cried out. "Their ranks have swelled with the masses of murdered victims throughout the ages. Here before you stand the mightiest warriors from throughout time."

Gavin could see her words were not exaggeration, for the long-dead carcasses standing behind the witch represented a variety of historic peoples, from Pictish barbarians to Roman legions. Their tattered and rotting banners flapped in the wind, while rusting swords hung about skeletal waists.

Thaddeus shook his head in disgust and bellowed, "Oh, bloody hell, here we go again. Take one egotistical witch with some marginally impressive magical skills, give her ridiculous robes and an equally silly maniacal laugh, throw in an army of mindless morons and we're supposed to shudder in fear."

The witch's face twisted in rage. "My forces will sweep your pitiful resistance aside and conquer all of this wretched island."

Thaddeus sighed. "Please. One despot after another has been saying that for centuries. Will you foolishly join the list of failed attempts to bring

England to her knees? Be it known that nothing so dramatic or violent shall bring an end to my glorious Briton. Her importance in the world will fade from lack of interest. The sun will not set on the British Empire because of war, but because the lack thereof."

Of course, the dragon's insight into the future did nothing to dispel the witch's delusions of grandeur.

"Kill them," she cried out. "Kill all of them! Let none survive."

Gavin looked up at Thaddeus. "I think she's mad at us now."

"So it would seem," the dragon chuckled. "Let's just ignore her raving lunacy and join your friends on that distant hill."

Sir Osbert picked up Gavin and placed him on his shoulder, before lumbering up the hill to join the others. A vast army of the dead was drawn up across the entire breadth of Bodmin Moor, the ranks assuming the battle formations of ancient times. They would use terror and fear to their advantage, creating panic throughout the land.

"I never imagined such hopelessness existed," Emily said as they looked out across the bogs and lowlands.

Tabitha took the teenaged girl's hand in hers. "We will set them free today. Goodness will make a difference, for all those who seek it."

Emily looked at the woman standing beside her in a different light just then. She interlocked her fingers with Tabitha's and squeezed.

The typical army of undead was made up of a wall of rotting corpses slowly shambling forward in mindless ranks, all at the whim of some fanatically evil leader. This time, however, the invading force was also bolstered by wights, devourers, and mohrgs, all highly intelligent creatures. Their shields caught the twinkling moonlight, swords and axes glimmering, skeletal faces glaring.

The undead were a walking plague. Their strength was derived literally from any human weakness, such as greed, hate, jealousy or lust. Skeletal spell-casters were sent ahead to soften up their opponents with hexes, diseases, and insanity.

Mounted on terrible skeletal steeds, armored knights sat waiting for the signal to charge. Rows upon rows of soldiers were prepared to die once again, without understanding why. They were incapable of rational thinking or feeling emotions, only able to obey magical commands.

"Onward!" Agnes shouted, pointing in the direction of the hill.

As one, the army of soulless forms moved out. Shields and bucklers creaked, swords clanged and spears clattered. The stomp-stomp, shuffle-shuffle, of hundreds of feet echoed across the bog and Bunty shivered.

"The wicked creatures of the grave are always seeking portals to the material plane of this earth," Tabitha explained to the gathered group. "Then they send the armies of the condemned through to harvest the living."

"It sounds like a train coming ever closer," Emily commented, her voice shaking with fear.

Thaddeus suddenly realized the advancing forces were being used as a distraction. For as soon as the formations of haunted warriors began marching forward to battle, Agnes scurried away towards a nearby stand of stone monoliths.

"Gavin, to me," the dragon roared.

The boy ran to him, kneeling. "What is thy bidding, Sir Osbert?"

Thaddeus smiled, for Gavin's words, though ancient in flavor, flowed from his lips as if he had uttered them a thousand times through the ages. "This attack is only a feint, meant to draw our attention away from the witch's true intentions. Use *Caladfwlch* to disperse those mindless ruffians and then join us by the *Hurlers*."

The dragon pointed to the distant rock formations.

"I shall do as you command, Sir Osbert," Gavin said.

"The witch has made her headquarters amongst those stones," Thaddeus continued. "I fear she conjures something more diabolical than previously imagined."

Gavin bowed deeply.

"Do not pay homage to me, lad," Thaddeus said. "You are Gavin Kane, Protector of the Blade and Guardian of the Lake."

The teenaged boy unsheathed *Caladfwlch*.

"Before you go, hack off one of my claws," Thaddeus commanded.

"I will not!" Gavin protested.

"It will grow back," the dragon reassured him. "You will have need of it."

The teen took a step back and chopped downward with all his strength. Whack!

Gavin picked up the severed talon and held it up to Thaddeus.

The dragon grinned. "Now place my claw inside your belt."

Gain obeyed without hesitation.

"Head directly into their midst and destroy them," Thaddeus instructed. "Do not doubt nor fear, for wondrous power you shall behold."

The boy turned and slowly began walking towards the ranks of undead. His hands trembled with uncertainty, as he pointed the mighty sword out in front of him.

"Where is he going?" Emily asked.

"To fulfill yet another step along the journey of his destiny, lass," the dragon replied. "Do not worry after him, for he is protected by dragon magic."

As Gavin marched forward, a bolt of green lightning from the clouds above him, hit the teen right at the beltline. Intense cobalt light surrounded him and in a burst of brilliance, he was instantly transformed. Instead of the simple clothes of a teenager from Cornwall, the boy was now encased in dragonscale armor. The enchanted material reflected a thousand rainbow sparkles from its polished surface, glowing with the power of Sir Osbert's magic.

Thaddeus looked down at Emily and smiled. "See what I mean?"

Gavin was no longer afraid, but was filled with enough courage to come face-to-face with Britain's legendary past. Confidently the boy wielded Arthur's enchanted blade, extending the tip outward towards the advancing army. *Caladfwlch* began to quiver and shimmer with pulsating blue light.

With shields on their left, ancient armies tended to lean to the right as they marched, so each man could cover his unprotected side with the shield beside him. In this manner, the opposing force instinctively favored their right, making them vulnerable to attack from the left flank.

Gavin had no recollection of how he knew the art of ancient combat, but he instantly understood where to concentrate his attack.

Sword fighting was often viewed as consisting strictly of brute force and ferocity, without style or tactics. Gavin believed that such opinions were highly inaccurate. Anyone who thought the medieval sword and shield were just slash-and-hack weapons was greatly misinformed.

"For England, home and beauty!"

With a mighty cry, Gavin charged.

He instinctively lifted his shield and blocked a devastating blow, before pouncing forward with *Caladfwlch*. The enchanted blade cleaved through the parting ranks. Each counterattack was parried, quickly followed by other skeletons hurling their bones into Gavin.

The clashing echoes of combat reverberated across the hills.

Emily watched in complete silence, mesmerized by Gavin's courage, but praying earnestly for his safety. Was it possible that her best friend in the entire world, was also an enchanted knight from legends and myths gone by? She would have so much to write about her hero, when the day was done.

Gavin's teeth rattled with each impact, one after another. He gasped for breath, before renewing the onslaught. Glowing with deadly intent, *Caladfwlch's* continuous song of death wailed across the bog and echoed amongst the stone monoliths. The moors had not witnessed such a battle for centuries.

The enchanted sword exploded into flames, destroying the skeletons in every direction. Gavin continued his attack, parrying and dodging the enemy's thrusts as if he was a veteran of hundreds of ancient battles. He did not know where the skills came from, but they were instinctual, as if he had been born knowing how to fight.

Forcing his way towards the center of the masses, Gavin's swing shattered one skeleton after another, bones splintering and turning to dust. The weapon's powerful waves of electrical charges set fire to the peat moss at his feet. Smoke wafted up around the boy, as the blaze licked hungrily at his passing. Still, Gavin pressed on, destroying all that faced him.

As he waded into the enemy, the teen suddenly realized he was completely surrounded, skeleton warriors fifty deep to either side, front and back. They were not alive in the real sense of the living, but as bones and skeletons without human form, which could not speak, yet moved all the same. Not as humans walked, but shuffling and scraping noisily along the ground.

They were all moving in for the kill, not because they thought Gavin was easy prey, for they sensed individually they could not match the boy's determination, but because they were a mindless army. They savored the brutality, because they knew that sheer numbers were on their side.

The rows of clinking bones advanced willingly to sacrifice hundreds to his sword, in the certainty that Gavin would eventually fall to their combined might.

Their cackling laughter echoed in his ears.

"Do you think I am beaten?" Gavin shouted in defiance.

This time the sword began to glow even brighter, changing colors to throbbing prisms of red and orange. Sparks cascaded in every direction.

Thousands of clacking jaws all snapped shut simultaneously.

With all his strength, Gavin swung the enchanted sword in a circle, as *Caladfwlch* launched forth a wide array of shooting stars, which disintegrated thousands of skeletons into a million shards of shattered bone!

Even with such power in his hands, Gavin could not avoid the grasping, snatching, and clawing boney fingers that locked upon his arms and legs, pulling him down to the ground. In that moment, the teen knew true fear and it swept over him like a cold wave.

"Thaddeus!" he cried out. "Help me."

The dragon appeared within seconds, hurtling himself into the midst of undead. Sir Osbert's four foot claws were used for ripping or slashing, or for grabbing and lifting an object, in the same manner as a bird of prey. If necessary, Thaddeus could lift several hundred pounds in each claw. Heavier loads could be handled as the dragon flew over the object and snatched it using his hind legs.

Now his wing claws, on the other hand, were only used for defense, to slash at an enemy who had ventured too close. In spite of the dragon's relatively fragile wings, Thaddeus often preferred using those talons to unleash yet another secret weapon.

Deftly, the dragon retrieved Gavin from the bog and tossed him up on his shoulders. The boy landed with a thud and grunted.

At that precise moment, Thaddeus reared backwards, his wings opening wide. He growled and roared, as if in horrible pain. However, just seconds before he was overwhelmed by the mass of recovering attackers, the dragon launched his wing talons, one after another, over and over.

Zip, zip, zip, out they went.

The fusillade of claws blasted the ranks of demons into splinters, which went flying in every direction. Each time Thaddeus roared, another volley reaped a harvest of grotesque monsters. The projectiles were launched at the same rate of fire of a modern machinegun, but the dragon's aim was incredibly accurate. Add to that, each talon was propelled in a circular motion, carving and drilling through bone with the power of a rotating scythe.

Now recovered, Gavin launched himself back into the battle, slashing and hacking in every direction, using Thaddeus to protect his back. They were a devastating pair.

Zip, zip, and zip, the dragon's talons buzzed past Gavin's ears.

The boy was dumbstruck by the sheer destructive power of the dragon's attack.

As quickly as it had begun, however, the combat was over.

There was nothing but the remnants of long lost and forgotten bones. Soon, the wind carried away even the dust and all that remained were memories.

Gavin patted the dragon on the chest. "Another surprise unveiled in the nick of time, eh old friend?"

"I'm afraid that's why sugar is so important to me, Gavin," the dragon gasped for breath. "Without it, I can't regain my strength or rebuild my special powers."

"Sugar does all that for you?" the boy asked with surprise.

"Indeed it does," the dragon replied. "In fact, I've used up about a month's supply of sugar just now."

"Well, we better get you some sweets right away," Gavin suggested.

"I'm afraid we don't have time for such measures," Thaddeus said. "As much as a few scones and jam would be quite useful right now, I'm afraid the witch is just getting started."

25

Tickling the Dragon

Clear across the globe, in the southwestern United States, tremendous changes were coming to the tiny little town of Los Alamos, New Mexico. US Army General Leslie Groves, the military commander overseeing the Manhattan Project, with physicist Robert Oppenheimer, were seeking a site to build a new laboratory. Once chosen, this would be where a terrible new weapon would be designed. The greatest minds in America were gathering to develop an atomic bomb, a program the US government believed was already underway in Nazi Germany.

General Groves wanted a remote, sparsely populated site that would be safe from enemy attack, and preferably lie in a natural bowl ringed by hills that could contain any accidental explosions.

Los Alamos fit the bill perfectly.

Under the wartime imperative, the privately operated Ranch School would cease to exist. Shortly afterwards, a government-approved construction company was engaged to erect the buildings which would house the top-secret research laboratory.

THIS IS A RESTRICTED DOCUMENT

The classified memorandum described the area chosen for the secret lab.

The country is a mixture of mountain country such as you have seen in other parts of the Rockies, and the adobe-housed, picturesque, southwest desert that is famous in many Western movies.

As the project got under way, Oppenheimer felt well protected by the constant presence of G-2 Army guards. They were painfully obvious, always wearing snap-brimmed hats, straw in summer, felt in winter. They were the only men in New Mexico dressed in three-piece suits and wingtip shoes, no matter what the weather.

The green barracks sat jauntily in a sea of mud, but the main lodge was quite nice. The interior surfaces of great logs used for the construction of the building were waxed to a warm honey color. In the dining room, massive, hand-hewn vigas supported the cathedral ceiling. Wrought-iron chandeliers hung from the vigas. A fireplace, built of varicolored tuff stone, dominated the south end of the room. The five-foot logs ablaze on the hearth cast a warm glow over the scene.

The top scientists lived in the Ranch School buildings extending north from Fuller Lodge and these were the only lodgings with bathtubs, hence the name Bathtub Row. Most of the scientist's wives had to make do with showers and preparing meals on the troublesome and messy wood-burning stoves nicknamed black beauties.

Life in the desert was very patient. The seemingly endless expanse of earth and sky, in unique and mysterious ways, was intensely comforting. The glorious sunset, in red and purple, polished gold, orange, and yellow, ushered in the approaching night. As the darker shades of evening dropped into the valley, the magical landscape suddenly became inhabited with scores of nocturnal creatures.

Within this forbidding landscape was now hidden a top-secret installation, chosen for its remote location, good weather, and because the American government already owned it. Los Alamos was located in the middle of the desert, in south-central New Mexico, far from any town or curious human eyes.

There were few research projects shrouded in more mystery. Here was the home of the Manhattan Project, where work proceeded at a slow but steady pace to develop an atomic bomb. Significant technical problems had to be solved, and difficulties in the production of plutonium, particularly the inability to process large amounts, often frustrated the scientists. Nonetheless, sufficient progress had been made to persuade the scientists that their efforts might succeed. A test of the plutonium implosion device was necessary to determine if it would work and what its effects would be.

Here too was the location of Wasabi Watanabe's greatest fear. The Eastern dragon was not only aware of what was going on at the top-secret base, he also knew what the end result would be. Wasabi felt so strongly that man was hurtling towards doom that he was willing to violate any dragon law to stop them. The humans must be prevented from creating atomic energy, or Watanabe reasoned that mankind needed to be exterminated.

Yet for scientists like Robert Oppenheimer, David Bohm, Leo Szilard, Eugene Wigner, Otto Frisch, Rudolf Peierls, Felix Bloch, Niels Bohr, Emilio Segre, James Franck, Enrico Fermi, Klaus Fuchs and Edward Teller, there were no moral issues with respect to working on an atomic bomb. Everyone agreed on the necessity of stopping Hitler and the Japanese from destroying the free world. It wasn't an academic question, because these men were desperately afraid of what the future might bring, aware that friends and relatives were being killed all over the globe.

However, as time went on, certain individual opinions started to change.

J. Robert Oppenheimer was noted for his mastery of all scientific aspects of the project and for his efforts to control the inevitable cultural conflicts between scientists and the military. He was an iconic figure to his fellow scientists, as much a figurehead of what they were working towards, as a scientific director.

Oppenheimer did not direct from the head office. He was intellectually and physically present at each decisive step. He stood in the laboratory or in the seminar rooms, when a new effect was measured or when a new idea was conceived. It was not that he contributed many ideas or suggestions, which he did sometimes, but his main influence came from something else. It was his continuous and intense presence, which produced a sense of direct participation, because he created a unique atmosphere of enthusiasm and challenge that pervaded the place.

Oppenheimer was also highly educated in fields that lay outside the scientific tradition, such as his interest in religion, in the Hindu religion in particular, which resulted in a feeling of mystery of the universe that surrounded him like a fog. He saw physics clearly, looking toward what had already been done, but at the border, he tended to feel there was much more of the mysterious, so he turned away from the hard, crude methods of theoretical physics into a mystical realm of broad intuition.

Dr. Louis Slotin was one of a select group of elite scientists invited to Los Alamos to work on a project aimed at outrunning the Nazi bid to create an atomic bomb. Slotin, who specialized in critical testing applications, worked quietly beside the other great scientists.

One day he met Oppenheimer in the head scientist's office, where they struck up a casual conversation about the solar system. Each discovered the other had a deep and abiding fascination in the stars. Their discussion quickly evolved into comparisons of alternative energy sources and travel through space.

"One day, we will break the bonds of earth," Slotin said.

Oppenheimer nodded. "Soon, I think. The Germans have perfected rocket engines, or so I have been told by General Groves. Such propulsion will lift a trajectory into space."

Slotin suddenly spotted a beautifully bound book on Oppenheimer's desk.

The volume's cover was very ornamental, with illustrations of red dragons spouting blue fire, Latin inscriptions and archaic rune calligraphy, all in the style of classical astronomy texts. The expensive leather binding was soft and supple to the touch, each page gilded with gold.

"Wherever did you get this?" asked Dr. Slotin, carefully flipping the pages.

"It was a gift, from an eccentric old British radar specialist I met years ago in London," Oppenheimer replied. "Dr. Lamken Rune advised me to refer to it on occasion, to keep my feet planted firmly on the ground, while gazing into the heavens."

"Good advice, I imagine," Dr. Slotin said.

"Dr. Rune also believed in dragons and heard voices in his head, which certainly made him crazy in some men's eyes," Oppenheimer added. "I guess that's why I liked him so much."

Both men laughed.

It was then that Dr. Oppenheimer's expression altered dramatically.

What is it, Robert?" Slotin asked with concern.

"I also recall that Dr. Rune warned me about accepted scientific methodology," the great scientist said quietly. "He was convinced that one day, in our attempt to replace God, we would go too far."

Slotin chuckled uncomfortably. "Well, you did say he was crazy."

Dr. Oppenheimer looked at his watch. "Yes, indeed. Well, it's time to go witness Otto's presentation. It sounds like he's onto something big."

The two of them casually walked to the Lodge.

It was at this session that Robert Otto Frisch suggested a dangerous experiment, allowing the Los Alamos group to get as near as possible towards starting an atomic explosion, without actually being blown up. It required an arrangement of Uranium-235 that would actually explode, but left a big hole in its center so that it wouldn't. The missing portion, a plug made exactly the right shape to fit the hole, was then dropped through the sample. The arrangement would become critical, but then the plug would fall out the other side, and the reaction would abate. It would provide valuable information about chain reactions.

Before actually conducting this phase, however, the experiment had to be approved by the entire committee. After Frisch presented his theories, one of his colleagues commented, "Sounds like we'll be tickling the tail of a sleeping dragon?"

Frisch replied, "In that case, remember, when tickling the tail of a sleeping dragon, you stand a chance of getting roasted!"

Everyone in the room laughed, even though the humor was tinged with a note of discomfort.

One hour later, after everyone voted, the experiment was unanimously approved.

It was thereafter known as the *Dragon Experiment*.

A refined version of the test involved bringing together two hemispheres of plutonium and uranium as critically close as possible, without starting a chain reaction. Its purpose was to observe the blue glow, which verified that the plutonium core of an atomic bomb was the right size to sustain the chain reaction among atomic particles, which would then cause an explosion.

As so many times before, the team gathered in the laboratory to perform the experiment, which created the beginning of a fission reaction. The trick was to bring the hemispheres close enough together, without allowing them to touch.

Dr. Slotin regularly pushed the hemispheres together, until they were close enough to produce the beginning of a chain reaction, which they detected by the blue glow set up in the air around the hemispheres. Then he pushed the hemispheres apart with screwdrivers.

However, catastrophe struck that fateful day. After successfully conducting this procedure dozens of times before, the screwdriver slipped and the experiment went critical, generating a vast flux of radiation. Instantly a glow, brighter than sunshine, filled the laboratory. Slotin and those present understood, all too well, what had just happened.

Slotin's reaction was to use his hands to separate the hemispheres. His body shielded the others from the neutrons that emanated from the plutonium. While the results would prove fatal to him, he was credited with saving the other seven scientists from an agonizing death.

Nine days later, Dr. Slotin died from the damage done to his body due to ionizing particles and the intense heat of uncontrolled pure energy.

In Iceland, this man-made accident had incredible repercussions within the dragon community. Up to this point, many dragons had been willing to let man solve his own problems, no matter what the outcome. Now, with human scientists tampering with the building blocks of the universe, many voices were calling for direct intervention.

Surprisingly, Korban Vex was not among them. While he had no love for humans, he feared a world without them. What's more, over the past several months, he was far more worried about the motivation of an Eastern dragon named Wasabi Watanabe.

26

Drawn to Death

Himmler's black dragon soared overhead, unseen, but circling his prey until the right moment presented itself. *Black Wing* prowled the skies over the doomed village of Lidice in Czechoslovakia, waiting to be unleashed.

How much longer must he wait to strike?

Hundreds of German security police surrounded the village, blocking all avenues of escape. The Nazis had chosen Lidice, because the residents were openly hostile to the occupation and were suspected of harboring local resistance partisans.

The entire population was rounded up, and all men over fifteen years of age were put in a barn and summarily shot. The women and children were shipped off to various concentration camps.

Once the village was emptied of every living soul, the dragon swooped down, breathing huge gouts of flame that incinerated rows of hamlets, consuming everything. When only charred ash and embers remained, Lidice was razed and bulldozed, leaving no trace it had ever existed. The black dragon settled upon the barren ground and savored death, absorbing all the energy that once had been life.

Such was the price innocent people paid for the death of Reinhard Heydrich.

Yet Heydrich's assassination was not simply the removal of a high-ranking and vicious Nazi official. It accomplished something that no human could foresee, by severing the link between the most evil man on earth and the foulest forces outside of earth. Mankind would never know how close the margin had been. The war would continue and millions more would die, but humanity had been spared the ultimate annihilation that might have been.

Out on Bodmin Moor, Thaddeus experienced this horrible event, as it wrenched his soul and knew that one day he must face all the abominations the Nazis were creating. Such a conflict would only have one outcome, but Sir Osbert preferred not to dwell on the negative.

To vanquish the dark witch was his only responsibility just then.

Lamken Rune wasn't too fond of anyone who brought harm to the natural order of things either. However, the wizard was also pragmatic. He would be willing to sacrifice his own life, if there was something to gain, but not if his death only delayed the inevitable.

Near the tiny village of Minions, once prosperous from copper mining, but reduced to a scattering of houses, was the Bronze Age stone temple known as *The Hurlers*. Old tradition that the circles were men turned to stone. The neighboring inhabitants termed them *Hurlers*, as being by devout and godly error persuaded that they had been men sometime transformed into stones, for profaning the Lord's Day with hurling the ball.

From inside this Megalithic portal, Agnes Olmanns had plotted the destruction and eventual enslavement of Britain. Joining the witch were thousands of England's lost souls. Their ranks were filled with the spirits of the condemned and unfortunate victims of historical executions throughout the ages. Gaunt reflections of men and women alike had gathered at this place. Their final memories were that of the gallows noose, the block and axe, firing squad, or even the burning fires at the stake. Lives had ended in misery and suffering, so when Agnes promised them retribution, these wandering ghosts answered her call.

"Who is that coming towards us?" the old man asked.

"Agnes Olmanns," Tabitha replied. "The witch was unsuccessful at halting the power of my revealing spells. At present she is invisible, so I can't be perfectly certain, but evil always smells the same."

"If it is her, she's likely to be quite angry that Gavin and Thaddeus destroyed her little pet army," Rune remarked.

"You must challenge the black witch to a formal duel," Tabitha announced. "Now that you have Elizabeth again, you can best her and the forces of the rift would be temporarily leaderless. Thaddeus can fight the black dragon while they are disorganized."

"What if the witch kills Dr. Rune?" Bunty demanded, appalled that Tabitha was suggesting the wizard should take such risks.

"It's a chance I'm willing to take," Lamken said. "I refuse to sit here watching the old hag make a mess of my dear England."

"What if she overpowers you?" Bunty asked.

"Please." The wizard's ego swelled.

"Master, you must prepare for any possibility," Tabitha warned. "The witch may have made an alliance with…"

"Just another risk I have to take," Rune interrupted her.

"He keeps offering to throw himself into danger to protect the rest of us," Bunty protested. "I, for one, am not going to let him do that alone!"

The wizard smiled at the red-haired boy and patted him on the shoulder. "You'll be at my side when we take her together, lad!"

"Remember, Master, that Agnes is stronger than any spell-caster you've ever encountered," Tabitha reminded Rune.

As Thaddeus and Gavin joined them, the dragon firmly stated his opinion. "The wizard must face her alone."

"Why, Sir Osbert?" Bunty wondered.

The dragon tried to explain, saying, "The black witch will accept the duel, because only Lamken has the ability to defeat her. Since her army of undead failed, she will call allies from beyond the rift, far more dangerous indeed. Besides, there's no one else. We are all that stands between that witch and the total destruction of Great Britain. We must stop her here or humanity will be forfeit."

Bunty looked up at Rune and started to protest once again. "What are you supposed to do against her?"

"Don't you see, Bunty, it's our only hope," Emily argued.

Thaddeus added, "If Lamken fails, the rest of us will engage her. Our chances won't be good, but if the wizard can't win, we're dead anyway, one way or another."

"Well, in that case, I'm sure to win," Lamken announced confidently. "I do my best work when it's a matter of life or death."

Bunty reached out and took the wizard's hand. "Please, sir, be careful." Then, he threw his arms around Lamken and sobbed, "I love you. Please don't die."

Rune knelt down before the boy and looked him straight in the eye. "Don't worry, lad. Because of you, I have found my Elizabeth and rediscovered love and friendship and loyalty. I do not intend to allow that old witch to take those things away from me. Besides, now that you're my chosen successor, I must provide a proper example and that requires victory."

Rune stood up. He winked at Thaddeus and cast an invisibility spell, before vanishing.

When the wizard reappeared, he was standing before the black witch.

Even though startled by his sudden arrival, Agnes surrounded herself with powerful magic. Holding up her left hand, she said, "Greetings, disgraced and fallen wizard."

"Is it really you, Morgause?" Rune asked, surprised by his own discovery. "I see you are doing quite well for yourself, in spite of our past encounters."

"So, you have uncovered my true spirit after all," the sister of Morgan le Fay replied, her voice full of feigned sweetness. "I knew we would meet again one day. Our last encounter was hasty and unresolved, leaving unfinished business."

"Who am I to disappoint?" Lamken asked sarcastically, knowing full well that Morgause would now accept his challenge.

The desire to kill him burned darkly in the witch's eyes.

Morgause looked past the wizard's shoulder. "Where are your little friends?"

"They're around here somewhere," Rune replied.

"Did you leave them with that ridiculous dragon?" Morgause chuckled. "You should pray I don't consume them as well."

"I haven't prayed in years, Morgause, but since you've suggested it, I don't mind if I do," Lamken responded agreeably. "Dear Lord…"

The witch interrupted him. "I have no time for this! Have you come to surrender?"

"Not bloody likely!" the wizard said.

"Is that a challenge I hear?"

Rune nodded. "I hereby invite you to partake in a formal wizard duel, without certain binding rules and regulations, to the death."

The rules for formal mage duels were really quite simple. One wizard would cast a spell and then the other would counter. Both would take a moment to recover and the order would flip-flop, until one or the other succumbed.

Sanctioned duels seldom ended in death, but such was not the case this time. Both combatants knew the fate of the world rested in their hands.

"Where is your wand?" Morgause cackled, instantly aware that Lamken was unarmed.

"Eons ago, some silly fool claimed that wizards could only fight with wands and suddenly it became accepted practice," Rune complained. "It's all poppycock."

Morgause couldn't help but smile, even if it was an evil expression of mirth.

She took a defiant stance and pointed her wand at the wizard's head. "What chance have you against me, you stupid, absent-minded, drunken old lout?"

Lamken put one hand on his chest. "Who's stupid?"

With a flair for drama, an ancient staff came out from behind his back.

Morgause took a violent step backwards, startled by this revelation. However, before she reacted in haste, her eyes narrowed to mere slits. First studying the staff and then the man, the witch came to an interesting conclusion.

She said, "Don't try your ridiculous parlor tricks on me. I know for a fact that Elizabeth was taken from you and destroyed by the Black Moot of Salisbury Plain."

"Just how would you know that, pray tell?" Lamken demanded, raising his hands over his head, the staff quivering with powerful vibrations.

Suddenly, the wizard began to physically change, his hair and beard turning as white as snow and his common clothes replaced by a splendid robe of shimmering blue satin. This spectacular transformation enthralled and captivated his audience. There was no doubt that great magic had been revealed.

At last released from centuries of bondage, the single greatest wizard in history was once again able to wield his incredibly powerful magic. He reveled in his freedom, aware that Bunty's love and Tabitha's loyalty had shattered the prison that held him for so long.

"Who is that?" Emily exclaimed. "What happened to Dr. Rune?"

Thaddeus answered. "He is still there, lass. It is his true self before you, the greatest wizard of all time. For Myrddin has returned!"

"Who is Myrddin?" Bunty asked.

The dragon grinned. "Oh, that's right, you would know him as Merlin!"

The teens were dumbstruck by this startling news.

Very slowly, however, Bunty sprouted a gigantic grin. "That's right."

Myrddin began the duel with a blast of energy from Elizabeth. The searing bolt was simply a display of power, nothing more, but Myrddin wanted to start with something grand and colorful. Besides, it was a neat little trick to uncover his foe's strengths. With a thunderous explosion, the bolt of pure energy streaked from the staff, arcing with lightning speed straight for Morgause's chest.

The witch merely raised her left hand and spoke a single word.

"*Dispendare!*"

The blazing energy simply vanished!

Both wizards took a breath, before Morgause began her own spell.

She recognized the wizard's strategy, but she had one of her own, by using overwhelming negative power. The witch hurled a potent spell, summoning forth the blackest magic. An aura of death and destruction surrounded her, as darkness flowed in and out of her body, while summoning her attack. Morgause's hands thrust out, sending forth waves of eerie green spirits, a form of death magic aimed at crushing the wizard's life force.

Myrddin quickly cast his defense. It was as if one thousand orchestras began to play, as the musical notes of Beethoven's 9th Symphony surrounded the wizard, instantly overwhelming the power of the witch's attack.

Myrddin's unusual counter-spell had succeeded.

He closed his eyes and conversed with Elizabeth.

"Morgause will anticipate my every move," he whispered.

"Yet the witch still fears you," the staff replied. "She will call on the blackest magic to defeat you. That will be her downfall in the end."

"How will we defeat her, dearest Elizabeth?"

The staff pondered the question for a brief moment, before replying, "When the time comes, you must trust me implicitly. Do you trust me?"

Myrddin smiled. "With my very life."

"It may come to that."

"So be it."

Myrddin suddenly pointed Elizabeth at Morgause. The staff emitted a rapid series of huge red hearts, pulsing with the power of love. They swerved back and forth, up and down, zigzagging in a complicated pattern known only to Elizabeth. It was highly doubtful the witch could defend against their random route. On impact, the spheres would be absorbed into Morgause's body and saturate her soul with forgiveness.

The sorceress reacted desperately, hurling her own defensive magic to counterstrike the attack. With perfectly accurate aim, her black orbs of despair collided with the red hearts, disintegrating them in fiery detonations. Morgause immediately began her next spell, casting a spinning vortex of purple and black negative energy. If this magic struck the wizard, he would forever be consumed.

Yet once again, Myrddin countered this attack with a spring shower.

The rivals threw themselves into each and every spell, with only a slight pause for rest and evaluation. Morgause tried to turn Myrddin's powers against him, by reflecting his energy back at him, but he merely blocked each counterattack.

This conflict continued for hours.

However, the increasing power of each spell was obvious to the spectators.

Shockwaves rippled through the air.

There was no doubt that each adversary was skilled and determined to win.

Gavin, Bunty and Emily were mesmerized, watching the duel unfold. They had witnessed Morgause's powers earlier, but seeing the full extent horrified them. As the duel progressed, the witch was joined by all manner of grotesque creatures from beyond the rift, horrible manifestations from the collective nightmares of humanity. These beasts viewed the conflict with mindless detachment. In contrast, Tabitha was kneeling in meditation, her forehead covered in the sweat of her spiritual endeavors. She felt her faith would aid the wizard in ways unimaginable.

"Is Merlin winning?" Bunty asked worriedly.

"I don't know," Emily replied. "Why can't you help him, Sir Osbert?"

The dragon sighed. "I have no strength left, I'm afraid. Without massive amounts of sugar, my secret powers won't return for days."

Just then, Gavin noticed that something was different, as if Merlin's confidence was ebbing way. The air surrounding them felt cold and unforgiving.

Had the tide of battle turned?

The concentration required to dispel Morgause's attacks was starting to strain the old man's features, while he still uttered colorful banter after each exchange.

Shattered by the mystical and magical combat before them, it's little wonder that no one noticed when Thaddeus invoked his invisibility cloaking and quietly slipped away.

"What's the matter, Morgause?" Myrddin snickered. "Have you run out of tricks?"

The witch sneered, "Fool, I will defeat you!"

She cast another spell.

This time it was a wave of black scorpions that covered the ground.

Myrddin jumped back and with a stylistic motion, flung the wicked insects aside.

Morgause looked bored.

She yawned and chanted another archaic spell.

Hundreds of carpenter nails came raining down from the sky.

Myrddin deflected the deadly shower with millions of hammers, which sent the sharp projectiles sailing back from where they came from. Upon hitting the outer atmosphere, they exploded like fireworks.

Merlin sighed with reluctant respect.

"Damn, woman, you're bloody magnificent," he loudly pronounced.

The witch politely bowed and countered with, "Why, thank you. You're not too bad yourself, old man. Perhaps you might consider throwing your lot in with me. The Nazis will win this war and we can reap the benefits."

Myrddin shook his head. "What utter nonsense! Those blithering idiots couldn't find the loo, even with a map. You've thrown in with losers."

Morgause didn't get angry. Instead, she frowned, as if something he said suddenly made sense. Perhaps that possibility changed the outcome of the duel.

Without warning, the witch sent forth her final spell, one saturated with vilest evil and darkest intent. "*Envelopous Infinitium!*"

As the seething, rancid, immoral force came hurtling towards him, Myrddin chanted the magical incantations to raise a barrier of light and goodness. It was the only defense that made any sense.

Unfortunately, at that critical moment, Elizabeth couldn't retrieve the energy necessary to invoke the spell. The death-force surged forward and there was nothing that could stop it.

Nothing.

Myrddin was standing there in his magical pose, hands before him, when his power eluded him.

Kaboom!

"No!" Bunty cried out.

Emily burst into tears and Gavin was too horrified to utter a sound.

Lamken Rune looked down in shock and realized that most of his body had been disintegrated. Only some unknown force was keeping him elevated. Fingers, which could no longer feel, released the staff and Elizabeth fell to the ground, her central crystal shattering into a million particles.

The wizard turned and looked up the hill, to lock eyes on the red-haired boy.

Then he died.

Bunty staggered forward in a daze. Tabitha quickly grabbed him, restraining the boy as he collapsed in hysterical sobs of grief. Emily reached out to take Gavin's hand, but her best friend was looking elsewhere and he had the strangest look on his face.

To her horror, Gavin Kane was actually smiling.

Befuddled by his unusual behavior, Emily looked in the same direction.

Morgause had been near exhaustion herself, but was still capable of realizing the significance of her victory. She raised her hands over her head in a signal of superiority and her minions screamed revolting cries of obedience and celebration.

"Excuse me," a loud booming voice spoke from behind her.

The black witch spun around.

Chomp!

Most of the witnesses later agreed that Morgause's demise by the voracious appetite of Sir Thaddeus Osbert was far less cruel than being burned at the stake. Still, it probably came as a bit of a surprise to be eaten by a dragon.

With a sense of timing that verged on miraculous, Merlin the Magician had created a magical slight-of-hand. Elizabeth had been instrumental, of course, for it was her power that made the trick work so effectively. With the invisible Thaddeus stepping in front of Morgause's deathblow, his scales took the full brunt of the impact, deflecting the spell. While that was taking place, Elizabeth projected the image of Myrddin being destroyed. It was all just smoke and mirrors.

"Look!" Tabitha called out. "Myrddin lives."

Bunty's mouth opened with elated surprise, but before a word escaped, he squirmed loose and sprinted down the hill towards Thaddeus, who was no longer cloaked. There, sitting high on the dragon's shoulder, sat Lamken Rune, or was it Myrddin, or Merlin? By any name, he was a wizard extraordinaire. Tightly clutched in both hands, he held the real Elizabeth. When the old man saw Bunty running toward him, the sorcerer dismounted, just in time to brace himself for the impact of the red-haired boy's mighty collision.

"Oof," Myrddin grunted. "You hit harder than any old witch!"

With Gavin and Emily in tow, Tabitha soon joined them.

What had become of the forces from beyond the grave?

They were nothing more than dark memories, perhaps spoken of only in outlawed books, local legends, or carried by the whispers of the unseen. Off in the distance, something inhuman howled, a mournful cry to mark the passing.

"Are you really Merlin, the most famous wizard in the entire universe?" Bunty asked in total amazement.

"I think I am, chum," the wizard replied hesitantly. "I've been imprisoned in stasis for hundreds of years and only set free by your friendship, trust, and love."

Bunty's eyes were wide with wonder.

Then he hugged the old man again.

Myrddin held the red-haired boy very close. The wizard looked over at Tabitha, who was smiling broadly. "I seem to have been forgiven after all."

"Yes, Master, you are free at last," she said. "Welcome back to the living."

Thaddeus rumbled up to stand over them. He winked at Gavin and flashed a mouthful of grinning teeth.

Then, quite unexpectedly, the dragon let loose an enormous belch.

"Thaddeus Osbert!" Emily exclaimed. "You should be ashamed."

"Excuse me," Sir Osbert said sheepishly. "I'm afraid I've eaten something that doesn't quite agree with my digestive system."

In spite of the macabre statement, everyone laughed.

"Good old Thaddeus," Gavin said as he scratched behind the dragon's ear.

Sir Osbert closed his eyes and purred, his grumbling growl music to everyone's ears.

Emily took Gavin's hand. "I'm so proud of you. You were so brave."

He blushed. "I was just doing what Thaddeus asked."

Merlin stepped forward and offered his hand to Gavin. "Not since Arthur was king, has anyone wielded that sword so bravely. May I?"

Gavin handed over *Caladfwlch*.

"Kneel, son," Merlin commanded.

The teen did so, surrounded by his friends.

The wizard tapped Gavin on his shoulders with the flat of the enchanted sword. "With the power invested in me by King Arthur, I formally declare you a Knight of the Round Table in the eyes of God. Rise, Sir Gavin Kane."

Thaddeus opened wide his great mouth, flashed his many sharp teeth and let loose a mighty roar, lifting his head skyward so that all might hear his proclamation. The sound of his triumphant bellowing carried through time and space, echoing in the minds, hearts and souls of all living things everywhere.

Even in far off Iceland, his fellow dragons knew that something monumental had just occurred. Every magical creature, in every land, stopped and listened as the news was carried on the wind, whispered from one to another, and pronounced to all that believed in the realms of fantastical wonder.

Emily and Bunty cheered.

Merlin grinned. "Well, that turned out quite nicely."

"We must be going, Master," Tabitha whispered to him. "The High Moot is calling the entire membership together for an emergency meeting. Your reappearance is having the same impact as an earthquake."

"Mustn't keep them waiting, what," Merlin chuckled.

"I must escort Myrddin to appear before our elders," Tabitha informed everyone. "There is much to be determined."

"Will Dr. Rune, I mean Merlin, be all right?" Emily asked.

Tabitha gave the teenaged girl's hand a squeeze. "He is the greatest wizard in all of history. I think he'll be just fine, once he's had a nice hot cuppa tea."

The sorceress stepped over to stand beside the former Dr. Lamken Rune. She whispered something in his ear. Myrddin turned and looked at Emily, then smiled warmly.

Looking down at Bunty, the wizard said, "It is time for me to go, son."

"No, please don't go," Bunty protested.

"Don't be sad, my lad, for I shall return," the old man said.

"Do you promise?"

"I do indeed."

Reluctantly, Bunty let go of the wizard's hand. "Please take care."

Myrddin smiled with abiding regard for the boy. "I will, Byron Digby. Your true heart has freed me from centuries of bondage."

The red-haired boy grinned from ear-to-ear.

With a chuckle, Myrddin took Tabitha's hand and they began walking towards the center of the Megalithic circle of stones.

"Goodbye," Emily called after them, waving.

Myrddin commented, "I think she is blessed with many gifts indeed."

"I shall cast a Circle of Protection to safeguard her," Tabitha promised.

The wizard affectionately patted his assistant's wrist. "You are an apprentice no longer, lass. I pronounce you Sorceress Tabitha, by the powers vested in me from the High Moot."

The young woman was speechless. Tears filled her eyes and she bowed before him.

"Rise, Tabitha, rise," he said. "You have wedding plans to complete, while I go forth to speak to the Grand Council on what I have learned these many years away. Truly, they had no inkling of what befell me before, or what has happened to me since. Powerful magic has restrained me for centuries and the members must be made aware of what is happening within their ranks."

"Shall we go before the High Moot now?" Tabitha asked.

"Might as well get it over with," Merlin replied.

Then, in a puff of lavender smoke, the two of them simply vanished.

Gavin looked up at Thaddeus. "That was a pretty neat trick, you old dragon."

Sir Osbert grinned. "Yes, it seemed to work exceptionally well. Now I will fly the three of you to Boscastle, but then I must continue on, for I have been summoned."

Gavin was worried. "Will you be in trouble with your fellow dragons again?"

Thaddeus chuckled. "Oh, undoubtedly, but this time I go to give witness on Merlin's behalf before the gathering of wizards."

"I must go with you!" Bunty said emphatically.

Sir Osbert placed a gentle talon upon the red-haired boy's shoulder. "Do not concern yourself with the outcome. It does not benefit wizards to argue with me, for I am a most unruly dragon when angered."

"I don't care about that," Bunty said stubbornly. "He is my friend."

Sir Osbert studied the boy's face, and then shrugged. "Oh, I don't see any harm. What are they bloody well going to do about it anyway?"

The trio cheered.

"Climb aboard then," Thaddeus beckoned. "I'm late as it is."

The teens scampered up the creature's spiny back, taking their places behind lifted scales. Once settled, they patted their dragon friend on the head.

"Here we go," the dragon roared. "Hang on tight."

A lovely village on the edge of the Cotswold escarpment, Long Compton featured several medieval thatched cottages, a 13th century church, and a two-story half-timbered lych gate. It was a quiet place, once steeped in the history of witchcraft, but now peaceful and silent.

Merlin and Tabitha suddenly appeared from a purple cloud of smoke, to stand near the parish church of *St. Peter and St. Paul.* From nowhere a sprightly breeze arrived to disperse the wisps of magic and then it was gone.

"Whenever I have visited Long Compton, it's always sunny," Merlin proclaimed. "I'm not certain what conclusion I should arrive at from that fact, but I enjoy coming around the bend in the road and seeing the valley lit up before me, with golden sunlight warming my very soul."

"Aye, tis a wonderful place, indeed, now that the curse is lifted," Tabitha said.

The village itself stretched along the road a fair distance. A short walk from the church brought the pair to the rectory, which was a very attractive Georgian building.

Tabitha sighed.

"What is it, child?" the wizard asked.

"You know what the mortals used to say about this place," she replied.

Merlin nodded. "Yes, they claimed there were enough witches in Long Compton to draw a load of hay up Long Compton Hill."

The pair was no longer alone, suddenly approached by a very elderly woman, whose hair was whiter than freshly falling snow.

The old lady smiled and said, "They are expecting you."

Merlin tapped his forehead with the crystal end of Elizabeth. "Where?"

"Avebury, of course," she replied.

"But, of course," the great wizard said. "The very place I betrayed Sir Osbert so many years ago."

"The dragon has been summoned once again," Tabitha pointed out.

"Yes, but the outcome will be decidedly different this time."

"There are some who will not welcome this change in power."

"Indeed."

Purposeful and enduring they stood, three circles of standing stones, along with the bumps, barrows, tors, cairns, caves, humps, hollows and hills that marked the countryside.

There were 19 stones, waist-high, in the round, and near the center a tilted monolith was angled on its skyward face. Leaning against this gigantic slab was an equally enormous red dragon, smiling from ear-to-ear and in the company of three mortal youths who waved.

Merlin couldn't help but laugh. "The last time I felt this happy was when I visited this place as a handsome young man, gazing towards the point on the horizon where Arthur stood before Druids, Saxons and Britons, to declare this land England."

Tabitha was not so certain it was yet time to celebrate.

For within the center of the stones, within the towering invisible walls, all the wizards and witches of England had gathered, to hold council at the Temple of Avebury. It had been hundreds of years since the entire membership had so met. In fact, Thaddeus Osbert and Myrddin had attended that last meeting too.

In one quarter-section of the throng, the magical members were all clad in red and purple. In another, all were attired in white. In the third segment the robes glistened with majestic golden hues, while in the final rear portion, sight would have only perceived blackness, ebony indeed.

Tabitha swallowed nervously and whispered, "Not many faces seemed pleased to see you again, Master."

Merlin had noted this fact, but said, "I suppose some of them fear my return, believing that I will once again defy them. Others appear undecided, fully aware that only love, pure and honest, could have set me free from my worldly prison. This perplexes them, for they did not think me capable of such emotion."

Myrddin picked up the hem of his blue robes and approached.

Tabitha knew she must remain behind. Once the great wizard had stepped within the circles, she flanked to the left to join the newly arrived dragon and his three teenaged escorts. Emily greeted her with a warm hug.

"Thank you, dearest," Tabitha said, holding Emily close.

"What will happen now?" Bunty inquired.

"They will mumble in riddles and blabber utter nonsense for awhile," Sir Osbert answered. "Then a few of the cowards will claim that black magic has freed Merlin, which is simply ridiculous, of course. They'll argue and spout rhetoric, but when I grow bored of all their cavorting and postulating, I shall rumble on over and bloody well set them straight."

Gavin patted Thaddeus with great affection. "I bet you will, you old grump!"

A hush fell over all in attendance, as Merlin approached the members of the High Moot, whose membership were all clad in blazing red.

"Blessed be," spoke Marcus Bogdash, Chief Wizard.

"Blessed be," repeated Myrddin.

"The prophecy has been fulfilled," Bogdash went on. "The innocent love of a child has set you free?"

Merlin looked over his shoulder at Bunty. "So it would appear, Grand Wizard. It is true that no more loyal a friend has walked with me since King Arthur himself!"

The gathering was awed to silence.

Yet one unidentified voice spoke from among the black-robed wizards. "What plans do you have now, rebel, upon your return?"

Myrddin smiled and replied, "No designs for power or stature, for certain. I wish to retire, to study only the magic of peace and harmony, nothing more."

"What know thee of the evil forces at work behind this human war?" the same person demanded.

"Show thyself," Merlin requested. "So that I may see thy face."

A solitary shape detached himself from the dark throng and approached. The hood was pushed back, to reveal a strikingly handsome young man. Yet this youth was not known to Merlin.

"I am Adicus Schinagel," the wizard introduced himself.

"We have not met," Merlin said.

"This is truth," the other man said.

"What was your inquiry again?"

"What do you know of this human war?" Schinagel asked.

"I know only this, that if the humans wish to kill themselves, then so be it…"

A loud murmur from the gathering interrupted him, so that he raised his arms to bring order. Once all were quiet yet again, he continued. "Yet it is not that simple, is it? We all know that there are other-world forces behind this conflict."

"I object," called out a voice from the crowd. "What proof have you?"

The gavel pounded.

Chief Wizard Bogdash raised his hand.

Order instantly returned.

"We are losing sight of why we are gathered here today," the head wizard reminded everyone. "Myrddin has returned from his exile, the magical banishment broken and therefore we must decide on our next course of action!"

Thaddeus stirred.

Without informing his companions of his decision to intercede, Thaddeus Osbert lumbered forward, stomp-stomping his giant paws downward with extra power, causing the earth to shake. Briefly looking over his shoulder, Sir Osbert made a silly face, which made Gavin, Bunty, Emily and Tabitha all giggle with delight.

"He's such a character," Tabitha managed to say.

"He is a grand old dragon," Gavin said quietly, tears suddenly forming in his eyes.

Emily scooted closer to him and looked worried as the tears rolled down his face. "What's wrong? Why are you crying?"

"Because, one day he will leave us."

Emily wanted to object, but everyone's attention was drawn to the mighty dragon's undeniably abrupt interruption of the proceedings.

"Excuse me," Thaddeus bellowed.

"This council recognizes Sir Thaddeus Osbert," Chief Wizard Bogdash said.

The dragon cleared his throat. He looked over at Merlin and winked. Then, with theatrics not witnessed since William Shakespeare, Thaddeus stood back on his hindquarters and flashed his teeth. With bravado and a gigantic lungful of air, he roared with all his strength.

The hills shook, trees bent and the echo of the dragon's cry shattered windows for a hundred miles in every direction. Hands clapped over ears were too late to prevent the memory of his call forever etched in everyone's mind. It was frightening and majestic, awe inspiring and terrible, captivating and shattering, as the very power of the dragon's growl left no one untouched.

Whether any of them would admit it later or not, without exception, every single witch and wizard in attendance flinched. The message was quite clear, no mistaking his intent.

Still, Thaddeus felt obligated to remind them with the spoken word.

"In case any of you have forgotten over these past seven hundred years," Sir Osbert said quiet calmly. "If I was of the mind, I could incinerate every single one of you in a heartbeat!"

Chief Wizard Bogdash swallowed nervously and said, "Please, Sir Osbert, speak your mind."

The dragon bowed slightly and then said, "Centuries ago, when I was a younger dragon and not as wise as my father, I stood before this very High Moot. Scores of those witches and wizards have since died, but many yet remain. Accused of betraying his own kind, Myrddin was brought forth to face the charges. During his trial, Merlin pointed a finger at me and claimed that it was I, who had betrayed the forces of light. In your haste to see justice done, and knowing that a dragon cannot tell a lie, you assumed that the great wizard was indeed guilty and unanimously sentenced him to a life without his powers or identity. You took from him his staff and banished him to wander the land without hope. Still, there must have been just the slightest doubt, because you also cast a backup spell, which if broken, would free Myrddin from imprisonment. Only the unconditional love of a child could return the mighty wizard to his rightful place amongst his peers. So for centuries, no such event occurred and many were comforted that Myrddin would never show his face again."

"This is all known to us, Dragon," Adicus Schinagel dared to comment.

With one eye focused on the brash young wizard, Thaddeus flipped through all his special lenses, evaluating Schinagel from every angle. In a voice just above a whisper, Sir Osbert spoke only to Adicus, "Be careful, mage. For I do not take too kindly to magic that originates from Germania."

Schinagel turned pale and backed away.

"As I was saying," Thaddeus continued. "I stand before you this day, to bear witness for my friend Myrddin. Instead of investigating the circumstances of his actions, you arrived at a hasty conclusion, not from justice, but from fear. The vast majority of you were threatened by Merlin's incredible powers. Still, he has his faults and when such weaknesses were used against him, this collective body was fooled by an ingenious conspiracy."

Chief Wizard Bogdash slowly stood. "Have you proof of this, Sir Osbert?"

Thaddeus shrugged. "You did not honor the word of a dragon then, so why would you consider my words any differently now?"

The wise old wizard sighed. "I did not sit in this chair when Myrddin stood accused, Sir Osbert. I cannot undo the injustices of the past, but only attempt to make things right this time around."

"Well spoken, sir," Merlin interjected.

"Were you aware of this plot to discredit you?" Bogdash asked.

"Not until quite recently, sir," Merlin replied. "Morgause told me that the Black Moot of Salisbury Plain destroyed Elizabeth."

"As was so ordered," the chief wizard verified.

"Then explain this!" Merlin demanded as he whipped out his staff for all to see.

Incredulous, the throng was aghast at this revelation.

Very slowly, Bogdash turned to look at the leader of the Black Moot.

"How do you explain this, Adicus?"

Poof!

Adicus Schinagel disappeared in a cloud of reddish-black smoke.

Thaddeus chuckled with disdain. "It appears that the wizard world is plagued with spies, traitors and covert agents as much as the human world. Be not so quick to judge."

Bogdash raised his gavel. "Unless someone has concrete evidence to the contrary, I hereby declare Myrddin innocent of all charges and restore to him the title of Grand Sorcerer."

No one objected.

Bam, bam, bam, went the gavel.

Then a very unusual thing happened. Clear across England, the clouds all dispersed over Bodmin Moor and the bog was bathed in glorious sunlight. The warmth chased the cold winds away, as they howled from fright. The plain no longer gurgled and belched obnoxious fumes of rot and decay, but green shoots burst forth and leaves sprouted on new healthy trees. Birds sang and for the first time in years, not a single enemy plane droned overhead.

An evil apparition appeared hovered in the shadows, frightened by the light. Demonic eyes were filled with the lust for revenge and Adicus swore he would return.

Suddenly, a chilling scream stilled every living soul that heard it.

In nearby Warleggan, Damien Dwellan's body was found in a crumpled heap at the bottom of the stairs at the rectory.

There was a dreadful expression of sheer terror on his cold dead face.

Epilogue

Deep within the imposing dark walls of Schloss Wewelsburg, Reichsführer Himmler was furious. The veins popped out on his forehead as he stomped around the room, looking for the right words to convey his anger.

"I will not tolerate another setback," he vehemently shouted. "If you fear for your very lives, then you will make certain the next operation is a resounding success!"

"*Jawohl, Herr Reichsführer,*" his entire staff voiced as one.

"Prepare my dragon," Himmler ordered. "It is time for him to strike."

Doctor Schumann stepped forward bravely and said, "*Black Wing* has not returned from his mission after Lidice, *Herr Himmler.* We do not know where he has gone."

Their leader's face was contorted with panic and desperation. "My dragon is missing?"

"*Jawohl, Herr Reichsführer,*" the doctor replied.

"You must find him," Himmler screamed. "You must find my dragon, do you hear?"

"*Jawohl, Herr Reichsführer,*" everyone called out, before scattering in every direction to search for the disobedient and willful black dragon.

Heidelburg had historically entertained a long-standing and unusual love affair with dragons, unlike most parts of Europe. For much of the early Middle Ages, the German city seemed to be the very epicenter of dragon activity.

It all began when Dragon eggs were found in the Neckar River nearby. When incubated in the home and raised properly, they grew into loyal protectors of their human hosts. The dragons all had the ability to breathe fire and were especially loved by the local blacksmiths, who produced the finest steel in the region, because of their helpers.

According to legend, a few of the especially brave city residents actually became dragon riders. Other dragons were water lovers and often helped nearby fishermen.

All this pleasant interaction between the people of Heidelburg and local dragons came to a violent end, when the Christian church moved into the area and clergymen convinced the people that dragons were actually the offspring of the creatures of hell. When they were betrayed by their former friends, the surviving dragons fled to Iceland and never returned. However, many residents in Heidelburg wished the dragons would come back and annual festivals were held to commemorate this ancient friendship.

It was because of this ageless bond that *Black Wing* traveled to Heidelburg. The black dragon was seeking answers to his very existence, without understanding why the motivation even existed. The flickering spark of humanity still clouded the beast's judgment and made him vulnerable. As chance would have it, the confused beast happened upon someone who would give him shelter.

Friedrich Drachenreiter was the *Oberbürgermeister*, or mayor, of Heidelburg. He was a good little Nazi and his name, freely translated, meant dragon-rider. His ancestors were known to have believed in dragons down through the ages. In fact, his great-grandfather had organized the dragon festival each season for fifty consecutive years, before passing away.

Friedrich loved everything about *lindwurm*, which was the German word for dragons. He was devoted to the winged beasts, almost as much as he was loyal to Adolf Hitler.

The mayor was sitting in his office, deeply concerned over the recent British bombing raids against Berlin and wondering when Allied planes would strike at Heidelburg. He had organized fire-fighting details and the construction of emergency stores, while selecting the strongest buildings for shelters. What more could he do?

Suddenly, Oberbürgermeister Drachenreiter felt cold, as if all the heat had been sucked from the air. He looked out the window and gasped, falling from his chair.

There before him, sitting perched on the ledge of the window, was a dragon, black as night, with blood-red eyes peering in at him. Instead of being filled with fear, Friedrich was elated as never before.

The dragon was an answer to his prayers!

At that very moment, a B-24 Liberator bomber was the first American airplane to arrive in England, when it landed at Prestwick Airfield, in East Anglia. The incoming medium bombers, along with B-17 heavy bombers, signaled the beginning of a concerted effort by the United States to make her presence known as soon as possible. In the coming days, weeks, and months, hundreds of planes and thousands of men would make the hazardous journey across the Atlantic, to take up residence all over the British Isles.

It was such a thrilling sight to watch the American bombers streaming across the skies towards their new airfields. They passed overhead in groups, trailing cirrus trails of pure white condensation from wing tips, against the deep blue English skies.

In St. Merryn, all eyes were cast skyward, witnessing firsthand the awesome power of the United States entry into the war.

Dymchurch Bixley looked over at his daughter. "Do you believe in omens?"

Tabitha smiled. "Yes, of course I do, Father."

"Then I think we are witnessing a very good sign," he said.

On one such incoming bomber, the American copilot turned on the BBC to listen to music. The crew smiled as they passed over the eternally green countryside. Perhaps it was odd that such a tranquil-looking land was about to become the staging area for a massive bombing campaign directed at the heart of Nazi Germany.

Britain's tumultuous history had often been enshrined in stone, forever inscribed across the battlements of castles throughout the realm. It was written in blood, right or wrong, innocent or guilty, then and now. Down through the ages, from Pictish and Roman slaughters, Catholic and Protestant civil war, Saxon and Norman conquests, right up to the recent Nazi aerial bombardment, so many had died. Magnificent castle towers, surrounded by impassable moats, were now nothing more than grassy ditches, but aptly represented a people who had defended their culture through siege and conflict.

In Cornwall, which represented Britain's past association with Celtic ways, a dramatic change was in the air. The howling winds across the moors carried a message of history that few were able to translate, but none denied. There was an excited undercurrent to daily life, as Cornish citizens realized they had been invaded after all. Yet this army hadn't arrived as conquerors, but rather friends. As England had successfully endured yet another year of war, a glimmer of hope sprang from within.

Americans, by the tens of thousands, were coming to take up temporary residence in preparation for the upcoming planned invasions of the European and African continents. Cornwall, of course, was the logical place to bivouac and train these young men, who had come from distant places as varied as their names, such as San Antonio, Texas; New Ulm, Minnesota; North Platte, Nebraska; Beloit, Wisconsin; Oakland, California; Champaign, Illinois, and Camden, Maine.

As different from the British as night and day, these Americans instantly became ardent tourists, wandering through picturesque coastal villages, or taking sightseeing excursions among Arthurian ruins. They were generous to a fault, handing out candy bars and wads of cash, but with the innocence of a nation discovering her potential to make a profound difference. These Americans were spontaneous and gregarious, full of fun and unwilling to take this war too seriously. None of them knew what the future would bring, but neither were they going to spend too much time worrying about it. They were a long way from home and ready to put an end to war, once and for all. They weren't supermen, but regular Joes.

Outside the little white cottage overlooking Tintagel Castle, three teenagers stood side-by-side, holding hands and watching the bombers flying overhead.

They were not alone, for an invisible dragon had joined them too.

This is not yet the end.
It is not even the beginning of the end.
However, perhaps it is the end of the beginning.

Historical Notes

In the 1930's, the only way to detect hostile aircraft approaching the English coastline was by sound location or visual sightings, both of which were inaccurate and of no use at all if cloud cover was present. By the spring of 1939, however, a chain of aircraft detection stations had been set up along the coast. The cover name for the operation was RDF, for **R**adio **D**irection **F**inding. In operation, a train of radio pulses was transmitted, bounced off the target, and detected by a receiver. The time between transmitted and received pulses was used to calculate the distance from the ground station, which could warn of incoming enemy planes 100 miles away at night or in periods of fog or storm. RDF was soon replaced by the American acronym RADAR, for **RA**dio **D**etection and **RA**nging, and the term RDF applied to passive directional receivers, which could take bearings on ships and ground stations.

The very short intervals to be measured were displayed on a CRT, for **C**athode **R**ay **T**ube, which was the forerunner of the TV picture tube. A beam of electrons was rapidly swung back and forth, impinging on a phosphor screen, which glowed when electrons struck the phosphor. The returning pulses moved the electron beam up, painting a "blip" on the screen. The time between blips represented distance to the target, as the display screen was calibrated in miles. Various improvements were made, so that range, height, and bearing could be measured as well.

The Germans had set up their own radar stations, but employed them in anti-shipping operations. German radar operated on a much shorter wavelength than the British and was transmitted from bowl-shaped parabolic antennas. To determine if the British had radar, the ***Graf Zeppelin*** made several flights up the coastline, listening for signals. The British were tracking the largest blip they had ever seen on their radar scopes. The Germans found nothing and concluded there was no British radar, which would cost them dearly once they started their attacks. They had been searching for the wrong wavelength!

The Germans had observed British coastal installations sporting some rather odd-looking antennas, none of which were bowl-shaped, and decided they couldn't possibly be connected with radar. Besides, they would be difficult to attack. This was to be their downfall in the Battle of Britain.

Already aware of German plans from decoded intercepts and radar information, the British were able to keep their fighters on the ground until the bombers showed up. German pilots couldn't understand how the British seemed to know exactly where they were going to be and when.

It has been said that radar won the war for the Allies in World War II. While that's an overstatement, it was true that radar had a huge impact on how World War II was fought on both sides. Radar was, in essence, a very basic way of obtaining information. That very simplicity made it highly adaptable and during the war, scientists and engineers found dozens of ways of using it.

Radar was essentially "seeing" with radio waves, but there were dozens of other uses in the war. It was used to aim searchlights, then to aim anti-aircraft guns. It was put on ships, where it was used to navigate at night and through fog, to locate enemy ships and aircraft, and to direct gunfire. It was put into airplanes, where it might be used to locate hostile aircraft or ships, or to navigate the aircraft, or to find bombing targets. Radar could be used to locate enemy artillery and even buried mines. Military meteorologists used radar to track storms.

One of the most important radar advances of World Wat Two was the movement to higher frequency radio waves, especially into the region of the electromagnetic spectrum called microwaves. The shorter wavelengths were easier to focus into narrow beams. This meant that a distant object would reflect more energy back. Even more importantly, higher frequencies gave greater resolution. Directing anti-aircraft and long-range naval guns entirely by radar required microwaves frequencies, as did displaying the topography below an aircraft when radar was used for navigation. The most important technical breakthrough in the move to higher frequency radar was the invention of the cavity magnetron.

About the Author

Secret of the Dragon's Claw is the third book in Derek Hart's dragon series of six. The incredibly positive reception for Thaddeus Osbert, Gavin Kane, Emily Scott, Bunty Digby and all the other characters in these books, has been immensely satisfying and the author looks forward to continuing the series.

Derek Hart would like to thank the people who volunteered their services, in one way or another, assisting the author. Without such dedication, these novels wouldn't benefit from creative minds and passionate hearts.

To **David Burke**, for his never-ending dedication in creating fantastic cover art. This friendship spans more than 14 years now and the author is convinced there aren't enough words in the English language to express his gratitude for David's contribution. Covers can make or break a book and it's obvious that Burke's talents have made quite a difference.

To **Sheila Seclearr**, who discovered the magic of a dragon named Thaddeus and threw herself, with love and conviction, to creating movie screenplays to capture both the story and the spirit. The author is very grateful for the friendship that has developed and the dedication that Sheila shows to the project and the future appreciation of the characters she helps bring to the screen.

Finally, the author would like to thank those increasing numbers of fans, loyal readers, and friends who make a difference in the writing process. The following list includes those people whose impact on the author's craft is monumental. To **Jodi Roth-Braun, Michele Desjardins, Eric Hammond, Josh Friedman, Barry Burden** and many others, a heartfelt thank you is offered.

The next book in the series - ***Secret of the Dragon's Scales*** – is coming soon!

(Preview)
Secret of the Dragon's Scales

More than Just Wind on Their Tail

The target today was Achersleben, the site of a major German Focke-Wulf aircraft factory. It was only 90 miles southwest of Berlin and represented the deepest penetration of American bombers up to that time. The members of the group were awakened by the cheerful cry from the orderly, "Briefing will be at 0230 hours."

The men numbly got out of their beds and stumbled into their flight gear, staggered to the Mess, to poke aimlessly at the unappetizing glob of powdered eggs, accompanied by stale, greasy bacon and petrified cold toast. Then the crews shuffled to the briefing room to discover where they might be ending their lives that day.

With the typical flare for the overly dramatic, a captain stood on the little stage in front of ominously closed curtains and announced, "Today, gentlemen, your target is…" He paused for just the right effect. "Achersleben."

There was an audible groan throughout the room, as the officer pulled aside the curtains and let the flight crews see the long strands of yarn pinned to the huge map of Europe, highlighting the dogleg course to Achersleben. The map seemed to have too many red markers along their route. Those infamous red crossed-guns indicated heavy flak concentrations, the most lethal aircraft killers. To the crews, it always seemed like the planners routed their flight paths so the German anti-aircraft gunners would get lots of practice shooting at them.

Once the briefing was over, Lt. Lennert's crew climbed into their jeep and rolled out to the hardstand, where their recently repaired bomber *Tailwind* sat waiting for departure.

Flashlights played all about her dark silhouette, as last minute ground checks were made on armament loading, engine ground checks, and radio gear. As the crews piled out of the jeeps, they took over and made their own inspections. Smitty checked the arming wires on the bombs hanging securely by their shackles in the cavernous bomb bay of the Liberator. The gunners again looked over the ammunition they had previously hand-loaded, ran oiled rags once more over the arming bolts before installing them in the breeches of the ten .50 caliber machineguns. The navigator laid out his maps, with his own little course deviations marked, which would keep them on the fringes of the worst flak concentrations. Bernie set up his radio log on his little desk, while Mario and Robert buckled into their seats and waited for the signal flare to start engines. They were leading the high squadron, which meant they would be number thirteen to take off.

Twin green flares arced off the little two-story building that served as a control tower, and down the taxiway, they heard the first thunderous roar of Pratt & Whitney engines jolting to life. The air trembled as the 1,200 horsepower engines began turning over. Shortly thereafter **Big Dipper** taxied by the lead aircraft of the middle squadron. In military precision, the clumsy-looking Liberators trundled out to follow the veteran B-24 in single file.

In a matter of minutes, thirty-seven B-24's were lined up from their takeoff position to a point far back along the taxiway. Another green flare went off, and **Big Dipper** slowly rolled down the runway. It hit the first rise in the runway and almost disappeared from sight as it dropped down the slope. Then at the second rise, it lifted off, and as the ungainly landing gear slowly folded up into the wells, the Liberator began its path-finding climb. Even before it became airborne, the lead B-24 was rolling, the entire Group taking off at 15-second intervals. All over East Anglia, a duplicate scene was taking place as 800 heavy bombers began the mission. It was as if the entire island that was England, trembled when this huge force of aircraft left the ground.

When it became Lennert's turn to take off, he lined up on the runway, having already checked the props. As the second hand ticked off on Valerio's GI watch and reached 15 seconds from the last roll, Lennert advanced the throttles and **Tailwind** was rolling. Speed built up rather slowly at first with a four-ton bomb load and a full 2700 gallons of fuel aboard, but they soon reached the first rise in the runway at the indicated 120 mph.

As soon as Lennert felt the controls take effect, he called for gear up, and at 300 feet retracted the flaps. The rate of climb was increasing altitude at a rate of 800 feet per minute. Then they began the long ascent to 20,000 feet, where they joined in squadron formation and finally group formation.

Eventually, thirty-six B-24's were nicely tucked in formation and their middle squadron lead preceded them to a radio beacon, where they would join up with their division, whose lead would, in turn, direct them to another beacon, where they would become just another one of 800 heavy bombers aloft. Then the awesome striking force was on its way to bomb Germany.

British Spitfires escorted them across the Channel and for a short time into Holland, where American P-47's and P-51's picked them up. Through disastrous experience, it was learned that the B-24 Liberator and B-17 Flying Fortress were unable to defend themselves without fighter escort. As they crossed the Dutch border, flak began to erupt in ugly black puffs amid their formation. Occasionally it came close enough to hear, and that was when holes appeared in the airplane. They kept going without being hit, but not every aircraft was able to match their luck. Up ahead they saw the long smoky trail of a bomber going down, as German fighters, literally hundreds of them, smashed into groups both in front and behind them. The sky above was crisscrossed with the contrails of both German and American fighters, as they maneuvered their way to targets of opportunity.

Flak was an acrostic for the German anti-aircraft guns known as *Flieger Abwehr Kanonen*. It meant exploding shells were fired upwards from cannons strategically placed on the ground around target areas. The little black puffs of smoke look harmless enough, but the chunks of steel that went flying through the air could knock out an engine or even collapse a wing.

Shortly after they passed through one of the heavy flak concentrations, the crew aboard *Tailwind* spotted about 200 Me109's and Fw190's hit the bomber formation to their right. The enemy fighters shot down twelve B-24's in a matter of seconds. The sky was filled with smoke trails from burning airplanes, both American and German. They witnessed another B-24 catch fire and slowly head for the ground. Two crewmembers managed to bail out, but one of them had the misfortune of his chute catching fire. The bomber burned fiercely and then exploded, debris scattered all over the sky. Several Me109's passed through their formation, but were sorely pressed by P-47's on their tails.

As the bombers approached Halberstadt, the group went into squadron trail formation, so that bombing could be accomplished by each lead bombardier. Flak became more intense, and the German fighters departed, so their anti-aircraft batteries could throw up more 88mm and 128mm shells.

Suddenly, *Tailwind* was flying through yet another wall of flak.

Explosions burst all around them

Pieces of metal went pinging off the aircraft, the echo reverberating in their ears.

Lennert could also smell…

He suddenly didn't want to think about it.

The flak was indiscriminate and getting through was purely a matter of luck.

Everyone just sat there, gritted their teeth and hoped for the best.

Lennert took some minor evasive action, but he was on the initial point to bomb, which meant he had to hold that position for three or four minutes without course changes.

Bernie held his breath and prayed aloud, though nobody could hear him.

Lennert remembered to call Benteen on the intercom. "Mike, put your flak helmet on!"

Kablam!

There was a terrific crash of an exploding 88mm shell, so close it shook the airplane.

Lennert again got on the intercom and asked, "Anybody hurt?"

Benteen's unnaturally meek voice replied, "Bob, you're not going to believe this, but part of the right tail is gone and the upper part of my turret is missing too!"

As Mike had bent down to pick up his flak helmet, the shell had torn through the area where his head had been seconds before and ripped off a portion of the right vertical tail, severing the control cables. Despite the autopilot automatically correcting, the B-24 was drifting off course.

Robert disconnected the autopilot, cranked in rudder trim and returned to the prescribed course for the bomb run.

Blam!

Boom, boom, boom, blam, boom!

A series of detonations went off all around them.

The flak was thick as bees.

Kablam!

There was another explosion directly ahead.

Both the pilot and co-pilot instinctively ducked.

Clang!

Shrapnel ricocheted off the left wing, punching a hole in the skin.

Kablam!

A huge cloud of black smoke enveloped *Tailwind* for just a moment, plunging them into complete darkness. The spinning props whipped it away and they were in daylight once again.

It didn't require Robert and Mario both to fly the airplane, even with part of the tail shot away, so they continued leading the squadron to Achersleben.

Wilcox called out, "Bombs away!"

Lennert immediately headed the B-24 into a standard evasive maneuver and descended one thousand feet in a long sweeping left turn.

The Germans were well aware this was common practice, and their flak batteries became even more accurate. After they had reformed and started the trip home, the crew took stock of the damage. Holes were all over the aft fuselage, and one of the gunner's parachutes was riddled, while several fuel cells in the wings were punctured. A large portion of the right tail was gone and the rear turret had no glass. After a quick tally, it was reported that *Tailwind* sported 63 holes in her, some of them large enough to put a man's head through, but the four Pratt & Whitney engines were unscathed and continued to drone steadily.

Just then, another group of German fighters came up. They knocked seven planes down, but didn't stick around for long. Two or three passes through the formation, and they bolted for their bases, chased by American fighters. The B-24 right alongside *Tailwind* was a mass of flames, and it just rolled over and headed earthward.

No chutes were seen.

Several minutes later, *Tailwind* started to shake, shutter, and rattle.

"I don't think she's going to make it," Mario hollered.

Lt. Lennert hesitated nodding in agreement, but gripped the wheel tightly with both hands. With his feet busy pumping the pedals, Robert constantly corrected with full power.

Several miles ahead of the returning formation, Sir Osbert and his passenger Gavin were closing quickly on the wounded bomber.

"There it is, Thaddeus!" Gavin shouted. "*Tailwind* is in trouble."

"I see her, boy," the dragon replied. "Hold on tightly, for I will be forced to make some erratic maneuvers,"

Gavin grabbed hold of the raised scale lifted before him.

Cloaked in invisibility, the dragon came up alongside *Tailwind*, making certain his expansive wings didn't interfere with the B-24's flight path.

Thaddeus could readily see the damage. The B-24 was riddled with holes and the tail was severely damaged. If the dragon didn't do something quickly, the bomber would break apart and crash.

"Can you do anything to help?" Gavin called out.

The dragon hesitated answering. Faced with his age-old conflict yet again, Sir Osbert struggled with his conscience. If he took action to save the plane, would his tampering change the course of human events? Yet how could he just idly watch the bomber disintegrate, probably killing everyone aboard? Especially since members of the crew had taken such an interest in the welfare of Gavin, Bunty and Emily.

"I'll see what I can do," Thaddeus shouted back, having made up his mind.

Gavin patted the dragon on the head. "Good old dragon!"

The giant beast tucked his wings tighter and in a burst of speed, closed the distance on the staggering B-24.

"Keep down behind my scales, Gavin," Thaddeus instructed. "I have to disengage my invisibility while repairing the damage, and I don't want anyone recognizing you."

"Very well, Sir Osbert," the boy agreed. "Good luck."

The dragon was almost on top of the bomber by then and after a quick survey of the critical damage, he decided the tail section was most in need of attention. Thaddeus reached back and plucked out one of his smaller scales from behind his neck.

"Grrrr," the dragon roared with pain.

"Are you all right?" Gavin asked worriedly.

"I'll be just fine, lad," Sir Osbert replied.

Thaddeus then spit on the scale and the acidic compound in his saliva dissolved the scale into a glob of sticky paste. While still maintaining pace with the B-24, the dragon deftly applied the goop to the damaged sections of tail and rudder controls. With just the right application of heat from the dragon's breath, the bonding agent instantly hardened, creating the perfect patch.

Inside the cockpit, Lennert felt an immediate change in the B-24's performance. He looked at the copilot and shrugged in disbelief.

Outside, however, Thaddeus suddenly became visible, as he focused his energies on conducting one more vital repair, rather than maintaining his camouflage. Reaching out with one talon, the dragon snagged the fuselage.

Bump!

The B-24 shook from tail to nose.

"What the hell was that?" Lennert exclaimed.

"I don't believe it!" exclaimed Benteen over the intercom.

"What is it now?" Mario demanded.

"Can anybody else but me see behind us?"

The top turret whirled around, allowing Bailey to see between the distinctive twin tails. His eyes were wide and behind his oxygen mask, his mouth dropped open in shock.

He couldn't find words to describe what he saw.

"Please tell me you don't see anything," the tail-gunner begged. "Please tell me I've merely lost my mind."

"It's a dragon!" Bailey suddenly exclaimed.

Lt. Lennert looked over at Mario, who rolled his eyes in anger.

"Quit horsing around, you guys," the copilot shouted. "Is the plane okay?"

"We're not kidding, sir," Bailey protested. "Have a look for yourself, dang it."

Mario was fuming by then. "I swear, you guys, I'm gonna have your stripes."

"Hey, Bailey's right, sir," came another voice, at the waist-gunner position. "It's a flying dinosaur or something."

"Have they been drinking?" Lennert asked in dismay.

"Must be, sir," Mario replied. "I'm going to beat the snot out of the entire crew, if we actually get back alive."

"Here it comes, you guys?" Bailey shouted.

"It's passing us on the left."

Mario unbuckled from his seat and strained to look out the pilot's side window.

"Oh, my God," the co-pilot suddenly exclaimed.

Then Lennert twisted in his seat to look.

There it was.

As big as life.

It was a gigantic...

"It just isn't possible," the pilot said, rubbing his eyes.

"But it is," Mario corrected him. "It's a dragon!"

Thaddeus slowed down just long enough to make certain the B-24 could continue flying without any further assistance. He lifted one of his front paws and waved, before reengaging his cloaking capabilities, disappearing in an instant.

Mario returned to his seat, blankly staring off into space as he buckled in.

"Well, did you guys see him?" Benteen's voice came over the headsets.

Mario looked over at Lennert.

The pilot shrugged, before speaking into his mouthpiece. "We certainly saw something out there. Perhaps it was a dragon, perhaps not. No matter what it was, this stays with us, nobody else. I don't want to end up listed Section Eight. Do we all agree?"

"Yes, sir," each member of the crew said, one after another, until all had agreed.

Lennert regained his focus and concentrated on flying. Using all the power he could get from the engines and partial flaps, Robert somehow managed to make it over the English Channel.

Tailwind had sustained several hits, but Thaddeus had repaired the most serious damage. One of the near misses had severed the rudder cables, but Lennert flew the B-24 using cowl flaps for directional control.

As they continued back to their base, the #2 propeller ran away, compounding their numerous problems. Lennert got the engine shut down and propeller feathered. A B-24 cannot maintain airspeed and altitude with two engines out, so Mario and Robert considered bailing out, but decided to stay with the airplane for a while and conserve altitude as best they could.

The weather over England had not improved, but they had little choice but to try to return there. The bomber was now due south of Norwich.

"There!" Mario shouted, when he spotted an airfield through a hole in the clouds.

"More good luck," Lennert commented.

The bomber descended through the gap, while everyone went through the pre-landing checklists. Lennert lowered the flaps to the landing position, lowered the landing gear and turned to line up with the runway.

Suddenly, the windshields and side windows iced up.

"It's too late to pull up now!" the pilot exclaimed. "Here we go."

Mario and Robert couldn't see through the iced-up windshields, but they were forced to continue their descent to keep the airspeed above stalling. Through a tiny clear spot on Mario's side window, he could see men running in every direction.

"We're gonna hit something," the copilot guessed.

Without thinking and relying strictly on instinct, Lennert pushed full left rudder, which caused the airplane to slew around to the left.

The B-24 touched down side-ways.

Crunch!

The landing gear snapped off.

Rip…Zing!

Both outside engine propellers broke away, cartwheeling across the field.

The B-24 slid on its belly through the ice and snow.

Crack!

The fuselage remained intact and without any warning, came to an abrupt halt. Mario squeezed out his side window, while Lennert went out through the left cockpit window. Pilot and copilot ran along both sides of the bomber, stopping at the waist window to make sure everyone was out. They continued around the tail and discovered all of the crew lined up as if for inspection.

Nobody even had a scratch.

On top of that, except for the earlier flak damage and the impact of the crash landing, the B-24 looked in relatively good shape. There was no doubt the bomber could be repaired.

The crew was amazed.

"This is not the first time our plane has escaped serious damage," Lennert commented.

"We almost had our tail blown off, sir," Mario said. "Now look at it. You can hardly tell we were hit at all."

The emergency rescue vehicles started arriving.

"Whatever it was, it helped us get back here in one piece," Benteen reminded them all.

One-by-one, the ten men looked at each other around the circle. Apparently, they were all thinking the same thing, because each man began to smile.

As impossible as it seemed, a dragon had saved their lives, and their airplane.

Peabody pointed to the fuselage. "After they put the wheels back on, I think we should give the girl a new name."

No one disagreed.

Several days later, after their B-24 was repaired, impressive new artwork decorated the bomber's fuselage, with the likeness of a gigantic fire-breathing dragon and a new nickname – ***Dragon on Our Tail***.

Pilots and crew stood admiring their plane.

Eventually they were joined by Colonel Stewart. "Good afternoon, men."

Everyone came to attention. "Good afternoon, sir."

Stewart looked at the B-24 and then at his clipboard. There was no mistaking that the group commander was specifically checking out the tail.

"Lt. Lennert, can you explain how the extensive damage to the tail section was repaired while still in flight?" Stewart asked suddenly.

Lennert shook his head. "No, sir, I can't. I have no logical explanation whatsoever. I just know that I had incredible problems keeping the bomber stable and then it suddenly stabilized, sir."

"The mechanics reported some kind of bonding agent or glue compound was spread over the hundreds of holes," the colonel went on.

"Yes, sir, I read the report," Lennert said. "Believe me, sir, none of my men crawled out there and glued it back together, sir."

The commanding officer laughed uncomfortably. "No, I imagine not."

"Is there anything else, sir?" Mario asked.

Stewart's eyes narrowed. He suspected they were not telling him something, but pressing the point probably wouldn't do any good either.

Shaking his head, the group commander said, "No, that's all. Carry on, men."

"Thank you, sir," the crew of the bomber all said in unison, saluting.

Then as a bunch, they walked away, heading for the barracks.

Colonel Jimmy Stewart returned the salute, but remained in place. He looked at the tail, and then at the new nose art. The intricate details of the dragon were amazing, as if the creature was real. The officer pushed back his cap and sighed.

"What's wrong, sir?" his aide asked quietly.

The group commander smiled and replied, "Oh, Frank, don't ask. You wouldn't believe me anyway."